DYNASTY KILLERS

BOOK THREE

of

THE THREE KINGDOMS CHONICLES

Baptiste Pinson Wu

To Isaiah,

My beautiful son who taught me the true meaning of the word happiness,
the day he was accepted into kindergarten.

Je t'aime, mon fils.

DRAMATIS PERSONAE

Characters from previous books appearing in Dynasty Killers.

263 CE

Liao Hua (Chun/Dun): General of Cavalry of the fallen Shu Han kingdom, narrates his life's journey to a scribe, starting from his childhood on a farm in Jing province. Received an education in Cao Cao's academy, then joined the army for a few years, before being given the command of Cao Cao's special forces, the Scorpions.

Chen Shou: Former official of the Shu Han kingdom, now in charge of recording the life's tale of Liao Hua.

Zhong Hui: One of the two generals of the Cao Wei kingdom responsible for the defeat of Shu Han. Ordered the recording of Liao Hua's story.

196 CE

Cao Cao: Cunning warlord of the late Han period, governor of Yan province, and General-in-Chief of the empire.

Cao Ang: Cao Cao's first son, former rival of Liao Chun, now one of his closest friends.

Cao Anmin: Nephew of Cao Cao from a dead brother. Briefly led Liao Chun as a section leader, but showed poor leadership skills.

Cao Ren: Younger cousin and officer of Cao Cao. Liao Chun's first division general.

Cao Hong: Youngest cousin and officer of Cao Cao. Led the diplomatic mission to invite the emperor to Xuchang

Xiahou Yuan: Jovial cousin of Cao Cao and his cavalry commandant.

Xiahou Dun: Cao Cao's cousin and closest ally. A ruthless man who fancies himself a soldier while his talents are more on the administrative side.

Lady Bian: Favorite concubine of Cao Cao and Liao Chun's first love. Gave birth to three sons.

Cheng Yu: Cao Cao's strategist. A tall, cold, and calculating man.

Xu Chu: Student of Cao Cao who joined his guard corps because of his imposing physique and skills in combat.

Man Chong: Prefect of Xuchang, and bastard son of Cao Cao.

Yue Jin: A short but extremely skilled warrior who quickly became an officer.

Li Dian: A young officer in Cao Cao's army, and Yue Jin's closest friend.

Yu Jin: Also called "The Bastard of Mount Tai". A professional soldier who loves the army above anything else. First trained Liao Chun's company as its Captain.

Xu Huang: A former *youxia* errant martial artist, first hired to protect the emperor during his escape, then joined Cao Cao's army as an officer.

Xun Yu: A former junior officer of Yuan Shao who joined Cao Cao after recognizing Shao's weaknesses. Gained famed after successfully resisting Lü Bu's attack on Yan for months.

Yuan Shao: Governor of Ji Province and childhood friend/rival of Cao Cao.

Yuan Shu: Half-brother of Yuan Shao but at war with him and most of the warlords in the empire.

Gongsun Zan: Warlord known as the Lord of the White Horse. Engaged in a brutal war with Yuan Shao.

Lü Bu: Former adopted son of Dong Zhuo, known as the mightiest warrior in the empire. Master of Red Hare, the best war horse in the land.

Chen Gong: Cao Cao's former secretary/strategist. Betrayed him for Lü Bu and planned the invasion of Yan province.

Liu Xie (Emperor Xian): Young emperor of the Han dynasty. Hostage of Dong Zhuo who used him as his puppet. Escaped Chang'an, traveled to Luoyang, then was invited to Xuchang by Cao Cao through Liao Chun.

Dong Cheng: Father of the emperor's favorite concubine and one of the most influential ministers of the court.

Liu Bei: Descendant of the imperial clan. Fought against the Yellow Turbans and joined the Loyal Rebels under the banner of Gongsun Zan. Later became governor of Xu province.

Guan Yu: Oath brother of Liu Bei. Target of Liao Chun's hatred after he killed his beloved uncle, Cheng Yuanzhi. Defeated Hua Xiong and thus earned fame among the Loyal Rebels.

Zhang Fei: Oath brother of Liu Bei and Guan Yu. Killed Deng Mao (Uncle Deng) in a duel.

The Scorpions

Du Yuan: Second in command of the Scorpions and childhood friend of Liao Chun. Despite his vicious nature, he and Liao Chun became close friends and have formed a deadly pair on the field of battle.

Pei Yuanshao: Childhood friend of Liao Chun. Has a tendency for larceny.

Two-knives: A deadly warrior

One-eye: Leader of the Scorpions' archers.

Tian Guli: A girl of Xiongnu origin. Saved by Liao Chun during the sack of a city. Later joined the Scorpions and became his lover.

Liang-the-broken: A great, fearless warrior who never leaves the battlefield without some kind of wound.

Meng Shudu: Eldest of the Meng brothers.

Meng Bobo: Youngest of the Meng brothers.

Duck: A young horse rider, formerly a messenger in Cao Cao's army.

Hu Zi: A former scout in the Dragon Fang division.

Guo Hai: Son of Guo Wen, nicknamed Sparrow by the Scorpions, which he joined as a servant.

Bu Luo/Pox: A soldier who joined the army to escape the life of a farmer and found himself in Liao Chun's section. Friendly and loyal.

Stinger: A dark, sullen man who joined the Scorpions under Cao Cao's recommendation for his unmatched talent in the art of torture and interrogation.

Guo Wen: One of the original soldiers under Cao Cao's command, and the first friend of Liao Chun from that side.

Lost an arm during the campaign against Dong Zhuo, then was hired by Liao Chun as his platoon and unit's servant.

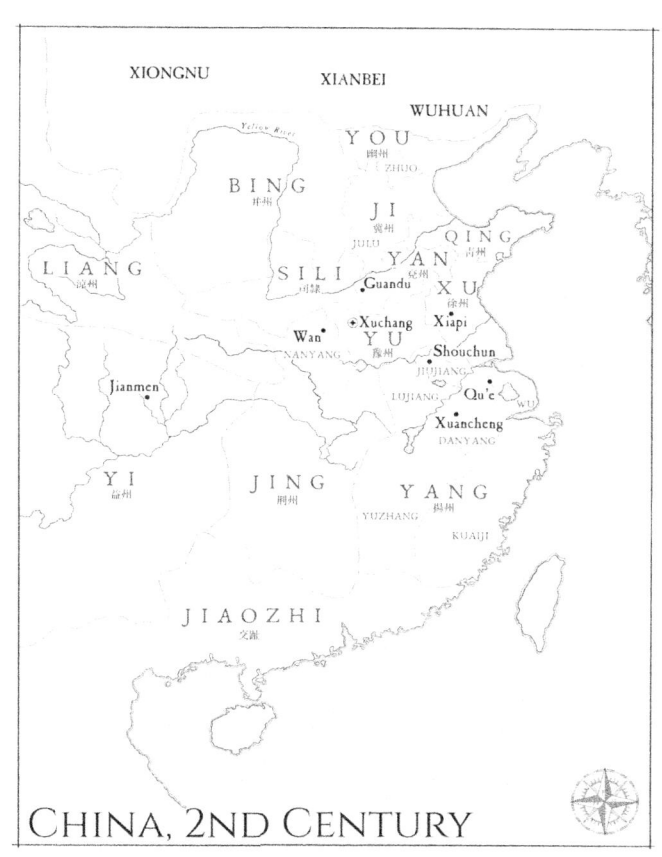

Dynasty Killers

The Three Kingdoms Chronicles (Book 3)

Copyright © 2023 by Baptiste Pinson Wu

All rights reserved.

No part of this book may be reproduced in any form or by any electronic or mechanical means, including information storage and retrieval systems, without written permission from the author, except for the use of brief quotations in a book review.

ISBN 978-4-9912768-4-2 (Paperback)

ISBN 978-4-9912768-5-9 (eBook)

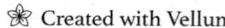 Created with Vellum

A Song of Seven Sorrows

The Western City fell into lawless disorder,
Jackals and tigers brought it to its knees.
Once more I abandon the capital,
And flee to uncivilized Jing.
My kin shed tears at my departure,
My friends cling to me as I leave.
Past the gates, nothing in sight,
But white bones covering the plain.
Down the road, a starving woman
Hugs her child, then leaves him in the grass.
She looks back to the sound of his crying,
Then wipes her tears and goes on alone —
"I hardly know where I am to die!" she says
"How could I look after both of us?"
I push my horse on, leave them and depart,
for my heart cannot bear her words.

Wang Can

PROLOGUE

Jianmen Pass, Yi province
12th month, 4th year of the Jingyuan era of the Cao Wei empire (263)

EVERYTHING HURTS. Absolutely everything hurts. Breathing is like pulling phlegm from my lungs, its passage blocked by thorns along my throat. My back and shoulders seem about to shatter, each shiver sending waves of cold agony through my skin. Coughing is even worse. Each bout feels like life's last attempt to get rid of me. Yet I survive, more or less. I have been sick before and on several deathbeds, but this one, I fear, is my last. I might never see the restored Luoyang after all. A pity, but not as much as the idea that my tale will remain unfinished.

"How much longer?" someone asks outside the wagon. I do not know his voice. He sounds old, though not as old as me. And he sounds impatient.

"We will know tonight," another replies. Him I know, though not by name. He is the physician who watched over me while I drifted into the fever madness.

So, I might not last the night. I thought death would not scare me after accompanying me for so many decades, but I must admit that I tremble at the idea of leaving this world, even though I have little to expect of it anymore.

"What if he survives the night?" the first man asks. "Can we move again?"

"I wouldn't advise it," the physician answers, which makes the other one click his tongue nervously. I don't like that man. "He needs rest, time, and—"

"We don't have time! We already lost weeks because of this cursed weather."

"General Deng, calm down, will you?" another voice says without warmth. That voice belongs to Zhong Hui, the young enemy commander who ordered me to dictate my life's account to Chen Shou. The other must then be Deng Ai, the old general responsible for my empire's fall.

"Don't tell me to calm down, *boy*," Deng Ai spits back at his comrade. There is no lost love between those two. It's a story as old as the world. Zhong Hui is young, educated, and from a good family. Deng Ai climbed the ladder through talent and perseverance. *He* is the one who defeated us through an amazing feat of arms, yet Zhong Hui will probably receive the accolades. In another situation, I would have sided with Deng Ai, but as the old hound wishes for my quick death, he can rot for all I care.

"Our orders were very specific about General Liao," Zhong Hui says in his suave tone. "He is to be given all due respect, and—"

"And my orders were to bring this convoy back to Luoyang before *chun fen*. The equinox is two months away. At this rate, we will never make it. If one old man prevents me from succeeding in my mission, I would rather leave him on the side of the road!"

"You will do no such thing!"

Ah, dear Zong Yu, my oldest living friend. Even in defeat, this comrade retains the fire of our youth. I can hear his rapid footsteps as he rushes to the two enemy generals, and I can imagine how they coil back at the sight of this old wolf sneering.

"That man is the most venerable of our veterans," he says as his steps stop. "He served your Emperor Wu, our Emperor Zhaolie, and studied with your leader's father. So show some respect, you brats!"

"Or what?" Deng Ai, who is well in his sixties and cannot be considered a brat by a long shot, asks.

"Or you'll have a full-scale rebellion on your hands," Zong Yu answers. I wish I could see the faces of the two generals.

"Is that a threat, venerable Zong?" Deng Ai asks.

"A promise," Zong Yu replies. "Liao Hua is like an uncle to our defeated emperor. If anything—" My friend is shaken by a bout of coughing. I was with him, sharing some soft wine, when I first coughed myself. I hope with all my heart I did not give him whatever disease bedrids me. "If anything happens to him, the whole convoy will rebel against your authority. So give the man a rest, or you'll have nothing to show for in your capital."

Well said, my friend. Though it is a bunch of nonsense, of course. Liu Shan, our emperor, would not give me the sole of his shoes if I walked bare feet on snow-covered sharp rocks. He hates my guts, and I can hardly suffer his presence, though it hasn't always been so.

Deng Ai growls like an angry bear but has nothing to reply.

"Can he make it?" Zhong Hui asks, understandably more concerned than his comrade. My life's tale will be appreciated in the capital, and he knows it. I know so much about the heroes from their empire.

"General Liao saw more battles than the two of you combined," Zong Yu answers. "In his youth, he would have snapped you in half with one hand. Yes, of course, he will make it. Nothing can kill that man."

"*Though the turtle lives long—*"

"Shove your poem up your ass," Zong Yu snaps. Like me, he doesn't fancy poetry. This time, Deng Ai chuckles. "He just—" Poor Zong Yu coughs some more. It sounds painful too. "He just needs some rest."

"Let's see how he feels in the morrow then," Zhong Hui replies, though it is clear he didn't like the remark about poetry.

"If he's still among us," Deng Ai goes on, almost threateningly, "I will take the convoy forward, and you will stay behind until he feels better. I am not losing any more time for an old fool."

Deng Ai does not wait for a reply and storms out, his feet marking a quick tempo through the muddy ground of the pass. Zhong Hui will not like it. Whoever reaches Luoyang first will give the details of the victory. No doubt the young upstart would want this role, but he will also follow his orders and show me due respect.

"If your friend is still with us tomorrow morning," he says, "let's ask the scribe to resume his task. We will wait three days, then follow the main convoy."

So, the enemy will split.

"Thank you," Zong Yu replies, doing a piss-poor job of sounding sincere. Zhong Hui leaves too, and so does Zong Yu a few seconds later. But before he does, my old friend knocks on the wood of my wagon three times, to which I reply in kind.

A simple, old code between us to say that everything is going according to plan.

PART ONE

TIGERS AT THE GATES

1

Xiapi, capital of Xu province
11th month, 1st year of Jian'an era (196), Han Dynasty

CONTRARY TO WHAT most rankers believe, being a leader is a tough role. What makes it such a living nightmare isn't the constant grumbling or the need for recognition. It's not even the subalterns' views on what is unfair or not. No, the worst, at least in my mind, has always been the moments when subordinates need to be trusted, left to do what they are trained for without supervision. It's never completely a question of trust, though. I trusted my men with my life but liked keeping them in sight. On that day, however, the Scorpions acting the plan set in the shadows for the past weeks were beyond said sight. Many walls separated them in the great hall of the palace from me at the table of a local watering hole.

"Will you stop?" Du Yuan asked through his teeth.

"What?" I asked, equally aggressively.

"Your foot. Will you stop tapping it?"

"I'm not tapping my foot."

"Not now. But you were driving me insane until I spoke."

"I wasn't tapping," I repeated, but a look at Pox, the third member of the table, confirmed that I was. "Sorry."

"We get it, all right?" Pox went on in a less off-putting tone than my second-in-command. "You'd rather be in the thick of it, with them, as usual. But we can't risk it this time. You said so."

"I know. It's just—"

"You don't like her taking all the risks," Pox finished for me.

He was right. It all came down to Tian Guli doing more than her share of the work and finding herself in the most vulnerable spot. I hated feeling as such. Time and again she had proven her worth, not only when it came to caring for the horses or shooting her bow with a deadly aim, but even on missions requiring a witty mind, as today. Usually, though, my lover was within my reach. I meant to drown my worries at the bottom of a fragrant beer, something I rarely drank but actually enjoyed. This particular cup, though, did not infuse me with confidence in our plan. I squared my shoulders and nodded as if I had managed to put my doubts behind me.

"Chun," Du Yuan said, knowing me so well after thirteen years of friendship that I failed to deceive him, "she can do it. And Pei Yuanshao is with her."

"Hardly a reassuring notion," I replied. Pei Yuanshao, maybe more than any other member of my squad, had made me proud over the past months with his natural talent for stealth, but it came at the cost of a terrible habit, thievery. Letting him loose within the palace of Xiapi might prove too tempting a playground for his expert fingers. As for Guli, while I knew she could usually do what was expected of her, this plan might be too complex a task for a foreigner. For a sixteen-year-old girl from the Xiongnu tribes, infiltrating a palace, disguised as a Han servant, was inviting a disaster.

I had been so proud of my plan. A simple, elegant plan, the kind that might even impress Lord Cao. Its success meant, as ordered, the end of peace in Xu province, with no risk of bouncing back on my lord. Yet, much was hanging in the balance. What if the powder proved too strong in taste, and our target felt it? What if it wasn't strong enough and had no effect on him? Stinger, our expert torturer, had assured me even a man like Zhang Fei would feel the alcohol rush to his head as if he'd been on an empty stomach. He said those herbs and mushrooms pounded together by his knowing hands could make a man talk when nothing else worked or exacerbate one's violence if taken with wine, and if there was one thing Zhang Fei was famous for, it was his love for wine. I put this worry in the back of my mind, confident in Stinger's methods. Even after two years, the man chilled my blood with his sole presence, the stench of his years within Cao Cao's torture department accompanying him like a second skin.

The powder would work. Pei Yuanshao would mix it with the right pitcher of wine, and Guli would pour it into Zhang Fei's cup and his alone. Then, once the drug's effect showed, the two of them were to leave the palace and find us here. All that would be left was for Zhang Fei to be Zhang Fei.

Our target was many good things, from a peerless warrior to a loyal brother, but a patient host wasn't one of them. Why Liu Bei, his leader and oath-brother, had chosen the brute to remain in Xiapi to take care of things while he and Guan Yu, my personal nemesis, went to push the army of Yuan Shu back south was a mystery, but it served us well.

Lord Cao's mission had been vague, to say the least. *Stir*

troubles in Xu. I had been tempted to bring the haziness of the mission to my lord's attention before we departed Xuchang, but I knew him well. This was as much a test for me as it was entertainment for him. Cao Cao wanted to be surprised. He wanted to guess how the Scorpions would handle the case of Xu province.

Xu had resisted my lord's conquest a couple of years ago, though one could call what we did to the province a massacre. My lord had, at the time, faced the cowardly Tao Qian who had murdered his father, thus giving us the perfect excuse for a punitive campaign. Had Lü Bu, the beast of the north, not attacked our home base while we fought in Xu, it would be ours now. But the beast had acted with the help of Chen Gong, my lord's former strategist, and with their combined skills, beast and tactician had nearly obliterated Lord Cao's ambitions. A year of hard fighting had seen those two unlikely allies pushed to a corner of Yan province, from where they fled to Xu and sought refuge under the banner of Liu Bei, the province's new governor. For a time, we all thought things would implode by themselves. No one in their right mind could handle the likes of Lü Bu. Arrogant and short-tempered, he had already killed two adoptive fathers. This was without counting on Liu Bei being a model of patience. This scion of the imperial clan from a distant branch had managed the beast well until now. It was just a question of time before Lü Bu showed his true colors and let his appetite for power drive his sword arm. Time or the right opportunity.

"Your plan is solid," Du Yuan went on as Pox gestured for a server to bring another pitcher of beer. "We all agreed on it."

"Even the best plans can fail," I replied.

We had first reached Tan, the capital of Xu, when Tao

Qian was alive, where we learned that Liu Bei had relocated the administration to Xiapi, closer to the border with Yan, in other words, us. Liu Bei was maybe a model of virtue, but he wasn't weak and would not shy away from a fight. Xiapi was thus a good move on his part. And to make sure his defenses were solid, he let Lü Bu man Xiaopei, a small town south, from where the beast and the imperial scion could help each other in case of an attack.

When we finally made it to Xiapi, I despaired a little. Despite being governor for just a few months, Liu Bei had gained the people's love. They would not rebel. And most of the former officials of Tao Qian also seemed content with his leadership. *Most of them*, not all. Finding the malcontent had become a specialty for me, and in this case, he wasn't hard to spot. His name was Cao Bao, though he had no link to my lord's family. Many saw him as Tao Qian's right-hand man, his chancellor, and he should have become his successor. So when the old man finally bit the dust, half a day after putting Liu Bei in charge of the province, Cao Bao became understandably disgruntled. In a not-so-subtle gesture, he had his daughter marry Lü Bu a few days after the beast entered the province, and that's how we knew where to find an unknowing ally.

A week after Liu Bei left to fight Yuan Shu, I personally wrote a letter, using the skills taught to me by Master Zhong Yao as a child. Copying the style of Liu Bei, I then sent the letter to Zhang Fei. In this letter, Liu Bei invited his brother to show deference to Cao Bao, who not only *deserved respect for his loyalty to the people of Xu,* but whose unhappiness *could be understood*. This pile of horse shit, as I wrote it, made my comrades laugh to the tears, and I had to rewrite it a few times as they shared some tempting ideas to include. I guess Zhang Fei wasn't too thrilled at the idea, but he was nothing if not a loyal man and sent an invitation to Cao Bao shortly after.

The rest was up to Guli.

"Seriously, Chun. Give it a rest."

"Sorry," I said again. This time I did notice my foot tapping.

"What is it now?" Pox asked.

"It's just ... Imagine for one second Zhang Fei touches her. Do you really think she would not react or act meekly like a proper Han servant?"

"Oh shit," Du Yuan and Pox replied together.

Guli would never just let that go; we all knew it. Maybe it wasn't such a smart plan after all.

For the fifth time in the last minute, I checked across the street, where two of my men were standing with a direct view of the palace's back door. Still no movement. I had instructed the Meng brothers to prepare some diversion in case things went south, but my instruction had been so vague that I would not count on them too much. The rest of the Scorpions waited outside the city, ready to ride back to Xuchang.

"I should have gone with them," I said, slamming the table and toppling the now-empty cup.

"Not that again," Du Yuan replied, eyes rolling.

"You said yourself it was a bad idea," Pox went on as he refilled my cup. "Zhang Fei might recognize you."

"Still worth the risk," I whispered in my beer.

It had been seven years since Zhang Fei and I had found ourselves in the same room, at least to his knowledge. I had been a thirteen-year-old boy then, serving Cao Cao as an aide. The chances Zhang Fei would have noticed me and even more remembered me were ridiculous but not impossible. I had served wine to his second brother, Guan Yu, in front of the council before the man became a hero, giving Zhang Fei a chance to see me clearly. But more, I had bested Guan Yu in combat during the battle of Tan. I did not recall Zhang Fei being around then, but Guan Yu might have mentioned me later on. It was thin but could tip our chances of success, so I remained on the sideline while others took the risks.

"I still doubt it will be enough anyway," Du Yuan said. The table shook, and my second winced in pain from Pox's kick in the shin.

I had no need for Pox's support because that part of the plan gave me no doubt. I could see it, plain as day. Zhang Fei would somehow insult his guest, potentially even harm him, and Cao Bao would leave Xiapi pride-wounded, gather the other malcontents, and seek help from Lü Bu. The latter, advised by Chen Gong, would quickly step up and pick a fight with Zhang Fei. One of the two might die, and I thought it would be Fei, for Lü Bu had more men, but this was of little importance. What mattered was that Liu Bei and Lü Bu would fight, thus weakening each other before my lord swooped in and took the prize. For each soldier those two lords lost, we were saving one of our comrades, I thought. Undoubtedly, we would be coming soon to take over Xu. Cao Cao had no other choice.

"Even after what we did here last time?" Pox asked, a little too loudly for my taste. I waved for him to lower his voice. The establishment was full of patrons, many of whom would have lost someone during the massacre.

"It is neither here nor there," Du Yuan replied in his usual merciless tone. "Our lord cannot let the threat of Xu on his side when the war with Yuan Shao begins."

Du Yuan was right. We all felt it; the war between the two greatest lords of the empire was coming closer by the day. The tension was building in the air, and rumors ran wild. For the moment, both Cao Cao and Yuan Shao, his childhood friend, pretended to be on good terms, but the Great Han land wasn't enough for both their ambition. One had to die, and the other would inherit an empire. On paper, Yuan Shao was stronger. He had more men, more money, more grain, and a more advantageous position. His only rival north of the Yellow River, Gongsun Zan, had seen his land reduced to a single city. It was only a matter of time before Yuan Shao squashed the Lord of the White Horse and turned his attention south. Cao Cao, however, was surrounded by potential threats. Liu Bei and Lü Bu east, of course, but also Yuan Shu in the south. While the toad got his ass kicked time and again, he was rich beyond words and could muster armies with a snap of his greedy fingers. On the southwest of Yan, Liu Biao, while never aggressive toward us so far, could also prove a threat if he decided, and the west of the empire was such a mess that it was difficult to know who could play a part in the coming conflict. Thus it was doubtless that before he moved against the illustrious Yuan Shao, my lord would have to clean his neighborhood.

"None of this matters," I went on. "Cao Cao might not be as fortunate as Yuan Shao in many ways, but he has two great advantages in this war." I said the last while holding two fingers up, waiting for the question I knew would come.

"He's a tactician now," Pox commented, elbowing the ribs of Du Yuan, whose eyes rolled to the ceiling once again. "All right, I'll bite. Please inform us, oh famous scholar, of Cao Cao's so-called advantages."

"First," I said, curling one of my two fingers, "he has the emperor and is thus both legitimate in his action and capable of summoning a great deal of support from other lords."

"Dong Zhuo also held the emperor," Du Yuan went on, talking inside his cup. I let it slip because I hated it when people made that point. It's not just that I found it insulting for my lord; it was also sadly true. While Cao Cao had welcomed the emperor with respect, things quickly changed. A few weeks after Emperor Xian moved to Xuchang, my lord had received several titles and gifts, many of which were self-attributed. And just as the Scorpions left the new capital, he had given himself the title of General-in-Chief of the empire. A terrible mistake, in my opinion.

"What's the second?" Pox asked.

"He has us," I answered.

"Us, the Scorpions?"

"Us, his soldiers," I said. "Trained men, solid men, ready to die and kill in his name."

"Not all of us get hard for him, you know?" Du Yuan said.

It was true that Cao Cao had few stronger supporters than me. I would have walked through fire for that man. He had not only saved me from certain death and given me a proper education but also offered more opportunities than this young fool deserved and made me the captain of my own special forces. Sure, I butted heads with him every chance I got and often cursed his name when I felt mistreated, but he was the greatest man of the land, a point I still believe sixty years later.

"You won't argue that he made us rich beyond our dreams," I said. Du Yuan could find nothing to say to that. Cao Cao's soldiers, especially during the massacre of Xu, had all managed to loot enough to double their pay, at least. Even at the end of their service, many had reenlisted, some as life-long soldiers. "Yuan Shao's men can't say the same. And *he* never fought with them." This, in my mind, was the greatest asset up my lord's sleeves; he had bled with us. Nothing gives more pride to a warrior than seeing his general waving a sword like a common foot soldier, sharing the torments of the battle with the lowest rankers, and fending for his life. Cao Cao had fought more battles than any other lord in the empire, and his men knew it. If the war took us to the *sidi,* the death ground, where the only choice is victory or death, our men would fight twice harder, while Yuan Shao's would run.

"Nevertheless," Du Yuan said, "this Yuan bastard is rich. Shoots coins out of his ass, that one. Enough to recruit all the barbarians from the north and then some more."

I was about to tell my second what I thought of those mercenaries and auxiliaries, but a shadow cast itself over the table, dragging my attention to Two-Knives, one of my best warriors.

"They're coming," he said, a small nod toward the end of the street, from where Pei Yuanshao and Guli were approaching. They looked unhurt, but their rapid footsteps and the way Pei checked behind him every few *bu* made me understand things had not gone exactly according to the plan.

"Two-Knives, you and Liang wait another three minutes before you follow us. Pox, Du Yuan, go first. We'll be right behind. If the city's gates are closed, take to a small street, and we will catch up with you." The night was approaching, and the gates would be shutting soon anyway, but if my plan worked, the city might be panicking sooner.

They obeyed right away. My men were the best I could have asked for, and two years together had turned us into a well-oiled machine. My two comrades left the table while I searched for a few coins to drop. I went after them, reaching the street a couple of steps behind Pei and Guli, who did not even check me as I did.

"All good?" I asked.

"A little too good," Pei answered.

"What do you mean?"

"I mean that we need to get out of here before things turn up in flame," he replied.

Pei Yuanshao was level-headed, not prone to panic, even amid battle. That he spoke as such was rare and made me more careful about my surroundings. Shops were closing for the night, soldiers patrolled up and down the streets, and dogs and children were returning to their homes. A normal evening, in a normal town. Yet I could feel it, too; something was coming. A storm we had summoned.

The explanation would have to wait. I did not want to attract too much attention as the three of us walked toward the western gate, a few seconds behind Pox and Du Yuan. But some things had to be said.

"You look beautiful," I told Guli, who had remained quiet so far.

"Shut up," she said, "I look ridiculous."

Tian Guli, as a proper girl from the northern tribes, liked her feet tucked inside warm leather boots and favored fur over any other fabric. In her land, clothes kept cold at bay and allowed people to ride horses and shoot bows with ease. I liked that Guli better, my huntress. But seeing her wearing small shoes keeping her feet tight, her hair coiled in intricate shapes kept in place by a long pin of silver, and clad in so much silk that she must have felt like a butterfly trapped in a spider web, worked up my appetite for her.

"It fits you," I replied.

"Don't get used to it," she said. "I'll throw it in the first river."

"Those cost me a fortune, you know?" I said.

"It cost Lord Cao a fortune, you mean," she went on.

"Will you two stop," Pei Yuanshao interrupted us, for once the voice of reason. "Chun, give her your cloak."

Half a *li* further down the road, the wall of Xiapi and its western gate drew themselves clearer. Our two comrades kept walking, no sign of alarm in their gait. I listened to my master thief, unfastened my cloak, passed in front of them, then let Pei pull it away from my shoulders. He would cover Guli with it, making her more discreet before we approached the guards in charge of the gate. At night, they would pay more attention to people trying to get in than out, but a pretty servant from the palace would stand out too much.

They barely looked at me as I strolled out of the city and offered little more than a side glance at the duo behind.

"What happened then?" I asked a couple of minutes later as Guli removed the pin to let her hair down, and Pei half-emptied my gourd of water.

"Stinger might have been too generous in his dosage," Guli replied.

What had happened, as they explained in turn, was a total success on our part. We had just missed one tiny piece of information. When Liu Bei left his brother in charge of the city, he forbade him from drinking. This had nearly killed our plan, but when Zhang Fei had caught Guli by the wrist and asked in his thunderous voice who had authorized wine to be served, she had cleverly answered the wine was a gift sent by Lord Liu Bei in celebration of his victory in the south. All too pleased with the excuse, Zhang Fei accepted the *baijiu* without second-guessing her words. And since he had refrained from drinking for the past couple of weeks, he went strong on it.

"You should have seen Cao Bao's face when Zhang Fei emptied his fifth cup," Pei said, finally breathing better now that we were out.

"And then?" Pox asked.

And then, as I had guessed, the host and the guest found a reason to argue, something to do with Liu Bei's exaggerated sense of virtue, I believe. Zhang Fei, uncontrollable now that he had drunk the spiked wine and some more, saw red and gave the thrashing of his life to a helpless Cao Bao. To listen to Pei, several bones had been broken before the guards intervened and restrained their commander.

"That's when we left," Guli finished.

Zhang Fei had been arrested by his own men and would be drunk for half a day, while Cao Bao, father-in-law of Lü Bu, had been beaten senseless. If that didn't work, nothing would.

The seven of us rejoined the rest of my men near the closest postal station, where our horses patiently waited for our return. Before we started our journey back home, I took my platoon to the south, where I had to check how well I had foreseen the situation.

Sure enough, as we observed the road south of Xiapi, a rider pushed his horse to its limits. His destination, I knew, would be Xiaopei, and his sender would be a wounded Cao Bao. Soon, Lü Bu would be coming to the capital of Xu with enough men to destroy Zhang Fei, and Liu Bei would have no choice but to punish the beast. War was upon the province again.

From the corner of my eyes, I saw Du Yuan reluctantly exchange a string of *wushu* coins with a beaming Pox.

"I still don't believe it will be enough," he said, crossing his arms over the mane of his mare.

"Trust me, it will work," I replied. "Better still, Cao Cao will be pleased with us."

"You hear that, boys? There is a fat bonus waiting for us in Xuchang," Liang-the-broken said, raising a cheer from our comrades.

A fat bonus, some days of rest, and maybe even a promotion, I thought. I had no doubt that my lord would approve of my plan and congratulate me on a well-thought strategy.

"You got him drunk?" Lord Cao asked, disbelief written all over his face.

"Yes," I answered.

"You got Zhang Fei drunk. That was your whole plan?" he went on. Suddenly I wasn't so sure of myself.

We had ridden hard to Xuchang, where I had not even bothered bathing before giving him my report. News from Xu province would follow us, but I wanted to be the first to inform Lord Cao of our success. Had I known how coldly he would receive me, I would have wasted a few *shi* in the comfort of our compound.

"Angry drunk, I would say."

"And?"

"And in the wrong company," I replied.

"I sent you on a mission to disturb Xu. You were gone almost three months, and all you have to show for it is getting a man drunk. A man, I should add, who is more often drunk than sober, to begin with."

"My lord," Man Chong intervened, "I think Chun's plan has merits."

I nodded my thanks to my old friend but wished he had not spoken. I could see Lord Cao's anger was not about me.

Something else bothered him. Over the years, I had learned to detect those swings, and while I felt the sting of his ingratitude, I knew Chong defending me would only make things worse.

"Oh, you think so?" Cao Cao sarcastically asked. "Then maybe I should let you handle all my affairs then?"

"Lord Cao, you are being unfair," the last person in the room said, which drew the air from my lungs. Guo Jia, Lord Cao's young secretary, was clearly overstepping. Even on a good day, Cao Cao would not appreciate being talked to like that. I thought this replacement of Chen Gong would not last long in my lord's administration, but the strangest thing happened.

"You are right," Cao Cao said as he pinched the skin between his eyes. "Chun, Chong, I am sorry."

I was so stunned by what had just happened that my mouth hung open for a while, absolutely motionless. Man Chong, however, pouted his thoughts about the young secretary in an obvious reprimand. My friend, now prefect of Xuchang, had spent years hating the sons of Cao Cao because he was, in fact, our lord's bastard son, but had recently made peace with the older of them. This left him without any target for his hatred until Guo Jia stepped into our lives. It was clear the secretary had filled the void.

Personally, I did not care much about him. Sure, I didn't appreciate how influential he seemed to be over my lord, but if it meant someone finally could rein his mood on bad days, I was all for it. Guo Jia had a slightly effeminate appearance, mostly due to his complete lack of beard, long, nimble limbs, brilliant eyes, and thin pinkish lips. But he also had an air of capability I could appreciate, like a veil of hidden threat. Maybe that's what Cao Cao had seen in him. Some claimed his influence on our lord was of a more carnal nature, but I doubted it for no other reason than Cao Cao loved women to an absurd degree. It didn't mean he could not appreciate a more masculine type of beauty, of course. And if one were into this kind of thing, they could do worse than Guo Jia.

"Since the two of you agree with Captain Liao," Cao Cao said, still working on his coming migraine, "what do you think is going to happen?" Lord Cao loved to test his men with questions of the sort.

"Lü Bu will take over Xiapi, and most of Xu, with the excuse of saving the city from the brutal hand of Zhang Fei," Man Chong replied right away. "Liu Bei will strike back, and since he has more men, will probably prevail, but it will be costly."

My old comrade echoed my thoughts exactly.

"I doubt it," Guo Jia said. If eyes could kill, Man Chong's would have made his head explode.

"What do you think then?" Chong asked, contempt dripping from his voice.

"The first part of your assessment is correct; Xiapi is probably under Lü Bu's control. But I do not believe there will be a battle with Liu Bei," Guo Jia went on.

"No battle?" I asked.

"Of course, there will be a battle," Man Chong replied.

"And I think Lü Bu will come out on top," Guo Jia said.

Cao Cao smiled his fiendish smirk as his eyes went from one to the other of his juniors, obviously enjoying the exchange. This had seemingly taken care of his headache.

"Tell us, Guo Jia," he said.

"Master Liao acted cleverly," the young secretary said, flattering me in a most seducing tone. "His actions will undoubtedly stir troubles in Xu. Lü Bu will take Xiapi, and since Liu Bei has more men, the legitimacy of his position as governor, the right to avenge his brother, and the support of the people, he would be right to fight back." So far, Guo Jia had followed my vision as well.

"But?" Cao Cao asked.

"But two things will prevent a battle from happening. First," he said, holding his index finger to the sky in a pose reminding me of what I had done in the drinking establishment in Xiapi. "Liu Bei will hear about it while battling Yuan Shu. He will have lost men in this conflict, putting his superiority over Lü Bu in question."

I had considered that already but had dismissed the point because I did not believe Yuan Shu could hold a candle to Liu Bei, especially with Guan Yu in the vanguard.

"And second?" Man Chong asked.

"Second," Guo Jia went on, taking a couple of steps to put himself in front of Lord Cao's chair, "Liu Bei's family is in Xiapi."

"Shit," I whispered, already knowing he was right. I had completely missed that point, and my whole plan would crumble.

"That wouldn't stop him from battling the beast," Man Chong said, waving his hand down. Except that it would. Guo Jia, Cao Cao, and I knew it. Man Chong was one of the greatest minds of our age, but he had one crucial flaw, his lack of empathy. Wives, concubines, and children were secondary assets in his world, and surely no lord would sacrifice his ambition for them. Liu Bei would, though, even if he was still without progeny at that point, just as Cao Cao would turn the world upside down if his children were under threat. Suddenly, I understood why Cao Cao valued Guo Jia's opinion. While the secretary gave me the same feeling of coldness as Man Chong did, his hardened mind was hidden under a soft layer of compassion. They were the two sides of the same coin. But when it came to assessing the motivation of a virtuous man like Liu Bei, Man Chong was at a disadvantage.

"What would you do if you were Lü Bu?" Cao Cao asked Guo Jia. The secretary pretended to think about it, but it was an act. He knew exactly what he would do should he be in Lü Bu's boots.

"I would treat Liu Bei's family kindly, return them to him without condition, and even invite him back to Xiapi as the rightful governor, claiming that I only acted to preserve the people from Zhang Fei's drunken fury. Liu Bei is a man of virtue, or at least he likes to pretend he is. If Lü Bu acts as such, Liu Bei will have no choice but to relent his control of the province; otherwise, people will see him as a petty lord." Guo Jia bowed in our lord's direction to show he was done. Lord Cao clapped hands with pride, but Man Chong and I found nothing to say. *That man*, I thought, *is dangerous*.

I could see it happen just as he told it. Without having even met Liu Bei, Guo Jia had perfectly grasped the kind of man he was.

"So my plan has failed," I sighed.

"Not necessarily," Guo Jia said as he resumed his spot on my lord's left. "They will try to settle for peace, or at least Chen Gong will push Lü Bu to strive for it. But I do not believe it will work for long. In a matter of months, or weeks maybe, one will chase the other from Xu. Your plan will work, just not as fast as you thought."

Light footsteps behind my back informed me of a servant's approach, but Cao Cao held his hand to stop him. He was enjoying the exchange very much.

"Who's gonna chase who?" my lord asked.

Guo Jia opened his hand toward Man Chong, inviting

him to speak first. My friend, the face of defeat, closed his eyes as he answered

"Liu Bei will have to leave Xu," he admitted, contrary to what he had first claimed.

"I also believe so," Guo Jia said.

"Do you know why?" Cao Cao asked, and it took me a second to realize he was talking to me. Frankly, I was at a loss. Guo Jia and Man Chong were thinking much faster than I could and saw a future that remained clouded to me. Even considering his potential loss of men, Liu Bei was still probably stronger, and since the people loved him, he could recruit them more efficiently. But if both my comrades claimed so, there must be a reason.

I closed my eyes and pictured the map of the Great Han like a board of *weiqi*, with stones of many colors rather than just the usual black and white. Man Chong had once advised me to think of the world as such. And the answer came easily.

"Liu Bei is alone," I answered. "He fought Yuan Shu in the south, so he cannot ask for help there. He fought you two years ago, so west is also out of his reach. And he fought Yuan Shao in the north as an officer of Gongsun Zan. None of his neighbors would help him, but Lü Bu could probably strike a deal with either of the Yuan."

Cao Cao stood, clapping his hands again, a crescent moon-shaped smile splitting his lustrous beard from ear to ear.

"Brilliant," he said. "Absolutely brilliant. While of different backgrounds, I have gathered peerless talents in my staff. With minds and blades such as yours in my service, my young friends, it does not matter who prevails in Xu. In the end, *we* will prevail."

My cheeks warmed up as I bowed in thanks to my lord's generous words.

Lord Cao had turned forty-two, and while still a strong man, age was taking its toll. The hair on the sides of his head had turned gray, as did the center of his beard near the chin. In comparison, the three of us facing him looked as fresh as the morning dew. Man Chong was a most striking figure, his resemblance to his blood father more obvious by the day. He could not grow a beard as rich, but it made his face even more angular and fearsome. I, on the other hand, had grown a nice beard, which I purposefully did not trim with too much care. My hair was slightly lighter than that of most Han people, as were my eyes, but many women had called me handsome, and since I was a warrior through and through, my arms and chest were thick, and my waist slim. Cao Cao saw the future of his ambition in us, and I was proud to be part of it.

"Only one question remains then," Lord Cao went on. "Where is Liu Bei going to go?"

I had yet to think of it, but it was an interesting question indeed. Liu Bei had a few thousand men, but more, he had a reputation. Wherever he went would make his host stronger. In the past, he had served Gongsun Zan, but the Lord of the White Horse was on the brink of defeat. If he had been ambitionless, he might have gone to Liu Biao, who was also a member of the imperial clan, but I doubted it. Liu Bei, for all his talk of benevolence, was as power-hungry as my lord, or so I thought.

"Let's make a game of it," Lord Cao said. "There are some wooden slips and a brush there." He pointed at a low desk where some scribe would take notes when asked. "Each of you, in turn, will write his answer, then bring it to me."

Typical Cao Cao. Man Chong, as the highest ranking among us, went first and in a rapid series of strokes, wrote his answer on a single strip of dark wood. Guo Jia went second, though he invited me to go before him. I refused, if only because I didn't have my answer yet.

Liu Bei, I came to realize, would either go to Yuan Shao or Cao Cao. While he had fought both in the past, he had done so as someone else's subordinate. No personal rancor existed between him and those two lords, and I knew Cao Cao would also see it as such. However, between the two, I could not distinguish which would offer him the best position. I picked up the brush, still not knowing my answer, knelt down, then bent over the low desk, keeping the position for a few heavy seconds.

The answer came as if whispered in my ear by a spirit.

We gave the slips to our lord, who made a game of slowly looking at them at the same time. I must admit, standing between Man Chong and Guo Jia, waiting for our lord's comment, I felt nervous.

Cao Cao barked a burst of heartfelt laughter, then another. Our answers, or one of them at least, pleased him.

"You managed to all disagree and agree at the same time," he said before lowering the three slips.

Man Chong had written the characters for Cao Cao, while Guo Jia had inscribed Xuchang as his answer. As for me, I believed Liu Bei would be coming here as well, but not for Cao Cao. In a calligraphic hand that would have made old Zhong Yao proud, I had written "Son of Heaven."

We had agreed on the destination but not the purpose.

Two months later, Liu Bei bowed in front of Cao Cao, who welcomed him outside the city's walls. He then went to kneel at the bottom of the emperor's throne. Everything had happened as Guo Jia had foreseen. Liu Bei handed the governorship of Xu to Lü Bu; they had given a chance for peace but had failed when the beast came to fear the popularity of the other. Lü Bu was now in control of Xu, but he was a threat we had dealt with once, and I could not wait to do so again. My lord, however, had other plans for us.

2

Jianmen Pass, Yi province
12th month, 4th year of the Jingyuan era of the Cao Wei empire
(263)

"So, why was Cao Cao angry when you gave him your report?" Chen Shou asks. So far he has not mentioned my health, which tells me I must look on the precipice of death. In my youth, I would have shaken a cold like that in a couple of days. Now, I know it will linger for the next month at least. If I survive that long. I hope I do, for there is much to do. General Deng Ai has gone ahead with the main part of the convoy, leaving Zhong Hui and a couple of regiments to watch over a few hundred of us.

"Exactly the question I asked Man Chong when we left Cao Cao's office," I reply. "His answer was *'Just another setback.'*"

"Yuan Shao again?" the scribe asks.

"Indeed. Though, for once, my lord had it coming," I reply while gesturing for my young companion to hand me a cup of fuming tea, as prescribed by the physician. "You might remember that Lord Cao gave himself the title of General-in-Chief, while he named Yuan Shao Grand Commandant."

"Which put the latter under him."

"Exactly. Well, Yuan Shao did not appreciate it one bit and refused the nomination. A clear message of the growing animosity between them. As I said, Lord Cao wasn't ready for that fight, so he made a gesture. He removed his own title and gave it to Yuan Shao, while he became Excellency of Works, which, among the Three Excellency, is the lowest one. And as if this sign of humility wasn't enough, the court granted Yuan Shao full authority over the four northern provinces of Bing, You, and Qing, as well as Ji, which he already governed. Because my lord had overstepped, he now had to make his rival the most powerful man in the empire, and that hurt his pride, even more so because he knew it was his fault to begin with."

As I speak, I manage to sit up, going as far as using my weak arms to push myself against the back of the wagon. The effort leaves me breathless, and it took Chen Shou's hand to help me through this excruciating movement. The scribe returns to his cushion behind his low desk, a frown full of concern wrinkling his clever face.

"We can stop here for the day," he says.

"No need; I can keep talking, if nothing else."

"General Zhong Hui said we would resume the journey in two days. Maybe you should rest as much as possible until then."

"Talking of my youth is the best way to regain some," I reply, making the young man smile. Since we left Chengdu on this journey to our new capital, I have come to appreciate that smile. A piece of me wants to tell the young man of the plan Zong Yu, I, and some others have set in motion, but my old friend has warned me not to trust the scribe. Some youth could be useful, though, if we are to succeed. Maybe when he knows more of our history, he will become a staunch defender of our values too.

"All right," he says, accepting my excuse. "So, tell me, how did Cao Cao welcome Lord Liu Bei? Not keenly, I suppose."

"On the contrary. He was thrilled."

Chen Shou did not expect that. It is easy, sixty-five years later, to remember Cao Cao and Liu Bei as the fiercest enemies, but at that time, they could have become the best of friends.

"Cao Cao valued Liu Bei. Remember that for Cao Cao, talent and guts mattered more than anything, and Liu Bei had plenty of both. After the loss of Sun Jian, I think Lord Cao was glad to have a man of Liu Bei's valor in his world. Sure, both of them had fought each other in Xu province, but Cao Cao did not take it personally, and if he could gain a commander of renown, you could be sure my former lord would treat Liu Bei as a king."

"What did he do?" Chen Shou asks, the brush once again in his hand.

"He first officialized once more the governorship of Xu to Liu Bei, thus making Lü Bu a rebel to the court. Then, and I believe this was the smartest thing he could have done to gain Liu Bei's loyalty, he introduced the man to the emperor."

"Liu Bei must have felt honored."

"Honored? He shook for the rest of the day. He was like a puppy after a walk in the countryside. Sadly, I believe this meeting was the origin of all the future problems between the two lords."

"How so?" Chen Shou asks. Now he has all but forgotten about my health,

"Emperor Xian could already feel his association with Cao Cao wouldn't be as pleasant as I had promised. So, in an attempt to gain a strong ally, he had Liu Bei's lineage checked, and when it was proven that Liu Bei was indeed of imperial blood, the emperor made a big deal of calling his new relative *Huang Shu*, imperial uncle. Many advisors of Lord Cao saw it as a potential threat and advised him to get rid of Liu Bei, but since Guo Jia counseled otherwise, the governor of Xu lived."

"How about you? It must have been difficult to once again be on Guan Yu's side."

"To be honest, I avoided them most of the time. I didn't know how I would react in their presence, and Xuchang was big enough that I did not need to worry about inadvertently crossing their path. Plus ..."

"Yes?" Chen Shou asks. I wonder how to express something I felt guilty about for many years.

"After the battle of Tan, where I had bested Guan Yu and so nearly killed him, a piece of my hatred had abated. It was there, but cold, dormant. I no longer fell asleep with the image of the bearded warrior in my burning chest. I was ashamed to feel as such, for Uncle Cheng had not been avenged, but I could not deny the truth: killing Guan Yu was no longer a priority. It would happen when it would happen."

"Is it possible that you were gaining in maturity?" Chen Shou smugly asks.

"Hardly," I answer, scoffing. "And if anything, my next mission would prove it. I was just twenty but acted like a brat on that one."

"Already looking forward to it," Chen Shou comments,

and I can see he is. "What did Lord Cao ask you to do this time?"

"Lord Cao?" I repeat, baffled to hear the young man call him so.

"Sorry," he replies, equally surprised. "I just wrote those words so many times it became a habit, I guess."

"I understand," I reply. "But be careful who hears you call him as such. Cao Cao might be the founding father of your new empire, but it doesn't mean his memory is well-loved by everyone."

Chen Shou doesn't really understand the meaning of my words. By the end of the journey, he will.

"To answer your question, Cao Cao actually sent me on a double mission. The first was to accompany Liu Bei back to Xu. While my lord appreciated the man, his rapidly growing popularity in Xuchang was troublesome, and he could use him in Xu, so he gave Liu Bei two thousand men, some supplies, and sent him to Xiaopei, which stood near the border of Yan and would give us a nice footing in Xu. I was to assess Liu Bei's loyalty and make sure he had what it took to hold Xiaopei against Lü Bu. For all his worth, Liu Bei had yet to gain any great victory, so some of my lord's advisors were understandably doubtful of his capabilities as a warlord. That mission, however, was given to me simply because I was going in the same direction on another matter. My destination was south, where a young lord was making a name for himself. A name my lord respected and one that would make a perfect ally against Yuan Shu, for the toad had made the greatest of a long list of stupid decisions, and it was time to do something about him."

*The border between Yan and Xu provinces.
2nd month, 2nd year of Jian'an era (197), Han Dynasty*

"Come on, Captain. Admit it. We're going to kill him, aren't we?" Meng Shudu asked in his big, resonating voice.

"Who are we going to kill?" I asked, for I had just joined my men's circle around the evening fire and had no clue what they were talking about.

"The toad," Shudu's brother, Bobo, explained. "It's got to be why the big chief sent us, right?"

I understood their remark and also believed it would have been a good use of our talents. But Yuan Shu wasn't our target this time; neither was our mission assassination.

People seldom talked of anything but Yuan Shu in those days. In retrospect, it should have surprised no one, for the man was nothing if not a first-class moron, but it did baffle the whole empire when he declared himself emperor. What he thought when he openly broke away from the Great Han and declared his own Zhong dynasty, I could not say, but it was certainly not the total isolation that followed. All his allies—what few he had left—abandoned him, and while he technically ruled Yang province in the southeast and part of Yu, his real power barely stretched over a few commanderies. And since he was hated by every lord in the empire, especially his half-brother, he found no support whatsoever. Still, a declaration of independence was dangerous and needed to be punished before the idea spread to other lords.

That, however, wasn't the Scorpions' purpose, but I could not reveal our goal to my men for the moment. Too many ears around us.

"Who has bet on Yuan Shu's murder?" I asked the circle

because, of course, they had bet on our mission. Those animals would bet on anything. Twelve hands rose.

"So?" Liang-the-broken asked. "Did we win?"

"Keep betting," I answered, amusing myself with the torrent of curses that followed.

I took my place next to Two-Knives, received a bowl of congee supplemented by a piece of chicken meat from the one hand of Guo Wen, and assessed the faces of those hard men by my side. We'd lost a few comrades over the past two years, but most had miraculously survived. With twenty-six men, I was the captain of the smallest retinue in the armies of Cao Cao, but we made in quality what we lacked in number. That number, however, would soon have to be split in two. Not all of them would accompany me to the south. I was hesitant about who to choose for this faraway mission, at least for a few of them, so I had left the decision in the hands of Tian Guli, who was presently checking our horses. The fresher and stronger ones would come with me, along with their riders.

The second group, close to fifteen men, would remain with the army of Liu Bei in Xiaopei and monitor the situation until I returned. Du Yuan, my second-in-command, would lead them. Only he and Guli knew about it so far. Many of them would hate the idea of being left behind, even more so because they would remain in Xu, a place we had very few fond memories of since most of us had fought in the massacre of the province. It could not be helped. I needed to move fast and discreetly.

While exchanging jokes with my men, I wondered who would make the best companions for the journey when a pair of feet planted themselves right behind me.

"Governor Liu requests the presence of your captain," a soldier said in a slightly trembling voice.

He was one of Liu Bei's original soldiers and knew not whom to address. Contrary to the rest of the army, my men wore whatever armor they wanted, so nothing made me stand out in this crowd. My helmet, which had belonged to Cao Cao before, might have tipped him off, but I had left it with our gear. When I did not react, One-eye, the leader of my archers, answered for me.

"And what does the governor want with us?" he asked.

"I don't know," the young soldier replied, confused.

"Does he know who we are?" Liang-the-broken asked, confusing the soldier even more.

"You are the Scorpions of Cao Cao," he replied, and this time I was the one to be shocked, and not just me. The circle of my men became suddenly very quiet, and an odd tension rose in a second.

"You mean you *do* know who we are?" Liang asked again.

"Of course I do," the soldier replied, scoffing. "Everyone does. The Scorpions are famous and feared."

My men looked at each other with something like awe, eyes round and white in the growing darkness. I did the same, exchanging a childish look with Du Yuan before one of us burst into laughter, pulling the lot of us into an infectious guffaw.

So the Scorpions were getting famous. And not just famous but recognizable. If I were to guess, I'd say one or several of my men had babbled about it during the previous days on the march. And now I understood the soldier's obvious discomfort. In his mind, he wasn't just speaking to a group of hardened soldiers but to the most dangerous bunch of agents working for Cao Cao.

"So what does the governor want with the *famous* Scorpions?" Meng Shudu asked.

"Maybe he wants us to remove a name from his list?" his little brother said.

"Or to visit a creditor," Shudu suggested.

"I really don't know," the soldier said, cold sweat running down his back.

"I think you do," Du Yuan said.

"Why don't we ask Stinger to question him," Pox said.

On cue, Stinger stood, quiet but threatening as death itself, and the soldier recoiled a little.

"Enough," I said, standing as well, forcing the enjoyment to slowly die down. "Take me to the governor."

Liu Bei, as a commander, was the opposite of Cao Cao. While my lord campaigned with enough items to turn his tent into a small version of his mansion, the imperial uncle traveled frugally. His tent was simple, barely bigger than his soldiers', and he shared it with his brothers. I did not see what he kept inside, but I would have bet it consisted of basic cots, itchy blankets, and simple three-legged stools, just like those he and his two brothers sat on as the soldier accompanied me to them.

"Liao Chun, captain of the Scorpions," the young man said as we both bowed toward the trio. Liu Bei stood, thanked his man, which I found odd, and invited me to sit on the last stool available around their fire. Liu Bei was maybe five years younger than my lord but looked both younger and older at the same time. Younger because of his naive, gentle eyes presently reflecting stars, and older because of the wrinkles at their corners. He was far from being a handsome man. Plain would be a more fitting description. But even then, long before I understood the depth of his grandeur, he struck me with the effect of his aura. Being in his presence was akin to a cold bath after a long summer day of work. It was soothing and energizing at the same time.

As I accepted his invitation, Zhang Fei handed me a cup of clay filled with fuming yellow wine. Guan Yu had not offered me a glance so far.

"What can I do for you?" I asked in a solid, perfunctory tone.

"It is you, isn't it?" Liu Bei asked.

I stiffened a bit at that. As I left my men, Du Yuan had accompanied me for a few steps and whispered for me to be careful. We had spent enough time in Xiapi recently that one of them might have recognized me. I hoped the armor and the sword would make me unrecognizable, but there was always a chance Zhang Fei had been more observant than I thought.

"Governor?" I asked.

"The soldier who so nearly took Guan Yu from us by Tan," he said, no trace of anger in his voice. I breathed a little at that, but it was Guan Yu's turn to stiffen and look the other way.

"I did fight your brother at Tan and had him at the point of my blade," I replied. I should have been more humble in my answer. I should have mentioned that luck had been on my side, and the whole point would have been brushed aside. But being in their presence was intoxicating, and I wanted it known that I did not fear them or care for etiquette. I hoped to provoke my nemesis, maybe even push him to another fight, but I poked the wrong brother.

Zhang Fei scoffed and spat a rich gob of phlegm into the fire.

"You got lucky, *pup*," he said. "If Guan Yu's shoulder hadn't been broken, he would have cut you in half."

"His shoulder broke because I threw a spear at his horse, and he fell. It was no luck," I replied.

"A cowardly tactic," Zhang Fei went on, wrinkling his nose.

"More than being rescued by your brothers during a duel?" I asked, referring to his fight with Lü Bu.

"What did you just say?" he barked, standing as if stung by a bee, fists tightly shut by his sides.

"I fought your brother fairly and won't have you take my victory away. Call me coward once more—I dare you," I said, taking a bold step in Zhang Fei's direction. He replied in kind, and when he next spoke, he stood so close to me that I could smell the mixture of garlic and *baijiu* on his breath.

"Or what? You would try your *luck* against me? Just say the word, *pup*, and you and I will go for a few rounds. If you last that long, that is." I maintained a facade of confidence and would not back away, but I could not suppress the knot in my belly. Zhang Fei was feral. I could feel the vibrations from his wrath through the tips of my fingers. His shoulders were much wider than mine, and his arms twice as big. If we were to fight, he would kill me, I thought. But I would not back down.

"Are you sure you want to throw another drunken tantrum? Last time wasn't enough?" I asked. I saw murderous flames rise in his eyes and took an involuntary step back. Zhang Fei raised his arm, ready to strike me down, but Guan Yu reacted faster and caught his brother by the wrist. I had forgotten how tall he was.

"Calm down, little brother," Guan Yu said in his deep, venerable voice. "This young man did defeat me. And luck is also part of the warrior's path." I did not like the way he implied the presence of luck in our duel but let it slide.

Zhang Fei did not immediately relent. But after a few seconds of staring at each other, he shook off Guan Yu's grip and stormed away to the gods knew where. I smirked at the sight of this angry man shaking with rage on his way to the closest jug of wine. My relationship with Zhang Fei did not start on a good basis.

"My apologies for my brother's behavior," Liu Bei said.

"It is fine," I said, though, again, I should have been more polite and apologized as well. "What can I do for you, Governor?"

"Please take a seat," he said, inviting me back to my stool. I realized then that despite the turbulence, Liu Bei had not lifted a finger.

I accepted, if only because my legs had weakened from the tension and my cup had been knocked away. Guan Yu refilled it and held it to me. When I took the cup, our eyes met, and my heart skipped a bit. There, deep within those two dark-brown irises, was more threat than any word could convey. For all his monk-like quietness, Guan Yu was barely controlling himself. A piece of his *white soul* tried to shake its shackles off and wanted to tear me to pieces. I got scared; I say it without shame. I looked into the abyss and saw my death.

"I return the favor for Hulao," he said, bringing me back to the now.

"And I won't let it cool down either," I managed to reply.

The moment passed, and I remembered to breathe. The wine was awful, but I did my best to hide my impression of it, promising myself not to anger them again for the rest of the night.

"Your name is Liao Chun?" the imperial uncle asked.

"That is correct," I said, fairly impressed that such a man would know me.

"When you ... fought," Liu Bei went on after I enjoyed some of their "gift," "you told my brother to tell Cheng Yuanzhi you sent him. Is that correct?"

"It is," I answered, wondering where this was going.

"Is this the Cheng Yuanzhi who led a division of Yellow Turbans in Zuo?" he asked.

"The very same," I replied. "And whom you killed on the way to Julu."

"Who was he to you?" Liu Bei asked. That he did not even flinch at the accusing tone I had just used was slightly infuriating but also quite impressive.

"He was my uncle. Not by blood, but by something stronger," I explained. "He showed the way to this peasant boy from Nanyang and took me under his wing. He and Deng Mao, whom Zhang Fei killed, treated me with respect, even though I was only seven."

"And you have since then sworn vengeance and hated us in your heart?" Liu Bei asked. The sorrow in his voice was genuine. I wanted to punch him in the face.

"I have and still do," I replied. Highborn can lie through their teeth, even when it is a matter of emotion, but I could not. Many had already told me my big mouth would get me in trouble, including Lord Cao, but keeping it shut was beyond me.

"We can never make it up to you," Liu Bei continued, leaning over. I copied him without realizing it. "But I am sorry we took your uncles away."

"Don't be," I replied. I so hated this sentimentalism of his. Men didn't speak like that, at least not warriors. Who was he to cheapen my quest for vengeance with base words? "You killed them in war; this is the way of things. And I will one day kill you in their names and in the names of Wu Rang and Cao Shuo, who died in Tan. For now, we are on the same side, but I know it will not always be so. Then, someone will try to kill me in your name. And so on and so on, as long as warriors exist and have a sense of duty."

Liu Bei sighed, his eyes lost in his cup of clay. Back then, I wondered if he was a fool or a liar, but as I got to know him better, I understood he was neither. His will to change the world was pure, and hearing a youngling talking of vengeance as I had filled him with dread for the future.

"Wait here, please," Guan Yu said, standing in a fluid motion full of grace. He took some steps toward their tent.

"How did you know my name?" I asked Liu Bei when his brother disappeared behind the flap.

Liu Bei's head rose from his thoughts as if I had interrupted him halfway through his meditation.

"The emperor told me about you," Liu Bei answered happily. "He even called you a friend."

"Liu Xie is a wonderful young man," I said, blushing.

"But he is alone," Liu Bei replied. "And will need friends. Can he count on you?"

"He has my friendship," I said as if it were an actual answer, not just empty words.

"But can he count on you against the rest of the world?" he asked, his tone dead serious. What he asked, but could not word, was if I would help Emperor Xian against Cao Cao if it came to that.

I wanted to curse him. Who was he to put me on the spot like that? And not just me, but my lord too had just been insulted. Despite his latest political blunders, my lord had done more for the emperor than anyone else. He had offered a safe haven to Liu Xie, while Liu Bei lost a province to an untrustworthy beast. Cao Cao had given land to the poor, while *he* had given up a city for the safety of his wife. *Screw him and his easy loyalty to the Han*, I thought. But just as I was about to storm out in a similar fashion to Zhang Fei, Guan Yu came back, a roll of bamboo slip stretched out from one hand to the other, his eyes lost in its contents.

"Under your uncle's name," he said as he handed me the scroll, "is that you?"

I turned the scroll the other way around, found the characters for Cheng Yuanzhi, then below it, a series of other characters forming the sentence *young boy on gray mare*, followed by a series of other descriptions, mostly men. *Old man with white droopy mustache; young spearman with broken nose; gang leader wearing brown gloves; young man bare chest*, and so on, and so on, slip after slip.

"What is it?" I asked.

"Every person I have killed," Guan Yu said with no trace of pride or remorse.

"Why?"

"When I die, I will have a lot of apologies to give in the afterlife," he said.

I found the idea astonishing, and I remember thinking it a shame I had not done the same, for already I could not recall the faces of all my victims.

"You can take that one off then," I told him as I handed the scroll back. "It was me."

Without a word, Guan Yu stooped down to the fire at the center of the small circle of stools, picked up a piece of charcoal, and rubbed it across the description of seven-year-old me. I could swear I saw the shadow of a smile through his magnificent beard.

"Young man," he said as he rolled the thing up, "if you manage to fulfill your vengeance, please bury this with me."

"You have my word," I replied. A promise I meant. "And if I fail, please write my real name there, Liao Chun."

"I will not forget," he said before stretching his empty hand to me.

I had seen people from the northern tribes hold each other's arms when saluting or agreeing to a trade, and while I found this custom barbaric, it felt oddly perfect in this circumstance. So, I reached for his arm and squeezed it for a couple of seconds.

Though I would not have recognized it then, the last of my hatred for the bearded warrior died that night. We had reached a tacit agreement. Whatever happened between us would do so without hard feelings; it would just be.

I left them feeling light and understood later this meeting had taken place so that Guan Yu could remove a name from his list. While I had not stopped thinking about him for the past thirteen years, Guan Yu also kept the memory of our first encounter in his mind, like a dark spot on the white canvas of his warrior's path.

The next day, the army stepped into Xu province, and I split from the main group with nine of my companions. I had a long road ahead. Hundreds of *li* to cross before meeting the man they called Xiao Ba Wang, the *Little Conqueror*.

3

Qu'e, Wu commandery, Yang province
3rd month, 2nd year of Jian'an era (197), Han Dynasty

EVEN THEN, before it became an economic and cultural center to rival cities like Luoyang and Chang'an, Wu commandery was described as *heaven on earth*, and I could only agree. Maybe luck made me visit the city of Qu'e on the days when flowers blossomed pink and white on the peach trees lining the many riverbanks, or maybe those people woke every day to a different sight of wonder. Whatever it was, I fell in love with that country. Few horses were parading the narrow streets of Qu'e, its inhabitants preferring the use of light barges to travel the city from north to south, east to west, and along the canals. Nature was ever present throughout Qu'e in the form of well-maintained ponds and rows of flowery trees, even in the southernmost part of the city where the less fortunate lived. As I strolled along the quiet canal, eyes half-closed to appreciate the fragrance of the blooming peach trees, any sense of urgency vanished from my travel-tired body. Qu'e wasn't the largest city I came across and could even be called a town in the north of the Great Han, but it was ... sweet.

From the moment we split from the main army and followed the southern border of Xu almost to the sea, my mind longed to be in Wu. I first looked forward to leaving south Xu, where I had committed the worst actions of my life during the year-long massacre of the province. Then, my second, maybe more urgent desire, was to be done with crossing the Dajiang, the *great river*. I had crossed the Yellow River a few times already and the Huai on a couple of occasions, but none of those experiences filled me with joy. I had long decided I hated boats and rivers, but there was no reaching the Little Conqueror without crossing the Dajiang.

I chose to cross near Moling, now called Jianye, the great city at the narrow border between Xu and Yang, but we did not even enter it. Instead, because the further south we went, the fewer chances of meeting Yuan Shu's men we took, I pressed my group of ten riders until the night grew dark.

The peaceful scent of spring and the sight of the waking meadow welcomed us at dawn. A double rainbow appeared with the sun and accompanied our ride for the rest of the morning. It disappeared shortly before we came upon the sight of Qu'e, where we would afford the first real rest of this journey.

Ten days from the border near Xiapi to Qu'e was a feat even I thought impossible, but we had ridden as if a dragon roared on our backs. My men and Guli were upset with me for the infernal rhythm, and they had every right to feel as such.

Sure, we were supposed to move as fast as humanly possible, but we had long crossed that limit. When the journey began, I granted us stops at postal stations and inns, where we pretended to be fighters willing to join the ranks of the local leader. This excuse allowed us to ask questions about the situation in the neighborhood.

We thus learned two things.

First, even close to Lujiang commandery in Yang province, the center of Yuan Shu's territory, the toad received no support from the folks. They spat at the mention of his name and cursed his ridiculous plan of naming himself emperor. No one was fooled; this would lead to war and very few bet on a victory from their new son of heaven. When we realized the extent of the people's animosity toward their ruler, we changed tactics and explained that we were traveling to join Sun Ce, the Little Conqueror, and more than once were offered drinks and supper at the news.

If folks hated Yuan Shu and talked about him like the plague incarnate, they loved Sun Ce as if he controlled the sun and rain. And indeed, there was much to love about the man.

Sun Ce was Sun Jian's first son. The one time I met the Tiger, he had told me about him. Sun Ce was a year older than I and made the pride of his father, which in my young mind had been enough to create the image of a worthy rival. When Jian died, I never thought I would hear about the Sun clan again, but it was without counting on Ce being the image of his father in more than one way.

Since Sun Jian had been Yuan Shu's vassal, it was only natural that Sun Ce served the toad. If their clan had been older and more illustrious, the young man would have found employment anywhere, but the Sun were nothing before Jian. They liked to claim they descended from Sun Zi, the genius who wrote *The Art of War*, but I could just as much declare myself the direct scion of Huang Di.

Sun Ce served Yuan Shu from the age of eighteen and quickly made a name for himself, a name which spread all the way to Cao Cao's ears. From his first military actions, Sun Ce showed promise and earned the loyalty of his father's officers, but the toad failed to reward his young servant properly and left him to his own self for two years. Then came a time, maybe a year before the moment I crossed the Great River, when he had no choice but to use the young man's talents.

Yuan Shu had been pressed on all sides. North, by us, and to some extent by Liu Bei, and south, by a certain Liu Yao, who had been named governor of Yang by the court when it still ruled from Chang'an. Liu Yao controlled the south of the river, the bigger part of the province, while Yuan Shu held the north. Nothing worked against Liu Yao, but Sun Ce declared with confidence that would have made his father proud that he could regain the southern commanderies for Yuan Shu. Veterans of the toad laughed at the young man's boast, and Yuan Shu probably did too, but, thinking he would at least get rid of an inconvenient officer, he gave a thousand men to Sun Ce and let him loose on his enemy.

As a sign of his charisma, on the march from Shouchun, Yuan Shu's capital, to the Great River, Sun Ce managed to gather eight thousand more men. With this strong division, the son of Jian crossed the river and began a campaign that would reshape our world in a few months.

No one could resist the Little Conqueror and his men. They first quickly regained control of Wu commandery, the home fief of his family, then Kuaiji, southeast of it. From there, gathering the forces of the vanquished under his own banner, he waged battle after battle in Danyang commandery, where Liu Yao had planted his flag.

When we entered Wu, people claimed Sun Ce had just

chased Liu Yao from Danyang as well and was now the real master of the southeast corner of the empire.

But this wasn't the reason why my lord sent me there. No, as far as Cao Cao was concerned, Sun Ce's value came from his unique position. While he had started as a servant of Yuan Shu, the instant the toad declared his own dynasty, the young man broke all allegiance with him and ensured the world knew he had nothing to do with that fool. He was thus something of an independent warlord, with no link to either of the two Yuan, Lü Bu, or Liu Bei, and he hated Liu Biao for his father's death. And since Ce wasn't a direct neighbor to Lord Cao, he was thus the perfect potential ally. My role was to make first contact with him and establish the basis of a beneficial friendship between Lord Cao and Sun Ce.

However, I was not, and would never be, a talented diplomat. Too much ass-kissing and bending-over for my taste. But my lord needed to act fast on this and hoped my firsthand meeting with Ce's father would help. Even better, according to my lord, the Conqueror and I were of similar age. I argued that Cao Ang, Cao Cao's first son, would make a better envoy or should at least accompany us, but Lord Cao had other plans for his son. All he could send at this time was the captain of the Scorpions, a verbal offer with simple terms, and complete freedom in case of negotiation. Lord Cao said he trusted my capacity to judge the young Sun and would know how much to promise him accordingly.

I did not leave Xuchang a confident man, to say the least. But I was enthused at the idea of meeting the Tiger's son and paying my respects to Sun Jian in Qu'e, where he had been buried. I knew Sun Ce would not be here, of course, but my lord had agreed to my idea of a small detour through the Sun clan's home base, even if this secondary task had to be done in secret. No one was to know of our presence until we met with the Conqueror.

To be honest, by the time we reached the burial ground, I was a little tired of hearing about Sun Ce. Everyone talked as if they knew him, and we heard many unbelievable tales. At one point, he was ten *chi* tall, with arms reaching to his knees and a chest as wide as that of a bear. Then we heard of his voice capable of shaking the mountains, his sight sharp enough to see the sun through the thickest clouds, and his hearing, whose acuity let him hear the hair grow on the back of sheep. All a bunch of nonsense. People had found a hero, and their imagination ran limitless. They all agreed he was handsome, especially the women, a point Guli did not ignore, and I think this was the moment I started to question the real value of such an extraordinary being.

It was one thing to be tall, and strong, and valiant, and daring, but it was another to be all of this plus handsome. Being a military man with a few years of experience, I knew his companions and subalterns would have accomplished many of the feats associated with his name, but even then, as I finally reached his father's stele, I'd had enough of him. And that was before actually meeting the man.

I put those thoughts for later as I knelt and kowtowed in front of the Tiger's resting place.

It was a very simple monument of granite, high as a man, with the Tiger's life written on it. It sat atop a small hill on the northern side of the city, from where Jian would protect his people. Climbing the hill was a simple affair and did not leave me winded. I had asked my men to remain at the bottom and would let them pay their respects after if they wanted, but only Liang-the-broken, who was from this commandery, asked to be allowed to.

The hill was quiet, with few such steles on it and even fewer people visiting them. While the sun still had a solid *shi* before it set, the evening's chill was already apparent through my bones. It felt rather good. I easily found the right mood in me.

I let my mind wander to that day, seven years before, when the Tiger gratified me with his infectious smile. I had started the evening thinking of him as my sister's murderer, but by the time he emptied his last cup, I was under the spell of his charisma and saw him as the only match for my lord in the world. I remembered his large back as he climbed on his stallion and left our camp, his cloak swiftly waving with the gentle wind like the promise of an outstanding future. One year later, he died, and the Great Han lost one of his most brilliant warlords.

I kowtowed a second time, slowly, as if touching the ground where his body remained with my forehead could connect me to him. Then I sat up again.

"Did you know my husband?" a woman said on my left. I was startled by her presence, then by her beauty. I only caught a glimpse of her face before the sun appeared through the clouds and forced me to lower my gaze, but it was enough to recognize Jian's great taste in women.

"Not as much as I wished," I replied as Lady Wu knelt by my side, a bottle in her arms. "My apologies," I then said, giving a last customary bow to leave the spot to her.

"Please," she hurried to say as I straightened up, "stay."

I thanked her and asked for only a minute to pay my respects, which she allowed with a friendly smile.

Lady Wu was a noblewoman in her mid-forties from a great clan of the region. As her family stood far above the likes of a young Sun Jian, she should never have married him. But her father, a great judge of character, knew the second he met the Tiger that he would achieve amazing things and granted his daughter's hand. She had borne five sons and one daughter to him, but you couldn't guess it by looking at her. The lady had the beauty of a golden tree and the energy to rival her late husband. As she sat by my side, I felt her electric aura like the gusts of wind before the storm and wondered if all great lords shared a talent for finding perfect women. I also wondered if maybe my appetite for older, married women was more than a mockery from my friends. While I still considered Lady Bian a more beautiful woman, Lady Wu had few rivals I knew of. She was on the shorter side, stood and sat straight as a soldier on inspection, and moved with the frankness most educated women lacked. Her hair, tied in the simple yet elegant style of the southeast, was kept together by a white pin shaped like a prowling tiger, and she wore rich red and golden silk clothes. Her eyes were very dark at the center of a slightly tanned face that had laughed often, and as she granted me a generous smile, I realized I had been staring.

"Apologies," I mumbled as I forced my attention back to the stele.

"I will take it as a compliment," she said, giggling discreetly.

"It is a beautiful place," I clumsily said.

"I think so, too," she replied. "My son wanted to build a mausoleum worthy of a king. But I said no. Jian was a free spirit, restless and bold. He would not have liked to be under a roof forever. He needs the sun and the wind, my husband."

"It sounds like him," I replied, ignoring the touching tear on her elegant cheek.

"How did you know him?" she asked as she put the bottle in front of her.

I saw no reason to lie. Many men, especially soldiers, had met Sun Jian during his campaigns.

"I met him in Hulao," I said, "and only spoke to him once. But once is enough with a man like your husband."

"Well said," she replied proudly. "But aren't you a bit young for Hulao?"

"I wasn't a soldier," I answered, refraining from using the word *yet*. "Just a boy helping great men before the battles. The Tiger left a strong impression on me, and I have long wished to pay my respects."

"We thank you, young man," she said, tapping the back of my hand with the tip of her fingers. "This," she went on, nodding toward the bottle on the ground, "was his favorite *huang jiu*. Even when he rose in the world, Jian preferred yellow wine, and no beverage of this kind pleased him more than Qu'e's. Every time before he left me on some campaign, he made me promise that should he fall, I was to serve him a cup every day until I joined him."

"I am so sorry then," I said, laughing happily, "for I believe I only served him rice wine in Hulao."

"Would you like to pour today's cup then?" she asked.

Even sixty-five years later, I cannot explain why, but it brought me close to tears. I have been given many honors in my life from the hands of three different emperors and some other great lords. But Lady Wu asking me if I wanted to pour a cup of yellow wine to her dead husband was one of the greatest. I think it was the way she asked, as if it were the most natural thing in the world, that almost undid me.

"It would be an honor," I replied before she removed the cup from the top of the bottle and filled it with honey-colored wine. She invited me to pick it up, which I did before standing. I then crossed the three steps to the stele and remained motionless in front of it for a few seconds.

"My lord wishes to express his respects to you, Tiger of the Jiangnan," I whispered to the stone, my hands extended in a military salute with the cup between them. "And his deepest regrets that you will not be part of this land's future." I do not think the lady could hear my words, but I am certain *he* did. "He hopes to come here in person someday and drink to your name, but should it not happen, please wait for him so that you two can share another few cups and exchange stories. As for me, I hope when we next meet, I will be worthy of sitting at the table with the two of you."

I slowly emptied the cup on top of the stone and watched the fragrant liquid wash over the Tiger's name. And now, as I am old, so many years after Sun Jian was given the posthumous name of Emperor Wulie and after they put him in a mausoleum, I cannot but wonder if I deserve a place at his table. I have many tales to share with him. I bowed again after taking some steps back and handed the cup to Lady Wu.

"Thank you," I said.

"It is I who should thank you," she said. "I'm sure he is happy to receive his wine from a friend for once." Lady Wu tilted her head, a curious light in her eyes as we stood in front of each other for the first time. "Have we met?" she asked. "You look familiar."

I could not stop a short laugh.

"Your husband said the same," I told her. "He thought I might just have reminded him of his first son because we were about the same age."

"Hardly," she replied with a scoff, and for a second I misunderstood her meaning. "You are far more handsome and obviously better mannered," she went on, and again I had to reply with a short burst of laughter. This was the first time I heard someone criticize the shiny Sun Ce, and I liked the lady even more for it.

"Would you like to dine with me?" she asked in a seductive tone. "With all the men of the family in Danyang, the company is limited at home, and I would love to hear more about your time with my husband."

I was tempted. I was extremely tempted. Lady Wu loved her husband deeply but had been a widow for six years and must have felt lonely. As for me, she was so exactly my type of woman that it hurt to resist her. If Guli hadn't been what she was to me then, or rather, if she hadn't been there, I would have accepted. I'm quite ashamed of admitting it, but I was young and passionate, and Lady Wu had me wrapped around her little finger and thirsty for her. Sun Jian was far from my mind at this very moment. But, on one of those rare occasions when I managed to control myself, I thanked her and told her I was in the company of nine comrades, and we could not impose on her. She said she understood and thanked me again for my presence, then squeezed my wrist a little before departing from the hill, leaving me breathless as if I had fought three rotations on the battlefield.

On that night, as I lay down with Guli, I must admit I thought of another woman. And on the next morning, as we departed Qu'e, I promised myself I would one day come back. A promise I never fulfilled.

But I would meet the lady again.

FINDING the Little Conqueror was the easiest thing in the world. One just had to follow the flocks of young men crossing the country toward the southwest. Meddling with them, we heard the rumors of Sun Ce's location in the very south of Danyang, where the young lord was preparing to push Liu Yao out of the commandery. This news displeased us because it meant going a few more days in the opposite direction from home, and the weather was turning hotter and more humid by the day.

Commanderies in the south were far bigger than in the north. So much so that Danyang was as wide as a whole province in the central plains. Back when our ancestors grew their influence beyond the Great River, counties and commanderies were delimited according to their population so that no territory held more inhabitants than the others, and I guess few Han people lived here then. This, however, had changed a lot over the generations. A fact the court had either ignored or never understood. Because I was born north of the Huai, I was considered a northerner and grew up with a distorted, arrogant vision of the south. We always joked about their eating habits, poor clothing, and beliefs, as if living here turned one into a barbarian. Nothing could be further from the truth. In fact, the south felt a lot more civilized than any other place I had visited so far, and the number of inhabitants was nothing to be ashamed of.

More than anything, I adored the abundance of rice. The further south and west we went, the cheaper it got, and one look at the countryside sufficed to see how easily it grew around here.

Towns were a little smaller, it is true, and people did wear fewer clothes, but anyone living in such a humid place would. And while I saw many non-Han people, those I met looked no different than folks from Fa Jia Po. In fact, many inhabitants of this region had come over the past decades, fleeing the violence in the north.

Even after a few years of petty wars, Jiangnan, south of the river, was a wonderful country. If my lord had not emphasized the situation's urgency, I would have called for us to slow down a little. Time, though, was of the essence, especially with the Little Conqueror being in the far south of Danyang Commandery.

Luckily enough, the rumors were outdated, and four days after leaving Qu'e, we came in sight of Ce's army near a town called Xuancheng. Sun Ce's men surrounded the town, and light camps had been built in the four directions around it, with many more activity spots between them. We followed the group of hopeful recruits funneling to the camps but did not simply wait in line and faced a wave of curses as we trotted past the lot of them. I had ordered my nine companions to look their best, with polished armor, well-trimmed beards, and horses as clean as possible, but even then knew we presented a poor diplomatic front. Not for the first, not for the last time, I thought my lord had made a mistake in choosing us, or me at least.

When I asked the officer in charge of welcoming the new recruits to see the camp leader, without saying who I was or represented, all it took was for him to spot the fine helmet on my head to get some answer. He invited us to dismount and ordered one of his subalterns to walk us to their commander. I did not trust those men yet, so I left Guo Huai, our little sparrow, and Two-Knives to guard the horses.

Walking through the camp allowed us to assess this army of newly recruited men and young officers. It was a lightly built affair, not a fortified camp as we used to do, but defense wasn't its purpose.

Besides the quality of the fortifications, I must say I was impressed with what I saw. While most soldiers had been warring for less than a year and had likely received a nominal training at best, they behaved professionally, practiced when not on duty, and carried an air of competence a veteran like me could appreciate. They might still be fresh but had seen more battles than most soldiers in a lifetime. It was off to a good start.

The army of Sun Ce was closing in on the last threat to his dominion of Danyang, the town of Xuancheng itself, where a great warrior still resisted the Little Conqueror. His name was Taishi Ci, and even I had heard of his valor. He was from the northeast of the empire and had made a name for himself as an honorable, loyal, and fierce fighter. The kind of man who never went back on his word, which, apparently, he had given to Liu Yao. Taishi Ci was, without a doubt, in a hopeless situation, but it wouldn't change his determination.

We were taken to the tent of command of the northern camp but did not even enter it, for the man we were to meet was hunched over a table outside, a map of the land stretching past the limits of the piece of furniture. No one was around him, and the officer was deep in his map, counting the distance between two points with a bamboo ruler.

"Chief Controller Lü," the soldier accompanying us said while saluting the officer, "those men asked to see you."

The bynamed Lü raised his head from the map, offering us a warm pair of hazelnut eyes framed by two strands of naturally gray hair. Despite this detail, the chief controller could not have been over thirty years old. Here was the man responsible for the army's discipline and thus, the one who should be congratulated on these soldiers' professionalism.

"Thank you," he told his soldier to send him away. "I am truly sorry for asking this, but would you mind giving me just a few seconds," he then asked, almost but not quite pinching his thumb and first finger to show us he only needed a short time.

"Of course," I replied.

Chief Controller Lü went back to his map and moved his ruler in a rapid succession of measures starting from the city to what I assumed to be a tributary of the Dajiang.

"Fifty-eight," he then told himself. With the tip of his right boot, he traced the characters for the number he had just mentioned in the dirt before bringing his attention back to us. "Sorry. What can I do for you?" he asked politely.

Even though this man was responsible for administering and disciplining two divisions' worth of recruits, he still felt the need to apologize for making us wait a few seconds. I quite liked that. Just like his soldiers, he was a competent man, and I thought Cao Cao would appreciate him.

"Our apologies for intruding. My name is Liao Chun, and I have been sent on a representative mission by Emperor Xian under direct orders from Cao Cao," I said, giving a *zuo yi* salute and bowing.

"All the way from Xuchang?" the man asked as he rendered the salute. "This must be very important indeed. My name is Lü Fan, chief controller of General Sun Ce's army."

This is how I met Lü Fan, a great friend of the Little Conqueror and the man responsible for much of his success. He was to Sun Ce what Xiahou Dun was to Cao Cao but stood a world above in manner and kindness.

"It is indeed important," I replied. "We hoped to meet your general to deliver our message at the earliest convenience."

A company of soldiers ran behind us, their rhythmical

stomping sending me back to my training year. Lü Fan waited for them to move on before he spoke.

"He is in the southern camp. If you want, I can take you there."

"You must be busy," I said. "Surely one of your aides can take us to him?"

"It would be my pleasure. And I have things to share with the general," he replied. "I suggest you bring two of your men, or woman," Lü Fan said, nodding toward Guli. "The others are welcome to use our facilities, though I'm sorry to say we did not set up much this time."

I accepted his offer and asked Liang-the-broken and Hu Zi, one of my two messengers, to accompany me. The first because he was my only warrior from those parts, and the second because he was discreet and could behave.

Lü Fan lent us three fresh horses, and in a matter of minutes, we left the northern camp. He rode well, contrary to what people said of southerners, which made sense when I heard more about him.

"I'm from Runan," he said as we circled around the town, "so I'm afraid I don't know much about boats. I still prefer horses and chariots to them."

"You've known Sun Ce for a long time?" I asked.

"I've been serving him for five years. Back then, he had less than five hundred men in his retinue, so when I showed up with one hundred more, he welcomed me with open arms."

"You've been with him since before he became the Little Conqueror, yet he makes you his chief controller?" I asked, trying not to sound too judgmental. This post was far from being prestigious, and surely a man of Lü Fan's talent could hope for more.

"I asked for it," he answered. "No need to look so

surprised; someone has to do it, and it wasn't going to be Ce. My general is many great things, but organized isn't one of them. He can't stay put for more than a minute, so if no one took care of discipline, in a matter of months, these soldiers would turn little better than pirates." Lü Fan, despite the jest aimed at his leader, spoke with obvious admiration, yet he was the one I was forced to respect.

"It is a bit rude of me to ask," Lü Fan said, "but when you meet the general, try to be as brief and direct as possible. He is very busy and does not care much for etiquette, though he doesn't mind flatteries."

"I can see he is busy indeed," I replied, a nod toward Xuancheng. "What's happening here? Surely this town cannot resist such an army."

"You know who is inside?"

"Taishi Ci, isn't it? I heard about him," I said.

"My lord dueled with him a few months ago, and it came to a draw. As you can guess, it both infuriated him and gave him great respect for his opponent."

"Let me guess. He wants Taishi Ci in his service?"

"Exactly. That's why, as we swept over Danyang, we left Xuancheng alone, but now it's all that's left of the enemy, and this Taishi Ci refuses our offers. We can storm the city, but the general would rather not risk killing such a valiant man."

I could understand Sun Ce's point and thought my lord might have acted the same. But it was also irresponsible to waste so much time and resources on one man.

"Oh, and try not to take anything personally when Sun Ce talks. His thoughts tend to pass through his mouth before he thinks them through."

"Uh-oh," I heard Liang say. He was right to be concerned. My short temper had become legendary among my platoon, and taking things personally was something of a specialty. I assured the chief controller I would keep his advice in mind just as we passed through the entrance of the southern camp.

Everyone saluted Lü Fan as we rode to the center of the camp, even some of the older officers. I actually recognized a couple of them from our time in Hulao and saluted them as if they were old comrades, though none of them would remember me. We dismounted close to the command tent, an impressive structure, twice bigger than the one Cao Cao used, with one distinctive difference; it had no door of any kind. I later learned that Sun Ce found them useless, for he never refused to meet anyone, kept no secrets, and hated the couple of seconds it took to open and close it.

I was a little anxious. On the one hand, everything, from the rumors to the assessment of the situation, proved Sun Ce worthy of my lord's attention and respect. The man would rise for sure. On the other hand, I had this gnawing feeling in my chest that no one could be that good, and this phenomenal ascension hid something I could not yet point out. I was still learning to trust my intuition, but it warned me to beware of the tiger cub.

As Lü Fan entered the tent, I pushed this feeling aside, determined to judge Sun Ce fairly.

The bottom of the walls had been rolled up to let some light in or the humidity out, so, contrary to what I was used to, I did not need to adjust to the light. There was little furniture in the tent. A table at the center, a large cot on the right side, a bunch of stools scattered around the room, and a few more narrower tables with platters of fruits, jugs of wines, and several rolls of wooden slips piled up. Two men stood toward the back of the room, hunched over the largest table in a very similar fashion to Lü Fan when I met him. One of them would be Sun Ce.

"General Sun, Lü Fan here, with the latest reports and bringing guests," the chief controller said with volume, which startled the two young men from their contemplation of what I assumed to be the town's layout.

I will say it with no shame; I was astonished at the sight of those two. The one on the left was the most handsome man I had ever met, and even in the future, I cannot recall another prettier one. He was lean but athletic, with full, red lips, gentle, dark eyes, eyebrows that could have been painted by a talented artist, and skin so pale he looked as if he had taken a milk bath. Women must be fainting on his path. I congratulated myself for not having brought Guli.

The other, who I assumed was Sun Ce, was another kind of handsome. Just like his mother, his skin was tanned by days under the sun, and he was as muscular as his friend was lean. In fact, he was one of the few men my age I was envious of for his musculature. His biceps bulged in his shirt, and his chest extended with each quick breath. He was like a wild animal, heat emanating from his body even in the quiet shadow of the tent. Sun Ce wore his hair in a simple bun tied with a piece of fabric, but many strands had displaced themselves, which made him look rather childish. This feeling evaporated upon the sight of his face. A generous face, with a strong jaw, no beard, a well-trimmed mustache, and a pointy patch under the lower lip. His eyes had a similar golden tint as mine, and I wondered if this was why I had reminded Sun Jian of his son.

I was impressed, but the feeling left me when he opened his mouth.

"I told you not to bother with this kind of thing," he told Lü Fan, a voice full of authority but not of respect.

"I needed to come anyway," Lü Fan replied, apparently used to his leader's tone.

"Well, since you're here, come take a look at this," Sun Ce went on, waving his friend to his side of the table and sliding a cup on his left where he expected Lü Fan to stand.

He completely ignored us.

The chief controller moved around the table, grabbed the cup, and whispered something in his leader's ear.

"Cao Cao you say?" Sun Ce asked. "Not Yuan Shao?"

"They come from Xuchang," Lü Fan replied, not as loud.

Still leaning on his fists, Sun Ce made a face, rocked his upper body, then fished a string of coins from his pockets and let it slide toward the pretty man, who took it with a wide grin of pleasure.

"Thank you, Lord Sun," the man said, exaggerating his friend's title.

"As if you needed more of that?" Sun Ce replied.

"If this campaign keeps on going, I will actually need coins," the other said. "Please, my friends, come closer." He said the last to us, and I was glad to move from my saluting position. By the time we reached the table, Lü Fan had already filled three more cups and handed them to us. To my surprise, it was actually water.

"So, what does Cao Cao want with me?" Sun Ce asked just as I was about to introduce myself.

"I bring words from the emperor," I replied.

"Is there a difference?" Sun Ce asked, contempt dripping from his lips.

"Please excuse him," the handsome man said. "He's a bit moody on account of Xuancheng resisting him and forgot to show a proper welcome to faraway visitors." That was said in an obvious air of reproach, which first slid over the Little Conqueror until his friend tapped Sun Ce's foot.

"Mmh? Right, my apologies, I have slept badly," Sun Ce said without meaning any of it.

"No need for apologies, Lord Sun," I said, searching deep within for a drop of patience. The little lord had *slept badly*, while we had traveled through half an empire to meet him. "My name is Liao Chun, captain of Cao Cao's special forces and loyal Han officer. I speak in the name of the emperor, but you are right to mention Cao Cao, who has some personal words for you, as a friend of your father, and as someone who respects your name." Now I wished they had given me something stronger than water to wash away the taste of horse shit.

"Well met, Captain Liao," Sun Ce said, giving me a half-hearted salute. "You know Lü Fan already, and this is Zhou Yu from Lujiang, my friend and second-in-command."

"More like personal patron," Zhou Yu replied, his perfect teeth showing inside a heartwarming smile.

So this young man, favored by the gods with a perfect physique, was also one of the sons of the famous Zhou clan from Lujiang. The Zhou were to Yang province what the Yuan had been to the Yu. Rich, influential, educated men who had served the Han government for generations and got fat on its rewards. The Zhou were said to be almost as fortunate as the Yuan, but since their land lay further from the capital, they had remained less involved in the affairs of the land.

I finally understood the secret behind Sun Ce's success.

Sure, the young man was brimming with brilliant charisma, and I could feel in my blood he was a talented warrior and leader of soldiers, but this could never have been enough to conquer three commanderies in a matter of months. Even including the former loyalties attaching strong men to the Sun clan, he must have had some help. Lü

Fan, Ce's left hand, managed the administration of the army and had the men trained and behaving while their general drove them ever forward. And Zhou Yu, his right hand, financed the campaign from the seemingly bottomless treasury of his family. All Sun Ce had to do was present a leading figure, fight the fights, win battles, and inspire all the young fools of the Jiangnan region. He was a sword, and the two others kept it sharp.

"Tell me then, Captain Liao, what the emperor wishes to offer me," Sun Ce blurted out. Did his arrogance know no limits?

"Emperor Xian first congratulates you on your victories in the south, and more, for having left the service of Yuan Shu when the traitor declared himself emperor," I said, reciting the message given to me by Cao Cao. While Zhou Yu and Lü Fan bowed when I mentioned the emperor, Sun Ce looked anything but impressed. "The Son of Heaven also acknowledges the rightfulness of your war against Liu Yao, who originally received his title from the bandits who controlled the court, and—"

"I'm sorry, Captain Liao," Sun Ce interrupted. "I know you rode a long way to meet me, and you're used to all this jibber-jabber of the court, but I am a busy man. Please get to the point or return to Xuchang."

"Sun Ce," Zhou Yu said reproachingly.

"What? I said please," Ce replied with a flick of the hand toward me.

I was astonished, and it took the last faint traces of my patience to keep myself from cursing him.

"Very well," I said, rocking my shoulders as I did before a training session. "I understand that time is important to you, though you are quite willing to waste some around a small town." Now it was Sun Ce's turn to look as if I had slapped him. Lü Fan gasped, and Zhou Yu snorted a discreet laugh, but I let none of them react further. "So let me cut to the chase. The emperor wishes to grant you—"

"What did you just say to me?" Sun Ce asked, not able to keep it in any longer. I already regretted my brazen words. He looked at me sideways like a rooster observing a worm. If only he had not been looking at me like that.

"I said the emperor wishes—"

"Not that. What did you say about my strategy, peasant?"

I could feel the heat increase inside the tent, and since none of his two friends dared intervene, I guessed I would have no help and might as well step into the shit with both feet.

"I said you are wasting your time, his money, and his talent," I replied, nodding toward Zhou Yu, then Lü Fan. "From the smoke coming from the town and the guards on the walls, I guess they have five hundred men, at best, while you have twenty thousand, at least half of them trained and experienced. Xuancheng's defenses are made of earth, hard to destroy but easy to climb. You could swarm it in a matter of minutes. Instead, just because you fancy a fighting man with whom you rolled in the grass, you do not dare attack. You are not short on talented officers; one more will not change your world. What you lack are supplies. Every day you keep your men from the farms at this period of the year is a week of grain you will need next year. This is what I meant." To his credit, Sun Ce listened to the end of my rant before he almost jumped over the table, a first raised in the air. Zhou Yu kept him in his spot, which did nothing to the following torrent of insults and missiles of spittle raining on the map. As usual, the angrier my opponent got, the quieter I became.

"I knew your father, you know," I said, loud enough to

cover Sun Ce's barking. It got him to relent a little. "Served him some wine at Hulao while he dined with my lord. And even though I only met him once, I knew he was one of the grandest men in the empire. He was proud of you, but I wonder what he would think of your attitude toward Xuancheng or toward an emissary of the emperor."

"You know nothing of my father, you pathetic worm," he spat. "Don't you dare invoke his name, and watch how you talk to me, you miserable—"

"No, you watch your tongue!" I said, pointing a menacing finger at his face. "One word from me, and the court will know you for the rabid dog you are. You will receive no title and no rank while your enemies will be granted enough support to crush you like a louse. So show some respect, *Little* Conqueror."

I thought the vein on his forehead would burst, and I wondered how long it had been since he last breathed. But I guess Sun Ce had a little more sense than I gave him credit for because he deflated a bit, grabbed his cup, turned around, and threw it against the closest piece of furniture. He took a couple of steps, then came back to the table, his fingers combing his hair backward again as he forced himself to swallow the bitter plate I had just served. I suddenly realized how quiet the camp had become.

"What does the emperor offer me?" he asked through his teeth.

"Emperor Xian, in return for your father's courage and service, grants you the title of Marquis of Wu. For your feat of arms, you are to receive the rank of Commandant of Cavalry and are granted the post of administrator of Kuaiji."

"That's a joke, right?" Sun Ce asked, once again leaning on his fists in a commanding pose.

"A joke?" I asked.

"Those petty *gifts* from the emperor. They are worth nothing," he said, his tone rising again.

"Sun Ce, calm down," Zhou Yu said.

"No," Ce replied. "I will not be disrespected by a lowly captain, then given less than what I have, *and* be expected to say thank you and kiss the emperor's ass. Not now, not ever!"

I could sympathize with him, for he spoke the truth. The marquisate of Wu was hereditary, and since no one had been named in replacement of Sun Jian, it was Ce's right by birth. He had himself conquered three commanderies, which he very much ruled, but was only given one of them to administer. And finally, he was supposed to accept the rank of commandant while he had acted as a general for over two years.

"This is maybe not as much as you expected," Zhou Yu said, "but it comes from the emperor. It's official, not something handed to us by a moron like Yuan Shu."

"But commandant?" he asked plaintively.

"If your rank does not please you," I said after puffing, "I'm certain we can come to an arrangement." While I disliked the man, he was also right in rebuking our gifts. "My lord has given me permission to increase the rank to that of General Who Exterminates Rebels. Would that be better?"

"Barely," he replied. "Can I name the administrator of Wu and Danyang?"

"I'm afraid not."

"Then no deal," he said right away.

I copied Sun Ce's stand, fists on the table, and leaned a little over so that our faces stood at arm's length from each other.

"Are you a betting man, Lord Sun?" I asked.

Sun Ce frowned, and for once, even Zhou Yu, who had

remained expressionless along the quarrel, looked confused.

"If I get you your town and the man inside alive, will you stop being a spoiled brat and accept what you are being given?"

"Shit," Liang whispered behind me. He knew where this was going.

The situation needed the Scorpions more than it needed diplomats, after all.

"You know you're just being jealous," Guli whispered behind my back.

"I'm not jealous," I countered. "The man is a real prick." I had to speak through my teeth and between breaths, the effort of pulling on the rope leaving me little focus for an actual conversation.

"But he's handsome," she went on, making me spit. "And he's already famous throughout the land as a great warlord while being only twenty-two. Surely that must sting your pride."

If I hadn't been the one asking her to watch the sentry walkway, I would have told her to help me with the rope rather than spewing nonsense. Since I had gathered my warriors, and thus since Guli had seen the dashing Sun Ce, she would not stop talking about him.

"Why don't you stay with him after this mission?" I childishly said. "Since he's so much better than me."

"I never said he's—"

"Will you two stop this?" Two-Knives asked as his arms appeared above the wall. "We can hear you all the way down there." I helped the warrior reach the platform we stood on, then let him take my spot and pull the next of us on top. While the remaining Scorpions climbed the defenses of Xuancheng, I disposed of the two bodies Guli and One-eye had shot before she and I ascended in their place, removing their armor first. Zhou Yu had informed me this was the least defended side of the town and also gave us his understanding of the defenders' rotation, proving that he wasn't just a coin pusher. He also told us what he knew of the enemy forces, which he judged at around four hundred and some men. Counting those who would be resting, I assumed three hundred were on active duty, with maybe half of them on the walls. This place was full of holes. A small plate of pickles, as some would say, especially for experienced warriors of the night like us.

"Remember," I said, "we don't kill if we don't have to."

This would have been more convincing if I hadn't been kneeling in the blood of a dead guard, as Liang-the-broken suggested by raising his eyebrow.

"We move in the dark by two. Our target is in the palace, but we don't know where, so we might have to split. Until then, I want complete silence."

"What? You think that's our first night out?" One-eye asked.

"For some of us it is," Two-Knives replied.

"I'll be fine," Guo Huai said in his cracking voice.

"I know you will," I said. "Stay with One-eye. Do as he does and watch your steps."

Guo Huai was maybe fourteen or fifteen, but looked younger because of his bony limbs. It was deceiving, for he was as strong as most adults and after two years riding with us, could fight just as well as any of my warriors. While he had joined the Scorpions with his father as a servant, I quickly saw the potential in him and started his training despite Guo Wen's disapprobation. I had chosen him to come south with us because, first, I didn't want to cook my own food, and second I thought some time away from his father would do him good. He had yet to bloody his sword, but it was time he joined us in the shadows. Tonight was a full moon, and usually, I would have waited a few days before risking such a mission, but I so despised Sun Ce that I took the risk.

We left Duck on the platform at the city's northwest corner, dressed as a guard, and hoped he would not be asked where the two others went by anyone. Duck wasn't a great liar, but he still lied better than he fought, so I left him behind. If the alarm was raised, he was supposed to get out of the city and inform Sun Ce of our failure, then ride back to Xuchang to tell my lord.

As we were nine, I moved alone, then was followed by Two-Knives and Guli. The guards were so few on the walls that we managed to get into the town easily. The rest proved slightly more complicated. Cities in the south were not as well organized as in the north. Their streets did not crisscross in perfect lines but rather formed a messy patchwork of houses built randomly depending on the individual needs of their owners. Using the moon, we still managed to advance toward the palace, but in a more regular town, our progress would have been faster. Of course, we did not aim for the main entrance, which I saw was guarded by a section of six men, but moved toward the back, then into the servant quarters, and finally, the kitchens, which would be empty at this time of the night. Contrary to the rest of Xuancheng, the palace was exactly what I would expect of such a building.

The palace corridors were almost empty of soldiers, and I guessed Taishi Ci was overwhelmingly understaffed to leave the building so unattended. It made our task easy, and besides a couple of patrols who did not bother checking beyond the limit of their main path, we saw no one.

I assumed Taishi Ci would be sleeping and so guided us toward the chambers, though, again, in which he would be, I had no way of knowing. My plan was simply to check each of them, starting by the furthest from the exit and thus the safest. But before we got to that part of the building, my steps took us by a small hall for private meetings, where I heard some voices. I crouched and invited my comrades to do the same with a hand open toward the ground.

"How much longer then?" one of the voices asked plaintively.

"Until Liu Yao comes back," the other replied unhappily.

"He's gone to Yuzhang! Come on, Commander, we can't expect him to come back before months, if at all," a third said.

"Nevertheless," the second replied, and I do not know what he said next because I twisted on my heels to face the Scorpions.

Using my hands in simple gestures, I told them I had heard three voices, and the target was one of them. I divided us into groups of three, each taking one of them. Guli, One-eye, and I would assault the one in the middle, which I hoped would be Taishi Ci. The door was open, and the shadows of the three men stretched almost to the corridor, not clearly enough to judge who was who.

On the count of three, we dashed from our crouch and stormed the room, grabbing the three men's attention in a heartbeat. I only had eyes for the one in the middle, who I now knew for sure was our target. He was taller than the two others, and wider of shoulders, with a squared face, a thick beard peppered with bits of gray, and eyes barely visible through his thinly shut eyelids. The first thing I noticed was his lack of reaction. Someone shrieked as we rushed in, but it wasn't him. The second was the low table by his feet. I meant to use it for support and potentially knee him in the face before he could react. But this great warrior reacted much faster than I had anticipated.

I was halfway through the room, or three steps from the table, when he kicked it toward me. The table flipped twice in the air before it crashed against my chest, sending me on my ass as the pain settled in. My men moved accordingly and avoided my fall. I shook my head to regain my senses and noticed the moment Taishi Ci caught One-eye's punch at the wrist and returned the favor by hammering his massive fist into my archer's face. One-eye's head rocked backward, a gush of red following its movement. The man on the right was falling backward, taken by the momentum of my comrade's lunge. But the one on the left got lucky. Guo Huai badly timed his attack. Or, to be more accurate, he had not seen how the man moved to his sword before we could reach him. Two-Knives saw it, though.

My warrior grabbed Guo Huai by the belt and pulled him with all his strength right as the blade from their opponent sliced through the air. Our little sparrow probably felt its wind on his face as his body was shoved backward. Two-Knives saved the boy, but the way he twisted his hips left him vulnerable, and his target noticed the weakness. The sword came back and pierced through his abdomen as his name escaped my lips.

I was up before I knew it and before Two-Knives fell on his knees. His face wrinkled with pain as I rushed past him, throwing my whole body against his killer and feeling the wind leave his lungs in a loud *humph*. He dropped his sword and raised his hands to grab me by the neck. I let him, oblivious to any pain this might have caused. Instead, I hammered his face with the bottom of my fists. His nose broke first with a crunch reminding me of chicken bones being snapped.

Guo Huai's voice came to my mind, the boy pitifully praying for Two-Knives to hang on while Guli cursed in her own language, though she also asked someone to stand down. I kept punching, shoved the weakening hand around my neck on the side, and used the extra space to strike harder, with both hands held together like a proper hammer. Each time I struck, my hands came back up slicker. One of his eyes popped; the other could not be seen behind his bruises. More voices joined the chaos in the room. Someone grabbed me by the shoulder. I shook his hand off, grabbed the dead man's face, and slammed it against the reddening floor of solid wood. Why did one of my men have to die for Sun Ce? Why couldn't this spoiled piece of shit simply take his reward and ally himself with my lord officially? Why—

"Chun!" Guli's voice screamed.

I came back to the now, breathless, the pain in my knuckles quickly settling in, and horrified by the sight of bones and flesh under me.

"Captain," Liang called, forcing me to acknowledge our situation.

The room was blocked by dozens of guards, each carrying spears and swords. But they did not dare go in.

Behind me, Guo Huai was rocking his upper body, tears pouring down his face as he held Two-Knives' paling head on his lap.

Then, where I should have been, Taishi Ci rested on his knees, one of his eyes as bruised as One-eye's and Guli's knife against his throat. She stood behind him, hair disheveled and blood running from a cut near her ear, but triumphant as she kept us safe with her hunting knife.

I stood from my victim, picked up my sword, then pointed it at Taishi Ci's face. He wanted to bite my face off; I could read it in his eyes.

"Tell them to drop their weapons," I said.

TAISHI CI WASN'T afraid to die, this much was certain, but I used his sense of duty to make him obedient. I reminded him that he was first a loyal servant of the Han empire and informed him that Liu Yao had been declared a rebel to the dynasty. This shook his world a little. After that, I only had to promise the life of his men was guaranteed, which I guess he had every right to doubt considering what I had done to his officer, but in the end, he agreed to open the city gates and let me take him to Sun Ce.

The Little Conqueror made a great show of welcoming me with open arms, a masquerade intended at impressing our prisoner, whom he freed from the rope we had tied around his wrists. He offered the warrior to join the ranks of the Sun clan, which Taishi Ci accepted, and thus the tiger cub finalized his conquest of Danyang commandery.

"I am sorry for your man," Zhou Yu told me as we watched Sun Ce introduce Taishi Ci to his staff, ensuring they knew the warrior had once fought with him to a draw.

"Thank you," I replied without warmth. Two-Knives had been carried by two of the Scorpions, a blanket covering his proud warrior's face. None of us spoke much after we successfully captured Taishi Ci. While we had fulfilled our mission, the price had been too high, and I think my display of savagery kept their mouths shut. Except for Guo Huai, who remained silent for another reason.

"Sun Ce officially accepts the emperor's gifts," he then said, handing me a roll of bamboo slips signed by Sun Ce, even though I assumed he had never even read its content.

"I'm glad he found them convenient," I replied.

"And please let the emperor know that when the time comes, we will stand with his armies to defeat the pretender," Zhou Yu went on. I knew he was trying his best to soothe my spirit, but I did not care much about his attempts.

"What of Cao Cao then?" he asked.

"Cao Cao?"

"You said your lord had some words for us. So far, all you mentioned came from the Son of Heaven," Zhou Yu said politely. I was too tired and quite frankly pissed to find a better way to put it, so I went straight to the point.

"Cao Cao is offering to bind his family to your lord's through marriage."

"A generous offer," Zhou Yu commented, offering his most charming smile, which I found forced. "Did Lord Cao have anyone in mind? And before you answer, I must tell you that Sun Ce is getting married soon."

"It is fine," I replied. What I could not say was that my lord had given me specific instructions on this topic. Should I find Sun Ce worthy of his reputation, I was to arrange a marriage between the Little Conqueror and my lord's eldest daughter, who was turning seventeen this year. If I thought Sun Ce lacking but his clan worthy, I was to offer the hand of younger children from the Cao clan in marriage. And if I found none of them of interest, I was not even supposed to mention the offer.

"My lord was thinking of his beloved niece. She is eleven

now and will be of age in four years. If I am not mistaken, Sun Ce has a brother named Kuang?"

"They will be a good match," Zhou Yu said. "How about Cao Cao's sons? The Sun clan has several daughters if your lord would consent to it."

"I will mention it to him," I replied, though I doubted my lord would agree. Not after my report, at least.

In the end, my lord did arrange a marriage between his fourth son, Cao Zhang, and a niece of Sun Ce. Cao Zhang was turning eight this year, and while he would become a brave man, and a great leader of soldiers, Cao Cao could already see the limits of his intellect, which is why he offered him up at such a young age.

"I know you probably don't feel as such," Zhou Yu said, finally turning to face me, "but I hope your path will lead you to Jiangnan again and that we may enjoy a few drinks in good friendship."

"You and I, Master Zhou, yes," I said. Zhou Yu, and to some extent Lü Fan, were the only reason I had offered those future marriages on behalf of my lord. Sun Ce was a dashing young man with a solid ambition, but I did not believe in a happy future for him. He was burning the candle from both sides. However, he had gathered many talented men under his banner, and *they* would ensure the clan's future.

"By the way," he asked, "have we met? You look familiar."

"To everyone in the south, it seems," I replied.

"Captain Liao!" Sun Ce shouted, his arm around Taishi Ci's shoulders as if they were childhood friends. "Magnificent work out there. Bringing Taishi Ci back to the path of righteousness as you did is commendable. Please, join us for a drink or two."

"You are too kind," I said, my voice full of sarcasm. "But I lost someone there and would be of poor company."

"My apologies for your man," Taishi Ci said. Now that we were on the same side, I could see he was a decent man, and his sorrow sounded genuine.

"And I for yours," I replied. I'm afraid I wasn't as sincere as he was.

"Soldiers die in war. Do not be so gloomy over their fate; it would tarnish their memory," Sun Ce said, warming the assembly with his victorious mood. "Come! Let's drink to their names."

I was too tired to argue, and I could not simply refuse a toast in honor of Two-Knives.

My fallen comrade had been a solid companion since the day he had joined the Scorpions under the recommendation of Li Dian. They came from the same commandery, but Two-Knives had never been interested in learning his characters and thus would never have risen in the army. They regarded him as the best fighter in his old company, which he often proved under my command. His name came from his cautious nature, forcing him to pack everything by two. Why he did so, even he wasn't able to say. I could not believe I would never hear the rhythmical sound of his stone against the edge of his knives as he sharpened them with something like love.

Two-Knives wasn't the most extravagant among us—some might even call him a discreet man—nor was he the cleverest, but he was a friend, as he had proven by saving Guo Huai. When we buried him the next day, at the edge of a quiet forest, one knife in each hand, all of us honored him with two handfuls of dirt.

We were soldiers and agents of the shadows, but we had

faced few deaths over the last couple of years, and it was a gloomy bunch who rode out of Sun Ce's camp at noon.

Two-Knives was our first fallen comrade in nearly a year, and as One-eye later put it, no matter how much it hurt, one loss per year was an acceptable ratio, all things considered. Little did I know Two-Knives was just the first of a long list. In the coming weeks, the empire would bathe in the blood of my friends, and many would never see the colors of the autumn leaves again.

4

Wan, Nanyang commandery, Jing province
3rd month, 2nd year of Jian'an era (197), Han Dynasty

THE MOST NATURAL thing happened on the way back from Jiangnan; we got over our brother's death. It always amazed me how quickly people resume their lives, even through grief. Two-Knives still came up in conversation, but as days passed by, it brought a few chuckles rather than heavy silences. We remembered his quirks rather than his unachieved dreams, and it was good to see how much they cared about both.

By the time we reached Xiaopei, only two of us had yet to get back to our old selves. The first was Guo Huai, who could not shake the feeling our comrade's death was on him. None of us thought so, not even One-eye, who had been Two-Knives' closest companion within the Scorpions. There was little to do about Huai besides giving him time and space. The second, however, worried me more. Liang-the-broken was not an outspoken man, but I barely heard his voice on those long days of riding.

When I finally found it in me to ask him what was wrong, he said, "I came out of it unscathed. Not a scratch."

"Surely that's a good thing," I replied.

"Two-Knives died," he went on. "Guli almost got her head bashed in, and One-eye nearly became No-eye. Even you took a table in the chest. But me, nothing."

Men, especially soldiers, are a superstitious bunch. Liang never left a battlefield without some sort of wound, which is why we called him *the broken*. His many scars told the stories of his fights better than words would, and what should have been a relatively handsome man had turned into a grotesque tapestry of white lines over a ravaged body. But Liang had survived every war and battle in his career without ever really nearing death. His wounds were the price of his survival in his mind, and with them came a prophecy that no man alive could kill him.

"We fought three men," I told him. "Hardly a battle."

"Yet, some of us didn't make it."

"What are you saying?" I asked, knowing that an idea was running wild in his broken skull.

"I think it's time I stop," he said.

I called him an idiot, for Liang was nothing if not a warrior. I told him if he left the army, he would still find his way to the field of battle somehow; it was in his blood. He had enough cash to live a good life for a few years but would need more at some point, and his talents left few options. While he agreed, nothing would change his mind, and we concluded that he would finish his three years of enlistment with the Scorpions and resume his life however he wanted. I was sad at the idea of losing such a reliable man but promised that for the next few months, I would keep him away from the action as much as possible.

We barely stayed in Xiaopei, where we gathered with the

rest of the platoon, rested for the night, and left the next afternoon. Nothing much had happened there during our journey south. Lü Bu had apparently sent an emissary to renew some form of friendship with Liu Bei, probably in fear of Cao Cao's support, which guaranteed the safety of the city for the time being.

I was longing to get back to Xuchang, where I hoped to get a few days of doing nothing, but it wasn't meant to be. We just reached the capital when Man Chong, its prefect, directed us toward Wan, in Nanyang commandery, where I was from and where my lord had led two divisions, the Qingzhou and the Dragon-Fang.

"Why Nanyang?" Pei Yuanshao asked as a disappointed group of twenty-five riders made a stop for the night on the open ground.

"Something to do with a certain Zhang Xiu," I answered, telling him and the others as much about the situation as I knew, which wasn't much.

In his effort to consolidate his base and clear his immediate neighborhood, Cao Cao had picked up a fight with what he considered an easy target.

Zhang Xiu was the nephew of Zhang Ji, who had been one of Dong Zhuo's main officers. When the tyrant died, Zhang Ji became one of the leading men controlling the Han court, turning it into a sham. But when the emperor managed to escape, those puppeteers fought among themselves, and many left Chang'an to avoid the guaranteed blood bath. Zhang Ji was one of them. Taking a few hundred men, he departed for Nanyang, where he offered his service to Liu Biao, governor of Jing. The old fox saw an opportunity and offered Nanyang to Zhang Ji so that he and his men could protect Jing province's northern front for him. Zhang Ji apparently died soon after, so Nanyang was handed over to his nephew, Zhang Xiu. This was Liu Biao's usual method. He would let others handle the fighting for him and take as little responsibility as possible. But this time he made one big mistake.

Cao Cao could not attack Liu Biao, who was not only strong, but legitimate in his post. Zhang Ji, however, was not, and worse, had been one of the emperor's tormentors, which gave Cao Cao the perfect excuse for a punitive expedition.

"I heard a rumor about that," the elder Meng brother said. It surprised no one. Meng Shudu was a well of unfounded rumors. Even if no one had invited him to, he would have informed us of his knowledge, but his brother asked what this rumor was anyway.

"I heard," he went on, "that Zhang Ji's wife came from the imperial harem as a gift from Dong Zhuo."

"What does it have to do with anything?" Du Yuan asked.

"Think about it," Shudu said, tapping the tip of his knife against the side of his head. "Who do we know, who is famous for his appetite for married women, and would kill to bed a beautiful widow famed in the whole empire?"

Most of my men turned in my direction, which put me in the delicate situation of swallowing my currently full spoon of congee while checking the murderous gaze of Guli.

"No, not him," Shudu said. "I meant Cao Cao."

"Ah," many of them replied in unison.

I didn't like my men spreading rumors about our lord, but in this particular case, I could not really fault them. Cao Cao was an incorrigible seducer of married women, especially if they or their husbands were famous.

"You think he'd wage a war just for a woman?" Pox

asked. Shudu shrugged, so they returned their attention to me.

"No," I said, though I felt anything but sure of my answer. "But I guess it might have facilitated his decision."

And sure enough, when we finally reached Wan, Cao Cao was unavailable for my report, too busy he was with Zhang Ji's widow in his bed.

There was no battle in Nanyang. Upon Cao Cao's arrival, Zhang Xiu surrendered, simple as that. He could not hope to win against the might of Cao Cao and opened the city gates for my lord. In a matter of *shi*, Lord Cao made the widow his concubine, and I heard it was near impossible to get a minute of his time since. For three days, my lord had enjoyed the company of Lady Zou, as she was called, and would not even bother granting an audience to Zhang Xiu who had so respectfully surrendered. I, of course, did not dare barge into the chambers of my lord, and remained outside the building, near its entrance, where a brasero had been set, and where some of my old comrades entertained themselves with wine and good stories until our general ended his mating retreat. The large square behind me saw little activity besides my lord's guards corps, whose members had been standing in order for I could not imagine how long. I wondered what they thought of their current assignment, standing like flag poles while their general plowed a beauty.

"Three days," Xu Chu said as he readjusted the cloak around his massive body to fight the cold, "that's impressive, isn't it?"

"She must have a cunt like a fine peach that one," Dian Wei replied, holding his groin with one hand. Being in this giant's presence was always a sure way for the conversation to turn vulgar.

"Not anymore," Cao Anmin replied, churning a loud guffaw from the rest of the assistance. Though not from me. I could not feel the joy of the moment, no matter how glad I was for the company.

While I didn't know Dian Wei well, he was a very easy man to like with his boorish nature and big-brotherly attitude. Anyone who ever saw him in battle would shudder in his presence, but since we fought on the same side, I appreciated his unnatural talents for war and for words. During the battle for Yan against Lü Bu, he had once made his unit wear a double layer of armor before leading them to break the enemy formation in a fearsome wedge attack. Half of them died doing so, but they had saved the day.

Besides him, though, all those present were old friends. Cao Anmin was there, and since he was no longer my superior, I had resumed my friendship with him. Xu Chu also sat with us, which, considering Dian Wei's presence, was not surprising, both being like the two humps of a calabash. And finally, there was my old rival, Cao Ang.

"Anything wrong?" he asked, probably flustered by my quietness.

"I just have no love for Wan," I answered.

"Why not?" Dian Wei asked, his hands open flat toward the fire.

"There is a hill right outside that wall," I said, nodding toward the west. "My father is buried there."

"Damn," Dian Wei said. "I'm sorry then, I took a big fat shit on that hill the other day." The others snorted when he said so, and it was so much like him to say something of the sort that I, too, chuckled a little.

"And my little sister's ashes are mixed with the soil of the city," I went on. This time the captain of the guards found nothing to say. None of them did.

No, I did not like Wan, no matter how much better it looked thirteen years later.

"So, what of the Little Conqueror?" Cao Ang asked in an attempt to change the topic.

"More like Little Prick," I answered, the tip of my cup against my lip.

"That bad, huh?" Ang said.

"Worse."

"Makes you wonder," Dian Wei said, "how come every lord's firstborn is such a tool."

The joke made us crack into another loud guffaw. Even Ang, the target of the jibe, joined in. Few people could make fun of him and get away with it. And Dian Wei was mostly right, firstborns of great men seldom lived up to expectations. Yuan Shao's son, Yuan Tan, was said to be brave but dumb as a rock, and Liu Biao's was a sickly little thing, I heard. Even the former emperor's first son had failed to impress so much that Dong Zhuo had him killed. Within this motley collection of disappointment, which included Sun Ce in my mind, Cao Ang stood out. He was brave, skilled in war and in the arts, could conduct himself with humility and authority, and was generous to his men. While he had been a real ass as a child, he had grown to be a worthy successor to his father.

Cao Cao on the other hand, I was having trouble following. His passion for women was a secret to no one, but I never thought he would put it before duty, and clearly, he had been lacking on that front. My lord, before he had become the emperor's protector, would have ensured his position to be safe, the surrenderees to feel valued, or at least the flags on the city walls to be changed before he took care of his own pleasure.

I was lost on this thought, my eyes aimlessly directed at

the building inside of which Lord Cao must have felt heavily dehydrated, when I spotted something strange with the roof. It was a cloudy night, and the light of the fire left me blinded to our surroundings, but I thought I saw the tiles of the roof moving as if they were slowly falling down. I squinted to try to make sense of what I was seeing, and then again detected some movement on the roof.

"Chun?" Xu Chu asked.

"It's nothing," I replied, blinking rapidly a couple of times. "I just thought—"

"What in the heaven?" Dian Wei asked, following my gaze and standing as he did.

The tiles moved again, and it took one of them to almost slip away for me to understand they were no such thing. Men, covered with dark drapes, crawling over the roof like lizards. I felt the air leave my body when they stopped moving completely.

"Guards!" Cao Anmin yelled.

A bolt ended his shout midway through it as it embedded itself at the base of his throat. The world stopped moving for a second during which Anmin turned around, his big white eyes full of surprise, screaming for help. My old comrade fell, head first, and the world spun suddenly really fast.

I unsheathed my sword just as Dian Wei threw one of his two short dagger-axes toward the assassins, catching one right in the chest. The closest guards copied him, and soon the roof looked like a hedgehog, though some fell back down, dragged by the weight of the men they had skewered. Most of the assassins, though, reacted faster and dropped from the roof, falling with no sound between us and the entrance of the building. I charged the closest, Xu Chu by my side, and while I could not see his face, wrapped in dark clothing as it was, I heard a faint tremor of fear as my giant friend caught his arm and I thrust my blade into his armpit. As I twisted it out, I felt more than I saw Cao Ang running past me. Xu Chu moved on to another shadow warrior, his face twisting with rage as he picked one of the spears on the ground and slammed it against his target's head. The pole broke, and I'm certain the assassin died on the spot.

I counted seven of them but knew there would be more. They were professionals.

"Chun!" Ang called from within, just as I noticed two more shadows infiltrating the building.

"Go!" Dian Wei yelled, his arms locked around the neck of a dark-faced assassin.

I dashed after Cao Ang, whom I could spot at the end of the hallway leading to his father's chamber. There was a dead body by his feet, but another of his opponents kept him in check with remarkable agility that left no opening to my friend's sword. The assassin moved like a cat, using the wall to jump away from Ang's blade, then rolled on his shoulder before bringing his short blade in an upward arch. Ang took a step back, then another, and before he knew it, he was the one on the defensive.

Without thinking about it, I unsheathed the small knife on my back and threw it toward the agile warrior. By some extraordinary reflex, the man parried it by raising his short blade. This left him vulnerable for the split second needed by my friend, who rammed his own sword upward and into his opponent's chin. The assassin did not even struggle.

"There's one more," Ang said, pointing toward the chamber as I meant to check him. Not wasting more time, I ran to my lord, feeling a burn in my chest and pushing any thoughts for later.

Without pause, I stormed inside the chamber and

shouted with rage at the sight of Cao Cao, lying on his bed, the last of the assassins straddling him. My lord was fighting for his life, both hands clutching the killer's blade as he pushed it toward Cao Cao's heart. I jumped at the assassin and threw him against the wall as we rolled with the momentum. His body crashed heavily, but I could feel this would not be enough. He still held the blade with which he had almost killed my lord. I would not let him use it. He rose up faster than I thought he would, but he was shaken. I could not see his eyes, but when he opened them, it was to see the rage in mine just before I headbutted him. I grabbed his sword wrist, then slammed him with my forehead again, hearing a satisfying crunch. Knowing he would not recover this time, I removed the long knife from his hand and planted it right where neck and shoulders meet, then left him to fall lifelessly. I was burning up with anger.

"Father!" Ang called as he entered the room.

Cao Cao was bleeding hard from the cuts on his palms, but the confusion in his features worried me even more. I had never seen my lord so shocked before. On the bed, Lady Zou's cadaver was paling already. I can only assume the assassin had cut her throat first.

"Ang-*er*," Cao Cao called in a trembling voice. "What's happening?"

"We're being attacked," Ang replied. "It was all a ruse."

"Or someone took an opportunity," I said as I removed the turban around my victim's face to use it as a bandage for my lord's hands. I cursed. The assassin I had just killed was a woman. "We need to go," I then said as I stood back up.

Ang helped his father, who was still quite shaken, so I took the lead. No one attacked us, for none of them was alive. At least none of the assassins. Zhang Xiu's soldiers, however, were coming. The square where I had been happily chatting with my comrades two minutes before was now the scene of a fierce battle between Cao Cao's guards and the soldiers of Wan, who very much intended to regain control of their city. As I stepped out of the building, our men were protecting the main entrance of the compound, but with only two hundred warriors against their few thousand, it was hopeless.

"My lord," Dian Wei called. The captain of the guards staggered to us, a cut draining blood from his neck. He made it look benign, but it was deep and would need some quick patching up. "We won't hold them for long. What should we do?"

Cao Cao did not reply. His eyes were lost on the unmoving shape of Cao Anmin.

"He died protecting you," I said, which was a slight exaggeration. "Don't let his death be in vain."

"We should ..." Cao Cao said but did not manage to finish his thought.

"We're getting out of here," Ang said in his most commanding voice. "We make for the stables then leave the city. Xu Chu, you take the vanguard, Dian Wei, stay with the general at all times, I'll take the rear, and—"

"I take the rear!" Dian Wei said. Ang was about to argue, but one look at the captain of the guards was enough to understand his feelings. He would probably not make it and wished to die protecting our lord's escape.

"And Chun, no matter how, you get out of Wan first, gather the armies, and come to us. We'll escape from the north. Understood?"

"*Zun min*," I replied, saluting my friend. I hated the idea of leaving them all here but knew my presence would make little difference, while I was probably the only man who could escape the city.

We had several soldiers in Wan, including a few Scorpions, but I could not lose time thinking about them. They would have to save their own skin somehow.

I shared no last words with Ang or my lord. Time was of the essence. When I climbed over the compound's outer wall, I spotted Xu Chu stepping through the mass of his comrades to take charge of the vanguard, and I pitied the enemies who'd find themselves on his path.

I jumped over the closest roof, which took a bit of climbing over a balustrade, then moved toward the east. The Dragon-Fang camp was up north, and between us, half a city, high walls, and a plethora of bloodthirsty soldiers, but east, I knew, would be different. From my vantage point of view, I could see lines of soldiers rushing toward my lord's location, but in a smaller quantity than I expected. I wondered if I should head back to my lord to tell them the threat wasn't as grand as we had feared, but considered the information wouldn't provide much and kept pushing toward my goal.

The further I went, the quieter it became; however, behind me the sky took on an orange tint as flames spread. This was the second time Wan burned in front of my very eyes, and I thought maybe this city and I were cursed in a way.

"Captain," I heard a familiar voice call right as I jumped from one building to the next. I doubled back, peered down into the narrow alley, and noticed three pairs of eyes looking in my direction.

"What are you doing here? I asked, recognizing the Meng brothers and Liang-the-broken as the cloud masking the moonlight gave us some clarity.

"Just like you," Shudu said, "getting out of here."

"Follow me, then, it's that way."

Of the four walls surrounding Wan, I knew the eastern one would be the least guarded because it led to a dead end. East of the city flowed the Bai river, so close to Wan that one could throw a rock in the middle of the river while standing on the wall. A bridge could be lowered from inside the city, but the mechanism would take too long to use for an escaping group and would be easily defensible. And I was right, we met no one until we reached the stairs leading to the walkway on top of the walls. Even then, it was an easy matter to deal with the two guards we came upon.

"What now?" Meng Bobo asked as we peered over the wall.

"We jump," I said, "and whoever makes it goes to the camp to tell them to bring the men."

"Is the river deep enough?" Liang asked.

"Yes," I replied, fast enough to cover the fact I had no idea about it. "Jump as far away as possible, and you'll be fine."

"Hey!" someone shouted from the walkway, followed by a set of heavy footsteps running in our direction.

"No choice then," Bobo said a second before jumping. His big brother went right after. I heard none of them hit the water, but neither did I expect to with all the noise coming from the city and the shouts from the approaching soldiers.

"Captain, I—"

"You'll be fine!" I said. I knew Liang was freaking out because of what he expected to be his fast-coming death, but I had neither the time nor the will to argue with him, so I grabbed him by the collar and forced him toward the edge of the wall, from which he did jump. I saw him splash into the river one heartbeat before I did.

For a few long seconds, all that made sense was Liang-the-broken waving his arms frantically above the current, and the coldness of the water. I struggled to regain my balance after so nearly bumping the back of my head against the river bed and thought that just maybe this had been a terrible idea. But this wasn't the first time I found myself in this situation, and the Bai's ferocity paled in comparison to the Suo in which I had almost drowned seven years before. Forcing myself to recognize I was in no immediate danger, I pushed on my legs, felt the bottom, and finally hooked a big stone with the tip of my feet. With this support, I waddled to the left bank, fighting the icy current while the two Meng brothers grabbed a helpless Liang and took him to the same side.

"I meant that I can't swim!" Liang-the-broken barked after spewing a cupful of water.

"I got that now," I replied.

The one good thing from this whole watery trip was how much faster we progressed compared to if we'd been on foot. The camp, I recognized, was two *li* inland. The land was flat and free of any structure, so we reached the Dragon-Fang division in a matter of minutes, though we almost got ourselves a nice collection of spears on account of not knowing the password. I told the *inbred moron* on watch duty to fetch Colonel Yu Jin unless he wanted to be marked by the Scorpions' sting. Luckily for both of us, Yu Jin was still the same old bastard with an apparent allergy to sleep, and sniffed the commotion at the gates like a hound after a fox.

"Colonel Yu, you need to get your men ready and moving," I told him as he appeared through the wooden poles of the palisade. I told him everything that had happened in Wan and the command from Cao Ang to get the army moving toward the city. As I recounted the events of the attack, more officers joined us. Most sent their seconds or aides to fetch the others or wake the men, so by the time I was done with my observation of the city, the camp was shaking with a chaotic energy. Even the most senior of them were shouting at each other.

"Shut up!" Yu Jin barked, stretching the last syllable until all his peers got quiet. "Company leaders, get your men in formation. We get this camp ready for defense. Tell the diggers to dig some more, and the others to prepare the heavy crossbows, ammunition, and the heavy shields. I want every surgeon's tent ready, and—"

"Sir," I interrupted, "what are you doing? We are supposed to move to Wan, not dig ourselves deeper."

"I'm doing what our general would ask for," Yu Jin replied. "You!" he shouted to a young captain. "Get two riders to the Qingzhou troops' camp to relay my orders. Will you remember them?"

"Yes, Colonel Yu," the captain replied before disappearing through the small crowd of officers.

I was speechless. This was the opposite of what we were supposed to do. Five *li* to the south, our lord was facing death and expected us to save him, but Yu Jin would have us take shelter behind a proper camp.

"Sir," I said again, "I must insist—"

"You must nothing, *smart-one*," he said. "How many of them did you see in there?"

"One to two thousand," I answered.

"Zhang Xiu has a little over twelve thousand soldiers. Where are the others?" he asked, raising his eyebrow rhetorically. "What happens if that was part of their plan and they expect us halfway through? Or worse, what happens when our two divisions engulf themselves in *their* city and the whole thing turns out to be a trap?" This was undeniable, we were playing into their hands and could not make a move without risking it all.

"But Lord Cao—"

"General Cao is either already dead or on his way here. What will better serve him, a winded division in the open or a strong camp?"

The bastard did think, and thought better than I, or Ang.

"So let me do my damn job or I shove my boot up your ass until you can taste its leather."

"Captain," Liang whispered in my ear, preventing me from arguing with Yu Jin, who immediately went back to distributing orders with efficiency. "What do *we* do?"

I passed my hand over my face as I tried to recuperate a little of my wits. Liang was right, there was probably something we, the Scorpions, could do. But first, we had to gather up. Some of my men would be half drunk in the followers camp, but most, I hoped, were around.

"Shudu, go to the red camp and try to find our comrades. Feel free to kick any soldier's ass back to their post on the way. Then come to the stables. Bobo, Liang, with me." I was certain a tent had been designated as ours within the camp, but I didn't know which. What I knew was the location of my mare.

"What's happening?" Guo Huai asked as he and his father strapped the horses' saddles. I counted seven Scorpions in the stable.

"Lord Cao needs us," I answered. "Everyone ready in two minutes! Armor, weapons, horses, everything ready. Not you, Sparrow. You run to the chief surgeon and tell him to get ready, and if you see one of the others on the way, tell them we're here. Go!"

"What's the plan?" Du Yuan asked as he worked the thongs on his armor's side.

"The army is staying put, but if I'm correct, our comrades in the city will need us on the way," I replied. Guo Wen handed me my helmet, then ran to Pox, who struggled with his own horse.

"No plan then. Got it," Du Yuan said.

"Chun, by the Blue Sky, you're alive," Guli said as she ran into my arms.

"Get your bow ready, *buga*," I told her after a short hug. When she saw the seriousness in my eyes, she simply obeyed, something she seldom did. "Guo Wen, when the others show up, tell them to gather at the southern entrance of the camp and wait for us." We were fourteen at that point, and I hesitated to wait a bit longer or leave one of us here, because fourteen is an unlucky number. At that point, though, we needed men more than luck, I thought, so we rode out. Exiting the camp proved troublesome because of the flurry of activity shaking it, but once we came out, it was five *li* of seemingly open ground toward the city.

"What if they're still inside?" Du Yuan asked, closing his eyes against the wind of our gallop.

"We get them out," I shouted back.

"Simple as that, huh?"

"No. But it has to be done."

We never had to enter the city, though. I saw the moment the doors opened, the light from the arson filling the opening space. Through them, from a dead start, dozens of horses bolted in our direction. I could not see behind the first line of riders, and even them I could not distinguish, but one thing was certain, they were in a hurry, not caring about keeping the line or matching each other's speed. Judging by the dark silhouettes against the bright fire, I'd say there were maybe thirty horse riders.

"That's Xu Chu!" Du Yuan shouted, pointing his spear toward the shape of our big friend. He was the first rider.

The distance was vanishing quickly, but not enough. Too

many horses and their riders followed the first group; they had to be the enemy. Between the march to the stables and the fight at the city gate, most of our comrades had perished already.

"They won't make it!" Liang said.

He was right, we would be too late. The enemy cavalry was swallowing the distance at an alarming speed.

I noticed how Xu Chu kept an arm stretched behind, then understood he held the reins of the horse behind him. It was Shadow Runner, my lord's mare, whom I had trained. On her sat a bent-over shape with two arrows sprouting from his back. The mare, too, was spiked with missiles, and I guessed it took Xu Chu's immense strength to keep her running straight.

"Faster, you bastards!" Du Yuan shouted.

My heart was pounding in my chest. Was Cao Cao dead? Were we all dead?

A horse put himself right behind the unmoving shape of my lord, and I realized it was Cao Ang, his back straight and a shield on his left arm to protect his father.

"Ang!" I shouted.

I don't know if he heard me, but his head moved in my direction.

He shouted something, to which Xu Chu reacted by shaking his head. Ang shouted again, then dropped his hand on his father's back, and I knew what he had in mind.

"Ang! No! Just keep riding, you moron!" I shouted.

Ang raised his sword, yelled his command, nodded at me, then pulled on the reins of his horse. On cue, all the guards still present imitated him, stopped their horses, forced them to turn around, and charged the pursuers.

I witnessed the moment Ang entered the enemy's line, beheading the first of his opponents with as good a stroke as

I would ever see. Then his horse and those of all these brave men disappeared in the mass, giving their lives away for us to gain a few precious seconds.

"Stop the charge!" Du Yuan commanded our men, for I couldn't. "And back!"

I obeyed, but my eyes refused to look away as my oldest rival left this world. Cao Cao's voice resonated in my mind. A voice from my childhood, the day I had slapped Cao Ang on his order. *"As you are now, you cannot trust my son, and he won't trust you. One day you might have to, and much will depend on it,"* my lord had said. He'd been more right than he could have known. Cao Ang had just entrusted his father's life to me.

We formed a line behind Xu Chu's and Cao Cao's horses right as they passed between us. Shadow Runner was pitiful to look at, but she ran straight on. As I rode next to her to check my lord, though, I realized with awe the mare was actually unconscious and simply moved out of habit or sheer nerves. She was the greatest horse there was, but she too would never see the light of the sun again. Cao Cao was breathing, and he would have to reward whoever had forged his armor.

"Xu Chu!" I called as I pushed Qilin faster.

The giant did not reply. His jaws were tightly shut, and two furrows of clean skin ran from his eyes to his beard.

"Dian Wei's dead," he finally said through his trembling lips.

"I know," I said.

"Out of the way!" Du Yuan shouted, waving his hands so that the guards at the entrance of the camp would let us through. I recognized Yue Jin as he ordered a path for us to ride through. We would make it, but the cavalry wasn't far behind either. They slowed when they realized they wouldn't catch us, but I knew the respite would be short-lived. Our soldiers had dug the trenches around the camp a little wider, but they couldn't have done much in such a short time, and behind the palisade, our crossbowmen were getting ready.

We emerged out of Yue Jin's company, and I let Xu Chu take our lord to the care of his medical staff. My place wasn't there. It was at the front, then later in the melee. I had friends to avenge.

I slid from my saddle, unhooked my shield, and left Qilin where she was.

"Scorpions, on me!" I yelled.

Pei Yuanshao, One-eye, and Shudu joined us as we unsaddled.

"This is not a shadow mission this time," I said. "This is not even a mission. This is just *us* butchering as many of *them* as we can. Those who shoot can join the missile troops, the others with me. Not you, Guli," I said as my lover removed the curved blade from her saddle. She was an archer first, but I knew if I let her fight, she would be by my side, and I could not lose anyone else tonight.

"I will fight," she said, shaking her blade to show me her determination.

"Shadow Runner is dying," I whispered in her ear. "She needs a friend."

It's not just that I wanted to manipulate Guli away from the battle; I truly wanted Shadow Runner's last moments not to be by herself. My lover nodded and ran after Xu Chu. I left her, the mare, my lord, and all the rest behind, blocking them from my mind as I forced a spot on the front line stretching across the camp's entrance. I only wanted to think about Cao Ang, Cao Anmin, Dian Wei, and all our comrades who no longer lived. I let the fire of their death burn bright in my chest and give strength to my arm, for it would swing my blade and paint Wan's ground red. I hadn't been part of such a battle in years, but I could feel the rage swell in me as the armies of Zhang Xiu gathered around our camp. They would come from every direction, twice as many as we were. *Let them come*, I thought; *twice as many would never be enough against the Dragon-Fang.*

"Cao Ang?" Yue Jin, who stood right next to me, asked. He was already famous as the toughest officer in the division and started every battle from the front line. On that day, I thought, he would probably not even accept to rotate.

"Cao Anmin, too," I answered.

Yue Jin rocked his shoulders and sneered like a wolf. For a little while, when we had been around ten years old, the four of us had been close comrades, and if my friend felt their loss as I did, I pitied those who would face him, for even I did not know how a furious Yue Jin fought.

"Fifth company, get ready!" he shouted. "They killed our lord's son. There will be no mercy!"

"No mercy!" his men replied in kind.

Du Yuan's spear fell on my shoulder, the comforting weight of the pole sending me back to our time in this division. On my left, Liang-the-broken was testing the balance of his *jian* sword, and more of my men found their spot next to or behind us. I nodded to Liang, but right then, the massive body of Xu Chu appeared between us. He forced his presence on my left, his face the promise of painful death.

"I got no one to protect right now," he said in response to my gaze. "But I got an ax." He raised said ax, a short-handle ax like those we display in the vanguard to let our enemies know we mean war.

This Zhang Xiu had managed to piss off the three best fighters among Cao Cao's former students, and as his soldiers breached the last step toward our line, I vowed to create a song of screams and pain Cao Ang would hear from the afterlife. I could see our foes were feeling confident, and why shouldn't they? They had forced us back to our camps after so nearly killing our general. They were twice as many as we were and got us relatively unprepared. Soon though, they would realize their mistake.

A volley of arrows passed over our heads and cut through the enemy ranks a few seconds before their first line reached us. Our archers, I knew, would not give them a second of respite.

"Form one!" Yue Jin called.

I braced the shield against my chest. Du Yuan nervously twisted the pole of his spear on my shoulder, its head making a couple of rotations before he stilled it. The moat around the camp forced the enemy to approach us with a fifty-men rank. Some would try the trench, of course, but our comrades behind the palisade would not make it easy for them.

In a testament to their bravery or their confidence, the enemy did not slow or temper their attack. They simply kept walking toward us. I locked gaze with my most direct foe, inviting him to check me and forget my friend's spear. Like most of his comrades, this soldier rushed the last steps, his shield forward to slam into mine. It never happened. They screamed. We screamed. He died.

Du Yuan jabbed his spear right through his eye and beyond, then retrieved it before the man knew he was dead. Xu Chu simply grabbed the top of his opponent's shield, pulled it away with ease, and brought his ax in a vertical strike that nearly cut the man in half. He kicked the bloody remains back to their line, forcing a few of his comrades on their asses. In the blink of time, when no one was facing me,

I thrust my loyal *dao* into the neck of the soldier facing Yue Jin, though my friend hardly needed it, then brought my attention back to my closest threat.

"Die!" Xu Chu yelled.

I punched the next man with the spike on my shield, ending his scream before it began by smashing his teeth and tongue in. All along the line, men were falling, those on the edges being pushed into the trench to leave space for more lambs to the slaughter. I stood in the middle, so to me, it looked as if the swarm of enemies would never end, but neither did I want it to.

"Rota—tion!" Yue Jin called after he retrieved his sword from a young man's thigh.

His men obeyed; I didn't. Neither did Xu Chu.

"Chun!" Du Yuan called.

"Not tonight!" I replied.

The giant kicked the shield of another soldier, making it bend. The helpless soldier squeaked when he understood what kind of beast he was facing, but I did not see how he died; too busy reaping my harvest of pain, I was. A spear nearly took my eye, but Du Yuan grabbed it and pulled until the spearman let go of it.

"Shit," I heard Du Yuan say. He would have preferred to drag the man with it.

The soldier I now faced was a beardless boy who knew he was in the wrong place and probably wished he was back in his farmhouse. He held his shield too high, so I kicked him in the shin and felt it break under the sole of my boot. His shriek could be heard above the tin of this bloody battle until I rammed the tip of my sword into his throat.

"Die, you bastards! I'll plow your wives over your cold corpses and piss in your skulls," Xu Chu shouted. He never swore, but I guess this is how Dian Wei, his mentor, used to behave when fighting, and this is how my big friend honored him.

Yue Jin was cold fury, methodical and precise, each gesture economical but lethal. I killed with just as much efficiency but could barely hold myself. I so wanted to take that first step forward and move from defending the camp to slicing through the enemy's ranks. Never before had I felt the heat of war so intensely. It was intoxicating. It was liberating. A few more strikes, I thought, and I would take that step. But Xu Chu beat me to it. *They* started avoiding him, and soon, a few steps of space of nothing but cadavers remained around the giant. This was their mistake. So far, my friend had killed without the freedom of movement. Now that he could swing his ax, there was no stopping him. Xu Chu stepped over a torn body at his feet and brought his weapon in a wide arc that ended in an enemy's skull. It went through helmet and bones, and if not for his immense strength, the blade would have gotten stuck. Instead, Xu Chu kicked the dead man away, blocked a spear coming from his left, pulled on it, and headbutted the spearman. Pox, who had followed the action, speared the unconscious man, but by the time he retrieved his dagger-ax, Xu Chu was already deeper inside the enemy line. I punched, and punched, and thrust to get more room and join my comrade, but no matter how much I struck, Xu Chu kept sculpting the field of battle with his ax. This was the night Xu Chu became known as Mad Tiger.

"With me!" I called, desperate to get to Xu Chu before they surrounded him.

"Spear on two, shield on three!" Yue Jin called, reminding me of that faraway day in Dong'e when we had breached the gates with that tactic.

"One, two..." Not just the spearmen, but everyone

holding a polearm or a blade jabbed it. It was like our line suddenly sprouted a wall of spikes.

"Three!" Yue Jin yelled. We pushed as one, using our shields, shoulders, and legs. The enemy in front took a step back, many of their soldiers falling between our feet and rapidly dying there. I do not believe my boots touched the ground, and I almost buckled because of this uneven floor of bodies. And yet I could hear the grunts of Xu Chu and the promises of death he shouted between each strike.

I lost count of my victims. I felt invincible. Some of our men were falling, but not nearly as much as theirs. Xu Chu was by himself killing their spirit while we showed them they would never enter the camp. Whoever said the brush is stronger than the sword obviously never met Xu Chu.

"Come on! Come meet your father!" Xu Chu yelled, his voice very close even though I couldn't see him.

Du Yuan thrust his spear toward the man in front of me, but I could feel the strength in his jab was weakening. I still had energy to spare, but it was purely fueled by the fire in my arms. At some point, it would wane, and I would be in trouble.

My next opponent wasn't even looking at me and stood sideways. I felt bad for killing him, but this was a battle. What he had been looking at was the fuming shape of Xu Chu, breathing hard, slouching slightly, both hands on his ax's handle. They formed a crude half-circle around him, and finally, it seemed, the giant had spent his rage and contented himself with waiting for them to come to him. They wouldn't. I saw so much fear in their eyes, no matter how much they outnumbered him.

"Xu Chu! Step back!" I shouted as I reached his level. I was dangerously ahead of the other, almost like in a wedge formation, and Xu Chu's spell of fear would vanish eventually.

"I ... can't ..." Xu Chu said, turning his head to look at me. There was not a piece of his skin that wasn't red. Some of it was his blood, but most belonged to his victims. His beard was a mess of gory substances, and I even saw a tooth lost in it. He was remarkably unhurt. However, I realized, he could no longer move. His legs would not let him go in either direction.

"Come on, big man. Think of Cao Cao; he still needs you to protect him," I said.

Xu Chu blinked hard as if awakening from a bad dream. He wiped some blood from his eyes with the back of his hand, but since his clothes were just as drenched, it did him little good. Then, he managed a step back and another. All the while, I could hear our enemies cursing at each other to attack us.

"Captain," Du Yuan called right behind me. "We need to get back." It was a testament to the direness of the situation that Du Yuan called me by my title. Men were still fighting, especially our comrades trying to reach our level, but I didn't think we could reform a line in time. Worse, while protecting the camp's entrance gave us the protection of the palisade on our sides, we had advanced so much that we now risked them engulfing us.

"Release!" Yue Jin's voice rang a second before a *whoosh* passed over our heads. It was too dark for me to understand what had just happened, but when the arrows fell like hail on the enemy just before us, I understood Yue Jin's men had used javelins. Contrary to some others, our people are not fond of this weapon, but Yue Jin had obviously found some interesting use for them and had his men trained in hurling javelins, for this volley came perfectly. It gave us some sudden space, and seeing the front ranks of enemy soldiers tumbling like bags of wheat woke Xu Chu, who followed my lead as we moved to resume our spot by the entrance.

We left a carpet of dead and dying in our wake, like a warning to those men who now hesitated to come at us. Most of the fallen wore Zhang Xiu's colors, but some were our comrades, and among them was a man covered in scars, though most were white and old.

"Shit," Pei Yuanshao, looking in the same direction, said when he realized Liang-the-broken was dead.

This warrior of great skill, the son of a fisherman from Wu, who had survived everything life had thrown at him, succumbed to the lucky thrust of a beardless boy. The blade had penetrated his abdomen, right under the ribs, leaving my comrade to suffer his last moments of life. Shudu, who had been by his side when it happened, later told us Liang gathered enough strength to snap his killer's neck before he collapsed. In doing so, he had preserved his legend; no one alive could kill him. I would mourn his death, but as the fire abated from my lungs, I started to feel the stings of all those tiny cuts along my arms and legs and wondered how long I could keep going. Worse still, it started raining then. It doesn't sound like much, but rain has the power to turn a desperate situation worse.

"That was good, your trick with the javelins," I told Yue Jin. My friend was panting, sweating, and breathing through a broken nose, but he was still cold and meticulous in inspecting the battlefield. The enemy had managed to remove a few pieces of palisade here and there with hooks and ropes, but fresh soldiers just as soon plugged the openings with the advantage of height, and none of them passed through. At least not on the southern side of the camp.

"We didn't have much to throw, though," Yue Jin replied.

"There's a breach in the west!" someone shouted behind us. "Breach!"

Yue Jin put his wolf-like eyes in mine, the drops of rain sliding along his muscular face down to his blood-smeared beard.

"Platoon six to eight, with Captain Liao!" he shouted. I nodded.

"You'll be all right?" I asked Yue Jin.

"He'll be all right," Xu Chu answered for him. "None of them will pass by me." He brought his ax across his chest, and I knew in my heart that our foe would never even dare approach the southern entrance as long as the *mad tiger* guarded it.

"Scorpions on me!" I shouted, feeling the words echoing the past few minutes.

With maybe a hundred men in my wake, I forced a passage through the packs of archers, wounded, and messengers crisscrossing throughout the camp and found the western entrance on the brink of collapsing. The enemy had punched through the defenses of Captain Li Tong with their heavy shield-bearers and was now forming a bridgehead into which more and more of them were gathering. If nothing were done, there would soon be more of them than us on that side of the camp. When that happened, they would open their shields and let a flow of fresh troops wreak havoc within.

A column of heavy shields is a bitch to fight because they don't really fight back. All they need to do is progress slowly, one small step at a time, making sure to tuck their feet and heads behind their protection. It's tiring work to be in one, but usually quite safe until the "gates" open. There are two weaknesses to this formation, though. One, the visibility is almost nonexistent. And two, there is no space inside the column; it's like a trap. I didn't know how best to use those two flaws when I ordered my hundred soldiers to join the melee but found a third one as I tried to pound a shield-bearer whom I could not see.

"Pox, Shudu, Bobo, go get me some wine!" I shouted.

"A bit early for celebrating," Bobo replied.

"Go to the closest supply cart and bring me all the pots you can find. *Baijiu* if there is," I said. "You two, go with them," I told a couple of young soldiers on my right. They hesitated for a second but understood when staring into my eyes they would have more to fear from me than from our foe if they didn't obey. "Pei, Du, get me some fire. Torches if you can." They, too, obeyed and squeezed through the crowded pack of soldiers. I did not go with them because that might have confused the soldiers of Yue Jin who had followed me here and because I was currently pushing with all my weight against an enemy's shield.

I tried thrusting my blade from above the shield but did not manage one good strike, the angle weakening my sword. My arms were shaking with fatigue when Pox came back to inform me they had found four full pots of *baijiu*. The column of shields had advanced an extra ten steps further, and it could not have been long until they let their warriors free. I gave my spot away and followed Pox to the back of our ranks, where they had found four pots, which were much bigger than I expected. Pei Yuanshao and Du Yuan came back with one brasero where six branches were burning. The rain had weakened to a drizzle, but I still feared it might soon extinguish those flames.

"We carry the pots by two and throw them inside their column, in the middle as much as possible," I explained.

"Those are heavy cows," Pox said.

"I know, but we'll manage. Shudu and Bobo, you take

one, the two of you as well. Pox and I work together. Pei and Du, you throw the branches where the pots land."

"Sounds fun," Du Yuan replied. It seemed we only agreed on a plan when it involved a lot of pain for our enemy.

I grabbed the neck of the first pot and despaired a little when I tried to lift it. Without Pox's strong peasant arms, I would never have managed.

"Move out," I shouted at the men between us and the shields. With pain, a path opened up around us. My arms were on fire by the time we reached the enemy. "On three! One, two, three!" Using all the energy I could muster, and in a neatly coordinated effort, Pox and I tossed the pot over the shields and heard it crash somewhere. Shudu and Bobo managed as well, but when the two other soldiers' turn came, a spear shot through the shields and punctured the first's throat.

"Du, Pei!" I called but didn't need to. My two friends tossed a burning torch each above our heads. They twirled in the dark sky, their movement appearing very slow in my mind, and landed perfectly.

The fire took in the blink of an eye. The screams soon followed.

"Keep their shields shut!" Du Yuan shouted.

I had only intended the sudden fire to create a sense of panic that would force the shields to open, but Du Yuan's idea was to keep them from escaping the flames. It was inhuman, but this was war.

So, instead of trying to crack the column up, we pushed on the shields to keep them as tight as possible, which was no easy feat considering the energy the enemy used to try to get out. They shrieked and jabbed through every hole, those dying men willing to die faster if it meant avoiding the pain of fire. Pox received a spear in the shoulder, but the way he cursed told me it wasn't a lethal blow. They called for mercy, some even tossed their weapons harmlessly, and still, we kept them trapped, the heat from the fire being unbearable, even on our side.

"Please!" someone said behind the shield I kept in place, all traces of pride long gone. I shut my heart to his plea, remembering the eyes of Cao Anmin when the bolt shot through his throat to harden my will.

The rain came back stronger again, and I could feel the fire weakening. There were still a lot of them alive.

"Let's finish them up!" I said.

I released the tension on the shield. A hand appeared through the gap, then the image of a charred face crying for mercy. I gave it to him in the form of my sword under his chin.

Most of those poor soldiers were more dead than alive as we plowed through their remains. I promised myself I would never use fire again if there was another solution. I still do not know if there was another way on that night. My plan saved hundreds of us, if not more, but death by fire is atrocious to witness and even uglier to carry in your heart.

It still took a long, arduous fight to push the shield-bearers from the west entrance, but Li Tong's men were brave and now believed in victory, while *they* did not.

I told the Meng brothers to take Pox to Cao Cao's surgeon, hoping the old man remembered me from the time I threatened him. Pox wasn't in immediate danger, but he bled a lot, and I would not lose another man. At least, this is what I promised myself. Reality, however, had other plans.

I didn't fight much at the western gate and couldn't have done more anyway. My *dao* sword had lost its edge a while ago, my lamellar was falling to pieces, and I had lost count of the cuts and bruises. I had also lost track of time and was amazed to see the first colors of dawn reflecting under the clouds. Pei Yuanshao and Du Yuan were the last of my companions by my side, and one look at them told me what I did not dare say; we were done. Not just us, but the whole army would soon reach its limit. Zhang Xiu had called more soldiers than we knew he had, and if it went on, they would eventually swarm us.

This realization filled me with regret, and I suddenly felt very lonely.

"I need to find Guli," I told my two friends, who simply nodded. I didn't ask them to follow me but knew they would.

Guli would no longer be with Shadow Runner, who must have departed the realm of the living a while ago. Once she had accompanied the mare on her last journey, my lover would have been looking for me. And since she had not found me, I hoped she had found One-eye and my archers, the section she belonged to. I grabbed a running crossbowman on an ammunition run and asked him where his regiment was fighting. He pointed at a spot near the corner of the south and east walls.

A ball formed in my stomach as I approached this part of our defenses. The enemy had managed to snatch wide pieces of the wall, and the melee's brutality could be felt from afar. Archers had defended this spot, but none of them shot anymore. Few yet had missiles to shoot anyway. Instead, those lightly armored soldiers made their officers proud with swords, knives, and spears. I later heard how astonishing our artillery troops had behaved in that fight. Some had permanently lost the use of their fingers due to the implacable rhythm of the volleys. Others had pulled muscles and kept on reloading and shooting through the pain. And when their bolts and arrows ceased, the enemy targeted them with a coordinated attack on the palisade, filling the trenches with their dead to gain access to the camp. A bloody mess followed; one my archers had been part of.

"Guli!" I shouted as I reached the back of the melee. The fight was still going on, but the lack of energy had slowed the battle. Soon, one side would falter, and the other would regain enough verve to smash the retreating soldiers to pieces.

"Tian Guli!" I shouted.

My bottom lip quivered as I scanned the battlefield, oblivious to the men around me. They could have been foes; I wouldn't even have cared.

"Chun!" Pei Yuanshao called right before catching my belt and pulling me back.

I rocked my head and felt the tip of a blade slice through the air. Du Yuan's spear got the swordsman in the belly, and my friend pushed him back into the melee, where he would die in seconds.

"Guli!" I called again as if I had not just escaped death.

"Chun, we won't find her like this," Du Yuan said. "Once the battle is over, we'll search for her."

"I need to find her," I replied, tears prickling behind my eyes. "I need to know she's fine. I need to—"

"Captain!" someone shouted, and while it was slightly distorted, I recognized One-eye's voice. The leader of my archers stood a few steps away, at the back of the line where he was just receiving a fresh delivery of arrows. As I moved to him, he released two of them over the melee, and when empty, his arms shook violently.

"It's good to see you, Captain," he said. "We lost Harelip, and I think I saw Zhu Pi's body lying somewhere over there." Those two archers had come from his original unit and had helped me when we had rescued Lady Bian a few years back. Their loss must have weighed heavy on him, as it would on me after the battle.

"We lost the broken," Pei Yuanshao told him, which forced One-eye to release the tension on his bow.

"Have you seen Guli?" I asked him. I saw something like fear passing over One-eye's face, and my lungs refused to inhale.

"I'm sorry, Captain," he said, "I told her to stay behind. I told her not to fight."

"Did you see her fall?" I asked, my words undulating as I fought to keep control of my voice.

"For all I know, she's still there," he replied, nodding toward the center of the melee. I did not wait for more explanations and jumped through the crowd. There were many of us still unaccounted for, and I particularly feared for Guo Huai and his father. Some of my men might have been inside Wan when it rebelled. Others would have been in the followers' camp, and I did not dare think about what happened to these people. But the thought of Guli's inert body lying in the mud, stepped on by wave after wave of soldiers, was too much to take. It gave me a surge of energy, and I moved like an eel between those tired warriors, slashing any who blocked my path.

"Guli," I called, knowing my voice would never reach her, even if she lived. I went from one shape to the next, searching for her braided hair, and listened for the sound of curses in a foreign language.

A man came at me. I chopped his hand off, then paid no more attention to him. This melee was chaos. Soldiers did not have any sense of rank or direction; they just fought wherever they stood until they were the last standing. I grabbed a warrior of Zhang Xiu by the back of his collar and pulled with all my strength. Someone would take care of him.

Then I saw her on the ground.

Her position made no sense, and I blinked a couple of times before I realized she was not only alive but very much fighting still. The man under her had his hands around her neck, but her thumbs were digging through his eyes, and he screamed like a slaughtered goat when she popped them out. She then moved to a knife lost in the mud and sliced it through his throat.

She stood, her shoulders rising and falling as she fought for air, and I thought she was the most beautiful, savage thing in the world.

"Guli," I called, dropping my hand on her shoulder.

She twisted on herself and snarled a curse, lifting her knife as if about to stab me in the chest, but all trace of violence left her face when she recognized me. Guli dropped the small blade and threw herself against me.

"I thought you were dead," she said, trembling like a leaf. "I thought you were dead without me." Her lips quivered.

"Guli, I'm so sorry," I said, though I had no idea what I was apologizing for.

I held her against my heart and patted her back while she sobbed on my neck. We remained motionless for a while, uncaring of the battle raging around us. I had no idea if some of my companions were protecting us or if we stood amidst a mob of enemies. I was just relieved that I had found her.

Then I felt a shift in the atmosphere; a moment when the energy seemed to finally agree on the direction to follow, and this time it was out of the camp.

"They're running away!" someone shouted.

Soon, cheers followed.

Zhang Xiu's soldiers were fleeing. They left just as fast as they had come, and while usually, it meant a pursuit, none of Cao Cao's men ran after them.

"We beat them," a young soldier next to me said to no one, his eyes showing his confusion. He had not thought to make it through the night.

In truth, as we would later learn, *we* hadn't beaten them. At least not alone.

Colonel Yu Jin kept sending messengers to the Qingzhou troops' camp with orders for them to come to us if they were not under attack. This went against what he had told them before, but he assumed by the state of our battle that most of Zhang Xiu's men were here. The Qingzhou came right away but were ambushed halfway through. Many of them fled, but this ragged division had at least one competent leader who saw the ambush for what it was, a diversion. He recognized the ambushers' lack of numbers and had his men push through. And, as I held Guli in my arms, the Qingzhou was so close to us that I could hear their cheers.

They came to a sorry camp, with more holes than walls, burning tents, red mud, and so many corpses they could not enter at first.

Yet we had survived, and Cao Cao too.

He came out of the surgeon's tent in the middle of the afternoon, bare chested, save for the bandages tightly wrapped around him. We all thought he would order the sack of Wan and the death of Zhang Xiu, but he did no such thing. For the rest of the day, we busied ourselves burying the dead, helping the wounded, and mending the gear. Anmin's, Ang's, and Dian Wei's bodies were not recovered, and in Ang's case, I guess there wasn't much to retrieve anyway.

The Scorpions had lost three men, the rest of the army, thousands. This was our first great defeat since the battle against Xu Rong in Xingyang, and it hurt even more, because this time we were trained and experienced. And while few said it out loud, everyone thought it was entirely our general's fault for his behavior in Wan. I kept those theories for later. I was relieved to find most of my friends alive. Guo Wen and Guo Huai had taken part in the action. Both of them got their swords wet, Huai, for the first time. Guo Wen promised it would be the last time he ever fought, and as far as I know, he kept that oath. Pox also joined us back that day, his shoulder fixed, but not by the surgeon. Stinger, our torturer, also carried the knowledge of medicine, a fact I ignored until that day. I guess it makes sense that someone who bleeds people to make them talk can also stop them from bleeding.

"His bedside manner is worth shit," Pox commented.

"Odd," Stinger said, feigning surprise. "My patients usually don't complain about it."

It was so out of character to hear him joke that I, and everyone in our tent, fell into a loud, uncontrollable guffaw.

We drank in honor of Liang-the-broken, Harelip, and Zhu Pi. Then, Du Yuan, Pei Yuanshao, and I went to Xu Chu and drank more in the names of Cao Anmin, Cao Ang, and Dian Wei. I wished Yue Jin would be with us, but as soon as he had finished his duty, my friend retreated to his tent in the company of Li Dian. I dared not get to him. He needed Li Dian's presence as much as I had needed Guli's.

Xu Chu shed more tears for his mentor and told us stories of their time together. Then, because he looked on the brink of collapsing, we left the big man to sleep.

"Will you visit Cao Cao now?" Pei asked me.

I shook my head in reply. Cao Cao didn't need me. Actually, I don't know what he needed, but it was certainly not a foolish young soldier reminding him of his son. No one saw him until the next day when he called for the march back to Xuchang.

With the bitter taste of defeat in our gullets, we burned the camp and marched back to the east. In the middle of the debris, Cao Cao had a stone engraved to mark this battle. Usually, he would have found poetic words to describe the sorrow of a fight or the bravery of the fallen. This time he was more direct.

"Here fell heroes.

Whoever touches this stone

Will face the wrath of Dian Wei's ghost

And Cao Cao's ire.

Disrespect the memory of the fallen

And share the fate of the people of Xu."

To my knowledge, the stone still stands on the road from Wan to Xuchang.

Jianmen Pass, Yi province
12th month, 4th year of the Jingyuan era of the Cao Wei empire (263)

"General Liao? Do you want to stop here?" Chen Shou asks. I guess I have stopped talking for a while now, though I did not realize it. Revisiting the battle of Wan, the second in my case, always shook me more than I dare say. Some events are too much to digest, even after a lifetime.

"I'm all right, my young friend," I reply.

I will never be all right when thinking about Cao Ang's death, but the story must go on. It has reached the tipping point of my youth, the period everything changed, and my friend's end had everything to do with it, though few seem to consider it nowadays.

"Where was I?"

"You were returning to Xuchang after the battle in Wan."

"Ah, yes. Well, to be honest, there isn't much to say about the march in itself. It was a morose moment. We feared Zhang Xiu might pursue us, but nothing came of it. Cao Hong met us halfway through, and my lord ordered him to preserve what little we had gained in Nanyang commandery for the time being."

"I'm wondering," Chen Shou says, taking a thoughtful pose. "Was the attack a ruse or a retaliation for Cao Cao's behavior?"

"We never learned the truth of it. At least I didn't," I answer. "Speculations went wild for a long time. Personally, I believe it was a mix of both. Zhang Xiu had probably surrendered to Cao Cao, hoping to gain something from it, but he also got his plan ready in case he didn't like his

Chapter 4.bis

reward. Cao Cao insulting him by bedding his uncle's widow helped him in his decision."

"A crafty one that Zhang Xiu."

"Hardly. The whole strategy was not his but came from the devious mind of his strategist, Jia Xu, another former officer of Dong Zhuo and one of the few you could call a clever man. He had planned the whole thing very accurately, and if not for the extreme bravery of our soldiers, especially men like Xu Chu, Yue Jin, and Colonel Yu Jin, this would have been our end."

"And you too," Chen Shou says.

"I did my part," I reply. "But I was just fixing things while the others truly won the fight. Yu Jin was especially pivotal in our survival. While many officers would have obeyed Ang's order, he remained calm and prepared the defenses. Cao Cao made him general and even enfeoffed him as the marquis of a small village. It was just a few hundred households, but it made him a wealthy man and a member of the nobility. The bastard laughed at that, but he took the riches happily enough."

"What of the others?"

"I believe Yue Jin was promoted to colonel, or lieutenant-colonel maybe. He was the youngest officer of that rank in Lord Cao's army, but no one ever complained about it. On my side, the Scorpions received a hefty bonus in cash and silk, but our hearts were not in it. We'd lost too many comrades in too short a time. I officially welcomed Guo Huai as one of us, but even then, between the dead and the wounded, we were now under twenty, and I was considering hiring some new members. Man Chong asked me if I wanted to return to the army proper, promising a bump in rank if I did. I was tempted, but I had gotten used to a certain form of freedom, so I remained a captain with a

Chapter 4.bis

generous increase in my salary. Oh, and Xu Chu was named captain of the guards. He asked for a short leave before accepting his new role, so a few Scorpions and I were added to the guard for a couple of weeks in replacement. Xu Chu came back a new man. His mourning of Dian Wei had given him a new strength, a more assertive aura, one could say."

"What of Cao Cao?" Chen Shou asks. How he manages to take all those notes as I speak and keep track of the conversation will always remain beyond my understanding.

"While I guarded him, I actually barely saw him. He kept to his private quarters, and even the ministers had to come to him for an audience. He would eventually need longer than Xu Chu to get over Wan, and I cannot blame him for it. To use a simile, Cao Cao was gestating in a cocoon of solitude, and what kind of butterfly would come out was all people talked about. Some said he was turning mad from the loss of another son; others pictured him turning into an even colder monster. As for me, I just ignored his red eyes and stinking breath when I saw him."

"No matter what people say about him, it must have been hard. Losing a son, I mean," Chen Shou comments. He starts to understand how twisted history has been taught to him. Few men are truly evil, and Cao Cao wasn't, especially then. He was a father as much as our general.

"One thing I could almost call positive came out of it, though," I go on. Chen Shou looks curious. "Lady Ding, Lord Cao's wife, left. She had raised Ang and Shuo with love, even though they weren't hers to begin with. Some might even say the few drops of love her dry heart contained were all for the two boys. So when the elder passed away, she grew even bitterer, and one day, a month after our return, she just left and went back to her family. Cao Cao

Chapter 4.bis

then married Lady Bian, and since I was mostly over her, it just made me happy for them."

"Did it help him recover?"

"I do not know if he ever did," I reply. "The pain of losing a child, you never truly get over it." The tears threaten to break free again, and my throat turns dry.

"My apologies, General," Chen Shou says after a few seconds of heavy silence. "I forgot about your—"

"Thank you," I say, interrupting him before we step on a topic I would rather avoid,

"So, you never had a heart-to-heart with Cao Cao about Ang?" Chen Shou asks, accepting to go back to the topic.

"We never did. In fact, I doubt he talked about it to many people. The guilt would make it impossible for him to open up, but I also think the transformation in Lord Cao's general behavior made him harder to approach. He could have become a broken man after Wan; instead, it made him more solid, as if he had used this great defeat as a shell against future drawbacks. I will admit he scared me a little when he finally left his compound with his dead, cold eyes and drawn features. He emerged stronger, but it cost him a piece of his soul. However, while my lord remained closed to me, another man visited me out of the blue, and shook my world a little with his kindness."

PART TWO

SLAYING THE BEAST

5

Xuchang, capital of the Great Han
5th month, 2nd year of Jian'an era (197), Han Dynasty

"Who?" I asked, leaning on my elbows while Guli grumbled her displeasure at waking so early in the morning.

"The governor of Xu," Guo Wen answered. "And the one I assume you call the bearded warrior."

"Liu Bei and his top commander are at our doorstep?" I asked, one eye closed because I had sat up too fast.

"Yes."

"Before sunrise?"

"Yes."

"Chun, go greet them or send them away," Guli mumbled. "But whatever you do, let me sleep in peace." I was about to tell her what I thought of her tone, but she snored right after her sentence ended. Probably a good thing I didn't, anyway. We hadn't been intimate since Wan and our daily life in Xuchang left me frustrated.

"Can you prepare some ... What do people drink at this

time?" I asked Guo Wen as I fumbled through a trunk for some passable *hanfu*.

"Hot water," Guo Wen replied, shrugging. "I heard in the south they drink tea."

"I'm not taking medicine for breakfast. Prepare some hot water and ask them if they're hungry," I told my servant. He left the room, and I heard his voice in the courtyard. Liu Bei's answer was short and polite. It took me a while to tie my hair in a correct bun, and for a second thought about wearing a hat to cover the mess underneath. But for a man such as Liu Bei, who had grown up poor as dirt, this wouldn't matter, I told myself.

It was still dark as I walked the passageway leading to the first floor, but dawn could not have been far. Liu Bei and Guan Yu sat on stools around one of the three tables of the Scorpions' courtyard, looking as comfortable as if it had been the imperial hall cushions despite our mansion's extreme mess. We never received guests. I had entertained the thought of buying a property for Guli and me, though it would have to be outside of the city, but since we were more often on a mission than not, I refrained. Our room was comfy enough, we had a proper hot water bath, a servant paid by my lord, and I could keep an eye on my men. They, however, treated the place with the care a horse does its paddock, and the courtyard drowned under the mess of training weapons, chicken bones, broken pottery, and the rest of yesterday's drinking on the floor. If it had been someone else than those two, I would have felt embarrassed.

"Governor Liu?" I said, saluting them after fastening my outer garment tighter to fight the morning cold. He and Guan Yu stood from their stool and returned my salute. I could not read them, but I guessed a certain discomfort from Liu Bei. "What is it?" I asked.

"I apologize for waking you, Captain Liao," Liu Bei said as I invited them to sit back down. "We cannot stay in Xuchang more than a day and will be busy for the rest of it." That they came here at all was quite astonishing. Not just this courtyard but Xuchang as well. Rumors were going wild about an alliance between Yuan Shu and Lü Bu, his two neighbors, and leaving Xiaopei was either foolish or necessary.

"It is fine," I replied. "You will have to forgive me for the state of this place. We never receive anyone, and my men are more dogs than courtiers."

Guan Yu chuckled at that, and it would take me to visit Liu Bei's private quarters to realize the man was as messy as a countryside butcher. The imperial uncle declared that no forgiveness was necessary since *they* had come unannounced, but when I asked what his visit was about, he stiffened a little.

"We would like to convey our condolences for Cao Ang's unfortunate death," Liu Bei said, his eyes diffusing a genuine air of sorrow.

"I see," I replied. "I'm no longer guarding Cao Cao, but I'm certain I can get you an audience." Ang had been dead for two months, and I knew for a fact that Liu Bei had sent a letter to express his sadness, but knowing him as I had started to do, I was certain he came to Xuchang as early as possible.

"No," Liu Bei said. "I meant to you."

"To me?" I asked, not understanding.

"We've heard he was your friend," Guan Yu explained, "and you were present when he fell." Guo Wen arrived then with cups in his amputated arm and a pitcher of hot water in the other. Liu Bei hurried to help, not knowing my servant could handle himself better with one arm than most people with two. I nodded my thanks when the governor handed me a cup and answered that Ang had indeed been one of my oldest friends.

"It must be a terrible thing to see a brother die," Liu Bei said, shaking his head.

"I appreciate your compassion," I told them, still not sure what to make of their presence. "But surely you didn't come to Xuchang for this reason?"

"We have to speak with the Minister of Works," Liu Bei replied, meaning Cao Cao. "But sharing a few minutes with you was also on our list."

"We've taken two uncles from you," Guan Yu explained as he understood that I doubted his leader's words. No one could be so considerate, I thought. "And now you've lost a brother. My brother wanted to see how you fared. Your family is smaller because of us; it is only fair that we check on you."

"I don't know what to say," I replied after a short time of confused, mouth-hanging silence. They had nothing to gain from this detour, at least nothing I could see. As the governor of a province, Liu Bei also had a mansion in Xuchang and could just as well have summoned me there. Ministers and officials never came to the southern part of the city, and even Man Chong, a friend, sent messengers to call me. This Liu Bei was an odd fellow, and I wondered if maybe he was as selfless as he appeared.

"Zhang Fei did not come?" I asked in an attempt to change the subject and mask my confusion.

"Well," Liu Bei answered, seemingly embarrassed.

"We needed someone to stay in Xiaopei," Guan Yu replied. This was only half of the truth. Zhang Fei would simply not bother with me after we so nearly pummeled each other in a fist fight the last time we met. I was surprised they let him take care of their base, though, considering what had happened in Xiapi.

"He is advised by good men," Liu Bei, who read my thoughts, explained.

The bell over the closest city gate announced the fourth *shi* of the day, *richu*, and right on cue, the sun's first rays caressed the palace's roof. Soon, the city would open to visitors less important than the governor of Xu, and Xuchang would brim with activity. Liu Bei picked up the *wuguan* hat from the table and set it quickly over his bun before readjusting his robes as he stood up.

"Captain Liao," he said. "We must sadly go, but please do not doubt the sincerity of my intentions. I simply wished to express my sympathy for a young man I respect."

"And I thank you for your kind words," I replied as I took a bow. Then, before Guan Yu could match my action, I offered him my hand, as we had done the last time. I had not realized how wide his hands were until he grasped my forearm again and squeezed it with strength. I accompanied them to the compound exit, a few steps during which I realized how peaceful it was to walk by their side.

Guo Wen joined me as I watched them leave, with no escort or carriage, I should say. They walked like simple folks, even though one glance at Guan Yu was enough to realize he was everything but.

"A weird man, this imperial uncle," my servant said.

"Very weird," I replied.

"And a good man, I would say."

"That he is. And one day, it will get him killed," I said, for that was exactly what I believed then.

"Goodness does not mean naive, Chun," Guo Wen said. "There might be more than meets the eye with this fellow. He wouldn't have climbed so high if he were just ... good."

I told Guo Wen I would keep his opinion in my mind and my eye on Liu Bei rather than his majestic brother. Maybe this was how he had reached such a powerful rank without loss in his reputation, I wondered, through the misdirection of his two brothers. However, as I watched him turn to rejoin the main street toward the palace, I realized something important about the imperial uncle; he walked side by side with Guan Yu. In fact, if one didn't know who the leader was, they would naturally assume it was the bearded one. This contrasted entirely with my lord, who refused to walk anywhere but a step ahead of anyone and carried his authority like people wear their belts.

I was starting to understand something that would shape the rest of my life and the future of the empire. Liu Bei and Cao Cao were two sides of the same coin.

While the debacle of Wan wasn't crippling in terms of men lost and would not make a huge difference in the great scheme of things, Cao Cao needed time to recover on a morale level. We were not weak, but for some time would not press on any attack. Instead, my lord worked on other ways to strengthen his position. To the east, south, and north, the only solutions were military by nature, but the west was different. Over there, past the former capital of Luoyang, chaos was omnipresent. Warlords came and went, eating each other's petty territories month by month until one could hardly call it the Great Han Empire anymore. It was time to resume some control of the northwest corner of our land, and this would be taken care of by one man.

Zhong Yao, my former calligraphy teacher, had returned to Lord Cao's service and would prove pivotal in his plans.

He had left us to become a county magistrate when Cao Cao was the lord of nothing in Chenliu but later returned to the emperor's service and by extension Cao Cao when the latter made Xuchang the new capital of the empire. I knew nothing of it because my old teacher was almost immediately sent on a diplomatic mission to the war-torn lands beyond Chang'an, where the emperor had previously been held hostage. There, he offered ranks and titles to all the petty lords who willingly submitted, and I cannot even imagine how this unfriendly man managed such a mission without angering any of those hot-headed leaders.

He and Cao Cao could never agree when it came to calligraphy, one preferring the flowery, stylish *cao shu* style while the other favored the straightforward *kai shu*, but Zhong Yao had other talents, as suggested by his triumphal return to the capital and his convoy filled with sons and relatives of our new collaborators in the west. His goal had not just been to bring control back to the northwest but also to secure our flank for when the conflict with Yuan Shao started. Without a single soldier lost, Zhong Yao had put more territory under Lord Cao's influence than we ever did with entire divisions. The calligrapher wasn't coy about his success, and Cao Cao drowned him with riches and titles.

This bloodless victory had a direct impact on the Scorpions and me, and put us in a fairly awkward position.

"And what am I supposed to do with him?" I asked a disgruntled Man Chong, who, as usual, had requested my presence in his office. The mansion of Xuchang's prefect was nothing to be ashamed of, and I didn't mind the journey north of the city. The reason for my presence, however, I could have done without.

"Honestly, Chun, I don't know," Man Chong replied.

The prefect was in a bad mood; this much was obvious. I

don't think I'd seen Man Chong smile since Guo Jia had reached Cao Cao's inner circle, but on this day, he was quietly fuming. Just a few months before, Man Chong had stirred the peaceful atmosphere of Xuchang by being very much himself. A few friends of Cao Hong had brewed some troubles in the city, thinking themselves safe on account of their companionship with Lord Cao's cousin. They pushed one step too far and gave Man Chong every right to arrest and sentence them to death. Even then, they believed all they had to do was invoke the name of their powerful friend to get out of jail and sent a request to Cao Hong for his intervention. When he learned about it, Man Chong sped up the trial process and executed them. Cao Hong wasn't pleased, but justice had been served, and Xuchang had gained in safety. People feared Man Chong's shadow, but to me, he remained the kid who found the recipe for a strong laxative to mix with our rivals' porridge.

"So you're just going to dump him on me?" I asked.

Man Chong dropped his head in his hands, just like his biological father did when suffering a migraine. It was unfair to me, I thought, it was unfair to Man Chong, who had more pressing matters to attend to, and it was unfair to the kid, who stood a couple of steps behind me and could hear the whole conversation. I say kid, but he was at least fourteen if I remember well.

"He can't stay here," Man Chong said, *here* being the northern part of the city. "But he has to remain in Xuchang."

"Why can't he stay here?" I asked.

"Come on, Chun, isn't that obvious?" Chong said, opening his hand toward the kid, who was presently looking at his feet in embarrassment.

It was, indeed, pretty obvious.

His name was Ma Dai, and he was a barbarian. Partially at least.

All the way in the northwest of the Great Han lies Liang province, a territory with lush, pine-covered mountains in the south and scorching desert in the north. It ends in a sleeve-shaped stretch of land called the Hexi corridor, from where merchants travel far and wide toward other cultures and realms. This corridor, no matter how much the Han fought for it, never fell completely under our influence. And as the empire struggled with uprisings, civil war, and tyranny, Liang became the theater of tribal conflicts and rebellions against the Han government. One man had managed to get a relative grasp over the region, Ma Teng, the kid's uncle. He had managed such a feat partly thanks to his mix of Han and Qiang blood.

I later learned these people hate being called as such because what we call Qiang are actually a diverse group of different tribes, their customs being too similar for us to care and too different for them to unite. Some were mountaineers who lived in the snow all year; others rode horses and camels across wide stretches of grass or sand. Ma Teng was from the latter's kind, as was Ma Dai, of course.

Master Zhong Yao had gotten Ma Teng to officially surrender to the emperor in exchange for a title of some kind. As insurance for his good behavior, this half-Han leader sent a few sons and nephews to the capital as hostages. None were from his wife, and most looked more Han than Qiang. Ma Dai, however, could no more pass for one of us than I could pretend to be a fish.

He was rather short, with bandy legs shaped by years on the saddle. His skin was darker than ours, with a leather-like hardness to it despite his youth. Two big, round eyes with a color approaching mine shone inside an honest face, and his hair, while just as dark as any of ours, was curling like the fur of a mountain goat. I'm guessing among his people, he was considered a handsome youth, and he was obviously well-educated according to our culture, but his life would be hard and unkind near the palace.

"And you think it will be better with my men?" I asked.

"You already have one barbarian within the Scorpions," he replied. "And he's good with horses, too, I hear."

"Are you?" I asked the silent Ma Dai.

"I think so," he replied. He had a low voice for his age. You could hear the dryness of the desert in it.

"What am I supposed to do with him?"

"As long as he remains in the county, whatever you want," Man Chong answered. I did not like that. It meant that I would either need to leave a man behind to watch him when we went on missions and as we were short-handed, I could barely afford it. Or that we wouldn't be going on a mission for a while. Since I had not been allowed to hire replacements yet despite my requests, I was inclined to believe it was the second.

"Well, consider him your newest recruit for the future," Man Chong commented.

"I can't make him one of us! Imagine he gets killed. Wouldn't it completely ruin our diplomatic effort with his uncle?"

"Hardly," Man Chong said, tilting his head. "Ma Teng sent us a litter of bastards and distant nephews. He won't cry over one of them disappearing."

I frowned to make him realize what he had just said. Man Chong could be a heartless piece of shit sometimes.

"No offense," he then added.

"It's fine, sir," the kid replied. "I know what I am."

If he hadn't said so, I might have argued the assignment

longer, but something in his tone made me boil within. Youths are supposed to be arrogant, angry by nature, and full of ambition. Ma Dai, despite his obvious education and martial training, lacked all of it, and I could only imagine what kind of treatment he had suffered to become so mellow. Man Chong immediately understood my silence and smiled his victorious grin when I dropped my eyes to his again.

"Fine," I said, lifting both arms in the air.

I so hated my friend's following chuckle that I rolled on the balls of my feet and turned around without even a salute. Five steps later, I was out of his office, Ma Dai on my heels.

"Don't you have belongings with you?" I asked the kid as we walked to his new life.

"The prefect said they would already be at your place," he replied. We were walking fast, but he did not complain or lag behind.

"A horse?"

"Yes, but I had to leave her outside the walls," he answered. He had said *her*, which earned him some good points in my mind.

"They probably put her in some military stable," I told him. "She'll be fed shit there. I'll get her with our horses. The fodder I get for our mounts costs me an arm, so you'll either pay for it or work for it. You got cash on you?"

"No, sir," he replied.

I stopped us right in our tracks and planted myself in front of him.

"Let's make things clear," I said, poking a finger into his chest. He was still looking at the ground. "I'm your superior, but you're in my care. I'm not *sir*. I'm Captain Liao in front of anyone or *big brother* Chun when it's just the two of us. And you look at me in the eyes when I speak."

As I said the last, I tried to grasp his gaze, but it kept fleeting, which forced me to bend over until he had no choice but to accept it. Even then, it lasted only a second before he looked away again.

"It's not what I learned," he said as an excuse.

"Ma Dai, I'm the son of a farmer, not a pompous bag of silk like *them*. Where I come from, people who respect each other make eye contact."

I waited until he managed to force himself to look at me and then relented the pressure a little.

"Good," I said, offering him my most sincere smirk. I felt so oddly old next to him, even though I was just twenty. "I've got only one empty room," I said, grabbing him by the biceps to force us back on the march. "If I manage to recruit a new member or two for my unit, as I plan to, you'll have to share my servant's room. Is that a problem?"

"Not at all," he answered.

"You'll eat with us, train with us, enjoy life with us if you got the coin for it, and we'll keep you safe until your uncle is judged trustworthy enough for you to head back to Liang." He missed a step when I said so, and I wondered if by the time it happened, he would be happy about returning home.

When he finally let go of the floor, his eyes went from one building to the next, an air of wonder painted on his face. He probably had never visited such a great city before.

"Do you have any questions before I introduce you to the others?" I asked.

"Just one," he said, and even that sounded like he had to push himself. "What kind of unit do you lead?"

"Oh, that," I said, pride drooling in my voice as we

reached the compound entrance. "Let's just say we are the Scorpions."

It wasn't long before we adopted Ma Dai. His inherent shyness made him the perfect target of our jibes, even though Guli soon took him under her wing. He didn't seem to mind much and rather enjoyed our company. Though I should have seen it coming, he also quickly fell head over heels for my lover. Suddenly I was Cao Cao, he was a younger version of me, and Guli was Lady Bian. She enjoyed his attention but never let me be jealous over it, even though the two of them were closer in age than she and I.

I had hoped to create a bond between Ma Dai and Guo Huai, but our Sparrow grew a natural hatred for the Qiang teenager. In retrospect, it made sense. Ma Dai, while looking foreign, could read, write, ride, shoot, and even recite some poetry, but Huai, while being as Han as one could be, didn't know his characters and could only sing bawdy songs whose lyrics he did not understand. It forced me to hire a teacher for him and any one of them who wanted to learn to read, but only he, Guli, and sometimes One-eye joined the class.

Even when it came to fighting, Ma Dai was superior to Guo Huai. He was actually better than most of us. With a spear or a *dao* in hand, Ma Dai was something of a genius, and his natural discretion gave way to a frank martial spirit when we practiced. Even I had to push myself to make sure he knew who he was dealing with. Better still, he could ride as few Han do. Not as well as Guli or I, maybe, but given time, I was certain he would become a phenomenal cavalryman.

"He rides like one of us," Tian Guli once said when we took the horses on a countryside ride. She was talking about her own people, who know horses better than any other.

There was only one thing I couldn't stomach with the kid; his constant babbling over one of his cousins, whom he obviously worshipped. Not a day passed by without him battering our ears with the merits of the magnificent Ma Chao, the first son of his uncle Ma Teng. Ma Chao rode better, fought better, sang better, and read faster. He was taller, people called him the most handsome man in the province, and his teeth were perfectly white and aligned. *Ma Chao this, Ma Chao that*, all day long, every day without rest. I had to forbid him from invoking his cousin's name. No matter how impressive a young man he was, Ma Dai suffered a heavy inferiority complex to his apparently brilliant cousin, and I already disliked this Ma Chao for it. Somehow, this kind of reputation seldom proves true.

Ma Dai was the perfect distraction for me, and I would have been glad to officially incorporate him into my roster of warriors.

Unfortunately, I couldn't manage to get the approval for any new hire, nor were we sent on any mission worthy of the name.

Soon after the autumn equinox, Yuan Shu, the self-proclaimed emperor of the Zhong dynasty, brought his troops north, forcing Cao Cao to meet him on the field of battle. From what I heard, it was barely one, and my lord pushed the toad south of the Huai river, thus increasing his control over the whole of Yu province.

While this happened, I got myself ready for what must surely come; our revenge over Zhang Xiu. I knew that any day now, Man Chong would send the Scorpions back to Wan and direct our blades to the bastard's throat. I studied maps to get us there discreetly, then interviewed people who used to live in Wan to better grasp the city until I was certain I could infiltrate it from any gate to Zhang Xiu's bedroom in the dark. I even worked with tanners and smiths to fabricate less noisy grappling hooks, climbing gloves, and shoes. But the order never came. Winter did, though, and with it, an incredible sense of boredom. For the first time in my life, I grew a little fatter. Guli's jibes pushed me back to training until the new layer of fat disappeared, though she claimed not to mind it. I am afraid I was not a great companion to her in those days, but the frustration of our inactivity weighed me down more than I knew.

Not just me, but even my men developed bad habits. Some invited women into the compound for the night, a practice I had previously forbidden but now ignored. One-eye even started a relationship with a courtesan from the red district. She claimed to love him and that he pleased her more than any customer ever had, and we never had enough of teasing him about his gullibility.

I became downright pissed when Cao Cao went back to Wan to deal with Zhang Xiu without even inviting my men and me to join. It was no secret I wanted to avenge my friends. The army left on the coldest day of the year and remained in Nanyang commandery for the next four months. They quickly took control of Wan, but besides this did not manage much. There was a lot of back and forth between him and Zhang Xiu's soldiers, whom Liu Biao's men helped for once.

We heard about our comrades' return a couple of days after the vernal equinox. I had just sat two wars out and felt as useful as a nipple on a male dog. I was tired of pouring my frustration on my men, so I found a new target for my displeasure and headed for the prefect's office. When I stepped into Man Chong's workroom, I saw something I had never witnessed before; my friend was drunk. And not just drunk but brooding.

"If it isn't Captain Liao," Man Chong said, leaning on his arm, his eyes barely visible over his sleeve. "Our *golden eagle*," he went on as he lazily sat up and pulled an empty cup from a tray, which he filled and slid to me. I knelt on the other side of his desk, accepted the cup, and emptied it in one gulp.

"Oh, that's strong," I said, breathing some of the alcohol out.

"Well, I need something strong before Cao Cao's return," he commented as he filled his own cup.

"What's wrong, Chong?" I asked. This was so out of character that I started to worry. I knew Man Chong had made some waves by interrogating a nobleman without much proof to accuse him of anything, but I couldn't believe that could get him so rattled.

"Nothing's wrong," he answered, wincing his nose and waving his hand.

"My friend," I went on, filling my cup once more. "You are drunk, and I am not yet. You will talk soon anyway, so why don't you save us some time and tell me already?"

Man Chong hesitated, frowned, burped behind his hand, and slapped his thigh. He had accepted my argument.

"I'm just tired, Chun, just tired," he said. "You, you complain all the time. You're used to it. But me ... never. I never complain. Especially to Lord Cao. My father ..." I had trouble hearing his words, which came in unarticulated stretches of syllables. Thankfully, I had been a soldier long enough and had practiced the secret art of drunk-chatting for many years. "But this time, I just have had enough."

"Enough of what?" I asked, the sensation of the wine reaching the back of my mind.

"I miss Ang too, you know," he went on, completely ignoring my question. "I didn't like him at first, but he was a good man. I would have advised him." He tapped his thumb against his chest as he spoke, then meant to grab the pitcher again, but I didn't let him.

"What in the heaven are you talking about?"

"Don't pretend you didn't notice," Man Chong went on, his hand on my wrist to remove my grasp over the pitcher. "You and I, we are being sidelined."

"Sidelined? By Cao Cao?" There was no denying this was exactly how I felt, but I never thought Man Chong shared the impression. He always seemed so busy. "You are the prefect of Xuchang, for heaven's sake; how is that being sidelined?"

"I was appointed prefect when Ang was alive," he answered. "I will never rise above that. Especially as long as this cock-sucker is by his side." Man Chong would usually not have used such a vulgar term. He would absolutely have called Guo Jia something of the sort, but using some metaphor or well-thought pun, not something as crude as *cock-sucker*.

"Chong, I can't follow you. What does Ang's death have to do with anything you just said?"

"Everything!" he replied, raising both hands like whips. "Chun, what did you think we were to Cao Cao?"

"His students," I said. "And some of the best, I dare say. You proved yourself time and again, so he made you a prefect, and I showed I could fight, so he made me the captain of his special forces."

"But why us? Why did he take us in, in the first place?

You know, he's never done that since, a school project like that?"

I had never considered this question. To me, Cao Cao had simply taken children to shape them into his future staff and officers. We were cheap labor back then, and he could model us any way he wanted. But it is true that Cao Cao, despite acknowledging the success of his project, never repeated it. Man Chong mentioning Ang is what told me where his theory went.

"You think he was grooming us for Ang?" I asked. Man Chong winked. It did make sense. Most of the students were around Ang and Shuo's age. Maybe Cao Cao had not meant us to become his men but his sons'. We had studied with them, fought with them, and shared joys and sorrow with them. When the time came for Ang to take his father's place, he would have a small army of devoted, qualified friends by his side. But this would never happen now. We had become obsolete, according to Chong's theory.

"Surely Lord Cao knows we can still be of use to him, or whoever his heir turns out to be," I said. Lord Cao had lost both his elder sons but had already sired more boys. The elder, Cao Pi, then eleven, was quickly becoming a worthy son. He lacked his father and older brother's charisma and looked withdrawn, but was praised as a good student in military and administrative affairs. Cao Zhi, the third son of Lady Bian, received even more praise on account of his poetical genius, and he too would follow in his father's steps. Even the cadet, Cao Zhang, had his merits, though they lay more in the military field. He was as dumb as they came but was eager to please his father and spent his days learning weapons and battle formations.

"Please, Chun, surely you know better," Man Chong said, cocking his head in a way suggesting that maybe I didn't after all. "In any case," he continued, grabbing the jug because I had let go of it, "Cao Cao will have to change his strategy, and I'm not sure how we fit in it."

"Why would he need to change his strategy?" I asked. My friend refilled my cup, and I gladly drank it down.

"Because his heir, no matter who it turns out to be, won't be ready for a while," he answered. "With Ang turning into a fine leader, Cao Cao was assured that his legacy was safe no matter what happened to him. I wouldn't even have been surprised if he had retired once the business with Yuan Shao was over. But now, he needs to consolidate his position until one of his sons proves himself worthy and gains the loyalty of the retainers. As I see it, he can do it two ways. The first is to strengthen his grip over the court and take out all those who might yet threaten him."

I shivered at the thought. Cao Cao was already pushing his role to its limit, and many saw him as little better than Dong Zhuo had been.

"What's the second?"

"He can declare himself emperor."

If I feared the first solution, I dreaded the second. Yuan Shu declaring his own dynasty was stupid because it relied on no bases, but Cao Cao was feared, respected, wealthy, and surrounded by the brightest advisors in the land. He had a solid claim to the throne based on his merits, and if the mandate of heaven had indeed shifted away from the Han, Cao Cao was the most likely candidate for it. This, however, meant the murder of the emperor and anyone who supported him. And since I was the reason Emperor Xian resided in Xuchang, his blood would be on my hands.

"He wouldn't," I said, not believing the words myself.

"Not everyone shares your moral compass," Man Chong

replied as he emptied yet another round of *baijiu*. "Some of us do the work, *then* ask ourselves if we should have."

I let his comment slide, knowing it came from a drunken mind.

"No matter which way he chooses," Man Chong went on, "Xuchang will bathe in blood at one point or another, and Cao Cao will have to harden himself even more. You mark my words, innocents will die, and you might not like whose hands spilled their blood."

Man Chong was more right than he ever knew he was, but before that happened, we had a beast to hunt down, for some news all of us expected finally broke out. Lü Bu had shattered the peace with Liu Bei and made a move to complete his conquest of Xu province. It was finally time to put an end to his rampage.

6

Xuchang, capital of the Great Han
9th month, 3rd year of Jian'an era (198), Han Dynasty

IN THE EARLY weeks of autumn, while the days still stretched with dry winds and late sunsets, Lü Bu once again showed his true colors. We all knew the beast would sooner or later break his peace with Liu Bei and us. It was meant to be. Xu, especially incomplete, would never satisfy his appetite. All he needed was an opportunity. It just so happened that we gave it to him, unknowingly. When we had pushed Yuan Shu south of the Huai river, we put the toad in a corner and forced him to seek alliances. He could not partner with Sun Ce, his most direct neighbor, who was not only officially our ally, but Yuan Shu's former officer, and one thing was certain, the toad would never ally himself with a former subordinate. As such, he chose Lü Bu.

Yuan Shu was still wealthy and strong in men, so he offered the beast a small fortune, and they exchanged a promise of mutual support in case of an attack. With the cash, Lü Bu hired every bandit sheltering in the Mount Tai region, and with his alliance, he grew bold enough to declare war on Liu Bei in Xiaopei.

Lü Bu sent one of his two top generals, Gao Shun, to besiege the imperial uncle, and while we all thought this battle would be short, Liu Bei and his brothers mounted an impressive defense and managed to last until Lord Cao sent reinforcements. My lord, however, made what I assumed then to be a mistake; he sent the division of Xiahou Dun to help our allies. Xiahou Dun never was, nor would he ever become, a military man. His men were brave but not trained to our standard, nor did they respect their general enough. In a matter of days, Xiahou Dun lost the battle and most of his soldiers, and because Liu Bei left Xiaopei to help him, they also lost the city. Tails between their legs, the remnants of the two defeated armies left Xu province and marched back toward Yan.

Xuchang was in turmoil upon the news of yet another debacle. People started claiming Cao Cao had lost the favor of the sky and would soon be attacked by all his enemies who now had witnessed his "weakness."

In reality, as I finally realized on the quiet evening before our departure to Xu, it was all part of my lord's plan. More accurately, Pox made me understand it.

"Has to be Lord Cao's idea," he bluntly said as we played a game of dice on a wooden board.

"What is?" One-eye asked, grumbling. He had been moody recently, both because his courtesan had dumped him, leaving him coinless, and because he was losing the game.

"I don't know," Pox replied. "All of it. Xiaopei, Lü Bu's betrayal, maybe even the beast and the toad's alliance. I don't know."

"Shut your noodle hole," Shudu, the last member of the

table, said, even more irritated than his neighbor because he was about to leave the game early. "Even Cao Cao cannot see that far."

"By the Jade Emperor's balls," I said, cursing myself more than anyone else.

"What is it?" One-eye asked.

"Pox is right," I answered.

"I am?"

"He is?"

And he was. I now had no doubt. It was all too perfect.

I always wondered why Lord Cao hadn't finished Yuan Shu, even though he had had many occasions. The simplest answer, and thus the most likely, was that Cao Cao wanted Yuan Shu to keep his position right between him and Sun Ce. The toad was an easy target and could be defeated whenever we wished. He was a buffer with the Little Conqueror, but also a magnet for our opponents. Only Yuan Shu would support a rogue like Lü Bu and help him make his move.

Lü Bu remained isolated in Xu province, but with Yuan Shu's help, he could resume his fight with us, thus forcing our hand in counterattacking. And by controlling Xiaopei, we gave an obvious target to the beast. We knew where the first blow would be dealt. Xiaopei was not of great importance, but it was the birthplace of Liu Bang, the founding father of the Han dynasty. By raiding it as he had, Lü Bu was declaring himself an enemy of the emperor for life, and such blasphemy needed a swift response.

Of course, it would have been suspicious if we hadn't tried to rescue our allies in Xiaopei, so my lord sent his cousin and his men. This too was part of a devious scheme. While our divisions were recovering from the battles in Nanyang, there were still more pertinent choices than

Xiahou Dun's. That, too, worked in Lord Cao's favor, though. This division was the weakest in our army. Thus, its defeat would not be a great blow to our dignity and would also get us rid of our least worthy soldiers. I shuddered at the idea that Cao Cao sent those men, knowing they would never return, but I had to acknowledge the possibility of it.

It all made sense, but I had been blind until a peasant soldier shone a light on it. I blamed my lord for keeping me away from his planning and Ang's death for taking the man who knew my lord the most from my circle of friends.

"Horse shit," Shudu spat, "even Cao Cao cannot plan so far ahead."

"Now, now, no need to implicate horses in your opinion of me," Cao Cao said as he stepped out of the darkness of the courtyard's round-shaped entrance. I thought my heart was about to leave my body through my throat as I leaped from my stool. My three companions did as much, and Pox almost choked on his sip of beer.

"My lord!" I called, kneeling and saluting.

Cao Cao laughed at our reaction, and for a second, I forgot we had not spoken to each other in a year and a half.

People in Xuchang claimed that whenever you spoke his name, Cao Cao would show up behind your back after hearing everything you said about his person. Until that moment, I always assumed they were talking of his spies.

"Please rise," he told us.

Now that he had stepped in the light of our lamps, I could see the last year had not been kind to my lord. He was still handsome but in a cold, mature kind of way. Gray was peppered all over his beard, some strands of it so clear they appeared white. He had turned forty-four that year and displayed all of them at the corners of his eyes. Yet he was still the man who had rescued me in Julu, and I felt grateful for his presence.

"Who is winning?" he asked, hands behind his back.

"I am, my lord," Pox replied, a face as red with embarrassment as I had ever seen it.

"Can you keep playing with only three people?" he asked.

"They can get someone else," I answered, guessing Lord Cao meant to speak with me, though what deserved his presence here, I could not imagine.

"Good," he said before nodding toward the exit as an invitation for me to follow. I emptied my cup of *huangjiu* and entered the darkness behind my lord as we stepped outside the Scorpions' compound.

Two sections of guards waited in the streets, one on each side of the exit. Further down the road, before the next intersections, more of them controlled the area. They would let no one come anywhere near their lord. I rarely experienced this side of the city so quiet.

"Why did you come here, my lord?" I asked.

"I have something to ask you," he answered. The rhythmic steps of our escort were the only sound besides our voices.

"I understand. But why did *you* come? Is everything all right up there?" By *up there*, I meant on the northern side of the city, in the palace and nearby mansions. I almost never visited those areas recently, besides on the monthly occasion of my riding lessons to the emperor, and those usually took place in his private hunting ground, where no one could witness their ruler's inability with horses.

"Just a migraine," he explained, nothing surprising there. "I am either stuck in the presence of sycophants and critics or sleeping in a cot at the center of a camp. A walk in the cool night air of the capital will make me feel better."

"So you think I'm neither sycophant nor critic?" I asked smugly.

"Oh, you are a critic, all right, I know that," he replied, equally amused. This was the lord I remembered and missed. "But at least you are not one to talk behind my back."

"I don't have much chance to speak in front either," I said.

"See what I was saying?" Cao Cao said, proud of himself. We turned left, following the wall protecting the capital. "I need you to tell me anything you can about Xiapi. As the captain of my special forces, you have spent some time there. What are its weaknesses, its strengths, how will Lü Bu defend his capital, what can we exploit there?"

Everyone guessed a great battle would happen in Xiapi at the end of the campaign against Lü Bu. This was his stronghold, his capital, and he would keep fighting until it fell, at least. But we were a few months away from such a battle, and I hadn't expected this question. It took me a while to remember the details of Xiapi. I had spent a little over two weeks inside the city and was not concerned with its defenses back then. Yet one thing was certain, it would be a tough nut to crack, as I told my lord.

"The walls are high and thick, and there is no easy way to sneak in. Liu Bei, when he was in charge of the city, made sure the defenses were fixed and strengthened, and I can hardly imagine Lü Bu let them deteriorate."

"I agree," Cao Cao said as he caressed the tip of his beard. "Especially with his current advisor."

"Knowing Chen Gong," I went on, "I'm ready to bet he even improved the defenses. I'm expecting heavy crossbows at each corner, in the garrisons and towers above the gates, and every ten crenels."

"It does sound like him, indeed."

"I'm no expert, but I don't think fire would do enough damage to the wall, and any poliorcetic tool would take forever to make a dent. It would mean a half-year siege, which I guess we cannot supply for the whole army, and if we send less than that—"

"We stand no chance against the beast," Cao Cao finished for me. "How about inside the city? Will fire work?"

A memory of the heavy shield-bearers from the battle in Wan flashed into my mind, the smell of their burning flesh coming first.

"I wouldn't advise it," I answered.

"Because?"

I hesitated to reply truthfully because I knew my lord would not like or care about my answer. But Cao Cao had come all the way to me, and the least I could do was be honest and frank with him.

"Because last time we went to Xu, we massacred its people. If you burn the town and its inhabitants, the province will never submit to you."

"But is it feasible?" he asked coldly. I could not even trigger his usual temper.

"It isn't," I replied right away. "Xiapi has wells filled with water, and I rarely saw water so clear run through such a big city."

"Wasn't it better just to tell me that, then?" Cao Cao asked. "You did not have to make it sentimental."

Because I did not reply, Cao Cao moved on to his next question, but I cannot say his attitude enthused me.

"You say the people will not support me. I agree. Will they fight for Lü Bu?"

"I don't know how he treats them and only heard rumors of his temper. What I know is that Xiapi's people loved Liu Bei. Bring him along, give him a spot where they can see him, and they might help us."

"Interesting," Cao Cao genuinely commented. He had not considered this. Cao Cao had long decided to inspire people with a mixture of fear and awe. Liu Bei treating his people with kindness had not been part of his appraisal of the situation. "Thank you, Captain, you've given me much to think about. Could you write all that down, map the city to the best of your recollection, and have one of your messengers deliver it to me while I march to Xu?"

"We're not coming?" I asked, sounding whinier than I wanted.

Cao Cao halted his walk, and so did the guards. We were a few steps from the city's eastern gate, where guards were monitoring the closed doors for the night.

"I need the Scorpions in Xuchang," Cao Cao answered.

"To do what exactly?" I heard his tongue click in his mouth.

"Just to be there," he said.

"So that's it?" I asked, walking to put myself in front of him. "We're just around to scare your opponents? Deterrent for anyone who might consider whispering against your name?"

"Isn't it what you wanted?" Cao Cao asked, apparently confused. "Bloodless results? The simple mention of your name or that of your group is enough to keep the peace. I might be away for half a year or more, plenty of time for my detractors to work behind my back. I need you and the prefect to make sure they do little else than whispering against my name, as you say."

"My lord," I replied, "when you made me the leader of

your special forces, it was to help you win future battles or bring your wrath against those who harmed you. We are not just daggers in the dark to be aimed at the throats of people who do not see eye-to-eye with you. I never asked for bloodless results; I just wanted to spare the blood of innocent people. I'm a warrior, for heaven's sake."

"Liao Chun," Cao Cao said, massaging his right temple, eyes closed against the pain.

"Please, lord, listen to me. You can ask the Scorpions to remain in Xuchang, but let me join you with the army. I cannot remain here doing nothing. Let me fight for you. If it goes on, I will never be more than an unknown agent of yours with no fame or title. Or send us to Wan to take care of Zhang Xiu at least. Make real use of us."

"I have plans for Zhang Xiu," he said, and I did not like the sound of that either.

"What about me, then? Do you have plans for me? Because it doesn't look like it." I knew how childish I sounded, but I could not waste this rare opportunity to speak my mind and heart.

Cao Cao licked his lips and gazed away from me. His eyes moved to the city gate, where guards were about to change shifts.

"Do you know," he said, "when I was your age, I was like him." He pointed a finger out of his large sleeve toward the officer who welcomed the fresh guards and directed them to their posts. "Back then, I was commandant of the northern gate in Luoyang. Now, as you know, Luoyang was bigger and more populated than Xuchang, but it was far from being a prestigious post. Do you know what I did?"

"Seduced a woman married to a powerful man so that she could push him to give you a better post?" I answered.

"Oddly specific, but no. What I did was my job."

"What are you getting at, my lord?" I asked, for I did not see where this story was going.

"I just meant that twenty years later, I became the governor of Yan, Minister of Works, and protector of the emperor. You, no matter what you believe, are still very young, and there is no telling how far you will get. For now, I need you to stay put so that I can use your reputation to keep the peace in Xuchang. Once Lü Bu has been dealt with, who knows what you might be able to do for me." He said the last while confidently dropping his hand on my shoulder, but I did not feel as such. My lord had basically admitted he had no clue what to do with me.

"I am leaving tomorrow, get your assessment of Xiapi sent to me as soon as possible," Lord Cao said.

"*Zun min*," I answered, saluting and looking at the ground as my lord left me by the eastern gate. I waited for a long time, even after his guards' footsteps could no longer be heard. Then I went back home and prepared my gear.

Cao Cao had made a mistake in telling me the story of his first position because it helped me remember he had climbed as high as he did by bending the rules. He had never been the obedient type and only rose when he decided to take charge of his destiny. I would follow his example and be damned if I didn't find myself with a bloody sword in hand in Xiapi.

7

Xiapi, capital Xu province
12th month, 3rd year of Jian'an era (198), Han Dynasty

"Would you care for a wager?" Xu Huang asked, his clean-shaven, darkened face barely visible in between the strands of tall grass.

"What about this time?" I asked, wondering how our newly promoted major-general intended to ignite his martial artist's spirit. It was always a question of competitiveness with him. Something I could not begrudge, not only because I shared this vice but also because it had served me well.

"On the number of them we both defeat," he replied in an obvious tone. "About time we reduce their numbers a little."

That point, too, I could not dispute. So far, the campaign against Lü Bu proved a boring affair. In a very uncharacteristic way, the beast had removed his troops from our path long before we reached them, focusing his effort on a single point, Xiapi, the capital of Xu province. Thus we did nothing besides making our presence known in the southwest corner of Xu for two months. It was smart of Lü Bu to regroup as such since there were three times more of us than them. Xiapi was easily defendable, and three times would never be enough for us to grasp an overwhelming victory, something we needed if we ever meant to fight against Yuan Shao soon. To make matters worse, Lü Bu had two small towns fortified into military camps at the edge of Xiapi. If we ever attacked one of the three, the garrison from the two others would come to the rescue, and the whole battlefield would become a mess of entangled troops. They would lose, but the price would be too high for my lord. This simple yet efficient strategy was, of course, not born of Lü Bu's intellect but that of Chen Gong, the former secretary and strategist to my lord, and my former teacher of tactics. I missed that scattered-brain man who treated us children with more respect than his peers, but he had chosen the beast as his new master when he started fearing Cao Cao and after I personally killed one of his friends in a drunken accident. Now he would die along with his new lord. At least when we managed to unlock the situation he had put us in with those two extra camps.

I believe it was Xun Yu who proposed we use an ambush. In the late evening, we had marched a whole division of men between Xiapi and one of the two camps, the one led by the mighty Zhang Liao, and since we offered no sign of aggressivity, no one attacked us. When we marched right between the two, just as we crossed a field of tall grass, the line of men at the center of the division discreetly crouched, then let the rest pass. To increase the chances of success, the foot soldiers who would spend the night kneeling in the cold mud were marching within a division of mounted auxiliaries. Those non-Han fighters were less organized than we were, which made the procession more difficult to count, and the horses hid us better. It was a moonless night, and we hoped the cover of darkness would render the maneuver invisible from the ramparts of Xiapi and Zhang Liao's camp, and since no one came at us during the night, it was fair to assume we had succeeded.

Even if we numbered under two thousand, I was confident in our chances. First, an ambush is such a confusing strategy for the victim that by the time they might realize they have the numerical advantage, they are already running in panic or dead. Second, those two thousand were Xu Huang's men, and they were tough. I had only heard rumors about this rather small division the *youxia* officer had named the Brothers of the Sword, a poorly chosen name since most fought with polearms. For once, the rumors proved true. Xu Huang was a former knight errant, or so he liked to say, but first, he was a martial artist of great skill, and so were his men. They lacked the coordination of professional soldiers trained under Cao Cao's more classic regimen but made it up in individual fighting capacity and spirit. Due to this particularity, they rarely fought at the center of pitched battles, but whenever my lord needed a crack troop to break the enemy through flamboyant actions, the Brothers were his men. Xu Huang had quickly risen thanks to his warriors, and he treated them generously in return. Despite his ascension, he had hardly changed since I first met and recommended him to Cao Cao.

"What do we bet?" I asked. Dawn was close, and so was the ambush. We should have been as quiet as mice, but we were also excited. Ambushes are as dangerous to their victims are they are exhilarating to those who launch them. Knowing that you will destroy unprepared foes has this strange way of getting the blood pumping. And, as I had said, we had grown bored with this campaign. So far, the most thrilling moments for me were when Cao Cao or another high-level officer came to meet with Xu Huang. I was not to be discovered, for both our sakes. Xu Huang had accepted my presence in his troops because I was a great warrior, but even more, because he owed me his presence under Cao Cao's banner and his great fortune. The point had nearly failed to impress him, so I reminded him of the time we had fought in Luoyang. While it had been a practice session, Xu Huang had bested me and had declared that was because I was a soldier and meant to fight on the field of battle. On the training ground, he had said, it was natural for him to win. So I challenged him to put me to the test during the war. His *youxia*'s spirit had taken the bait and swallowed the line, and I joined his section of guards. They were good men, easy to befriend, serious in their training, and I looked forward to seeing how they behaved in battle.

"Your horse," he answered, his teeth flashing white at the center of a mudded face. *Damn youxia*, I thought, they always had to make things so serious in a competition. He knew how much I loved Qilin and had set his eyes on her from the moment I snuck inside his regiment-size division.

"I'll take your *dao* in that case," I replied. Xu Huang fought with a great-ax, a weapon he adored so much that he had even taken it with us for the ambush, no matter how clumsy it proved as we hunkered in the cold grass field. But besides his favored tool of death, he boasted an amazing collection of blades and armor, at the center of which sat a magnificent single-edged blade. Up to that point, blades were nothing more than tools for me, and I cared very little about their appearance or the technique behind their fabrication. I often changed blades from one battle to the next, didn't give them special care after the killing, and broke many during practice bouts. Seeing that one changed my mind. It was a slightly curved blade with a solid back and a supple, razor-sharp edge that would keep its bite after many assaults. The back of the tip was also sharpened, and when I saw it, I wondered why most were not forged the same. The pommel was shaped in a perfect ring, the hilt made of dark wood. The blade part was also darker than most I had seen so far. A glance had been enough for me to recognize its quality. The waves on the blade were unique in their pattern and gave me the same impression of perfection as Cao Cao's calligraphy. It was a treasure of craftsmanship only appreciated by true warriors. But more than its appearance, its aura drew me to it. I feel silly speaking of aura for a weapon, but I do not know how to express it better. The closer I got to the *dao* set at the center of the collection, the stronger I could feel its pull. I could almost hear it; a low, vibrating buzz like the call of a male bullfrog on a summer night, but with a metallic tone to it. I remember stretching my arm and feeling a comforting warmth at my fingertips. The edge of the blade was calling for the skin. I shivered when Xu Huang told me to be careful, my hand a *cun* away from the sword, and I still shiver now from the memory of it.

Xu Huang had won it over the cadaver of its previous owner, the leader of a large group of bandits rampaging eastern Yan, though how the latter came into its possession is a mystery. The *youxia* gave it a name, something I always found ridiculous, even though the choice had been well thought.

"If you want *Yingzhao*, you'd better give it your best," Xu Huang answered, though I could see he wasn't against the idea of this bet. *Hawk Talon*; I craved it.

"And if you want my mare, you'd better not slack off, my friend," I said.

"Older brother," a warrior of Xu Huang called from his left, interrupting our childish banter. Everyone in this division called the others *brothers*, though Xu Huang was the only *older brother*. "Almost time." This was his second-in-command's way of telling us to shut up, and he was right, of course.

Xu Huang and I went back to the observation of the enemy's camp, a former village turned stronghold with a solid wall of earth and thick poles to cover it. They had installed watch towers at regular intervals, roofs for the archers, two gates north and south, and had probably stocked it with months' worth of supply. I could feel my old teacher's hand in the camp's design, and we would be lucky to see its inside if we tried to storm it the regular way. Even more so if the enemy's reinforcement attacked us simultaneously. Our only chance was to assault it while they were out, and this is what we hoped to do. The Brothers of the Sword's role was simply to scatter and destroy Zhang Liao's division and prevent them from returning to their camp while Yu Jin's Dragon-Fang took their camp.

Dawn drew near, its faint light appearing against the clouds over Xiapi. The bells from the city rang, interrupting the peace of the slowly awakening nature. Our comrades had launched their diversion assault on the capital. Then would come the enemy's banners calling for reinforcements. I could not see the gate of the camp we targeted, but from the commotion, I guessed that Zhang Liao was dashing out of it, first with his cavalry, then the foot soldiers. We were to let the horses pass by and wait for the second, bigger group. The Dragon-Fang needed twenty minutes to reach the enemy camp, which we had to give them, plus some more for the assault.

I almost lay down in the cold earth—turned mud by the

previous day's rain when the horses trampled on the path to the city, their riders cursing their mounts to go faster to rescue their comrades. Our lines went parallel to the road, and I was in front, so I felt their passage like the rumble of the thunder. I tried to catch a glimpse of Zhang Liao between the tall strands of grass, but they all came in a flash and were gone.

This man, who some called Iron Heart, was the terror of our soldiers around the evening fires. Of course, everyone feared Lü Bu, but since we had defeated him on several occasions and because he had chosen to hide in Xiapi, some of the dread he used to inspire washed down on his top officer. I remembered how, back in Hulao, the soldiers who had fought Lü Bu quaked in fear at the mention of the beast but just as much when speaking of his two officers. Zhang Liao was one, the second was Gao Shun, and together they had defeated Liu Bei and Xiahou Dun's army. I was curious about this man who had followed Lü Bu since his very youth and who some claimed could make children start and stop crying with a simple gaze. As he rode by, though, I was left to wonder if I would ever meet him in battle at all.

"Get ready," Xu Huang whispered before he tapped the side of his helmet, a sign taken over and repeated by all his men along the line. Once enough of the enemy's foot soldiers stepped in front of our line, we would reap death.

I cocked the string of my crossbow as discreetly as possible and nocked the only bolt at my disposal. We would only have time to shoot once, then charge. While I was no expert with this weapon, I could use it well enough to fulfill my role. Those men would be less than ten steps from us, a hard target to miss. We also had a spear to throw each. While Yue Jin regularly trained his men with javelins, it hadn't become the norm in the rest of the army, and I didn't expect amazing results. Then I had a regular *dao* sword and a *gou-rang* hook shield. I was armed, armored, and ready, but felt nervous, and it took me a few anxious seconds to realize it was due to the one asset I lacked, my comrades. I had never fought without Du Yuan or Pox by my side. One-eye was always at the ready with his bow behind me. I missed Shudu and Bobo's regular banter before some kind of battle and missed Guli even more, for her presence helped me focus. I acted unfairly when I left without any warning and would need to apologize profusely on my return.

Thinking of my lover and my friends quieted my mind just before I heard the first rhythmical footsteps of our targets. Somewhere by the wall of Xiapi, men would already be dying while we executed our part of the plan, and if I hated the idea of those brave soldiers sacrificing their lives as bait, something had to be done about the two camps.

The man on my right frowned as Zhang Liao's men came ever closer. I shook my head to ask him what was wrong, and he came close enough to whisper.

"It sounds wrong," he said.

I was about to ask him what he meant but noticed it too. The sound of their march was slightly off, as if they were limping. Their progress was also slower than I expected for an army marching to the rescue of their comrades. Something *was* off. I meant to share my worries with Xu Huang, but one look was enough to understand he did not feel as such. The *youxia* officer stared through the grass with the eyes of a wolf, licking his lips in a bestial way, and before I could say anything, he opened his hand to signal the man in charge of calling the action. The soldier raised his *bo* cymbals and banged them in one loud, sky-piercing sound.

We rose as one, pointing the crossbows in front of us

swiftly and released. I felt the pressure of the trigger go off before I understood how doomed we were.

The bolts came almost all at once; a gush of missiles that planted themselves into the heavy shields of the foot soldiers or simply bounced back. This was the origin of their slowness and the odd sound of their march.

"Spear!" Xu Huang shouted, recovering from the shock of the trap faster than I did.

I had yet to see the face of the enemy, who kept themselves behind their shields, but I threw the damn thing with enough strength to force my target on his ass. He wouldn't die, but I bet his arm broke. Some of his companions fell as well; others screamed, but most remained in their spot, adequately protected against our ambush.

"Brothers, charge!" Xu Huang shouted.

We could have turned back. Frankly, this is what I would have ordered. Those shield-bearers would never catch us with their gear made for defense, but the major-general still meant to accomplish our mission. He trusted his men, and in this, he was right. Not one of them hesitated. The Brothers rushed to the carapaced foes, blades and spears in hand. I, too, dashed toward the open space I had created, hoping it would remain so until I engulfed myself in their lines and spread even more chaos. The first of my comrades reached their lines, and some jumped over the shields with a grace known only to martial artists. Our enemy had not expected it, and some shields opened up in a panic. I had to shoulder my way through but found myself in the melee.

Not thinking twice, I slashed my sword in a wide arc and felt it bite into the flesh of the soldier facing me, near the hip. I punched the spike of my shield through his mouth before he could recover, then turned around and kicked low into the shin of a shield-bearer. It snapped under my boot, and the man buckled pitifully, his shriek replacing any other sound from my vicinity. The Brother coming behind me took care of him, but I still counted the victim as mine for my personal tally.

The enemy had been prepared and knew they would be ambushed but had never faced men like Xu Huang's warriors. The shock of this agile, efficient, and uncoordinated attack tore through them with speed, and I think we dispatched a third of their numbers before they rallied. Sadly, few of them ran away as we had hoped, and the resistance would be terrible.

I killed a third, then a fourth man, before a Brother pulled me back on time to avoid a synchronized attack from two shield-bearers. I was about to thank him, but the warrior had already moved to the offensive. He stabbed his spear in the foot of the shield-bearer, who then lowered his protection, offering his head for the taking. I did not hesitate and thrust my sword between his eyes. His companion yelled and raised a short blade but fell to his knees, life fleeing from the puncture wound through his ribcage.

"You can thank me later," Xu Huang smugly commented as he pulled the spearhead part of his great-ax from his victim's abdomen.

"I'll thank you for your beautiful blade," I replied, using this moment to catch my breath. Xu Huang looked as if on a beautiful morning stroll, his mudded face still perfectly masked, while mine was dripping muddy pearls of sweat.

"How many?" he asked, a frown comically appearing between his two very white eyes.

"Five," I said.

"Ha! Six," he replied. I was about to call him a liar, but a sound washed over the battlefield and turned my bowels to water.

Horses.

"Watch out!" Xu Huang shouted, just as he used the flat of his great-ax to shove me on the side a second before a tall gelding charged through from our rear. Xu Huang saved my life then, but the beast bumped into his chest and sent him flying into the melee.

More horses charged through us, tearing us apart and claiming easy death in their wake. They also killed many of their men, but we would never recover from such a charge, then from the following fight. I avoided two more horses by twisting and skipping away but knew we were as good as dead if we let the horse riders dictate the flow of the battle. Already some jutted their spears and swords through the ranks of the helpless Brothers.

I now stood at the back of the melee, and the temptation to run away came strongly into my mind. We had no way to win or survive this fight. Even less to accomplish our mission. However, the sight of Xu Huang lying motionless in the mud forced my next steps. He had just saved my life, after all.

I cursed his infectious *youxia* righteous spirit and dashed back into the fight. A mare tore from the confusing pack of horses and placed herself between Xu Huang and me. Her rider, I saw, was about to spear him through even though the officer was clearly unconscious or worse. I did not let him. Using the cadaver of a shield-bearer as a stepping stone, I jumped over the mare and slashed through the rider's neck in as perfect a swing as I ever managed. His head bounced by my feet as I landed, and a flow of blood showered me and the unconscious *youxia* before the body toppled to the side. Using the stirrups for once, I climbed on the panicking mare and pulled on the reins to tell her she had a new master.

"Brothers! On me!" I shouted from the bottom of my lungs, raising my sword toward the sky.

The sight from the saddle filled me with dread. Our men were being slaughtered, stuck between the cavalry and the foot soldiers. The former group, I knew, would soon pull out, for nothing is more useless than a horse that doesn't move. Then they would charge again, and our thin line would vanish.

"Kill the horses!" I shouted an order I would regret for the rest of my life because I hated harming those animals. In a matter of seconds, the first of them fell, their legs and bellies being savaged by my comrades' blades. Their riders were crushed in the fall or taken care of before they could recover.

"Retreat!" Xu Huang's second-in-command called.

"No!" I shouted. "If we run, their cavalry will pick us one by one. Brothers on me!" I called again. Our only chance was to mount some kind of resistance until their camp fell and they abandoned the fight or until some of our allies came to rescue us. This, however, was where Xu Huang's troop showed their weakness. They knew very little about formation and could hardly unite on cue. Yet, many of them managed to come closer, and soon a circle of spears formed around their fallen leader.

"Pick the shields," one of them said.

Zhang Liao's cavalry pulled away and would soon return for another charge. I had to stop it somehow, or we were all dead.

"Protect him with your lives," I told the circle of warriors around Xu Huang before kicking my mount to a gallop. I picked a spear sprouting from a dead body after I passed the blade in my shield-hand and followed the mass of riders as they tore through the field of tall grass. One of them would be Zhang Liao; if I took him out, their attack might falter. None of them noticed me at first, but then, under their leader's command, they slowed to a halt and turned around to get the next charge ready. They were maybe a hundred of them, but I could easily spot my target. He rode a sturdy yet swift stallion, a gray-coated beast with a dark mane. His helmet was mounted with two pheasant feathers marking him as a commanding officer, and his dark-blue cloak flew behind him like a fishtail. When his horse turned, I could spot his impressive face and knew for certain this was Zhang Liao. It was a hard face marked by a sharp-edged beard squaring a pair of pinched lips. He saw me, so I threw the spear sooner than I would have liked. It was a perfect throw, but the man simply sat back a little and let the missile pass by harmlessly. Harmlessly for him, at least. The horse rider behind him received it right in the sternum and bolted away from his saddle. Zhang Liao did not even check his fallen comrade, his eyes remained on me, and I shivered.

"Zhang Liao!" I called, putting my sword back in my right hand as my mare slowed down to a walk. Fifty steps away, their line reformed in front of my eyes. Behind me, the battle raged on between the Brothers and the shield-bearers. Any second I could gain would give my comrades a fighting chance. "Fight me, Iron Heart!" I shouted, opening my arms in invitation.

Zhang Liao twisted his head on the left ever so slightly, though he never let me go from his glare, and he whistled. The rider by his side raised a northerner short bow, lifted it up in my direction, and pulled on the string until his hand reached his cheek.

"Oh shit," I whispered, a heartbeat before the string twanged. I meant to bring my shield in front of me, knowing how little protection a *gou-rang* offers against arrows, but the trait wasn't meant for me. It thumped into my mount's right eye, and she died without as much as a neigh, taking me in her fall. I kissed the ground, shoulder first. The grass and the mud cushioned my fall, but not enough to prevent the inevitable crush of the horse's dead weight on my leg. The pain shot from my knee as if I had been stabbed with hot metal, and my scream rang pitifully in my confused brain before being replaced by the sound of Zhang Liao calling for the charge.

"*Sha!*" he shouted, a voice like a hammer striking the anvil. The earth shook with the horses' coordinated charge.

I pushed on the dead mare, kicking and cursing it to no avail; my leg remained stuck. I had dropped both my shield and sword in my fall, though they would have been of little use against the trampling of a charging cavalry. Twisting my head, I witnessed the charge of Zhang Liao, who himself rode straight in my direction, no emotions drawing on his hard face and a short dagger-ax bouncing in his hand with every step of his stallion.

"Move, you ass," I said through gritted teeth as I attempted one last effort. I thought if I could free my leg, I could meet the charge and dive between the horses' legs. It was stupid, but the only way providing me with a chance. My leg remained stuck, though, and it sounded as if the number of horses doubled as they approached. I closed my eyes, cursed again, a few dozen horses neighed, and the world became suddenly silent.

I opened my eyes again, wondering why nothing moved. Zhang Liao had called the charge off, ten steps from me, and a small cavalry unit stood between us. They were the reason I felt as if the number of mounts had doubled, and at their head rode a man wearing green robes. His beard and sideburns flew backward with the wind, and he held a crescent-moon halberd, which he kept low.

"Master Zhang," Guan Yu said, bowing his head respectfully toward his counterpart.

"Master Guan," Zhang Liao replied in kind. The tension between the two lines of horses was clear, and it is a wonder the clash had simply not happened. Within the troops of Guan Yu, the animals were breathing hard and tossing their heads nervously. Wherever they came from, those beasts had been ridden hard to come here on time.

"Congratulations on defeating the ambush," Guan Yu said, just as I finally managed to extricate myself from under the dead horse.

"We were prepared," Zhang Liao replied. "Now, if you don't move, I will have to go through your cavalry to finish what I started." There was no threat in his tone, only the perfunctory tone of a professional warrior. It sounded almost as an apology for what was about to happen.

"It won't be necessary," Guan Yu said. "The general-in-chief has called off the attack on your camp. You may get back to it in peace. Enough blood has been spilled for one morning."

I limped toward Guan Yu, my leg functioning, though not without pain. Zhang Liao observed me with his steely eyes, and I thanked the gods or the spirits for putting Guan Yu on his path when they did. Without the bearded warrior, *that* man or his horse would have killed me.

"Agreed," Zhang Liao commented. He flicked his *ji* downward to remove some of the blood, and his men seemed to relax as one. "When this war is over, if both of us survive, let's share a drink."

"With great pleasure, Master Zhang," Guan Yu replied, bowing his head once more. Those two obviously knew and respected each other a great deal, probably from the short time Lü Bu had served under Liu Bei. "Let us hope we do not meet again on the battlefield then."

"Ha!" Zhang Liao barked in what passed for a laugh for him. "Indeed, though one can hardly call this skirmish a battle." The last he said while staring at me. I looked away in shame, my anger not being enough to overcome his victory. I should have died and had no right to speak against his taunt.

He clicked his tongue, and Zhang Liao's cavalry veered around Guan Yu's small forces. One of them raised a pennant as they resumed their march, calling for their foot soldiers to disengage, which they did with efficiency. One look was enough to understand the magnitude of the carnage. I could spot the circle I had left Xu Huang with and another, though smaller, but most Brothers of the Sword lay motionless in the muddy and blood-splattered ground.

"How is your leg, Captain Liao?" Guan Yu asked.

"I can still feel it," I replied, though I used his saddle's swell for support. "Without you and your men, I wouldn't feel much of anything. Thank you." It hurt my pride to thank the man I had long vowed to kill someday, but not doing so would make me a very petty man. He acknowledged my gratitude with a nod. "What are you doing here anyway?"

"When he realized the ambush had failed, Lord Cao Cao called back the different attacks and sent us to rescue you," Guan Yu said while dismounting. His riders were already moving toward the broken Brothers, except for a couple who remained around us as we walked back.

"Well," I said, "you did rescue some of us, but not all."

"No," Guan Yu replied. "You misunderstood me. Lord Cao sent us to rescue *you*."

"Shit. He knows I'm here," I said. Not a question.

"He knows," Guan Yu confirmed.

Just then, the circle of Brothers broke up as two of them brought a shield on which they dropped Xu Huang, who had yet to regain his senses. At least he was breathing.

"Mi Fang," Guan Yu called. One of the two riders pushed his horse closer, and a vigorous young man with a thin mustache saluted his officer, the reins of his mount between both hands. "Ride back to Lord Cao and ask him to send a healer for the major-general."

"*Zun ming,*" Mi Fang said, acknowledging his order.

"And tell him the rescue was successful," Guan Yu went on before sending his messenger away.

The rescue might have succeeded, but I was far from safe. I had once again disobeyed my orders, put myself in danger, and got caught red-handed. If I knew my lord, and if Man Chong had been right about what we meant for him now, this could brew troubles on a personal level.

"Once your lord is done chewing you up," Guan Yu said, reading my face to perfection, "come share some time with us. Brother Liu will be glad to know you are well."

"Some time?" I asked ironically. "I might have to hide with you for a while."

"It is fine. We have enough wine for one more brave man," Guan Yu went on, dropping his massive hand on my shoulder.

When he rode back to his camp, a strange feeling of loneliness took me in. I had not shared more than a few weeks with the Brothers of the Sword but knew they were done as a unit for the time being. There were not enough left to carry the dead, so I helped a warrior with a deep wound in his thigh back to our camp. The poor man was more dead than alive when I helped him down into a cot in the surgeon's tent, and sure enough, he did not make it through the day, though I would only hear of his passing in the evening after I got *chewed up* by my lord.

It was oddly reassuring to know he still cared enough to bite my head off in front of his staff, but I would have liked to remain anonymous a little longer.

8

Xiapi, capital of Xu province
1st month, 4th year of Jian'an era (199), Han Dynasty

"Will you stop that; it's making me nervous," Xiahou Yuan said, though his eyes remained on the horizon.

"Stop what?" I asked.

"This," he said, nodding toward the sword hanging from my belt. "I swear, for the past ten minutes all I hear is this *clink, clink, clink*. Either take it out or leave it in its scabbard."

Xiahou Yuan was understandably anxious, a trait he was growing fond of as the years took him away from a blessed, carefree youth. More than any other member of his family, Cao Cao had trusted this cousin with extreme responsibilities, sending him away with personal authority wherever my lord could not be. And this was on top of his usual position as our main cavalry leader. Some said he had felt relieved when being "only" given the Commandant of Cavalry rank for this campaign. This, however, gave him some room for extra assignments, such as keeping an eye on me or barring any sortie attempts from Xiapi while our foot soldiers surrounded it.

He didn't really need to watch over me. Even my disobedience had its limits. I might not have gained much goodwill from Cao Cao upon his remonstrance, but he also acknowledged my presence could prove beneficial if it ever came to an infiltration of Xiapi. And, as Xu Huang and his crack troops were out of the fight, an extra warrior would not hurt.

After this campaign, Xu Huang, who had survived with nothing worse than a concussion, would reevaluate his drilling method and incorporate more soldiery discipline into his martial arts practice. Before he left to rest in Xuchang, the *youxia* paid me a visit as I accepted Guan Yu's offer for a drink and used this opportunity to thank us both for our actions, claiming we had saved him and many of his Brothers' lives. Guan Yu deserved his gratitude, but I did not, for he had saved my life first. Xu Huang did not see it that way and rewarded me with Yingzhao, the *dao* sword I craved. I accepted it, if only because I had killed more foes than he had, and so won our bet. From that point on, and for the next two weeks, I would go nowhere without it, and my left hand was never far from its hilt.

"Chun, let it go, or I turn your ass into its new scabbard," Xiahou Yuan said through his teeth. I had not even realized I was doing it again. Even the sound of the blade leaving its scabbard enticed me.

"Sorry," I said, returning my hand to the saddle. "Not my fault things are so boring."

"Boring is good," Xiahou Yuan commented. I disagreed entirely but did not mention it.

The cavalry had been placed at five different points around the city, though to avoid any confusion, we had only taken Han riders. Members of the barbarian auxiliaries were far more talented than my countrymen but did not always respond in a timely or precise manner to our orders, and since Lü Bu's forces also contained Qiang and Xiongnu riders, Cao Cao asked his cousin to keep only Han soldiers with him. This, however, left us with just over four hundred cavalrymen to dispatch over the five points.

We sat over a hill with no trees, from where we had a panoramic view of Xiapi and its surroundings, though it was mostly a desolate land blanketed by snow at the moment. Two months of siege had left little vegetation for entire *li* around the city, and whatever structure used to dress the plain was now either burned or dismantled. Even the two villages turned camps by Lü Bu's men were nothing more than a darkened memory across the frozen, white-covered ground. A week after our failed attack, Cao Cao had grudgingly ordered a full assault of the second camp. Lü Bu and Zhang Liao came to Gao Shun's rescue, and the fight was fierce but hopeless for the enemy. We lost many comrades. Some even said this was Cao Cao's most costly victory to date, but at least we had destroyed this camp and captured its commandant, who now waited in our temporary jail. Since Chen Gong's plan relied on three camps, Zhang Liao abandoned his useless one and regrouped with Lü Bu inside the capital of Xu.

It was only a matter of time before Xiapi fell, but neither army possessed this luxury in great quantity. On our side, morale was high, but food low, and the opposite was true for Lü Bu. Which is why my lord expected some reaction from the beast and his strategist, the most plausible being an attempt to send messengers to Yuan Shu in the south.

A few months before the campaign, Lü Bu and the toad

striking some kind of alliance had been the flint stone rekindling the fires of war. Confident in his new ally, the beast had attacked Liu Bei and declared his wish to pick a fight with us, but Yuan Shu had yet to send any help, and Lü Bu must have grown both fuming and eager to see the toad's promises being held. Our task was to stop those messengers before they made it past our lines. So far, none had tried.

From where I looked, Xiapi was doomed, no matter what. It was a great city, and enough soldiers manned it to protect its walls for years if need be, but the difference in might was just too great. I believe we had close to thirty thousand men currently tightening the noose around the capital, moving like ants in regiment blocks. The presence of siege engines slowed their advance, and they, in turn, had made our lives impossible. I say *ours*, but I had, thankfully, nothing to do with those behemoths. Xiapi was mostly bare of trees, and two rivers flowed nearby, making the ammunition resupplying and transporting beams a nightmare for the soldiers assigned to the teams of engineers. All of it for nothing because when, by some luck, they hit their target, the wall remained stubbornly intact. The towers worked a little better, if only because the enemy feared them so much they actually left the cover of the city to destroy them, giving us the few opportunities for real battles we had experienced over the past weeks.

But today, under the gray sky of early spring, something would happen; I felt it in my bones—Xiahou Yuan too, which is why he seemingly blinked less than twice per minute.

"Um, I'm sorry, sir," a little voice called behind us just as I leaned over my saddle to stretch my legs and back. Xiahou Yuan did not react to his son's call, and it took the young boy to call once again for me to understand he had been addressing me.

"Did you just call me *sir?*" I asked, faking a frown of displeasure. "What happened to the boy who called me *big brother*? You're Xiahou Heng, right?" I asked, suddenly realizing I might have been confused. Xiahou Yuan pupped sons and daughters yearly, and they all tended to look alike. They shared their father's easy smile, glowing eyes, and rather large nose, but thankfully neither his over-friendly attitude nor his gluttony. The young boy sitting on a black mare behind us was still lean, though his armor made him look tougher, and his well-crafted helmet covered in lamellar hid how thin his face truly was. It was hard to judge, but I guessed he was around eleven or twelve years old.

"I'm, uh, I'm Xiahou Ba," he answered, almost sorry for not being who I thought he was.

"Apologies. You look very much like your brother." Or at least he looked like his brother five years ago when rebels had taken the Cao and Xiahou families hostage. Xiahou Heng had then spent the following days proudly calling me *big brother* and following me around with no rest. I vaguely remembered this younger brother of his walking in his shadow nervously.

"None needed," he replied, cheeks turning red, though it might have been because of the morning's freshness. He meant to say something, but his eyes refused to stay on mine long enough to start a conversation. I was making him nervous.

"Come on, boy, spit it out," Xiahou Yuan told his son. "Since you saved my litter, this one can't stop asking questions about you," he then told me, moving his gaze away from the horizon for once.

"Is that true?" I asked, feeling stupidly gleeful inside.

The boy nodded. "What do you want to know, *little brother*?" When I called him that, his chest filled with air, and he sat straighter. Finally, he looked at me. He had good eyes, beaming with curiosity and now pride.

"Is that true you were a Turban?" he asked.

"Ah!" Xiahou Yuan barked, startling the boy's mare. Xiahou Ba barely flinched and regained control with a tug of the reins. At least he rode well. "He sure was. You should have seen him then, tall as three apples stacked together, covered in dry shit from head to toe."

"So much gratitude for the man who saved your family, *commandant*," I replied, a comment he waved as of no importance. "I was a Turban indeed until your father and uncles begged me to tell them what their spies ignored."

Xiahou Yuan snickered but did not reply. This was typical soldiery banter, and he appreciated it. This officer had been the first man to offer me a drink, which I had immediately puked. He had chosen my first courtesan and saved my life in Tan. I would never tell him because warriors don't say this kind of thing, but I truly saw him as a friend.

"And is it true you killed your first man at thirteen?" Xiahou Ba continued. I gestured for him to walk his mare closer, for I was tired of looking over my shoulder.

"It's true," I replied when he put his horse between his father and me. "At the battle of Xingyang."

"Oh, that was a bitch of a fight," Xiahou Yuan commented with an exaggerated shudder. And that it had been. Our first defeat and my first battle. I made an effort to remember the name of the man I had killed and sighed when I failed to picture his face clearly. How many battles since? How many deaths? I had just turned twenty-two the week before, but suddenly felt as old as the stones of Xiapi's wall.

"You'll have to give it your best if you want to do better than me," I told the young man with a wink.

"Hey," Xiahou Yuan snapped. "Don't encourage him. He's only here because his tutor gave up on him, and because I have sons to spare. But he is in no way allowed to fight. You hear me, boy?" The last he said while looking at his son, the murderous gaze of a loving father in his eyes.

"Yes, sir," the boy replied, his chest deflating and his shoulders slumping again. I felt sorry for Xiahou Ba. I knew he wanted to emulate his father and me, but he was indeed very young. I had been like him once, thinking myself ready while I was not.

"Don't worry," I told him. "When I killed that man, I was also forbidden to draw my sword."

"How did you do it then?"

"I used my knife," I answered. We both laughed, and I heard some discreet giggles from the riders near us. Xiahou Yuan waved his head as he sighed, but I could see the corners of his lips angling up.

"And is it true that you—"

"Silence," Xiahou Yuan said, raising his hand and kicking his horse a few steps further. The tension came back at once.

The two visible gates of Xiapi were opening, and soldiers poured out of them. Groups larger than Lü Bu had gotten us used to stormed out of the city and formed bridgeheads around small units of cavalrymen. As far as I could see, those riders were lightly armored and were, without a doubt, the messengers my lord had charged us to take care of. Once the soldiers surrounding them managed a path through our defenses, the messengers would bolt out and gallop southward in an attempt to reach Yang province and Yuan Shu. This, I thought, was too obvious, too direct. I didn't feel any cunning from this blunt attempt, nothing that reminded me of Chen Gong.

"Get ready!" Xiahou Yuan shouted as he fastened the strap under his helmet.

I copied him, then freed Yingzhao, the satisfaction of its weight in my hand comforting me as we prepared to ride down the hill.

The bridgeheads from the south and west gates turned to circles as their soldiers peeled away from the walls. Our men had yet to reach their level, but it would be a hard fight. Men focusing on defense are hard to kill; if they are patient enough, they can turn a battle around. Seeing how far from their defenses they moved, those soldiers must have known they were doomed. It was a suicide mission to get some messengers away. A sacrifice I could only respect and honor.

"They must be desperate in there," a rider on my right commented. He was absolutely correct. This kind of action only happens on the *sidi*, the death ground, where the only choices are death or victory. We had turned Xiapi into a *sidi* and backed our foes into a corner. They were now more dangerous than ever.

The circle south of Xiapi suddenly disbanded and charged their most direct opponents, Li Dian's regiment, I believe. They probably hoped to block our approach and give some room for their dozens of messengers, who would then slip on the sides of our unit before another came to block their path. Our regiments in charge of the eastern gates were already moving toward Li Dian's position and would eventually link up with our comrades. They would be too slow, I thought, and the messengers would likely pass in between. Those riders would, however, never pass our cavalry.

"On my signal," Xiahou Yuan said, raising his *jian* sword.

"Father, wait," Xiahou Ba called. "There's something there."

He pointed toward the east of the city, where we had seen no action yet.

"Ba-*er*, not now," Xiahou Yuan snapped.

Then I saw it too. Or at least I thought I saw something. It went fast, but a movement caught my eyes through the debris of a former camp of Lü Bu. I squinted to get a more focused view, and just as I told myself it was probably nothing, it flashed into my sight again. A horse and its rider, using the cover of everything standing around to mask their movement. I lost him as soon as I recognized the horse.

"It's Red Hare," I said to no one. "Commandant, your son is right; there is someone there. I think it's Lü Bu."

"Horse shit," Xiahou Yuan said. His arm must have been killing him by then. "Lü Bu is awaiting news of his messengers from his palace."

"I saw something," I insisted.

Xiahou Yuan gave a brief glance in the direction his son had been pointing to earlier but shook his head in disbelief. Just then, the messengers we were to watch broke away from their line of defense and rode past Li Dian's regiment, two of them tumbling from the start, their bodies pierced by bolts. We would have to ride soon if we hoped to catch them.

"*Xiongdimen!*" Xiahou Yuan shouted.

"Commandant!" I called again.

"Fine! Take four men and go chase your ghost!" he barked.

"Four men with me!" I shouted, then kicked Qilin to a gallop from a dead start.

The sound of the four horses following me preceded that of the rest by a couple of seconds, drowning any other noise from our surroundings. The hill was steep, but the ground was soft enough for my mare to get a good footing, and I trusted her with choosing the perfect path as we sped through the freezing morning air. If I was right, Lü Bu would veer south before reaching the bridge over the Si river. On the other side was Xiahou Dun's motley division, what was left of it, and even *they* would manage to stop one rider. Lü Bu was a fool, but he had a good instinct. He would follow the river south and cross it at the point where no threat would prevent him from doing so. I would not let him, and I rode directly east, hoping to intercept him.

Qilin did not like when I forced her to the right a little. We would have run through a patch of land where the engineers had worked not long ago, and the place would be littered with nails and shards. She barely slowed down and eventually obeyed. One look over my shoulder confirmed the closest of my comrades followed me well enough. I lowered myself on the saddle to fight the wind whipping my face. Qilin's breathing was oddly reassuring in this cavalcade. She knew what she was doing, and I could focus on spotting my enemy.

The river was getting closer, right in front of me, but still no Lü Bu. *Had I dreamed him? Did Xiahou Ba's call make me see things?* I was about to slow us down a little, wondering if we should follow the river up or down when Lü Bu appeared again through the mist floating by the river. He rode so close to the water I wondered if Red Hare ran on it. I pulled on my mare's reins to force her on the right again; otherwise, I would never catch Lü Bu, but even then saw him pass me by a long shot. I went from wondering if he had been there at all, to thinking he would probably escape me as well. Qilin was a marvelous beast, but Red Hare was in a world of its own.

My mare ran so fast that I could barely open my eyes. Knowing of Red Hare's presence ahead, I used the sound of its hooves hitting the wet ground near the river to guess the distance. Lü Bu did not gain ground, but neither did I.

"Come on, girl," I said in Qilin's ear. "Just a bit faster."

If she did increase her speed, I did not feel it but realized the gap between me and my prey had shrunk when the cold mud and snow from Red Hare's back hooves rained down on my face. Then I heard something like a whimper coming from Lü Bu's direction. I raised my head long enough to get a good look at my target, and what I saw nearly made me lose focus.

Ten *bu* ahead, staring right back at me from the top of Red Hare, sat a girl. Her eyes screamed with panic, and her hair flew in my direction as if she meant to attack me with it. Her arms were stuck against her chest, tied tight by a thick rope on the other side of which sat her father, for this was without a doubt the daughter of Lü Bu.

She yelled something I could not understand, probably begging us to stop this mad chase, and whenever Lü Bu whipped the reins of Red Hare, she closed her eyes with fear. We had heard rumors Lü Bu's daughter and Yuan Shu's son were to be married to seal their alliance, but the natural distrust of the two men had pushed the marriage to a later date. That or the fact she could not have been more than thirteen years old.

My eyes filled with water and stung hard as I observed this scene of madness, but at least I now knew why I could keep up with Red Hare. It only came then that I had no clue what I was supposed to do when I caught up with the beast. Even five to one, we stood no chance against the greatest fighter in the empire, and Lü Bu had been smart when he chose his path. The river protected his left, while he could protect the right by himself using his wicked halberd presently dangling against his knee. No matter what, I had to get closer and meant to kick Qilin once more, hoping she had it in her to run a little faster.

But just then, another horse passed me by, a black mare, running with grace as if floating over the snow-covered earth. I cursed when I realized she could run so because her load weighed less than Qilin's or Red Hare's.

"Xiahou Ba, come back, you moron!" I shouted.

My lord's nephew was blasting toward Lü Bu, a short sword in hand. He was riding to his death. Lü Bu would kill him in one stroke, no matter if his daughter slightly hindered his movements. The usurper of Xu turned his head when he realized the approach of the kid and raised his halberd.

"Qilin, faster!" I shouted, and she must have felt my eagerness, for she did increase her speed.

The ground between us vanished, but not fast enough. Lü Bu brought his halberd down with extreme brutality. By some amazing reflex, Xiahou Ba's mare took a step to the side, and I heard the boy's curse when Sky-Piercer grazed his cheek. He was a brave young man, and this did not scare him away. He hacked his blade toward the beast but being right-handed could hardly reach him. In other circumstances, this would have made a great story. A feeble youth against the mighty beast. But we were not in a story, and my friend's son would die if he did not relent.

I forced Qilin between the two other horses, even though she neighed upon passing between their flanks. At least, with Xiahou Ba's presence, Lü Bu had naturally slowed down a little. Qilin pushed hard when she understood the only way out was forward, and she put me between the beast and the boy right in time to intercept the halberd coming in a great arc. I blocked the pole with my *gou-rang* shield, but the blade was so wide it still nearly cut Ba's neck.

"Get out!" I shouted.

"Let me help you," Xiahou Ba shouted back. I had to give it to the boy; he was brave beyond words. He had so nearly been slain twice but still wished to fight. Xiahou Yuan would be proud of his second son if he didn't kill him first.

"Get out, or I kill you myself!" I said, then raised my shield to take another hit from the beast. How someone could strike so hard while on a full gallop was beyond me. I thought my arm would snap in half, and the top hook of the *gou-rang* did break clean off. I had no time to lose on a brazen boy, not if I wanted to survive the next few seconds, so I kicked as hard as I could toward the face of Ba's mare. A weak blow it might have been, considering my precarious position, but I caught her in the eye, and she reeled away. I heard Xiahou Ba cursing in panic as he tried to regain control of his mount, but finally, I could return my attention to Lü Bu.

Upon getting my eyes on him, I realized that I had never approached the man from up close before. I had seen him at Hulao when he tore through our ranks as if they were made of paper, then again when he fought Zhang Fei and his brothers. I took part in the capture of Puyang, from where we ousted him, then saw him several times from afar when the Scorpions worked in the shadows of Xiapi. I had come to think of him as a regular man, like the rumor of a distant family member. Lü Bu had been such a strong presence in my life, yet we had never exchanged a gaze. When we did, I wished to be anywhere but here.

His face was nothing but burning anger. Some said he bore a kind of handsomeness, but I saw none, only the hard features of a man aware of his imminent doom. Lü Bu had lost weight recently, judging by his angular cheekbones, and the darkness around his eyes spoke of short nights. Yet his brutal strength poured out of his skin. Usually clean-shaven, he had let a stubble beard grow, which did nothing to hide his strong jaw. Added to the red veins popping in the white of his eyes, he gave me the impression of a man about to drop of fatigue, but his arm said otherwise. Even encumbered by his daughter tied to his back, the beast fought like a demon.

My position was weak. I fought with a sword, but Lü Bu rode on my left, so I had almost no reach. He had chopped half of my shield, which I let go because my arm got numb from the second strike. Red Hare, while it puffed clouds of hot air through its nostrils, kept running strongly, and since it stood a hand taller than Qilin, Lü Bu had the upper hand. As far as I could see, I had only two advantages. The first was the men behind me, though I could not even check how far behind they now rode. And the second was the river.

I kept on the defensive, doing my best to parry every strike from the beast while pushing Qilin always more to the left. We got so close, he and I, that I could smell his sweat and hear the whimpers of his daughter with each step.

"Get lost, you maggot!" Lü Bu shouted, surprising me with a voice cleaner than I would have thought.

I had neither the energy nor the wits to reply. All I could think was getting Red Hare into the water, where it would inevitably slow down. Lü Bu quickly realized what I attempted and pushed his terrible horse against mine. The stallion picked up on his rider's attitude and began snapping its big, yellow teeth at Qilin, but for once, its size proved more of a hindrance, and when my mare understood she was out of its reach, *she* bit Red Hare in the neck. Lü Bu meant to attack her then, wielding his massive polearm like an ax. I stopped it with the back of Yingzhao, and if it had been any other *dao*, my blade would have broken under the impact. Sky-Piercer bounced back up, and I used this chance to unsheathe the knife on my back and plant it straight in Lü Bu's thigh. He screamed like a wounded animal, covering even the sound of his daughter's voice shouting at him to stop.

Lü Bu recovered before I could take the knife out and shot a straight jab in the side of my face. I call it a jab, but it felt like the bottom of a hammer shattering my cheekbone and making me see blips of light as my head bounced uncontrollably for a few steps.

"Brother Liao!" Xiahou Ba called, bringing me back to the moment. I meant to curse the runt for coming back but sensed Lü Bu's halberd just before it almost stabbed me through the neck and lowered myself as flat as possible on the saddle. How this man could fight so nimbly after riding hard for so long, with a deep wound in his leg, and while carrying his daughter on his back was prodigious.

Before I sat back up, I noticed the ice-covered water under my mare and realized we were getting into the river. It was time to push a little more.

I grabbed the hilt of the knife sprouting from Lü Bu's leg and twisted on it viciously, pulling a shriek out of the beast. By some miracle, Qilin chose this moment to bite back at Red Hare, and both the stallion and its master lost control of the fight. I heard the splash stronger, then, in a matter of seconds, felt the water reach my ankle, and the horses just stopped. Qilin pushed a few more steps, and I made her turn around to face Lü Bu, who shook with rage.

"You'll never pass," I said, fighting for breath as the taste of blood invaded my mouth.

"I'll kill you," Lü Bu replied. His hand moved to the knife in his thigh, which he pulled out without wincing and threw into the brown water of the Si river.

"You won't," I replied. "Not fast enough, at least. Soon, both sides of the river will fill with my comrades, and this will be your end. The mighty Lü Bu will be shot down like a dog, and his body will wash down this river, his daughter stuck under him."

Oh, he did not like that. He snarled like a wolf, and I thought I may have pushed him too far with this image, but my four comrades joined us then and formed a semi-circle around the beast. Xiahou Ba was the closest to me, and I saw Lü Bu's gaze stopping for a heartbeat on my friend's son.

"What are you waiting for, then?" he asked, opening his arms to invite us to resume our fight. Truly, this man was magnificent. Blood poured freely from his thigh, his horse was struggling for air, its muscles twitching after such a cavalcade, and his daughter whimpered behind him, yet every inch of his body meant to fight. "Come at me, you fool! Don't you want to be the man who took Lü Bu down?"

I wanted it. I wanted it from the bottom of my soul. My name would ring throughout the empire, my lord would have to raise me to a generalship at least, and I would, by default, be recognized as the strongest warrior in the land. I could feel it at the tip of my fingers—fame.

But the cost might be too high. Even in his desperate situation, I feared Lü Bu. If we attacked together, or if I asked the two riders with me carrying spears to throw them, we would eventually kill the girl, and no matter my ambitions, I had long vowed never to drag children into it. And more important still, I knew who Lü Bu would target first, and *that* was a price I wasn't willing to pay.

"Go back to Xiapi, Lord Fengxian," I said, pointing my sword toward the besieged city. That I had used his *zi* name, and spoken without threat, made him hesitant. "We won't let you pass, but you can still make it back to the safety of your walls."

"Why?" the beast asked, his head perpetually checking if any of my men moved. Red Hare lowered its mouth and drank long gulps of water, its breathing already back to normal, while my mare still fought for it.

"We don't fear you," I replied with contempt. "We know of the situation in Xiapi. Your men don't trust you anymore. Soon they'll turn on you and will either drag you out or replace you." I knew of no such thing, but his eyes told me he was picturing the faces of all the potential traitors in his entourage. I wondered if Chen Gong was one of them. "Your end will come without a fight, and I look forward to seeing your face when you kneel by my lord's feet, ashamed and finally beaten down. Go back, hide; we'll get you out soon enough."

The beast's face turned into a mask of hatred again, and his grip on the pole of Sky-Piercer tightened. Red Hare reacted by raising its head.

"If he moves, throw your spears through his daughter!" I shouted. My two comrades changed their grip and held the spears ready to throw. Lü Bu did not make a move.

"I will rip your heart out," he said through his teeth. "You hear me, boy! Even if you are the last man I ever kill, I will make it the bloodiest death I ever inflicted. Your head will leave your body still screaming; I will pull your guts—"

"All right, we get it," I interrupted him. I was pushing my

luck, but I think his daughter's sob got the better of him, and soon his shoulders slumped a little.

"Your name?" he asked.

"Liao Chun," I replied. "Captain of the Scorpions."

"I'll remember you," he said menacingly.

"Remember me as the man who took your last hope away. Now go before I change my mind."

Lü Bu struggled for a few seconds. He checked Xiahou Ba again, then past us. It was an impossible stretch of flat land from here to wherever he meant to go. More of our riders would come soon. And despite his face of steel, he was hurt, and the blood had yet to coagulate. I saw it trickle from his boot to the water, then float by me. We were connected. I knew he thought of picking up the battle, just as I knew he wouldn't. Too much to lose, not enough to gain.

"Father," the girl called. Lü Bu's mask of rage peeled away when he heard her voice. Inside the beast was a loving father. "Let's go back home."

He looked back at me with no trust in his eyes, so I sheathed Yingzhao as a sign of my resolve to let them go unharmed.

"We'll be fifty *bu* behind," I told him. He nodded, then pulled on the reins of his terrifying stallion to make it turn around. They walked away in the river for a time, a sign that he did not mean to try anything other than heading back to Xiapi. All the while, the girl looked at me, a maelstrom of mixed feelings drawing on her young, innocent face. Before I asked Qilin to follow them, she nodded in my direction, and I even thought I saw a smile across her tear-smeared face.

Xiahou Ba rode next to me as we came out of the water, head down, but his anger obvious from the rhythm of his breathing. The three others came behind us. I nodded to them in gratitude for going along with my plan.

"Why did we let him go?" the boy asked, his short sword still in hand.

"Some, if not all of us, would have perished," I replied.

"But it's Lü Bu! We could have ended the war!" he shouted.

"And who do you think he would have killed first?" I asked, which had the benefit of silencing the boy completely. He remained with his mouth agape for a few steps, finally understanding how close he had come to an early death. "What are you doing here anyway?" I asked.

"My father asked four riders to follow you," he answered. I pretended not to see the tears pearling at the edges of his eyelids.

"Your father asked for four *men*," I said. "You are not one!" My anger was rising. It was unfair to the boy. He had shown bravery and skill. And even when he could have turned back he chose to follow us. But the heat was returning in my veins with a vengeance. The fury that takes a man after a battle grabbed my bowels and twisted them in every direction. Never before had my hands shaken so violently after a fight. This is what it meant to fight the greatest warrior under the sky.

"You killed someone at thirteen," Xiahou Ba whispered, too stubborn to let it go.

I shot my hand and grabbed him by the collar of his oversized armor, then twisted on it to tighten the leather around his neck a little.

"I killed someone to save my friend, and because I had no choice! You threw yourself in pursuit of your target. And the man I killed was a nobody, not mighty fucking Lü Bu!"

Then the tears came out, and there was no stopping

them. He meant to hide them inside his hands, so I let him go, feeling a little ashamed of this bout of anger.

"I thought this was the kind of thing you would have done," he said through his sobs. He was absolutely right, and I could not reply to that, so I just let my hand fall on his shoulder and squeezed a little before leaving him to process his first battle. Soon, I knew, he would be bragging to his friends and brothers about having fought the legendary Lü Bu and seeing his back as he retreated.

Every bone in my body screamed with fatigue as we rode back behind Lü Bu. Somewhere, halfway through maybe, he picked up some speed to avoid our troops, and while I never saw him pass through the city gate, I know he made his way without any issue. His mind, though, would be full of doubts and suspicion, and I would hate to be one of his officers in the coming days.

"Should we keep all this between us?" Xiahou Ba asked as we rode back toward our main camp, where I guessed Xiahou Yuan would be.

"Oh no, young man, you're not avoiding this conversation," I replied, amusing myself with the veil of fear falling over his smooth face. "And you can be sure we'll have some things to explain to the general-in-chief as well."

"Shit," Xiahou Ba said.

I laughed at his misery, but this brought a strange discomfort in my mouth. After some working on it, I pulled out a back tooth with two fingers and looked at it with awe. This was the first tooth I lost in my adult life.

"A tooth and a black eye," one of the riders commented when he saw it. "Not bad for a fight with the northern beast."

It suddenly came to me that I had not only survived an encounter with Lü Bu but had even forced him back. I hadn't acted alone, and Lü Bu was not fighting at his best, but I had done something very few men could brag about; I lived to tell the tale. I patted Qilin's neck as we rode through the field of battle where all the messengers had met a gruesome death, forever grateful for her fighting spirit. Without this great mare chosen for me by a younger Guli and without the sturdiness of my new blade, I am certain as one can be I would be feeding the worms by now.

Ningqiang county, Yi province
12th month, 4th year of the Jingyuan era of the Cao Wei empire (263)

The silence is heavy around the fire. None dare to speak, but I can see the desire to ask questions in their eyes. None more so than General Zhong Hui, to whom I owed this audience. Some are old friends, and they've heard this story before; the others are the officers of the Cao Wei empire who remained behind as I recovered. Of course, they did not choose to do so out of their good heart for an old, feeble veteran. Not so long ago, we fought on opposite sides of the battlefield, and for the more advanced in age among them, I might have killed some of their comrades. No, if they remained behind it was out of loyalty to Zhong Hui. Two factions exist within this Cao Wei army, but that's what you get for sending two generals with a similar level of authority on a faraway campaign. As long as they worked together, they would be hard to break, but separated, we had a chance. Now that Deng Ai and his faction had taken the road ahead, we could work on Zhong Hui and his followers. We had a lot to prepare if we wanted to put our plan in motion before reaching the border of our former state; many old friends needed a spark of hope to rekindle the fire of their patriotism. And while I regaled this small crowd, Zong Yu would be busy visiting those potential allies. I would give him as much time as possible.

How ironic that the future of our great war resides in my storytelling skills. Truly, I'm thinking we are doomed.

"To think we are sitting across a man who battled Lü Bu," Zhong Hui says, shaking his head in wonder. "I am without words."

"That's a first," one of his officers comments, which brings a few chuckles from the audience. Zhong Hui is not what could be considered a friendly man, and if the man who had spoken were anything but a close ally, he would have been thrashed by his leader for such a jest. I believe his name is Tian Xu. I will need to keep an eye on him. He could prove useful.

"We are talking of Lü Bu here," Zhong Hui goes on. "The greatest warrior this land ever saw. The bane of Dong Zhuo, the beast of the north, the master of Red Hare! And you, old general Liao, fought him. A toast to a hero!" he calls, raising his cup and inviting the others to do so as well.

I humbly thank him for his gesture, wishing I could accompany them in their wine. My disease, while it served our plan well, was not faked. I had recovered enough to take a few steps out of the wagon, where Zhong Hui, upon hearing me talk of Lü Bu, insisted I retell the story in the evening, but at my age, one never truly recovers, and I have to be careful if I ever want to see the end of our dealings.

"What did the Grand Ancestor then say?" another young officer asks. He meant Cao Cao, who has long been called as such now. That man is Wei Guan, and he sits a little further from the rest. Until the split in the convoy, I thought he was a staunch follower of Deng Ai. If there is a spy here, it must be him, and he, too, we will have to watch.

"The conversation went better than anticipated, to be honest," I reply. "I made sure all the cards were in my hands before I presented myself to his command tent. Xiahou Yuan was there, and Lü Bu's whereabouts were confirmed within the city. Our scouts also confirmed that no messenger made it out of the siege."

I gesture to Chen Shou, who sits next to me, to hand over a cup of warm water. My throat starts to hurt again.

The young scribe did not need to be here, he has heard and recorded all of this during the afternoon, but he seems to enjoy it all right.

"Cao Cao could not reprimand me for acting in a way that saved his nephew, not in front of the boy's father, at least. Xiahou Yuan did admonish the boy, but I could see he was more relieved than angry. Later we got drunk, Yuan and I, and he thanked me profusely, telling me how much he loved his son and what a brilliant future he foresaw for him, though we all know how it turned out by now."

I see a few headshakes in the audience. Most have known Xiahou Ba, and there would be very mixed feelings on this topic within this particular crowd. I guess they will ask for another public retelling when the time comes to recount his part in the drama of the three kingdoms.

"But surely Lord Cao regretted that you let Lü Bu go, no? No offense, but you did let the enemy leader retreat in peace," Tian Xu says.

"You are right. It was a tough sell," I reply, handing the cup back to the scribe and extending my hands toward the brasero. "If I'm honest, I believe I outmaneuvered Cao Cao a grand total of four or five times in my life. This was one of them. The idea came just as I entered his tent. I told him what had transpired of my exchange with Lü Bu, especially how he reacted when I mentioned potential traitors within his ranks. I then offered the idea that we were better off with the beast in charge rather than a clever man such as Chen Gong. Better still, I hoped the seeds of discord I had planted would sprout into open discontent inside Xiapi."

"Did it work?" Zhong Hui asks.

"It did, but I don't think I had much to do with it. From what we later heard, for months already Lü Bu's officers had whispered behind his back. He was a great warrior but did not instill confidence, and many would have preferred Master Chen Gong or another to take his place and seek peace with us. Lü Bu knew it, of course, and had many flogged even before we besieged his capital. Plus, though I should have guessed it, Cao Cao had people within the city to fan the flames of mutiny. If we had enough supplies, we would just have waited for them to destroy themselves."

"So what did you do?" the general asks again, eyes beaming with curiosity.

"We destroyed Xiapi," I answer.

"You what?" Zhong Hui asks as a wave of murmuring spreads through the audience.

"We had to act fast. We were out of food, our morale started getting lower by the day, and we still had enemies on our borders, especially this son of a whore of Zhang Xiu. So we acted radically."

I amuse myself with another sip of water while they await my explanation. I might not be the greatest *pinghua* performer in the land, but I know how to entertain a small crowd of soldiers.

"I believe it was Xun Yu's idea, though it took Guo Jia to validate it, but my lord reluctantly accepted to flood the city. We changed the course of the Si and Yi rivers and let them flow toward Xiapi. And this time, I say *we* for real, for I took part in this back-breaking engineering feat with a spade in my hands. With thirty thousand pairs of hands, plus the help of the auxiliary and some of the camp followers, Xiapi turned to a pile of freezing mud within a week, and if one thing ruins the morale, it is living with your feet constantly soaked."

"Genius," Zhong Hui comments.

"It was a rather radical yet efficient solution," I go on, "but ruining a city such as Xiapi meant losing the support of the people from the province forever. No matter what, Xu would never love Cao Cao. Of course, at that point, he cared more about slaying the beast than getting the people's support, and at least we seemed to be getting closer to that goal. A few days later, on a quiet morning, what we had hoped for for months finally took place; the city gates opened."

9

Xiapi, capital Xu province
1st month, 4th year of Jian'an era (199), Han Dynasty

"COLONEL LIAO, WHAT DO WE DO?" a man twice my age asked, his spear red halfway through the pole and his face squinched with a mix of pain and elation. To a soldier, nothing gives more joy than an open city to loot, and I guessed this was what he wanted me to order. He was to be disappointed.

"To the palace!" I shouted so that he and his comrades could hear me well over the din of Xiapi falling to our swords. "Captains, get your men moving north!"

"You heard the colonel," one of them said as he ran across his pack of warriors and kicked them in the right direction.

Cao Cao had promoted me to Colonel of Cavalry for my actions against Lü Bu, a bogus title in appearance because I had no cavalry to lead and technically still led a platoon-size force. In reality, though, I was flattered. The bump in my salary was more than correct, as were the benefits coming along, and the Scorpions would more likely forgive my abandoning them if I came back with some rolls of silk and ingots of gold to distribute among them. But what truly pleased me was the choice of title: Colonel of Cavalry. This had been Cao Cao's rank when we met, and, of course, he had given it to me as an echo of our conversation in Xuchang before we left for this campaign.

For the rest of the war against Lü Bu, I was put in charge of Xu Huang's Brothers, though at this point, between the dead, the wounded, and those who accompanied their leader back to the capital, only five hundred remained. I divided them into three companies and named as many captains. This was actually what I had been doing, reorganizing this small regiment when the first shouts came to inform us of Xiapi's gates opening. The camp came to life in a couple of minutes, and before we knew it, we were ordered to assault the city with all we had and destroy Lü Bu's forces.

The Brothers of the Sword and I stormed Xiapi from the south, and the only soldiers we spared were those on their knees, outside of the city, for they had opened the gate. The rest, we slaughtered, turning the flooded city red. I doubted many civilians survived this attack, and Xiapi would be left bare of anything of value. But I would take no part in it. I told Lü Bu I would be here upon his defeat, and the Brothers deserved some measure of vengeance. So I led them toward the palace.

My arm was tired of striking men running away, but we passionately pursued them. Sieges, especially in winter, have this way of making a soldier angry. Everything was the enemy's fault, even the weather. So when we could finally let out our frustration, it became a battle of rage and fire. I paid no attention to the Brothers, trusting their captains in keeping the pack together, and stood at the front as we waddled through the filthy, icy water of the city.

A gentle snow was falling, but it did nothing against the fires consuming the buildings around us. Feminine screams could be heard at every two houses at least, and I lost several soldiers to their appeal, but most obeyed and followed.

We never entered the palace, for some of our comrades had already invaded it. Instead, we followed the rumor of Lü Bu's presence further north. We joined the mass of soldiers from the Dragon-Fang as they ran toward the exterior wall. Pulling rank, I forced them to let us pass through and arrived by the stairs leading to the gate tower right at the same time as my old comrade, Colonel Yue Jin.

"We heard Lü Bu's up there," he said, answering my question before I asked it.

Up there was the top of a tower built against the wall. A three-story tower called White Gate, from where the officer in charge of Xiapi's defense would have a panoramic view of the city and its surroundings. We could either reach it from the wall or the bottom of the tower itself, both paths probably brimming with archers, spearmen, and, at the end of it, the beast himself.

"Which do you take?" Yue Jin asked in a playful tone, completely ignoring the rain of arrows pouring down on us from the wall and the arrow slits of the building. The soldier protecting him with his shield held at arm's length must have felt otherwise.

"We take the tower," I replied.

"To the wall!" Yue Jin shouted through a grin full of soldier-joy, raising his sword and commanding his men toward the stairs tugging the wall up to the crenels.

"Brothers! With me!" I shouted just as enthusiastically.

Yue Jin's men had been working on the tower's door

already, and it took only a few ax blows to break it apart. Soldiers were expecting us on the other side, and some of my men died on their spears, but once the first of us passed through the ruined door, the slaughter resumed. I was in the thick of it, shoulder to shoulder with some of my men, none of us giving each other enough space for a real fight to take place. It was madness. We all wanted to be the first on top. Men screamed as they killed, and died, and struck. I lost count of the men I wounded in the fight for the first floor, just as I lost count of the cuts I received along my arms, legs, and face.

Out of breath, I let some of my comrades go first up the stairs, where Lü Bu's soldiers were retreating. The Brothers were implacable in their advance; this was their realm. They fought like demons in the narrow staircase, jutting their spears through every back offering themselves to their well-trained arms. Soon, the defenders plugged the stairs with their mass of bodies alone, and when the doomed soldiers realized the way up offered no safety, they turned around, and the battle regained in viciousness.

This was neither pitched battle nor the ransack of a rich city; this was just the last remnants of Lü Bu's army fighting on the *sidi* and making us pay each step forward with blood and death.

"Vengeance for the ambush!" I yelled, hoping to fuel my men's ire.

"For Big Brother Xu!" one of them replied.

The same man died two seconds later, and his body fell down the staircase, giving me his spot at the front. I avenged him immediately, thrusting my sword into the belly of a young soldier with fewer summers than I even boasted. He joined his own victim when I shoved him to the side.

The next few minutes passed in a blur of blades, red

gushes, and shrieks. I turned off the part of my mind that thought and let the years of practice take over. My reactions came faster. I dulled my senses to pain, stopped shouting, and thrust again and again. Knowing how cumbersome it would be, I discarded my shield at the bottom of the stairs and wielded a knife in my left hand. This had been a clever idea, and I believe more than Yingzhao, this knife claimed lives that day.

I almost stumbled when I reached the second floor, thinking I had yet a few steps to climb, and this almost proved to be my undoing. A soldier picked up on my mistake and brought his dagger-ax down as if to hammer the top of my head. Despite the quality of my helmet, the one Cao Cao had given me, this would have, at best, knocked me unconscious. The Brother behind me reacted faster and stabbed my foe through the neck with his spear. I thanked him and pushed deeper, my rage rekindled by my near death.

Some of Lü Bu's men threw their blades on the ground and dropped on their knees when they understood the inevitable, but none received our mercy. We were unleashed, bloodthirsty, and had no compassion to spare.

The more my comrades made it to the second floor, the weaker the resistance became. Then, just as I spotted the path to the third floor, I felt the enemy's attention shift and realized the door leading to the outer wall was wide open. I thought some of them were trying to escape that way but soon understood soldiers were coming in, not out. Yue Jin and his soldiers had made it up the wall and brought the action to the tower. Lü Bu's soldiers were doomed, stuck between Yue Jin's men and mine.

"Come on!" I shouted. "Do you want the Dragon-Fang to be the first up?"

The uproar from the Brothers and whoever accompanied us was deafening. A surge of energy passed through us. My comrades struck as if possessed, knowing this was their last chance to shine during the campaign. I heard more coordinated shouts from Yue Jin's side, followed by shrieks from the foes facing them. We didn't care who raised their hands in a plea for mercy, who meant to take some of us before their eventual death; we just kept hacking and thrusting. My feet lost their balance twice upon the slick wooden floor, and I almost tripped over a thick rope of bowels, but the press of soldiers was so dense that I remained on my spot. The battle could not have lasted more than a few minutes, but it felt like an entire *shi*. I spotted the helmets of our comrades, a few ranks of enemy from us. It was over soon.

"Almost there, Brothers! Lü Bu is right up those stairs!"

"We surrendered!" a big, bearded brute shouted, though he kept thrusting his broken sword.

"Tell that to my friend, you son of a whore!" one of my comrades replied.

The sounds of life lost themselves to the metal on metal, the flesh reaping apart, the last breaths of broken men. Everything was still, but swarming at the same time, like a bucket of eels. I felt sick in the stomach but kept thrusting, no longer feeling any specific pain but that of my victims. There were no more curses, just bellows of wild beasts ripping each other apart. I thrust, I parried, I thrust again. They fell and died on their knees. Some called their loved ones, but most could not even do that. I thrust again, and—

"Yue Jin! Liao Chun! Enough!"

I blinked in confusion, snapping out of my savagery. I had been hacking at a corpse. The poor man was still standing, kept in this position by the press of his comrades who still fought. Most didn't even do that. Many among them were simply kneeling, faces lost in their hands while waiting for the inevitable. They were broken.

The voice had been so strong, so full of authority, that not only I but all the soldiers nearby pulled their arms back, and a sudden, eerie silence fell on the second floor. I searched for my lord, for surely he had been the one speaking, but found him not. Instead, I noticed Chen Gong standing proud on the stairway leading to the third floor. He looked unhurt, his back straight, hands behind. Next to him, slumping like the carcass of a hunted deer, Lü Bu. The beast had been tied up with thick ropes, the end of it being held by a man I didn't know, but from his side, an officer by the look of it. He breathed, but the trickle of blood running down his mouth led me to believe his capture had been a hard bargain. Chen Gong's wrists were also bound, but the strategist had obviously given the captors less trouble than Lü Bu.

"Is this what I taught you?" Chen Gong asked. "To butcher men who surrendered?"

Following our old teacher's gaze, I found Yue Jin in the crowd. He actually stood three or four steps from me, and the same sense of shame forced his eyes down. Yue Jin wiped his gory blade inside the crook of his elbow, then sheathed it back.

"My friends," Chen Gong called, taking another step down, "drop your weapons and get on your knees. They won't hurt you anymore."

He was right. Now that the killing had stopped, none of us would have the stomach for more. Guilt and shame would prevent our blades from striking again. I imitated Yue Jin and let Yingzhao rest in its scabbard as the few dozen living foes dropped to their knees, the crash of their weapons hitting the floor the only sound to be heard for some time.

Lü Bu looked away, but I could see his whole body tremble. The officer behind him pushed his former lord down the stairs, but I felt no animosity from him. Of course, Lü Bu would never willingly surrender, but I'm certain those few men who had secured him hated the idea just as much. They, however, wished to live.

"We surrender," the man holding Lü Bu's leash said before his closest comrade tossed Sky-Piercer toward us. The great halberd landed pitifully by Yue Jin's feet, bouncing a couple of times before becoming still. It was truly over.

"Do you accept our surrender and guarantee our lives in exchange for those two?" the second man asked.

"I can guarantee you safe passage to our general-in-chief," Yue Jin answered as he picked the halberd up. My short friend was dwarfed even more by this colossal polearm. "The soldiers must wait here for our lord's decision."

"It is fine," Chen Gong commented, again, walking down by himself. "Mengde will not harm them." I wasn't so sure. Maybe the Cao Cao Chen Gong used to know would have spared them, but my lord had changed; the world had hardened him. Now that the fire in my chest had abated, I hoped he did spare them.

I passed through the mass of kneeling men to stand by Yue Jin to meet with our old teacher, who naturally came closer. But before I could exchange a word with any of them, Lü Bu seemed to regain some of his senses.

"You!" he shouted, testing the limits of his binding as he stretched his whole body in my direction. He snarled in hatred, and I thought he might try to bite me, though he was still too far for that.

I thought of a rebuke, a smart way to say *I told you so*, but could not find the heart to mock him. That man was a living legend. The slayer of the tyrant, the man who fought the Liu-Guan-Zhang trio and survived, the master of Red Hare. Already people said, *"Among men Lü Bu, among horses Red Hare,"* as a way to call the greatest of both realms. But here he was, in chains, defeated without even fighting, as I had foreseen. No matter how chaotic he had turned our empire, he deserved better, I thought.

"Lord Fengxian," I replied, bowing my head.

"Liao Chun, is it?" he asked, his snarl still in place. I nodded. "My daughter," he then said. His warrior mask suddenly peeled off. The corners of his eyes went down, filled with tears, and Lü Bu dropped his head against his chest.

"Where is she?" I asked, kneeling to see his face under the curtain of his unbound hair. He worried for her.

"Her room. End of the palace's right wing."

"I'll find her," I said. Lü Bu did not thank me. I don't think he had it in him.

I stood and exchanged a meaningful gaze with Yue Jin.

"Go," he said, "I'll tell the general what you did here."

There are very few men I would have trusted in that situation, but Yue Jin was one. So I left him in charge of the situation in the White Gate Tower and went back down the way I came, avoiding as much as possible lingering on the scene of carnage of our making.

Cao Cao's officers were running wild in Xiapi, trying hard to get a semblance of order from all this chaotic mess. I knew a few floggings would accompany the eventual rewards of the coming days. Without surprise, Xiahou

Dun's division was the one currently looting the palace, and a ball formed in my stomach when I thought of their presence near the families of Lü Bu's officers. I ran more than I walked past the main hall, where my lord's cousin was amusing himself with Lü Bu's famous pheasant-feathered helmet on his head, then increased my gait as I followed the narrow corridor leading to the palace's right wing.

It was already mostly empty of soldiers, and the few rooms I could see were nothing but a heap of broken furniture and dead bodies, very few of them being soldiers. Some of Xiahou Dun's soldiers were laughing as they left the hallway. I let them go, even if they did not salute their superior. I had better things to take care of, and I probably looked more like a corpse myself than a colonel with all the gore and sweat drenching me.

Three rooms before the last, I heard more laughter coming from the end of the hallway. My hand went by itself on the hilt of my sword. Between the waves of laughter, I noticed some rhythmical grunting. I knew this sound all too well and dashed through the open door. The scene awaiting filled my nightmares for the rest of my life.

Two soldiers were standing, one with his thumbs tucked in his belt, the other arms crossed over his chest, both of them heartily laughing at the sight of their comrade kneeling on the ground. The man was the one grunting, in rhythm with the back and forth of his naked ass. And the only other person in the room was the girl I had come to save, bending over the bottom of her bed, face on the side as they raped her.

Lü Bu's daughter was looking in my direction, her young skin terribly pale, and old traces of tears running down her cheeks. Her eyes had no life, and her mouth remained open in terror. Under her chin, though, a red smile welcomed me into the room. She could not have been over thirteen.

"Get out," I said.

The two men standing noticed me then; the other did not even react and kept at his labor.

"Sir?" one of the two asked.

"Get out!" I shouted. "Get out now!"

I could barely control myself as it was, but the grunting from the third man was drilling through my brain and putting me back into the murdering mood I had left in the tower.

"Sir, it's almost our turn," the second said plaintively, his hand opened toward the girl's corpse.

"I swear, if you don't leave now, I will kill the three of you myself," I said. The pair felt the ire in my voice or noticed the intense will for blood in my eyes, and they took a step back. The third one, however, could not care less about my threat; he had other priorities.

"Will you all shut up!" he barked, intensifying his rhythm. "I can't finish will all this—"

My blade went through his neck, and I twisted viciously as I ripped the sword away. He died with his pants around his ankles, and I hoped he would wander the *land of shade* as such for eternity. His gurgling accompanied his fall satisfyingly. His two comrades hesitated on what to do next, and if they had remained petrified as such, things might have turned different. Unfortunately, one of them dropped his hand on his sheathed sword. It was all I needed.

I killed them. I killed those animals. And when I was done, there wasn't much left of the men those three had been.

I dropped my blade, unable to carry it any longer, and moved toward the girl. I first dragged her onto the bed, then flipped her on her back and pulled the blanket over her face to hide her eyes from me. Her hand fell to the side. I picked it up, but instead of putting it back as intended, I kept it between my dirty palms and knelt.

"I'm sorry," I whispered as fresh tears washed over my shame. "I am so sorry."

If I hadn't stopped her and her father, she would be in Yuan Shu's palace by now, getting ready for her wedding with the toad's son. Instead, she now lay dead in her bed, ravaged by gods knew how many men. The three I had killed were platoon leaders, and I guessed the first to get over the girl had been higher up the chain of command, maybe even Xiahou Dun, who now rejoiced on more of Lü Bu's treasures.

"Your father will join you soon," I told the girl as I stood back up. "And no one will ever hurt you again."

I placed the three dead soldiers against the side of the bed facing the door. A clear warning for anyone thinking to abuse her more. When I passed by the hall again, Xiahou Dun was waving a cup of wine toward his officers. This time he saw me, and the way he grinned confirmed everything I suspected. I kept my eyes on him, hoping he understood what I promised in my heart I would do to him one day.

CAO CAO WAS STANDING on the stage of the forum when I entered the camp, Liu Bei and some high-ranking officers by his side. I shuffled my way through until I reached the first ranks of onlookers, emerging right next to Li Dian, who stood with a genial smile on his lips and a face as dirty as the bottom of my boots. Yue Jin, his best friend and, according to the rumors, his lover, could be seen at the bottom of the stage, Sky-Piercer in his hand.

"He just pardoned the surrenderees," Li Dian told me when he noticed my questioning gaze.

"What of those four?" I asked, nodding toward the men on their knees, hands tied behind them. Lü Bu and Chen Gong were at the center of the quartet. On their left knelt Gao Shun, whom we had captured a few weeks before, while on the right, straight as a column, was Zhang Liao.

"We're about to find out," he answered.

I could barely hear the voices of my lord and the prisoners over the crowd's murmur but guessed things were not going well for Lü Bu. He squirmed and thrashed the ground with his feet, cursing my lord and calling him a coward in many variations of the word. Cao Cao asked something to Liu Bei, who I assumed would intervene in favor of the beast, if for no better reason than he was the kind of man who always seemed ready to forgive, but I was wrong. From what I later heard, Liu Bei reminded Cao Cao of what happened to those who had trusted Lü Bu, and the beast's reaction matched his reputation. It took Xu Chu to put him back down on his knees, and even then, the flow of insults did not dry up for some time.

When it was his turn to speak, Chen Gong laughed, which seemed to anger my lord, but pleased me inside. It was so like him to react so frivolously at the very end of his life that I felt proud of him for some reason. Cao Cao turned his face to Gao Shun, who spat in his direction, and Zhang Liao kept his face of steel, and no words passed his lips. The four of them, it seemed, were fated to die.

My lord raised his hand and called for our silence to render his verdict. But before he could speak up, Guan Yu, standing behind his brother, overstepped and took a knee in front of my lord, arms extended in a respectful salute. Again, I could not hear his words, but when he was done, my lord nodded, then ordered Zhang Liao to be released from his bounds and taken away. Iron Heart had been spared by the good grace of Lord Cao and the intervention of Guan Yu.

There would be no pardon for the three others, though.

"So that's the end of the mighty Lü Bu," Li Dian commented as guards came to help the three condemned up and brought to the gallows.

I wished to salute Master Chen on his last walk, but his gaze never met mine since he walked head straight and proud. However, Lü Bu did see me, and the anguish drew itself on his warrior's face when he recognized me. I then managed one of the hardest things I ever did in my life to that point; I faked a reassuring smile and nodded to make him understand his daughter was safe. This lie nearly broke my heart, but I could not send him to his death knowing it came after his daughter's. Lü Bu nodded back with something like gratitude in his stare, and then he vanished behind the line of soldiers forming after the trio. One of the reasons I feared death for the rest of my life was the idea I would stumble upon Lü Bu in the afterlife, knowing his anger would still be fresh for me not saving his daughter.

"You're not coming?" Li Dian asked.

"Had my fill for the day," I replied, the taste of bile making itself strong in the back of my throat. He gently touched my elbow and went after the procession.

For many years, I regretted not having witnessed the end of Lü Bu, but back then, I would have rather suffered Guli's wrath than watched the hanging of such a great warrior. From what I heard, Chen Gong and Gao Shun went with dignity, though some said my lord offered his old secretary a last chance of pardon, which he refused. The story claims that Lü Bu made more of a mess of his last moments on Earth, but I believe those rumors are unfounded. He was a force of nature, a god among men, and in my mind, died like a warrior.

"Once again, you shined through your disobedience," Cao Cao said, his voice barely making it to my ears over the sound of the pipa, its player himself struggling to cover the hundred or so drunken men laughing and cheering.

"Only way I know how," I replied without enthusiasm. My customary congratulations hadn't been any warmer, but Cao Cao was tipsy enough not to mention it.

Xiapi's palace, because of its elevation, was the only building protected from the water. Engineers and soldiers would be working on putting the rivers back on their natural courses in the morning. For now, they, too, celebrated our victory in the various camps. As for their commanding officers, they enjoyed wine, music, and dance from the comfort of the palace's great hall, the latter part being the reason I could not partake in the festivities.

"She isn't to your liking?" Cao Cao asked, pointing his cup toward the single dancer entertaining his guests.

"I can't say she is," I answered, looking over my shoulder to take another glimpse at poor Diao Chan, graceful in her art, even for the benefit of her captors. The most famous courtesan in the empire was dressed in rich silk, with sleeves reaching to the ground, and her hair was bound in an intricate pattern held by a jeweled phoenix-shaped pin. She wore makeup to smooth her skin, and while I found her all too plain to my taste, I could see why high-born men appreciated her subversive beauty. However, my lack of interest for the spectacle had nothing to do with her looks. Her tears were just drowning my will to celebrate.

"My young colonel," Cao Cao went on, pointing his finger at me but looking at his neighbor, "prefers them a bit more exotic."

"Or a little older," I replied, a barb to my lord, who knew how I felt about his wife. Diao Chan's age had been the true surprise of the evening. Her fame had spread for so many years that I had imagined her to be in her thirties at least, while in reality, she must have been around my age. It meant that while Dong Zhuo and Lü Bu presumably fought for her, she had been fifteen at best. Whenever her dance brought her face in my direction, I saw another girl instead, an even younger one, with a red smile across the throat to my benefit. "Or willing, at least, contrary to your cousin," I finally said. I did not need to specify which cousin I was talking about. My lord knew of my hatred for Xiahou Dun, and while I am certain he understood my feelings, he could not condone my comment, and the way he licked his lips warned me to watch my words.

"Xiahou Dun actually complained to me about three of his men being murdered today," my lord said, his joviality already a distant memory.

"A lot of soldiers died today," I replied.

"They were *murdered* after the battle, here, in the palace already under our control," he went on. "And it so happened that you were seen in the vicinity. From what I've been told, you fought valiantly in the White Tower, so naturally, I told the administrator of Dong he was mistaken, but you know him; he is as stubborn as you are. So, what should I tell him?"

"You can tell him they died screaming like slaughtered pigs," I answered matter of fact before I could stop myself.

"Liao Chun," Cao Cao said, bringing the tip of his fingers to his forehead. "You can't simply kill three platoon leaders on a whim."

"Executing would be a more fitting description."

"Chun, you butchered them. From what I have been told, even their comrades struggled to identify them."

"If I may?" Liu Bei, who, as Xu governor, sat alone next to Cao Cao, intervened. So far he had remained silent and oddly stoic. "Why did those men warrant an execution?"

"A fair question," Cao Cao commented.

While the two lords sat on the hall's elevated dais, Liu Bei's table had been slightly angled as to leave no doubt who led here.

"They raised their swords against me," I answered. This was actually a fair point. As a colonel, I only had to invoke this fact to walk free of any accusation, and I had to thank Liu Bei for cooling my quickly rising temper. Unfortunately, Cao Cao did not bite.

"Even the one with his pants down?" he asked, cold fury settling in his voice.

"No," I replied. "That one was too busy raping the dead corpse of Lü Bu's daughter." Liu Bei shook his head, though I do not know if it was for me talking back to my lord or because of the nature of my words.

"I gave no orders to spare the civilians," Cao Cao said, pinching his nose.

"Well, you should have," I replied.

"You do *not* tell me what I should or shouldn't do!"

Cao Cao's shout, added to the smacking sound of his palm striking the table, called an abrupt silence throughout the hall. I did not need to turn around to know they all looked our way or pretended not to, at least. The music resumed slowly, as did the murmurs, but neither my lord nor I relented our staring contest.

"Lord Cao," Liu Bei called softly. "Even if young Colonel Liao's actions were ... rash, I believe he acted to protect your illustrious name."

Cao Cao released his glare and turned his intention toward the governor in an invitation for him to explain his meaning.

"The mistreatment of a defeated leader's family is a highly disapproved behavior. Such barbaric actions would have tarnished your reputation, through no fault of your own, of course. But since Liao Chun here, a famed officer of yours, killed the culprits, your name remains clear. In fact, one might even say you sent him to protect Lü Bu's family and punish their wrongdoers, thus acting as a true gentleman."

Cao Cao tilted his head in my direction as he pondered Liu Bei's words. And while he did, the governor of Xu discreetly shook his head as a warning for me not to push my luck any further.

"Would you accept this being the official statement of your actions?" he asked.

The temptation to refuse caressed my mind. Once again, my actions would help Cao Cao's cause, though he had done nothing to deserve it, while I would be seen as some hound to be sent after blood. In my mind, I had acted with honor and killed three dogs, thus making the world a better place. A place a young girl would never experience because she was as dead as the rest of her family, which was, in big part, also my fault. I was tired of this war.

"Yes," I answered, bowing in salute.

"Good," Cao Cao went on. "And, Liao Chun. I owe this

victory to you as much as to anyone else here. So, I insist you remain with us until the end of the festivities."

I snarled as I bowed my head low but resumed a mask of gratitude by the time I showed my face again.

"Thank you, my lord," I said. This was the only way this troublesome conversation would ever reach its end. An end that didn't see me in jail or hanging from a rope, that is. Cao Cao waved me away, and I saluted both him and Liu Bei, the latter honestly, before leaving my spot for the next sycophant willing to congratulate our lord on *his* victory.

I was to stay in the hall and suffer Diao Chan's humiliation, but I could not feign my pleasure, so I went to the only table where officers did not seem to enjoy this shameful show.

"Some wine?" Zhang Fei asked. I sat across their low table on a piece of empty cushion. He handed me the cup before I could accept, which I very much intended to do anyway. The third brother of the trio and I had mended the bridge between us during this campaign. I wouldn't have called us friends, but on the morrow of my fight with Lü Bu, this burly warrior accepted me as worthy of his respect, and I was glad to find him so welcoming here.

I quickly saluted him, Guan Yu by his side, and Zhang Liao, who sat next to me, before emptying my cup of *baijiu* in one sip.

Iron Heart had not only been pardoned but had also been recruited by Lord Cao, who offered him the title of General of the Household in his army. I believe he did so because he knew otherwise this fearsome warrior would join Liu Bei, if only because he and Guan Yu respected each other deeply. The least I can say is that Zhang Liao was treated with the utmost respect by my lord from then on, and Iron Heart returned the favor on many occasions, which is why he, like Yu Jin, Yue Jin, and Xu Huang, is now considered among Cao Cao's five elite generals. Back then, though, I could not see if Zhang Liao enjoyed the evening or not, but the way he kept his back to the show, as I did, led me to believe he did not approve of Diao Chan's treatment.

The crowd laughed when the dancer fell, her exhaustion getting the best of her. She stood up again and resumed her dancing, so I drank until I could no longer hear their laughter.

"What do you think will happen to her?" Zhang Fei asked sometime later.

I had dropped my head on the table at this point and struggled at the border between puking and sleeping.

"She'll be sent to some harem," Guan Yu replied, his face even redder than usual. "Either the emperor's, Lord Cao's, or someone of note." He did not seem to find solace in her fate.

"At least she'll live," I spoke through a bubble of saliva.

I never found out what happened to poor Diao Chan after this evening, but it could not have been an enviable life.

"I heard what you did for the girl," Zhang Liao said, for the first time looking me straight in the eyes. I sat back up, fighting the pain of the movement in my sorry brain. Guan Yu and Zhang Fei were also looking at me. They had all heard. The whole army had probably heard. "It isn't much, but on behalf of my former lord, I thank you."

Zhang Liao extended his cup for me to knock. I meant to reply that nothing came of my actions—the girl was just as dead—but Iron Heart guessed my mind.

"You tried," he went on meaningfully. "No one else did. Remember that."

"To trying," I said, a voice full of sarcasm as I drank with a man who had so nearly ended my story a few weeks before.

I got drunk that night. Drunk enough that I could not speak my mind anymore. But not drunk enough to keep the memory of the girl and her red smile from my dreams.

PART THREE

GUANDU

10

Xuchang, capital of the Great Han
3rd month, 4th year of Jian'an era (199), Han Dynasty

I CAME BACK to Xuchang with the army, a knot in my stomach. The march had been an odd moment for me, to say the least. We had slain the beast, secured our eastern border, and proven our might to the rest of the empire, but I felt no joy in my heart. On a personal level, I came home with a promotion, bonuses to fill a trunk, and a name shining brighter from my battle against Lü Bu, yet none of it mattered. I felt as if I had lost a piece of myself in Xiapi. But as the *li* separating us from the capital shrunk, my worries were less and less in the past and more targeted at my reunion with the Scorpions.

I'd been gone for four months without any instructions or notes for my comrades besides a vague promise to "be back soon," and a bag filled with some gear as the sole clue of my purpose. By then, they would have heard of my exploits in Xiapi, but since I had received no message from any of them, I was at a loss as to what to expect.

Some kind of mutiny was my major worry. The Scorpions existed to serve Cao Cao in the shadows, but to us, it was, first and foremost, a chance to get richer using our various talents, without the usual risks and issues of war. Yet, it had been over a year since we'd been used, and besides a regular salary, my men had gotten no chance to better their lives. This winter in Xuchang must have been as dull as they get, and I had no doubt their days had been long and boring. Few things instill a desire for mutiny stronger than boredom. The second thing that preoccupied my mind was Tian Guli. I half expected my room to be empty upon my return, with my lover gone back to her people in my absence. I had not only left her; I had left her in the presence of animals. Since our first encounter, Du Yuan had tried his luck with her, and who knew how far he was willing to go to bed her?

I entered Xuchang at the back of the triumphant officers and even then dragged my feet all the way to the compound. But, to my great surprise, nothing much happened.

I was welcomed with friendly waves and pats on the back. Life had kept its course, training had been respected, and some might even say a certain sense of professionalism could be spotted here and there. The weapons racks were stacked, and the floor was clear of chicken bones and vomit. Even the fuming bathwater looked as limpid as on the first day.

My men greeted me with smiles, each asking for a retelling of the events in Xiapi, which I promised to give around a few cups of yellow wine in the evening. Guo Wen happily took my bundle and kicked his son's butt to force his help with my sword. Ma Dai, the hostage from the governor of Liang province, avoided my gaze, as usual. I noticed his shoulders had filled nicely in my absence, and when I pointed out the bruises on his cheeks, he laughed and told me it was just the fruits of Du Yuan's training regimen. My second had been up to the task, and I could see from how the others took their spot by his sides that he had turned himself into a reliable leader during the winter. I felt a little jealous but knew it was my fault. Du Yuan received the lion's share from my trunk of silk, jewels, and gold, which he completely deserved, then the rest took what he told them to and left enough for the absent. Du Yuan complained of his absence in Xiapi, claiming he would have given all his rewards to take part in the sack of the city. I said I believed him but knew he would have acted exactly like the three platoon leaders I had "executed," which killed the joy of our reunion. When I dragged the conversation as far as I could, Pox nodded for me to move to my room, where my lover waited.

The way up reminded me of the battle of the White Tower, and I reached the second floor with a heartbeat similar to that fateful day. No one stood on the second floor, which I knew was a way to give me some space. Some of my men even left the compound, Guo Huai, Ma Dai, and the Meng brothers among them.

My heart was in my throat by the time I reached the door of my room. I thought of knocking, but the idea of asking permission to enter my own bedroom bothered me more than the potential harm, so I just pushed the two doors and prepared myself for the storm.

It never came, though.

Guli was there, on our bed. I was going to apologize before she could open her mouth, but my words remained stuck inside, too astonished I was by the vision awaiting me. She was entirely naked, posing languidly, a hand between her legs as she feigned to ignore my presence. I slowly walked to the bed, wondering where the trap lay, keeping her in my sight as I would a feral tiger. I had given my armor to Guo Wen and my blades to his son, which left me with civilian clothes, and nothing to hide my feelings for her at this instant.

"I am really—"

"I know," she said, interrupting me. She flipped on her belly and walked on all fours toward the feet of the bed.

"And you're not—"

"Not anymore," she said as she raised her beautiful chest, then pulled me to her angry mouth.

For the next *shi*, I wondered if I was experiencing a dream. Everything had happened so much more smoothly than I had feared, and my love for Guli, which I had thought broken on her side, seemed as fresh as ever. Even the way she straddled me felt new. The gods in heaven sometimes smile on us and must have been watching me, I thought before calling them *pervs* in my mind.

But, as I later lay in my bed, Guli sleeping in my arms, a sense of loneliness took over me. It was the same feeling of not-belonging I had felt after coming back from my first campaign; the one against Dong Zhuo. It was a horrible thought to entertain, but part of me wished my friends and lover would have worsened in my absence. Had they gotten lazy and fat, had she yelled and insulted me, I would have felt at home and of some use. They had done well without me, maybe even better, and from what I heard, Man Chong actually kept them busy.

For the first time, I wondered if the Scorpions were better off without me, and this thought gave birth to another. Maybe Cao Cao would as well.

A man only sees things clearly when his balls are empty, and my clear mind did not allow me much sleep that night.

In the morning, I stepped outside before anyone awoke in the compound, shortly before the sun rose too, and let my feet take me through the city. I thought of Diao Chan dancing until her feet bled and Xiahou Dun laughing to his heart's content with Lü Bu's helmet on the head. I thought of Chen Gong smiling on the path to the gallows and his lord nodding in gratitude, believing I had saved his daughter. I thought of her as well, though she rarely left my mind anyway. And I thought of Zhang Liao thanking me for having tried and Guan Yu, who had saved me from him. My brain refused to consider the obvious truth, but it was there in my heart; I could no longer follow my lord blindly.

More than anything, Cao Cao's voice telling me he had not ordered the civilians to be spared resonated in my skull, and I felt sick in the stomach at the coldness of his statement. Chen Gong and even Zhou Cang, my childhood friend, had warned me, but part of me still hoped there was goodness in my lord's heart. Not benevolence, this I knew, but maybe a goal to which he aspired that would explain how he could accept all this cruelty. I debated with myself, arguing that Cao Cao had, in fact, done nothing despicable himself; he had just gone with it. As he had once told me in the jails of Puyang, he was riding the chaos, and the younger me had accepted the idea. The people of Xu might see it otherwise, but no one was closer to bringing peace and stability to the Great Han land than Cao Cao, and this granted him the right to some mistakes. One might even say a certain coldness was necessary to harness the winds of change and bring the world back to a more natural state. When the realm was one again, I told myself, Cao Cao would become a decent man once more and punish those who were not. It was a foolish thought, but it gave me hope.

I raised my head after a long walk, and, to my surprise,

my tired feet had taken me to the front gate of a mansion, that of Liu Bei.

The governor of Xu had been invited back to Xuchang after our victory in Xiapi. Soldiers and workers needed to rebuild the city, and the population, while at first adoring Liu Bei, was slightly less favorable after he took part in the flooding, if only by standing next to my lord. While the tempers cooled down and a semblance of life resumed in the province, Liu Bei would remain with us, close to the emperor. This was the official argument. In reality, my lord feared to leave the governor out of his sight. He had no cause to doubt Liu Bei, but Cao Cao doubted his own shadow at this point. I believe Liu Bei would have preferred to remain in Xu and take care of his people, but he was wise enough to obey and bide his time. And the emperor was here after all.

I looked to my left, then to my right, and, satisfied that no one observed me, knocked on the governor's door.

For the next couple of months, twice a week maybe, this is where I went when my world stopped making sense. I became a regular guest in the mansion where the three brothers lived, and not once did they spurn me. There was always a cup of wine and some millet for me there. I got acquainted with some of Liu Bei's staff and particularly appreciated the wits of Liu Bei's brother-in-law and advisor, Mi Zhu. While born into one of Xu's wealthiest families, Mi Zhu was easy to befriend and simple of taste. He must have been in his mid-thirties then, and while his chin and cheeks remained beardless, he boasted an impressive pair of whiskers, which he joked was his attempt at competing with Guan Yu. His brother, Mi Fang, was Guan Yu's aide, though the latter clearly thought little of this slow-minded comrade. Liu Bei showed astonishing deference to Mi Zhu, and I quickly understood their relationship went deeper than simple brothers-in-law because the advisor was also, in fact, Liu Bei's main creditor. No point was ever made of money within the mansion, but Liu Bei must have owed the man a fortune to have granted him such a place in his staff.

Mi Zhu, however, was absent on a particularly stormy afternoon, just a couple of days before *lixia*, the beginning of summer. It was my weekly day off, and I had chosen to spend some of it drinking a few cups of expensive *mijiu* with Zhang Fei to cement our blooming friendship and because we had a cause for celebration.

"Oh, you got to bring some of that wine at the wedding," Zhang Fei commented after smacking his lips in pleasure.

"Cost me an arm and a leg to get that one," I replied after burping through my sip. "We'll need another war so that I can afford more. Besides, you owe me for your wife-to-be, not the other way around." Zhang Fei grunted in reply and found nothing to say. He did owe me his good fortune. At least partially.

It happened during an imperial hunt I had been invited to as the Son of Heaven's unofficial horse-riding instructor. This event went terribly bad because Lord Cao shamed the Son of Heaven with his archery skills, but while the court raged at the treatment given to Emperor Xian, I saw none of it because I rode at the back, where the women and youngsters walked. I kept company with Zhang Fei, a rather poor rider himself, or at least I thought I was, for the man could not be bothered with a conversation. His focus was somewhere else.

I quickly realized his attention was all for the benefit of the women from the Cao clan, and it took me a few minutes to realize that one, in particular, kept his head from the game.

"Tell me if I bother you," I had said.

"What? No, sorry, it's just ... who is that lady over there?"

I followed his nod and struggled to find exactly who he was talking about; there were many of them.

"Which one?" I asked.

"Beautiful young lady in blue, right behind your lord's wife. She keeps throwing me some glances," he answered.

"No offense, Yide," I said, using Zhang Fei's *zi* name, "but no one is—" Then I saw someone was indeed looking furtively at us, or more accurately at Zhang Fei, and I could not have been more surprised. She was indeed beautiful but could hardly be called a lady, being still a year from a marriable age. The young lady blushed, something I didn't think she could do, for I had known her as the bravest, most brazen girl from her clan. Yet there was no hiding that her appreciation for Zhang Fei had struck her so strongly that she could no more care about following the hunt than Yide could.

"That's Xiahou Yu, Xiahou Yuan's eldest daughter, though we all call her Lady Xiahou," I replied, amusing myself as Zhang Fei repeated her name in a whisper, as lovestruck as the young lady was.

"Chun, you have to introduce me!" he barked, scaring my mare with the sudden volume in his voice.

"Are you crazy? We're on an imperial hunt! There's no way we can approach the women of the Cao clan on such an event. Plus, I'm sure it's a mistake, and she's actually looking at your horse."

But there was no mistake. Lady Xiahou was blushing with each timid gaze, batting her eyes like the wings of a butterfly escaping its cocoon. I could still recall the girl I had saved from Puyang's old temple, and how much she had impressed me on the road to Dong'e. She had been a child then, and of course, was nearly a woman now.

"Chun!" Zhang Fei went on. "She's the love of my life! Get her to me, and everything is forgiven between us!"

"I've got nothing to be—"

"*Shush-shush-shush*, less blabbering, more matchmaking," he said, slapping my mare's rump to force me on my way.

I did not, in fact, broach the topic during that hunt in the imperial forest but worked relentlessly on Xiahou Yuan for the next few days. At first, my lord's cousin had been curious as to the reasons for my visit, and I believe he thought *I* was interested in his daughter. When I finally mentioned Zhang Fei, he nearly threw me out the window. I came back the next day, having worked my argument in between. Zhang Fei was *a hero of the empire, a peerless warrior, and the right arm of a governor.* But all arguments fell on deaf ears. It took young Lady Xiahou to intervene for her father to understand how serious the situation was. She was, by her own words, in love. I could not believe it any more than Xiahou Yuan, for surely no worse match ever had existed under the sky, but love sometimes has a way of uniting very different people. Yue Lao, the old man under the moon, must have been drunk when he tied his red cord around Zhang Fei's and Xiahou Yu's ankles, but it proved to be a sturdy link, and when Cao Cao consented to the marriage, Xiahou Yuan finally relented. It was to happen later that year, after Xiahou Yu's hairpin ceremony, but I know for a fact the lovebirds managed to meet long before that, though I had nothing to do with that part.

I often thought some women tend to be attracted to men resembling their own fathers, and in the case of young Lady Xiahou, this was the best explanation I could come up with.

Whatever the case, I took it as the greatest of news and happily acquired an expensive jar of *mijiiu* to present to the future husband. We had cracked it open a few minutes before a lightning bolt pierced the sky and announced the first drops of a rather heavy rain.

"What about you, Lord Guan? Should I also find you a match within my lord's clan?" Because of his majestic stature, everyone called Guan Yu *Lord Guan*, which he claimed to dislike, while in reality, I could see how much he appreciated it. Despite his best efforts in hiding it, the bearded warrior was arrogant to a fault.

"I decline," he answered. "Like my young brother here, I will marry when the time is right. Not before."

"Second brother, you're almost forty," Zhang Fei said, elbowing Guan Yu in the ribs, making him lose some precious wine. "Maybe it's time to push Yue Lao a little, eh?"

"In love, like in war, one must be patient, Yide," Guan Yu replied, caressing his beard as a teacher facing his students.

It was quite astonishing to hear these two warriors speaking of love so casually. I would have thought them above those petty concerns and always assumed Liu Bei intended to marry them to gain some favor from their future wives' families, but the governor was not this kind of man and would never have forced them on such a private decision. Liu Bei, however, was stricter with himself. His wife, Lady Mi, could hardly be called a beauty, and his favorite, Lady Gan, was no better, but both had gotten him a fair amount of financial and military support. This would have been a good deal for many men, but like Cao Cao, Liu Bei was a woman's man. In fact, one could say this was their only common point; they were real goats.

Everything else made them stand apart. While Cao Cao had consciously committed to instilling fear in people's hearts to gain their respect, Liu Bei chose kindness, making all decisions with this idea in mind. He led by example, and as far as his two brothers were concerned, it worked. Without a doubt, had a man like Zhang Fei followed another lord, he would have turned into a brute instead of a big bear to be smitten by love at first glance from a young lady. I wondered how I would have turned out had I grown under his leadership.

I was still glad to be Cao Cao's officer, for I believed Liu Bei's vision was horse shit and would lead him to a pitiful death. He was less naive than he appeared, as he had proven when arguing in favor of Lü Bu's execution, but he was still too ... soft for our world. In fact, I could even say he was the only member of his household I had trouble with, and more often than not, I ended our conversations with an eye roll. I especially had trouble with their core belief that should one of them die, the others would, by some mystical means, too. If a brother of mine died, I would bring the full wrath of my vengeance upon his killer before even thinking of joining him.

So, when Liu Bei returned from his lunch with my lord, soaked to the bone, I thought my time with them was over for the day.

"Didn't see that one coming, right, brother?" Zhang Fei said, chuckling at the sorry sight of Liu Bei shaking the water from his sleeves.

"Not the only thing I didn't see coming," Liu Bei replied, insinuating that something surprising had happened. A servant ran with tiny steps toward the governor and offered a dry robe of average quality.

"Something happened?" Guan Yu asked.

"You could say that," Liu Bei replied.

"And since when do *we* buy this kind of thing?" Zhang

Fei asked, pointing his little finger toward Liu Bei's waist while holding his cup with the others.

What he referred to was hard to miss. Liu Bei's clothes were never of the best material, and he wore them many times before acquiring new ones. His belt, however, was a masterpiece. A magnificent piece of dark leather, incrusted with small plates of gold and passing through hoops of jade. Even at court, I had rarely seen such luxury.

"Oh, that?" Liu Bei asked, looking at the belt as if he had forgotten about it. "A gift from the emperor himself. Can you imagine? Given to me by a servant of the General of Chariots and Cavalry just as I left Lord Cao's mansion. Truly, the Son of Heaven is too good." He said the last with a salute toward the palace of Emperor Xian.

I found it odd. Not that Liu Xie gave such a gift to his imperial uncle, if only because I knew the young man was always looking for allies outside of Cao Cao's sphere of influence, but about Dong Cheng being the one delivering it. Liu Xie had enough servants to carry a present without having to rely on his favorite concubine's father.

Guan Yu picked up on my frown and changed the topic.

"Why don't you dry up first, then tell us about this lunch?" he offered his brother.

"I will need more than a few towels to get over this meal," Liu Bei replied, apparently not following Guan Yu's lead. "Without this first lightning bolt, I might actually have made a fool of myself." He stretched the last word as he finally noticed my presence.

"Let me take my leave, then," I said as I stood from my cushion. Guan Yu and Zhang Fei copied me, and I saluted them with a bow each.

"Liao Chun," Liu Bei said with something like regret in

his voice. "My apologies. I do not wish to put you in a difficult situation."

"None needed, Lord Liu. I need to get back to the compound anyway," I lied.

I bowed to him as well, arms extended in a *zuoyi* salute. Liu Bei dropped his hand on mine before I could break the salute; it was still cold and wet.

"Can I ask you a favor, Colonel Liao?"

"Of course," I replied, straightening up. I stood half a head taller than Liu Bei and was supposed to look below his eyes, but the man would just not let it happen, and whenever my eyes went under his, he would catch my attention back and force it up again.

"When we are back in Xu," he said, "watch over our emperor for me, will you?"

"Brother," Guan Yu said, a slight tone of rebuke in his voice.

"It is fine," Liu Bei replied still keeping my gaze. "Liao Chun is a friend of Emperor Xian, and so of us as well. The Son of Heaven trusts him. I do too."

So the reason Liu Bei was so shaken by his meal with my lord had something to do with the emperor. Not only the three brothers, but half of Xuchang could seldom talk of anything else but Cao Cao's treatment of Liu Xie. While at first, when the young man had just arrived in Xuchang, Cao Cao showed proper deference toward him, things had quickly changed, and not always in subtle ways. Man Chong kept tongues still in the capital, but even my talented friend could not suppress every whisper targeted at Lord Cao. However, I was his man, and Liu Bei's words and trust were dangerous. Only one thing would keep me from retelling this conversation with Lord Cao: guilt. The sole reason Liu Xie lived inside the walls of Xuchang was my convincing him to do so. Whenever the rumor of another abuse from my lord came to my ears, a sense of shame took me over. I was Cao Cao's officer, but I was a supporter of Liu Xie as well. I owed the latter some discretion, if only because I was sorry for the part I had played in his presence here.

"Liu Xie thinks of you as a friend and blames you for nothing," Liu Bei then said. It sucked the air from my lungs. Cao Cao could read your mind, but Liu Bei saw through your heart. An equally destabilizing talent and one that left me searching for words on that day.

"Thank you, Lord Liu," I said, bowing again.

The moment passed with another strong gust of wind outside the building. I saluted Guan Yu and Zhang Fei, telling the latter I was looking forward to his wedding and promising the trio I would be back soon if they allowed, which they did.

This, however, was not meant to be. Five days later, they left Xuchang without a word for me. News had come from Yang province, where Yuan Shu, the usurper, once again attempted something foolish. Thinking Xu province weak, the toad had directed his army north, and my lord replied by sending Liu Bei at the head of a division to stop Yuan Shu. I watched Liu Bei's army departing the capital from the ramparts, wishing them luck and wondering if I would next see them again at Zhang Fei's wedding or before.

Little did I know that on our next encounter, we would stand on opposite sides of the battlefield once more.

11

Xuchang, capital of the Great Han
5th month, 4th year of Jian'an era (199), Han Dynasty

"Chun, wake up, something's happening," Pox said, startling me from a dream when he stormed inside my room.

The city was in turmoil. Messengers were crisscrossing through the streets, their hands empty of messages but the urgency of their mission clear from the width of their steps. No bell was ringing from the wall, but otherwise it felt as if we were under siege. No word had been sent to the compound yet, but I would not wait for them.

"We don't know what's happening," I said from the center of the courtyard where my men were gathering. Guo Wen was helping me don my armor, and his son brought Yingzhao for me to take. I gestured for him to take it away. I wouldn't be allowed in the palace with it, and if I judged the situation correctly, this was where I was headed. "But I want everyone ready for battle. Guli, Ma Dai, Hu Zi, and Duck, get the horses ready and stay there. We'll get your things."

The four of them obeyed right away; they had picked up on the urgency of the situation as well.

"Du Yuan, take care of things here. I want everyone ready for battle by the time I return. Pox, Pei, with me."

We were out of the compound before Pei Yuanshao could fasten his belt and joined the mass of curious striding toward the palace.

The palace doors were wide open, an event in itself, which, of course, did not mean every living soul in Xuchang was welcomed inside. It took me a few curses and a bribe for the guards to let the three of us pass after they made sure we carried no weapons. Even with the strict protocol of the palace and the great number of people being forbidden within, the Square of Heavenly Favor, the greatest empty space of the place, stretching from the Gate of the Supreme Harmony to the hall bearing the same name, was full of onlookers. Everyone of note and their cousins were present, all staring in the same direction toward the stairs leading to the great hall, where a circle of fierce-looking guards kept the public from approaching any closer. Because of all the hatted heads in the crowd, I could not even distinguish the upper stairs and had to elbow my way through until I reached the first line of onlookers.

"*Tian na!*" Pei Yuanshao, who could see better from his extra height, said. My curse was less polite when I saw what had made him blanch.

There were nine stairs leading to the great hall's terrace, nine stairs of alabaster stone, already polished by thousands of feet despite the palace construction being less than five years ago. On each of those wide steps knelt a man dressed in white, each gagged, hair falling unbound on their shoulders. They knelt near the extremities of the staircase, the first on the right side of the first step, the second on the left side of the second step, and so on, so they could watch each other. Behind the kneeling men stood members of Cao Cao's guard with broad swords in hand, in case anyone had doubts about what was about to take place. There would be blood.

"Who are they?" Pox asked.

"Ministers and officers," I answered. "At least those I recognize."

Of the nine men about to depart the realm of the living, I actually knew four and remembered them as supporters of the emperor from his time in exile. On the upper step knelt the one I knew best; Dong Cheng, General of Chariots and Cavalry, father to the emperor's favorite concubine and my lord's greatest opponent in Xuchang. Not for long, though. The condemned behaved in various ways, from the ones crying heavy tears, slouching so low their foreheads touched the stone, to the prouder ones, like Dong Cheng, who sat straight in defiance, eyes lost over the horizon.

More guards appeared from the top of the stairs, flanking the terrace left and right as if about to protect some invisible defenses. I had to fight a few knocks on my back as more people gathered to witness the macabre show, but a hard look over my shoulder was enough to gain some peace.

"Enjoying the view?" Man Chong, who had appeared from seemingly nowhere on the other side of the cordon, asked me.

"I'm guessing it's as good as it's going to get," I answered.

"You don't know the half of it," my friend replied, though at that particular moment I could not think of him as such. I recognized a glint in his eyes from our childhood, which usually preceded the result of his cunning preparation. It always ended badly for someone.

"What is all of this?" Pei Yuanshao asked, probably recognizing the same threat in the prefect's behavior.

"Retribution," Man Chong answered vaguely.

I meant to ask *retribution against who* when a gong called for our attention from the terrace. I knew *who* anyway. And just as I thought of him, Cao Cao appeared above the stairs, taking a genial pose as he observed the crowd and paid no attention to the condemned. Next, his *mianguan* crown announcing him, came Emperor Xian, and, without being asked, the crowd fell to its knees, and we all kowtowed and wished the Son of Heaven a life stretching over ten thousand years. Man Chong, the guards, and Cao Cao remained on their feet. I glanced at young Liu Xie, daring this blasphemy because I worried about him more than about the protocol. His face was a message of sorrow, features pulled in a mix of anger and terror. Even through the beads of his crown masking his face, I could see how much he had cried very recently. Cao Cao nodded to him, and the emperor told us to rise. We thanked him before standing back up. The Son of Heaven was not even given a chair to sit on.

Another blow of the heavy gong called for our silence, and when it was achieved, Cao Cao took a series of steps leading him to the third march from the top. He wore his *jian* sword, of course, an honor given to him by the emperor when we had welcomed Liu Xie in Xuchang. An honor the Son of Heaven probably regretted. My lord kept his hand on the sword's pommel as he addressed the crowd.

"People of Xuchang!" His voice rang as strong as ever. "Noble servants of the Great Han dynasty! Today is a great day, for today, we become stronger. Evil men have worked in the shadows of the palace, plotting to weaken the unity of our great nation, plotting against me!" Cao Cao took another step down, for the first time throwing a murderous glance at the kneeling man on his right. "While our illustrious army fights to bring order back to the land, while my staff works tirelessly to punish the rebels, those men here, kneeling in front of you, conspired to have me killed. Me! Cao Cao! The only man capable of putting the empire back under the rule of its rightful leader."

So this was the reason for this masquerade. Some men had been brazen or stupid enough to think they could take my lord's life, acting in the very city he controlled. Every whisper was reported back to him; every thought of sedition came to his office before the wannabe rebel finished it. Frankly, while I did not envy their fate, I could hardly defend their stupidity.

"If not for the efforts of your prefect," Cao Cao went on, opening his hand toward his bastard son, who bowed in gratitude, "they might have succeeded. And then what would have happened?"

He let the crowd think about it as he took another series of steps.

"In a realm without Cao Cao, how long until the likes of Yuan Shu manage to storm the capital and destroy the four-hundred-year legacy of the Great Han? How long until an ambitious man like Yuan Shao declares his own dynasty? How long until our beloved Son of Heaven falls in the hands of another Dong Zhuo, another Guo Si, or Li Jue? Is this what you want?"

Cao Cao made himself angry as he spoke, and the crowd answered as he wanted, of course.

"To conspire against me," he then went on, stopping his walk on the second step from the bottom, "is to conspire against the emperor himself! And if it was not enough, they did so claiming to act in the name of the Son of Heaven."

"Maybe they did!" someone shouted from the crowd,

forcing Cao Cao to turn just as he was about to climb the stairs again. A thick murmur passed in a wave through the spectators as they searched who had spoken. They probably thought the man would not live long, but from the discreet smile on Man Chong's lips, I knew this was all part of the show.

Cao Cao pretended to remain calm and waved his hands down for our silence.

"If Emperor Xian wishes me dead," my lord said, just as he drew his *jian* sword theatrically, "he only needs to ask." On this, he brought the sword against his throat, pointing upward, and turned toward the Son of Heaven. Liu Xie's hands had turned to fists; I could see it from the folds of his sleeves. "I am and always have been your humble servant," Cao Cao shouted so we could hear even from his back. "If I have disappointed you, you may order my life to be taken by my own hand right now."

Lord Cao dropped to his knees and waited for Liu Xie to speak. There was a pause, unscripted I believe, during which the young emperor probably thought of some dramatic action, but my lord must have held something against him, and Emperor Xian played his part.

"The Minister of Works has always greatly supported our cause. He has protected us, offered us a haven of peace after years of captivity, and even now, while many would enjoy the fruits of their labor, he alone carries the burden of gathering the empire back together." While his voice remained as smooth as ever, I could detect the frustration shaking his throat, just as I could guess the same words forming at the tip of Man Chong's lips. At this moment, I hated him. "We would never conspire against him. Lord Cao, please rise."

"Thank you, *Bixia*!" Cao Cao said as he stood and

sheathed his blade. He then turned again in our direction, and I could feel in my heart his next words would carry consequences far in the future. My palms turned wet like before a battle, my mouth dry.

"For fomenting an assassination against an Excellency, the punishment is death!" he shouted. On cue, the sword-carrying guards stood straighter and brought their instruments of death against their chests. "For falsely using the emperor's name, the punishment is death!" The guards put one foot on the lower steps to get a proper footing. Some of the condemned screamed through their gags, their tears pouring even more freely, while others offered their necks in a last gesture of defiance.

"Each drop of the blood about to be spilled will make the empire stronger!" Cao Cao shouted. He turned once more and climbed the first step. The first guard acted on cue, bringing his wide blade through his victim's neck.

A gush of disgust flashed through the crowd as the blood erupted from the severed neck, flowing freely behind my lord, who took another slow, measured step up. The second condemned joined his comrade, and the people shook in horror. I heard a man puking somewhere behind and knew more would follow.

"You should know," Man Chong whispered in my ear. "We're still missing some names from the conspiracy." A new tremor in the crowd informed me of the third man's death. "And some that we know of aren't in Xuchang, of course."

"Such as?" I asked, not understanding why the prefect was telling *me* this.

"Ma Teng of Liang," he whispered back. My heart missed a beat at the name.

"You're coming after Ma Dai," I said. Not a question.

"As long as your men don't resist, you have nothing to fear," Man Chong said, and I didn't like the sound of that. The fourth man was struck, but the guard had botched the execution, and a piece of the head remained attached by the skin. Someone standing right behind me passed out at the sight of the dangling head.

"Let me send one of my men to make sure they hand the boy over quietly," I said, to which Man Chong replied with a nod.

I turned to Pei Yuanshao, whose eyes would not steer from the spectacle of blood and death unfolding in front of us.

"Ma Teng is part of the conspiracy," I whispered in his ear, and that brought his attention back. "Go to the stable first and tell them to get as far away as possible. The boy is never to come back. Then go back to the compound and tell the guards Ma Dai was on his way to his ancestors' temple at dawn. That should keep them busy for some time." To the best of my knowledge, the Ma clan had no temple in Xuchang. The stable where our horses remained was outside the city wall, the inner ones being far too expensive for us, and this provided me with a semblance of hope for the young man.

Pei Yuanshao nodded and left, using his nimble body to slip through the crowd, which shook again when another fell.

"That's what you do now?" I asked Man Chong. "You hand me a boy to take care of, then just get him killed because of his uncle's mistake?"

"I thought you didn't want him to begin with," my friend replied.

"This is neither here nor there. He's not even a man yet. Since when do we kill teenagers?"

"Oh, it's about to get much worse," Man Chong replied, a spiteful smirk across his well-trimmed beard. Even then, guessing the level of horror he had hinted at, I could never have imagined how far my lord was willing to go.

Cao Cao reached the upper stair, where Dong Cheng waited his turn. My lord faced the kneeling man and ordered his executioner, who turned out to be Xu Chu, to remove the general's gag. I could not hear their exchange but guessed Cao Cao was asking for the other conspirators' names one more time. Dong Cheng spat at my lord's face, and for the first time, I thought well of this courtier. Lord Cao straightened up, wiped his face with the back of his sleeve, and gestured somewhere toward the great hall. Less than three seconds later, Dong Cheng yelled like a wounded beast and cursed Cao Cao, forgetting all his previous bravado as he shamed himself with his pitiful reaction. And he wasn't the only one.

Emperor Xian nearly faltered as two guards dragged a young woman toward my lord, then dropped her between Cao Cao and her father. I did not know her, but this had to be Lady Dong, the emperor's favorite concubine. If Liu Xie and Dong Cheng's reactions were not enough to realize who she was, her heavily pregnant belly removed any doubt about her identity. She could not have been more than a month from giving birth.

She crawled to her father, crying as much as her lord, then embraced the older man whose bound arms prevented him from returning the gesture. Liu Xie knelt at Cao Cao's feet and took my lord's hand as he pleaded for his concubine's wife. This was an utterly miserable scene.

"What have you done?" I asked Man Chong, rage making my voice tremble.

"She's the daughter of the conspiracy leader," my friend replied, matter of fact.

"She's the concubine of the emperor," I replied. "She carries his seed, for heaven's sake."

"Chun," Man Chong went on, "what do you think is happening right now to all their clans? How many children and women, old and young, are being slaughtered while this pantomime takes place? Don't get sentimental about one girl and her not-yet-born baby; it's unbecoming."

In other circumstances, I would have punched him in the face. Of course, those people's families would die; this was the way of things. But why make a show of it? And how could he show so little guilt about it?

Liu Xie, on his knees, meant to reach his favorite, but Cao Cao stood between them, then asked the guards who had dragged the young lady to help the emperor back to his feet. The young man searched through the crowd as the two soldiers pulled him from his beloved. His eyes found mine, or at least I think they did, and I could no longer stop myself.

I meant to intervene; throw everything up to the winds rather than stain my soul further with the murder of an innocent woman and her baby. Man Chong grabbed my wrist before I could even start.

"If you know what's good for you," he said menacingly, "you won't make a move."

"So that's how you intend to remain in his good graces? By killing women in front of their husbands and fathers?" I asked, shaking his hand off me.

"What has happened to you?" he asked in reply, a frown showing his confusion. "Since when are you so ... soft?"

I did not reply to his insult because I knew my words would have carried more vulgarity than his and also because I wondered if maybe he was right. Maybe the world, Lord Cao, and Man Chong himself hadn't changed. Maybe I had.

They strangled the lady with a rope.

It took a long time. She was blue when they released the tension and let her body drop lifelessly on the palace's stone. I can still hear the whimpering of Emperor Xian and the shrieks of hatred from Dong Cheng as it happened. Xu Chu chopped his head off next. Then silence fell. I had rarely witnessed such an eerie silence from so many people gathered in one place. Very few still looked up the stairs, but I did. And when they dragged the emperor back to his palace, he looked at me again, and I knew he no longer thought of me as a friend.

I don't know how long I remained there afterward. Long enough to see the servants clean up the blood from the staircase.

Pox remained with me, quiet. I sent him back to the compound to ensure everyone was safe and asked him to return if there had been trouble. A *shi* later, I was still alone and chose to believe my comrades were all safe.

My mind went blank for a while, then I revisited my past, thinking about all the times I had seen the good in my lord and wondering if it had been the imagination of a boy willing to ignore the obvious if it meant a better life for himself. Zhou Cang's voice came back, claiming that Cao Cao was not a good man, and I wondered if the peasant boy had been right all along. It was never about being *good*, but surely such evil could not be condoned.

A palace servant informed me it was about to get dark and they would close the gates, so I left.

I do not remember the walk back to the compound, only the sorry look my comrades shared with me in the courtyard. None spoke or tried to stop me as I climbed to the second floor, so I assumed there had been no trouble. The room was empty, of course, and would remain so until Guli returned from escorting Ma Dai as far away as possible. Knowing her, I wouldn't have been surprised if she took him back all the way to his uncle.

I missed her. I missed her very much.

The call of the wilderness suddenly grew loud in my mind. The room's walls shrunk around me. The place smelled of iron, my furniture was full of dust, and the noise from the streets, while being quieter than ever, was deafening. I needed to get out of this place, find my lover, lose myself in her arms, and curse Cao Cao openly without risking jail.

Pouring the contents of my wardrobe on the bed, I chose two sets of clothes for traveling and punched them inside a bag of linen, then scanned the room and wondered what else I needed. My sword, of course. My armor maybe. Not my helmet, though, for it used to protect the head of a monster.

My newest knife was nowhere to be seen. I searched through the contents of a drawer from my desk, then again, but found it not. I threw the drawer against the wall, spreading the brushes, ink stones, candles, and all its contents across the room. I moved back to the wardrobe, broke my fist against its side, then slammed the piece of furniture on the ground. I was yelling when Guo Wen entered the room.

His gentle, understanding face undid me.

I turned toward the windows and finally cried.

Guo Wen said nothing for a while. This was the second time he came to me as I broke down. Last time, he had walked into the sea with me; this time, he simply put his hand on my back and waited for me to be done. It took a long time, but when he judged the time right, he put my broken hand in the crook of his amputated arm and bound it with some rag he had picked off the floor.

"It's all my fault, you know," I said as he tightened a noose over my wrist with his teeth and one hand. "I convinced Liu Xie to come here. Without me, he would still be in Luoyang. Far from that *monster*."

"In that case, it's my fault first," Guo Wen said. "If I hadn't spoken well of my lord to a snotty rebel kid, maybe he wouldn't have tried to join him." There was no way I could blame him for that, and he knew it. "Chun, you can't blame yourself for actions you thought were good at the time. All that matters is how you will react now."

"What do you mean, old man?" I asked, sniffing some of my tears back. Any reaction I could think of went against Cao Cao, and I did not believe he meant this.

"I mean, there has to be something you, and only you, can do to make the world a little better. You don't need to find what it is now," he said, putting his hand on my shoulder. "But I know you, Liao Chun, you'll make the right decision. In the end, you always do."

I doubted it but thanked him for his kind words.

Old Master Qiao once said I could light the path for my comrades or burn it to the ground. At this very moment, I knew what I was tempted to do.

"If it makes you feel any better, you saved Ma Dai's life today. That must count for something," my servant said as he helped me raise the wardrobe back up. "Though I guess you'll have to think of an explanation about this disappearance, and fast."

Guo Wen was right, for the next day, I received a summons from Cao Cao, served to me by two city guards.

I TURNED my nerves to steel the next day as I was accompanied to my lord's office by two guards unknown to me. They were neither friendly nor rude and barely spoke at all. The summons they carried was so fresh I could still smell its ink, and its urgency could not have been made clearer. It was from Cao Cao's hand, in his elegant style I had learned to appreciate but never to copy. And if I thought the message to be short, almost rude, it in no way conveyed any form of threat. Without Guo Wen's warning, I would have been confused as to what my lord expected of me, but of course, my one-handed friend had been right, I was to explain Ma Dai's disappearance, and I had to explain it convincingly if I meant to avoid any further problem.

I was ready, I thought. I would say Ma Dai, probably aware of his uncle's machinations, had asked for a day of leave to pray at his family's temple in Xuchang, then, of course, had left the city before we knew it. How was I to know the Ma clan had no such temple here? Since when did I pay attention to this kind of matter? If need be, I would curse the youngling, call him a halfwit barbarian, an ungrateful piece of turd. Ma Dai was safe, but my men and I weren't if my lord understood we had helped him. Our lives were worth a few dishonest insults.

Man Chong, I thought, might have noticed the absence of the three others. I would tell them Guli often took a few days off to ride, which was true, even more so recently. And my two messengers were known for their loving relationship, as their military records stated, nothing surprising in them leaving on short notice for some privacy.

If my lord asked about my behavior at the executions, I would not lie, as doing so would seem out of character. He knew how much I hated violence against children and women in general. I just had to find the perfect balance between insubordination and betrayal.

The problem wasn't the conversation about to happen but what came next. I had yet to understand what I was supposed to do or if I was supposed to do anything at all. Now that my lord had breached the line of obvious cruelty, should I try to stop him, or should I work tirelessly to make his vision come true faster?

The two guards left me to wait in the courtyard leading to my lord's office, where more of their comrades watched me while Cao Cao finished his current business. As I was made to wait outside, the voice of Liu Bei came into my mind. He had asked me to protect the emperor in his absence, and I had already failed him.

A cold feeling in my guts warned me about the next few minutes, and I suddenly wondered if I had been summoned to talk about Ma Dai at all.

When I was brought across his desk, my lord confirmed this feeling.

"We have some news from the east," he told me a heartbeat after I saluted him. Cao Cao wasn't alone in his office, and even with the sharpest blade, you could not cut through the thick layer of tension floating around. I took my time, saluting the different advisors present, starting with Guo Jia, then Xun Yu, Cheng Yu, and finally Man Chong, out of spite. It almost looked like a military council.

"The toad is dead at last, or just back to Shouchun?" I asked, thinking my lord meant *that* east.

"He has been defeated, yes," Cao Cao confirmed with a small wave of the hand. "But since he was not with his army, he still lives."

"A mission for the Scorpions perhaps?" I asked, truly

hoping it was the case. Nothing would please me more than a return to a semblance of normality. Even an assassination of the usurper would have suited me at that point.

"Eventually," Lord Cao said. "But that's not why I asked you here. I wasn't talking about Shouchun but about Xiapi."

I closed my eyes at the name of this cursed city and sighed. When would we be done with Xu province? I wondered.

"What happened?" I asked.

"We believe," Xun Yu said when Cao Cao asked him to explain, "that Liu Bei has rebelled against us."

"Liu Bei?" I asked, confused.

"Yes, Xuande, the imperial uncle, that big-eared straw-sandal-weaver, has betrayed me," Cao Cao went on, barely containing his ire.

"I warned you to get rid of him," Cheng Yu grumbled, not even bothering to mask his tone of rebuke.

"And you were absolutely right, old friend," Cao Cao said. "Others told me the opposite, but this time I should have listened to you."

Guo Jia stiffened a little, and I wondered if he had been the one defending Liu Bei against the cold, calculating Cheng Yu.

This was unbelievable news. Yet I could not figure out how Liu Bei would already have heard of the events in Xuchang, acted on it, and been found out less than a day after the fact.

"It was obviously planned," Cheng Yu told me when I asked as such.

"Do you mean that Liu Bei was part of the conspiracy?" I asked, shocked.

"That is what we think," Cheng Yu replied. "In fact, we believe the conspiracy was less than a week from taking place. Our spies reported the advance of Ma Teng's army, who, as you know, was part of the assassination plans. And Liu Bei acted as soon as he came back from his victorious campaign against Yuan Shu and killed the temporary governor of Xu. The timing is too perfect."

"Which means we have to attack Xiapi. Again," I said. I hated that city that would not submit despite having swallowed so many lives. "Wait," I said, snapping from my reveries. "Why did you ask for me?"

They all looked at each other, hesitating on who should speak first, and, without surprise, the role fell on Man Chong.

"You did spend an awful lot of time with Liu Bei in the past months," he said accusingly.

"So?" I asked. I had failed to veil the aggressivity in my voice. Nothing sounds more guilty than a defensive tone.

"So you may have heard or seen something that might help us understand why or how Liu Bei rebelled so efficiently," Guo Jia answered in his typical consolatory tone.

Cao Cao had his back to me, but I could see his thumbs nervously dancing around one another inside his palms. If he was accusing me of anything, I thought, he should at least look at me in the face like a man. Then I remembered he was no longer one.

"So?" Cheng Yu asked impatiently.

I was about to say that I could not think of anything pointing at Liu Bei's plan. Of course, I knew Liu Bei had been unhappy about the emperor's treatment from my lord, but that would have been like saying the chicken is displeased by the fox's presence. Then it hit me.

"Damn it," I whispered, looking at the floor. Cao Cao's thumbs interrupted their incessant loops.

"Yes?" he asked.

"The belt," I answered.

"What belt?" my lord asked, turning around.

So I told him about the gift from the emperor, given to Liu Bei through Dong Cheng. A fine piece of leather with plates of gold and loops of jade. One could easily have slipped a message inside. When I told my lord it had happened after he and the imperial uncle shared a meal during a stormy day, he did not look surprised. My silence on the topic, however, he did not appreciate.

"How come I only hear about it now?" he asked, his mask of cold fury back over his face.

"You didn't ask," I replied in kind. Two could play this game.

"I am supposed to ask you if a governor not affiliated with me directly receives a belt from the most vocal of my opponents?" he asked sarcastically.

"I don't know," I went on, feigning confusion. "That's not how it works nowadays? You ask, we answer. You order, we obey. Even when it comes to killing unborn babies and their mothers, isn't it?"

"Careful," Man Chong whispered.

"Chun, I have had enough of your insubordination," Cao Cao replied, a migraine obviously making itself known to him. "If you don't have the guts—"

"The guts?" I asked, interrupting him mid-sentence. "This has nothing to do with guts!"

"What is it then?" he asked, the volume in his voice reaching mine.

"It's about not killing innocent women and children. Especially not in front of their loved ones! How is that weird?" I asked, taking a difficult step closer to Cao Cao.

"She was just a concubine!" Cao Cao said.

"So was Lady Bian!" I shouted, slamming his desk with

the flat of my hands. The one I had broken the day before screamed with pain, but I managed to keep it unnoticeable. For the first time in my life, I believe, I had rendered Cao Cao speechless. "Your wife was once *just a concubine*. Lady Dong's baby might have been our future emperor. Even if it had been a daughter, you could have had her marry one of your sons someday. *This* was a way to fulfill your ambition peacefully. Or are we not even looking for that anymore?"

"Liao Chun," Xun Yu called in a warning, but I paid no attention to him. It was all for my lord, who stared back at me with an equal level of defiance in his eyes.

"I am outspoken," I told him, "but you used to appreciate that part of me. So, please, lord, listen to me. One day you will wake up and realize your cruelty went far deeper than you thought, then it will be too late. For generations, people will not see Cao Cao's greatness, only his evilness."

"Chun, enough," Man Chong said, but him too I ignored.

"Do you remember, my lord, when you came back from Luoyang with Chen Gong, you gave a speech in the hall of your mansion in Chenliu. You called Dong Zhuo a dog and a dynasty killer. Guess what people say about you now?"

I heard the guards approaching me from behind and finally let go of my staring contest with Lord Cao, who had yet to speak. When he did, he broke any hope I had for us.

"Liao Chun," he said. "It was just a concubine, and the baby was just a girl. A small price to pay for order to remain in Xuchang and the empire, wouldn't you say?"

"I wouldn't," I answered. Man Chong sighed, and I saw Xun Yu shaking his head.

Cao Cao stretched the folds of his robe under his belt and caressed them as if to remove some imaginary dust. This was his way of calming his nerves.

"Thank you, Colonel, for bringing this belt story to our attention," he said. "You and your men will soon be needed and are to remain within the walls of Xuchang until such a time. If anything else regarding the conspiracy on my life comes to mind, please inform the prefect. You may now go." He politely invited me out, so I respectfully bowed and saluted him before following the two guards from before.

I was not even out of the compound when I heard the crack of a piece of furniture smacked against a wall. This made me feel a little better, but I now knew my life was about to either change or be shortened.

12

Countryside of Lujiang commandery, Yang province
9th month, 4th year of Jian'an era (199), Han Dynasty

ONE HAD to appreciate the irony of the situation, as Pox had justly pointed out when we had left Xuchang about three months before. The last time we had traveled through Yang province, our efforts were targeted at avoiding Yuan Shu. Now, all we wanted was to find the toad. For a man who had lived a life of luxury and extravagance, his exile was surprisingly low-key.

No one knew where Yuan Shu had left when, on a regular evening after being pushed back by Liu Bei and my lord's men, he removed his *minguan* hat, dropped it on his throne, and vanished. Whenever we asked, people told us more or less the same thing.

"Hopefully he wanders the shadow land, and his body feeds the fish of the Dajiang."

This would not suffice for my lord, so we kept searching, not hoping much. From what we had gathered, Yuan Shu had lost his mind. Out of options, we interrogated some of his former staff, who were still figuring out what to do with their shoddy realm, and all claimed our hunt was a waste of time. Even if he lived, they said, he wasn't Yuan Shu anymore. And the more we went, the more I was inclined to believe them. Following the trail of some odd money, my men and I, half of the platoon, per Cao Cao's order, ended up in a typical village. A day of hard riding from Shouchun, this settlement was inhabited by farmers, a relatively successful tanner, and a former emperor, judging by the two horses tied to the entrance of a shack.

"Guess we got the right place this time," Stinger commented, his black gelding walking peacefully next to Qilin. The dark man was pulling the horse by his bridle, as we all did. We came in peace, despite our intent, and did not want to frighten the people of this village.

"Hopefully," I said.

"And then back home?" Bobo asked.

"Or maybe we can push to Qu'e, eh?" his brother replied impishly. His jest was targeted at me; even from my back, I could feel it. I had made the mistake of telling some of the men of my encounter with Sun Jian's widow, Lady Wu, and they, in turn, made sure to bring the topic back whenever Guli wasn't around. She, on the other hand, was the reason I longed to ride back to Xuchang as soon as possible.

Even if we had left a good month after the execution of Dong Cheng and the rebellion of Liu Bei, Guli had not returned. I had almost requested Du Yuan to be put in charge of our current mission, preferring to wait for my lover's return before leaving, but the gap between my lord and me had only widened since our altercation, and I knew he would have scoffed at my demand. Besides the worrisome absence of my lover, I was glad to be out of the capital.

Cao Cao would not start any campaign for the time

being; this much was certain. He needed to gather more food and recruit more troops. The past few years of warring east and west had left him weakened, and since the conflict with Yuan Shao could not be far, he had to show some restraint. The governor of the north, the official general-in-chief of the Great Han empire, was almost done with his interminable battle with Gongsun Zan. The Lord of the White Horse now only ruled one city, a fortified citadel from which he stubbornly resisted Yuan Shao. For years the conflict had reached a stalemate, but Cao Cao's spies were categoric; the citadel was about to fall. Meaning Yuan Shao would turn his attention south sooner rather than later, and the inevitable battle between the two most powerful lords of the empire would shake the earth.

The quiet anticipation was taking its toll on my lord's mood, and I heard his migraines hardly left him alone more than a day per week, at best. The atmosphere in Xuchang worsened accordingly, and I could not imagine how thick the tension was by now. Yang's countryside was more to my taste. We were still north of the Great River, so the humidity was still bearable.

However, the anxious, angry stares of the onlookers were quickly getting on our nerves. I knew what those people were thinking: they were about to lose their hoard and were right.

"Remember," I said, loud enough for the closest farmers to hear my words, "they may look harmless, but get ready for blood."

"Don't look so harmless to me," Meng Shudu replied.

They did have a look in their eyes, the glint of people who had found a trickle of liquid gold in their well and would die rather than letting it dry out. I, and some of my men, knew firsthand what motivated peasants could do, just as we knew they would try nothing against menacing-looking veterans.

To be honest, I was more afraid of what we'd find around our target. Even destitute, weakened, and depressed, Yuan Shu would never have left his palace by himself. We were only twelve, and I did not like our odds against a potential platoon of guards, especially if the villagers took part in the battle. I had sent One-eye and Guo Huai to watch the place earlier in the morning and from their observation spotted two war horses and no soldiers.

"That's the place," One-eye said as we reached the end of a beaten path leading to the shack. The building, if it could be called as such, made me feel nostalgic. I had spent a part of my childhood in a similar house. It looked ridiculously small and broken.

"Soldiers," Pox said as if I had not seen them.

Soldiers might not be the best term for the two men stepping out of the shack. They wore armor and carried sheathed blades, but they were no more warriors than I was a seamstress. One of them put a finger in front of his mouth to ask us to be quiet. I twisted a little and gestured for my men to remain in their spot. Stinger and Guo Huai, as agreed, would come with me.

The two soldiers walked to us and the three of us to them, leaving our horses to the care of our comrades. One of the two, the one who had asked our silence, saluted us respectfully. I did not reply immediately, fearing a trap, but when the second joined, and after I could read their eyes, I finally gave them a *zuoyi*. They were not bad men, those two. One could say they looked relieved to see us.

"May I ask who sent you?" the first asked, a diction speaking of a well-educated man but a politeness pointing at one without power.

"The Minister of Works," I replied. "Cao Cao," I then added, thinking that another Excellency bearing this title would be in exercise here.

"Told you it wasn't the Little Conqueror," the second replied. "Too discreet to be his men." Yuan Shu and Sun Ce had been at war for some time now, though the conflict remained cold, both parties content in observing each other from the banks of the Dajiang separating their territories.

"You were expecting us?" I asked.

"We've been expecting someone for the past month. Since we arrived, really," the first answered. "We just didn't know who it would be. Cao Cao, Sun Ce, Yuan Shao, or even someone from Shouchun. The emperor isn't short of enemies." It took me a second to remember he was talking of Yuan Shu when he said *emperor*.

"We came as soon as possible," Stinger said in his usual, menacing tone. The two of them recoiled at his grim smirk.

"May I ask who you are?" I asked them.

"Apologies," the first replied before bowing once more and remaining in a bending position. "I am the General of the Vanguard of Yuan Shu's army, and this is the General of the Rear. Though, as you could guess, I am no military man."

"Never held a sword until last week," the second replied, "until my predecessor left with half the treasury."

"I was Yuan Shu's physician," the first said as he finally straightened up again. "And my comrade here was his cobbler."

"His cobbler?" Guo Huai asked with a scoff.

"He offered good money," the cobbler replied.

"The emperor thought he would be gone on a long journey to regain the favor of heaven," the physician-turned-general explained for his comrade's presence.

"You know you can stop calling him that," I said. I could not say much about the shoemaker, but the physician was obviously a man of good morals, and I did not envy his current situation.

"The world might have abandoned him," he replied, "but I haven't. My lord is sick, and whether I use a blade or a scalpel, I will serve him until his death. Which, if I'm not mistaken—"

"Is near," Stinger went on.

The physician clicked his tongue inside his mouth and looked away. He was tired, hungry, anxious, and near the end of his rope, but he still cared about a fool like Yuan Shu. I put my hand on his shoulder to let him know I felt his pain.

"Can I ask you," he said as I walked past him. "Can I ask you to make it quick and painless?"

"If he doesn't make a fuss," I replied.

"Oh, he'll make a fuss all right," the cobbler said.

A look over my shoulder let me see Pox opening a bag of food for the two generals' benefit just before I stepped inside the dark, foul-smelling shack where an emperor would die.

Two crude holes had been dug on the sides of the house to serve as windows, but the current occupants had plugged them with rags, leaving the inside of the building in complete darkness. The door was the only source of light, and as I stepped in, not much of it filtered through. Guo Huai pinched his nose when he also penetrated the shack, frowning against the pungent smell of fresh shit. The buzz of flies indicated the emperor had emptied himself in the furthest corner of the one-room house, right at the foot of the plank of wood serving as a bed. The "Son of Heaven", however, was crouching at the center of the wall facing the entrance, his beautiful *hanfu* of silver and gold stained to the point they appeared brown. Yuan Shu's hair hung on his back, and his legs were opened like those of an unmoving frog. In fact, the only parts of Yuan Shu that did move were his arms, which he did not seem in control of. His left hand went frantically to his skull, scratching his unruly mass of hair before ultimately bringing it to his mouth. His other hand caressed the wall without rest. Or so I thought.

As I stepped closer, I realized the wall was marked with hundreds of small scratches and lines. The toad was digging through the baked earth with his nails or what was left of them. This whole side of the house was marked, and if the light had allowed, I would probably have noticed the same phenomena on the other three.

I whistled for Guo Huai to remove the rags from the windows.

When he did, Yuan Shu hissed like a wounded cat and waved his left arm defensively as he crawled toward the corner of the room; the one with the shit, in which he then sat and curled into a ball.

"Heaven," Guo Huai commented.

"Leave me alone," Yuan Shu said from behind his shield of arms. "I am not holding court today."

"He's not sick," Stinger said. "He's lost."

Since no one approached him, the toad released the tension in his body, rearranged the hair framing his hollowed face, turned around, and dug in the wall again, the flesh at the tips of his fingers scrubbed raw.

Now that I got used to the sudden light, I could see the same two characters applied all over the shack. Every inch of baked earth was marked with the title "Son of Heaven," and most had then been scratched off. Sometimes, Yuan Shu has had his fun by removing a stroke or adding another.

I saw one *hanzi* for "sky" thus transformed into "dog," and another he had simply changed to "man."

Son of a man. Son of a dog.

Somehow, I thought the reunion between Yuan Shu and his father in the land of shades would not be pleasant.

"Pssst," Yuan Shu went on, his eye half-closed, throwing glances at the young boy. "Tell the General of the Rear to come and get rid of you, will you?"

"Uh, Colonel?" Guo Huai asked, confused beyond his wits.

I didn't like the idea of killing a man who had lost in mind, but maybe it was kindness. And it was an order, after all.

Yuan Shu waved his arms like a child when I came closer and crouched to his level, so I waited for him to calm down again. It took a long time, and a glance at Stinger confirmed I wasn't the only one at a loss. Our only order was to end Yuan Shu's life, but it all seemed ... unfair. Not the killing part, of course. Few people deserved death more than the toad. But killing him without even a few words, a last chance for this once powerful man to speak, felt wrong.

"Lord Yuan," I called, seizing him by the wrists to force his hysteria down, which, of course, did the opposite until I used enough strength to pin his arms against his body.

"Let me go, peasant!" he then shouted.

"I've been sent by the Minister of Works," I said, hoping he would think the Excellency was the one from his court. "We're here to help you." Yuan Shu relented his struggling, so I let him go. He blew a strand of hair from his face, and finally, I could take a good look at him.

The toad had never been handsome, but the years since the war against Dong Zhuo had been harsh on him. The abuse of drugs, alcohol, and delicacies had taken a toll, but the last few weeks of errancy had probably achieved the transformation from human to breathing ghost. Yet, even inside this decrepit face shone a petulant light.

"About time," he said. "We're wanting of everything here."

"Do you know where you are?" Stinger asked from his standing position.

"Of course, I'm on a pilgrimage," Yuan Shu replied, matter of fact. "The mandate of heaven is waiting for me at the end of the road. But don't you worry, I have good shoes." After he said so, the usurper wriggled his toes in my face and only then seemed to realize he was barefoot.

"Do I know you?" he then asked.

"We met in Suanzao," I answered. "You were our General of the Rear then."

"I don't recognize you," he said.

"I didn't expect you to," I said. "I was just a child."

"But I remember Suanzao," he said as if I had not spoken, a glint of happiness in his eyes. "Such a wonderful time we had there. Until the bastard turned on us." He meant his half-brother, Yuan Shao, though who turned on who first was up for debate. "They're all monsters, you know? And your master is the worst of them. He is a *mogui*, the evilest spirit plaguing *my* land."

So he did know who sent me.

"I was so close," Yuan Shu went on, opening a small space between his thumb and first finger. "So close to defeating him."

Stinger scoffed, which Yuan Shu did not seem to like.

"Lord Yuan Shu," I said, feeling sorry for him. "You were never a threat to him."

The toad hissed again, though this time in defiance.

"You were dancing inside my lord's palm the whole time.

He only let you live because you served him better alive than dead. You were a target for the whole empire's hatred and a buffer against the southern province. And since you were so easy to predict, *we* let you believe you could be an actual emperor. But now you are spent, and it is time to remove—"

"Colonel," Guo Huai said, interrupting me from my rant to notice the two streams of tears pouring down from the toad's eyes. I don't know why, but I needed him to hear those words.

"But I have the imperial seal," he whimpered. "The mandate of heaven is mine."

"No one cares about that," I replied, more gently this time. "The mandate isn't something given to you, and it is certainly not a piece of stone. One must grab the sky's will with both hands and tug on the dragon's tail until the world submits. You were never worthy." I heard my lord's words spoken with my voice.

"But Cao Cao is?" he asked. I did not reply. Cao Cao was worthier, if only because my lord relied on more than his name and wealth. But if heaven really chose him to hold their mandate, it spoke volumes about the gods' sense of morality.

"One day," Yuan Shu went on, "the world will see Mengde for who he really is. A devil."

"I don't know about the world," I said, then lowered myself to whisper in his ear, which proved a mistake because the toad smelled like a week-old dead mouse, "but *I* already have."

Yuan Shu's face, when I peeled from it, greeted me with the most unpleasant grin I ever saw, yellow teeth as stained as the bottom of his feet, and lips he had bitten to the blood repeatedly.

"That is good," he said, nodding.

"Good?" I asked.

"You are death," he answered. "And one day you will bite the hand of the lord that feeds you."

Mad people sometimes speak the most ominous prophecies, this is known, and I did not like Yuan Shu's. It suddenly became personal, and it was time to end it. I drew the knife from my back, for I would not stain Yingzhao with the fool's blood.

"I'll take care of it," Stinger said, taking a step closer.

"No need," I replied, lifting my arm to stop him. "He's mine."

"Killed by a peasant," Yuan Shu scoffed, "ridiculous."

He was not even fighting it.

"Lord Yuan. This," I said, showing him the naked blade of the knife, "is for Sun Jian."

"Sun Jian," the toad whispered as if the name would burn his lips. "Another disappointing piece of—"

The knife pierced skin, flesh, and heart in one swift movement before Yuan Shu could finish his insult. It was more than he deserved, but his death came fast and as painless as the situation allowed. He slumped against me as I retrieved the blade, his last breath foul and putrid already.

First Lü Bu, then Yuan Shu; the great lords of the empire were falling like flies, and I was cursed to witness their ends. For a second, as I stood and let Yuan Shu's body drop on the shit-covered floor of the shack, I wondered if I would be present at my lord's last moment on Earth and whether I would be holding a bloody blade as well.

I WOULD HAVE PREFERRED to leave this wretched place as soon as the deed was done, but the physician asked our help in burying his lord. I accepted, if only because I would unburden these two of their coffer. The cobbler complained about it until I remarked that I knew he had buried some of the treasure somewhere around and would not press him to find out where if he did not pursue the point. That got him quiet. I still warned him to be generous with the folks around here if he wanted to leave on his two feet. The physician asked for nothing, so I told him he should come with us and I would introduce him to my lord. There again, he refused, claiming that he still had patients in Lujiang commandery, but accepted our escort out of the village.

Yuan Shu was put in the ground near a pigsty, absent any riches because we knew the folks would dig him up before sunset. I did not feel the same sympathy for him as I had Lü Bu, so I did not even offer a prayer for his soul. It was just disconcerting to realize I would never hear of his foolish actions again. Yuan Shu had been the butt end of jokes for years, but at least he had lived with strong convictions and the guts to act on them. Not many do as much.

WHEN WE MARCHED BACK to Xuchang, three pieces of news awaited us.

First, Gongsun Zan had been defeated at last. Yuan Shao had all but destroyed his great citadel with underground passages, then burnt the fortifications of the Lord of the White Horse. Zan, as we heard, killed every last member of his family before offering his body to the flames. By the time the news reached us, Yuan Shao was already working on resupplying his massive army.

Second, Zhang Xiu, the son of a whore responsible for the death of Cao Ang, Cao Anmin, Dian Wei, Liang-the-broken, and thousands of others, surrendered to Lord Cao. I thought my lord would have arrested the bastard and let him hang from the northern gate of Xuchang until his body rotted, as I would have suggested, but instead he welcomed him with open arms and offered him titles, a rank in our army, and even the promise of a marriage between one of his younger sons and Zhang Xiu's daughter. I could not stomach this decision but quickly got over it because the third piece of news pleased me greatly. Guli and my two messengers had come back while we were away.

Guli buried her face in my chest when I hugged her, but her tiredness was obvious. They'd been back for a fortnight, so I could not guess why she still looked so, but that too I put behind us. I was back home with the woman I loved in my arms, and no matter what, I knew my lord would not send his armies to fight until spring.

We had one winter to get ready for the greatest battle of our time. And I had one winter to decide what to do about my lord.

13

Xiapi, capital of Xu province
1st month, 5th year of Jian'an era (200), Han Dynasty

I SPAT a rich gob of snot in front of Qilin's head in Xiapi's direction. I hated that place. If I closed my eyes, I could still hear the laughter of the officers cheering for the exhausted dancer, the screams of the Brothers of the Sword as our ambush backfired, and, of course, the rhythmical grunting of the platoon leader abusing the corpse of Lü Bu's daughter.

I did not close my eyes because I wanted those things to leave me alone for good, just as I wanted to depart this place and never see it again. If I acted to my lord's wishes, we would be gone before the end of the day. But that, too, I would have preferred to avoid. Following his orders, I mean.

To say that I harbored strong negative feelings for Lord Cao would be putting it mildly. We had avoided each other for the first half of winter, which I spent in Xuchang because Guli had trouble recovering from whatever ailed her. It did not appear life-threatening, but my lover hardly got out of bed in the morning, spoke to no one in the compound, and refused my affection more often than not. The Scorpions still received missions, none of them taking us far, but I handed them over to Du Yuan or One-eye.

However, when Cao Cao named Man Chong administrator of Runan, where the Yuan clan still cultivated some influence, and failed to decide on a replacement for his dealing with us, I was forced to meet the man face to face.

It went ... politely; this is all I can say about this reunion of sorts. My lord informed me of our imminent departure for Xu province, where we would crush Liu Bei before Yuan Shao could react. It had to be swift and merciless, of course. But it would also have to be done with a limited number of men. All winter long, Cao Cao had dispatched troops along the Yellow River, the natural border between his and Yuan Shao's territory. Xiahou Dun had been sent west to contain any sign of rebellion there; Yu Jin took the Dragon-Fang north of Chenliu, Cheng Yu the Tiger-Claw to Dong commandery, which he divided into several camps, and many other officers thus departed east, south, and to other locations in preparation for the great war. We left for Xu with Zhang Liao and Xu Huang's forces, both still under training and half full at best, Cao Hong's division, now that he didn't need to protect Nanyang commandery, and Xiahou Yuan's cavalry. My lord would lead the Qingzhou troops himself. And I was to bring the Scorpions with me to be used however he saw fit.

My men and I took no part in the action, which was indeed swift and merciless.

We destroyed Liu Bei's army in Xiaopei, the place he had been occupying once again to stop our advance. At the end of the battle, I saw him riding away, surrounded by a diminished guard. Zhang Fei, who had also been fighting there, was not counted among the dead or prisoners, so we assumed he had escaped as well. Cao Cao sent me among the corpses to ensure whether the man who should have married his niece lay there. While he wasn't, I recognized some of the soldiers from Liu Bei's retinues and offered libation in their names in the evening.

Next, we moved to Xiapi, which Guan Yu guarded.

By our estimation, less than a thousand men kept the city. Even if they focused on the palace's citadel, they would not resist us for long. My lord, however, had other plans. To preserve his strength, maybe, or because he thought I would dislike it, he sent a delegation to meet with Guan Yu and offer terms. I was part of this small delegation, and the other half consisted of Zhang Liao, our General of the Household.

"General of the Household," Zhang Liao repeated with a discreet air of derision. I sputtered a laugh at that. Iron Heart had a subtle sense of humor once you got to know him. "Why not General of the Kitchen?" He, of course, knew what *household* meant in that context.

"Should we introduce you as Marquis Zhang then?" I asked, enjoying Zhang Liao's face greatly. So far, he had done little for my lord, but Cao Cao insisted on rewarding him with titles and honors. I believe he used Zhang Liao as a symbol, proof to the world that Cao Cao was a forgiving leader ready to welcome worthy men.

"I feel indebted to him," Zhang Liao replied when I said so. "It will take me a lifetime of servitude to deserve those titles."

I wanted to tell him this was also part of the point but refrained. Zhang Liao was a man of honor, and I did not want to drag him into my secret conflict with our lord. He was no fool, though.

"I guess it explains my presence in our current delegation," he said. "Lord Cao wants a fresh recruit to offer terms to Master Guan."

"That and the respect existing between you," I went on.

"Is this why you are here?" he asked.

I didn't know how to tell him that Lord Cao had sent me as a punishment. In Cao Cao's mind, I was still the boy who would have given anything to kill the bearded warrior. Little did he know my respect for Guan Yu had grown each time we met, and I now considered him among the worthiest men of the empire. It was a strange feeling, and I would never forgive him for Uncle Cheng, but I could not deny I respected Guan Yu above most warriors, not only for his skills and courage but, first and foremost, for his unwavering sense of honor. Liu Bei, in my mind, was naive, and Zhang Fei was driven by emotions, as I was, but Guan Yu stood above, the perfect balance of duty, benevolence, and strength. Now that Lü Bu was dead, Guan Yu was a fair contender for the spot of the greatest warrior in the realm. The few others who contended with him in terms of reputation were Sun Ce, a general of Yuan Shao named Yan Liang, who was said to be undefeatable, and Zhang Liao himself.

"What do we tell him of his brothers?" Zhang Liao asked as we approached the bridge standing over the moat surrounding Xiapi. We were within shooting distance of the ramparts but hoped our slow approach had given enough time for Lord Guan to recognize us.

"We tell him the truth," I replied. "They probably live, but we don't know where."

"What do you think of our chances?"

"You know him better than I do," I answered.

"I know the warrior, the officer," Zhang Liao said just as the city gates opened. In between them rode Guan Yu, his massive halberd in hand. "But that's not who we are talking to today."

Zhang Liao was right. If we appealed to Guan Yu as a warrior, he would refuse our demands. His honor would not let him. We had to address the loyal brother.

"Greetings," Zhang Liao said as we both extended our arms, fist in hand.

Guan Yu did not reply but returned the gesture. He was as unreadable as ever. He clicked his tongue to order his horse to a stop, closer to us than I would have expected. In doing so, he put us within striking distance and told us this was his land, not ours. Mi Zhu, the long-whiskered advisor of Liu Bei, rode right next to him, and *he* saluted me with a warm smile.

"If you came for negotiating," Guan Yu said, "I'm afraid you tired your mounts for nothing. My brother trusted Xiapi to me, and nothing will make me betray his faith."

"Before we start the negotiation," Zhang Liao said, "you have to know your brother lives and has fled to the north. My lord wishes you to know that. I'm also supposed to tell you on behalf of my lord that he is glad to see you well and hopes the current conflict has not weakened your friendship. Now, we all know this is a pile of horse shit, but it had to be said."

Guan Yu nodded, and I scoffed a little. Noblemen have a strange sense of imagination. As if warriors actually said those things.

"If that is all," Guan Yu went on, lifting the reins of his horse as if about to turn around.

"Liu Bei trusted you with Xiapi," I said, "but the city is not all he entrusted you with, is it?"

The bearded warrior did not move and gave me the

same look I had received when we fought each other in Tan, half sorry, half deadly.

"You also watch over his family," Zhang Liao went on. "His wife and concubine are here, aren't they?"

"They are," Guan Yu confirmed, not liking where this was going.

"I hope Lady Mi is well," I said.

"She is," Mi Zhu replied. "Thank you for your concern, young Master Liao."

"What is it to your lord?" Guan Yu asked.

"If you submit and join us," said Zhang Liao, "they will be spared and remain in your care."

"I said no negotiation," Guan Yu replied, his voice hard and cold.

This was not going as planned, so I overstepped. Zhang Liao was a fearless warrior and an imposing lord of war, but, as he had rightfully pointed out, I knew Guan Yu, the man, better.

"I'm sure you've heard what happened to Lü Bu's wife and daughter," I said. Guan Yu and Mi Zhu stiffened at that. "Is this what you want for your brother's women, for your sister?" I then asked, looking at Mi Zhu. His gaze wasn't as friendly anymore. I could hear the grip of Guan Yu tightening around the pole of his weapon.

"If I give Xiapi to Cao Cao to save my brother's household, people will say Liu Bei lacked honor and put his family above the good of the people. A man lives and dies by his reputation. I will not harm my brother's so."

"Lord Cao has already promised to keep the people of the city safe," I replied. "No harm will be done to any of them, no matter if you resist or not. They and the population of Xu have already been given amnesty for following Liu Bei in his uprising. Lord Cao promised no taxes would be collected from Xu for the next three years, and no levy will be imposed for the next five. Xu is to be a haven of peace under his and the emperor's rule."

"Is this true?" Guan Yu asked Zhang Liao, which I found vexing.

"It is," Iron Heart replied. "You are not fighting for them."

This was the whole reason for Cao Cao's "generosity." If Guan Yu kept the fight going in Liu Bei's name, they would do so against the greater good of the people. They would say Cao Cao had offered generous, fair terms, but the ambitious Liu Bei refused them. His reputation would never recover; my lord would make sure of it. Cao Cao bet on Liu Bei caring as much about this reputation of a benevolent, just man as my lord cared about his name spreading fear.

"Fight," I said, "and your brother's reputation is gone. Submit, and your own reputation as a loyal brother will spread. Everyone and their cousin know Guan Yu does not admit defeat. They will say you acted only to protect your brother's family."

This had not been part of the strategy, but I also wished to appeal to Guan Yu's pride. Zhang Liao barely reacted when I improvised, but he, too, must have known how risky it sounded. Guan Yu could have chosen to take it as an insult.

Thankfully, he did not. I believe to this day, this was actually the argument that won him over.

"If I am to comply," Guan Yu said, to which Mi Zhu reacted by slumping a little in relief, "I have three conditions."

"Please, tell us," Zhang Liao said, taking the reins of the negotiation back in his hands.

"One," Guan Yu said as he slammed the butt of his

halberd into the ground and raised a finger with his other hand. "My brother's family is never to be harmed. No matter how my brother acts in the future. They will never be hostages to threaten him with. And no one is to approach the two ladies but me and my staff."

"Agreed," Zhang Liao said. He had spoken fast enough for our two counterparts to understand Cao Cao had guessed this demand.

"Second," he said, raising his middle finger. "I am serving the emperor, not Cao Cao. I want it known."

"We are all serving the emperor," Zhang Liao replied.

"It will have to be recorded, though," Mi Zhu said.

Zhang Liao nodded in reply. Cao Cao might not like that, but in the end, it was a trifle in the great scheme of things.

"And three," Guan Yu went on. "When I learn of my brother's whereabouts, I will be free to join him."

Iron Heart scoffed, and Mi Zhu sighed. This was preposterous. Guan Yu had basically asked to be given the right to betray Cao Cao whenever it sounded the most advantageous. Guan Yu did not represent as much as the conquest of Xu, but this would tarnish my lord's reputation more than I thought he would accept.

This, however, gave me an idea. Suddenly, I knew how to deal with my lord.

"We will present Cao Cao with your condition," I told the bearded warrior before our hesitation showed. "But I have one more for you if this negotiation is to succeed. No matter what happens in the future, even if you do join your brother again, you, Lord Guan, will never harm Cao Cao. This is a promise you have to make on your honor."

Guan Yu looked me straight in the eyes, attempting to guess what I was trying to do. Mi Zhu behaved the same way. They could not understand. Frankly, I wasn't certain either. All I knew was that the plan forming in my mind as we spoke required me to regain some trust from my lord. Forcing Guan Yu to swear never to take arms against Cao Cao was a good first step, though what mattered to me wasn't the oath in itself but Zhang Liao mentioning it to my lord. I had spoken for Iron Heart's benefit, not for them.

"Agreed," Guan Yu said, albeit reluctantly.

I thought I had taken the first step of a bold plan.

Little did I know I had just sealed the fate of the empire.

14

Xuchang, capital of the Great Han
2nd month, 5th year of Jian'an era (200), Han Dynasty

To the best of my memory, this had been Cao Cao's shortest campaign ever. Altogether, I believe we remained in Xu province for less than a week. It also happened to be the last time I set foot in that cursed province.

Since we had taken some of our fastest divisions, the march back to Xuchang was one of the swiftest I took part in. Our movements had a sense of urgency, so Cao Cao did not order any camp to be built. We swallowed the road, my lord actually riding ahead and leaving us to advance under the lead of Cao Hong. I spent those short evenings with Zhang Liao, Xu Huang, and, of course, Guan Yu, though the latter never left the wagon used by his sisters-in-law from his sight. I think fondly of this march, where warriors of renown shared cups, bowls, and stories as good comrades.

Because we still marched slower than the small party led by Lord Cao, I wasn't in Xuchang when he read the now famous call-to-arms sent by Yuan Shao throughout the empire. The general-in-chief had his secretary, the eminent scholar Chen Lin, write a manifesto attacking Cao Cao personally in an educated, petulant, yet insulting way. Everything my lord had done, and many things he hadn't, were described in this text. As usual, my lord was criticized for his ancestry, especially his eunuch grandfather. Cao Cao was also compared to another eunuch from the old times, who had allegedly caused the premature end of the Qin dynasty, and, of course, Yuan Shao was associated with some hero who brought the empire back on the track of peace. This document, I once heard, was the most copied text of our time, and Cao Cao had a lot to do with it.

While the story claims the document was so well-written, it helped my lord get rid of a migraine, some people who were present at the time told me he had nearly burst a vein long before reaching the end of the text. It wouldn't have helped his cause to bark at such a document, and, after some time pondering, my lord did decide to praise its quality and even had it copied. Even then, as I chewed through my blooming hatred for Cao Cao, I had to admit the genius of the man. I could never have reacted so politely to such an attack on my person.

From a warrior's point of view, it was a rather boring piece of propaganda, but I must admit Chen Lin's style was fascinating. However, the scholar, or rather his leader, made two mistakes in this document.

First, he claimed the heroes of the empire would rise upon receiving his call and even named two, Zhang Xiu and Liu Bei. The call-to-arms had taken too long to be sent, and of the two said heroes, one had already submitted, and the other had been utterly destroyed. It completely discredited the rest of the document.

Second, to us warriors, it felt forced. The constant

comparison between Yuan Shao and Cao Cao's forces, which the text claimed inferior, confused, and ill-led, sounded like the boasts we throw before a duel, and while it is a common practice before a fight, it is known the loudest barker is usually the most afraid. We could all feel Yuan Shao's anxiety in this declaration of war.

Yuan Shao, I believe, should have acted right as the document traveled to us to gain the upper hand in the battle. Instead, in a very typical manner for the flamboyant Yuan Shao, he took his time. My lord, however, sent warnings and reinforcements to every outpost along the Yellow River. And a few days after we arrived in Xuchang, he redirected the divisions toward their new destinations. Not me, though, and not Guan Yu either. In fact, one could say the only personal thing taking Cao Cao's time on those few days was showering Guan Yu with gifts and honors.

It wasn't just a question of turning Guan Yu into another symbol of my lord's generosity and respect for talented people; he genuinely hoped to seduce Guan Yu and thus prove he was better than Liu Bei. For that purpose, Cao Cao promoted Lord Guan to the rank of Lieutenant-General, offered Liu Bei's women enough silk to fill a room, and even proposed Mi Zhu become administrator of Taishan commandery. This happened on our first day back in Xuchang. On the second, Cao Cao invited Guan Yu to meet the Son of Heaven and asked the young emperor to elevate Guan Yu to a marquisate. Now there was no stopping him being called Lord Guan, and some even used the nickname of "Lord of the Magnificent Beard," following a comment from Liu Xie himself. Guan Yu was shaking upon returning from the meeting, the first time I saw him so perturbed.

And as a final gesture to gain the favor of the bearded warrior, Cao Cao gave him what I would consider a poisoned gift, Red Hare, Lü Bu's infamous steed. Guan Yu was touched most by the gift, although I know for a fact it had meant little to Lord Cao, if only because no one had managed to ride the stallion.

I know all this because I spent my days with Guan Yu. Not out of choice but because the new marquis had asked the Scorpions to guard his mansion, a request my lord accepted. Thus the Scorpions became glorified guards for Guan Yu's household, something they uniformly despised and pestered about to no end. I, too, could not stomach this assignment that kept me from the front line, though it gave me time to refine my plan.

Whenever I managed some time off, I generally spent it in Guli's company. She looked much better than before winter, at least physically, but I could see something bothered her to the point of depression. And if I, a man as knowledgeable about women as I was about the fabrication of silk, could see it, it must have been utterly evident to others. I did not relish those days with her. She barely spoke, ate even less, and refused the simplest gestures of affection from me. I think Guan Yu saw how miserable she made my life, which was why he invited me on a windy morning of early spring to a training session with Red Hare.

The stallion had been given to Lord Guan three weeks before, but he had yet to climb on it. He could tie the bridle and force the bit in its mouth, but that was it. Red Hare followed me and Qilin to a pasture outside the city, but whenever we got too close, it would try to bite us, probably remembering the last time the three of us had met.

"You should sell it," I said as, for the third time, Red Hare bucked when Guan Yu meant to pat its neck.

"It will take time, but I will conquer the horse," Guan Yu replied, eyes riveted on the horse's ears. He knew what he was doing; nothing speaks clearer of a horse's intentions than its ears. This detail so absorbed Guan Yu that he forgot to check the beast's teeth, which it bared a second before snapping them toward its new master's face. I tugged on the rope connected with the bridle to force it down, but it was all pointless. Red Hare was all muscle, and I could do little to make it obey. Guan Yu took a couple of small leaps back to get clear of the stallion's reach and twisted his head as if saying I may have been right.

"Can you imagine what it must feel like to ride it into battle, though?" he asked, arms akimbo.

"I'd be more afraid of my horse than the enemy."

"And they'd be more afraid of it than of you, which would be an amazing advantage, don't you think?"

"Perhaps," I replied, unwilling to concede such a good point. "Not that you or I will see some action anytime soon."

"You believe so?" Guan Yu asked, his breath back under control.

"Surely you have noticed all the officers have left the city already," I said. "If Lord Cao intended us to fight, he would have called us already. And by *us,* I mean *you.*"

"He may soon not have the choice," Guan Yu went on. "Have hope, young Liao Chun."

This was something I was in dire need of, hope. I was losing control of everything that mattered. My relationship with Tian Guli was turning savorless in front of my eyes, my men were getting dissatisfied with their lot, and while I needed to regain the trust of my lord, he was on the frontline while I attempted to break the most stubborn and brutal steed in the empire from a peaceful pasture of Xuchang.

Lord Cao would not call Guan Yu because, just as he had done with Zhang Liao and Zhang Xiu, he hoped to make the Lord of the Magnificent Beard feel indebted to him. And if Guan Yu ever set foot on the battlefield and fought in my lord's favor, it would reduce the said debt. Guan Yu was right, though; maybe my lord would soon have no choice. After all, his new officer was one of the empire's greatest warriors.

So far, the grandest war of our time proved a rather boring business. Skirmishes had taken place on both sides of the river, but little blood had been spilled. Cao Cao and Yuan Shao were playing a game of sorts with each player advancing and removing his pieces in search of a weakness. According to the latest report, a large division of men had crossed the Huang He and now threatened Xuchang from the northeast, but my lord was presently answering this threat himself with Zhang Liao and Xu Huang's men.

Despite what I claimed regarding Yuan Shao's apparent fragility, every report confirmed his army was stronger and well-supplied. They may not have our experience, but they benefited from the Yuan clan's immense fortune and would be thus well-equipped. It was also known for a fact that the four provinces under Yuan Shao's leadership harbored a pool of talented men and genial scholars. I doubted any of them could hold a candle to the likes of Guo Jia or Xun Yu regarding strategy, but disregarding Yuan Shao's tacticians would have been foolish. So far, they had kept our attempts in check.

Among the fighting men, our enemy also boasted a few renowned warriors. Yan Liang was their most famous, but his oath brother, Wen Chou, was said to be nearly as imposing. An old comrade of Cao Cao was also supposed to be a skilled leader of men under the banner of Yuan Shao. His name was Chunyu Qiong, and he, Yuan Shao, and Cao Cao had been colonels in the Western Garden Corps back when the world made sense. And finally, there was a name making itself spoken of more and more often around the campfires; Zhang He. This officer, a great martial artist, we heard, had distinguished himself against Gongsun Zan, and some bet *he* was actually Yuan Shao's top warrior. Both sides thus prided themselves with zealous champions willing to test their courage and skills in battle for the glory of their leader, and mostly for their own. I felt a hint of jealousy at not being among them.

"Lü Bu must have trained him viciously," Guan Yu said, taking me from my reveries as he scratched his head pensively.

"You want to borrow a slip from his scroll?" I asked.

"I would rather not," he replied. "But maybe ... Liao Chun, get on your mare."

"Yes, my lord," I replied instinctively.

"My lord?" Guan Yu asked, frowning and smirking at the same time.

"I meant *Lord Guan*," I stumbled, feeling the red coming to my cheeks.

Yes, this was the first of many times I would call that man as such.

I understood his idea immediately and could have kicked myself in the butt for not having thought about it in the first place. Red Hare was a war horse, above all. It would respond to any threat coming its way but would also expect its rider to meet their opponent from its back. So I climbed on Qilin in a nimble jump and unsheathed my blade, making it scrape loudly as it exited the scabbard. Red Hare picked it up right away, its ears pointing up and then scanning the area until they froze in my direction.

"That's it, look at me, you ugly bastard," I said, hitting the part of my armor covering my legs to keep the beast's attention. Keeping my eyes on the stallion, who started foaming at the mouth, I saw Guan Yu walking toward it from the mounting side, stepping lightly. Soon, even Qilin responded to the rising tension by tossing her head to the side and fighting against the reins in my hand. I raised my arms to look more menacing, then waved them in a wide arc. Red Hare snarled its big yellow teeth in a wolfish manner, and just then, Guan Yu dropped his hand on the beast's neck and jumped over its back before it could react.

For a second, everyone present held their breath, men and horses. There was absolute silence as we all wondered what would happen next. Guan Yu looked as surprised as I felt, and Qilin froze on her four legs. Red Hare reacted first by rearing so high it looked as if about to walk on two legs. Guan Yu held for a few seconds before ultimately flailing his arms and landing on his ass. He rolled away to avoid the beast's hooves, and I only allowed myself a snort of laughter when he stood back up, his face even redder than usual.

"Maybe it will take more time than I thought," the Lord of the Magnificent Beard declared, slapping the mud from his hands. "But you'll see, young Liao Chun, with a bit of patience, I always manage."

And with a bit of patience and a lot of our time, Guan Yu did get what he wanted. Three days later, Red Hare let its new master pat its neck without resisting. Another two days and he could ride it. Another week and Lord Cao called us to Boma, where Guan Yu, to my great surprise, was to fight.

15

Boma, Dong commandery, Yan province
3rd month, 5th year of Jian'an era (200), Han Dynasty

As I scanned the battlefield, I wondered if my intentions toward Cao Cao were so smart after all.

Cao Cao's genius shined bright across the plain through the waves of confusion shaking Yuan Shao's army. Messengers were running wild from one officer to the next, increasing the anxiety of the bewildered soldiers who stood without order or direction. This was Cao Cao at his best.

A few days ago, the enemy had established a beachhead by a ford of the Yellow River near a fortified town called Boma. The place had been evacuated a while ago because Cao Cao had ranked the ford among the most likely crossing points for Yuan Shao, meaning the city was now fortified and garrisoned by Zhang Liao's men. With a little over two thousand warriors, Iron Heart's chances stood low against the ten thousand who had already crossed the river, but this was without counting on our lord's cunning. With a celerity worthy of my former division, Yu Jin's Dragon-Fang marched at double speed a little north and east of Boma, toward another ford, then across the river as well. While Yuan Shao's men, led by the famed Yan Liang, worked on establishing the first step of an invasion, with all the logistics and baggage complications it implies, Yu Jin moved unburdened and would be ready to smash into Yan Liang's rear, on the other side of the river, in a matter of days, thus cutting the supply route of the enemy and leaving them stranded on our side of the river. When he heard about this fast-approaching threat, Yan Liang ordered the interruption of transportation so that he could send some men back to the northern side. From the slightly elevated city of Boma, it was easy to notice their numbers diminishing as boats carried men instead of supplies.

Yan Liang, confident he could protect the beachhead against Zhang Liao's two thousand soldiers, sent back two regiments. A grave mistake. One he would pay for dearly, though I guess it made sense from his point of view, and I don't think I would have acted otherwise. He may have been in control of the ford and the dike protecting the plain against the mood of the river, but this did not help his view of the city, and while his earlier estimation of our forces must have been accurate, he probably never noticed how many men joined Boma from the rear, one section at a time.

We, the Scorpions, Guan Yu, and a handful of his men were among the last men to make it to the fortified city, and it is nothing short of a miracle that we managed a spot inside, especially with the aggressive stead of Lord Guan among us.

Cao Cao was jubilant when we reported our presence to him. He knew his trap was about to shut on his prey. It had to happen the next day before Yu Jin could launch an attack he actually had little chance of winning by himself.

Guan Yu had one objective, killing Yan Liang.

On the first day of the battle for Boma, right after he had crossed the river, Yuan Shao's top commander had proven to the world his reputation wasn't overrated. My lord had, of course, given some resistance, if only because a landing force is a weaker target, but Yan Liang had crushed our efforts by fighting Xu Huang to a draw. This must have hurt the *youxia*'s pride, but, as he repeated when the story was shared, Cao Cao had only asked him to stall the enemy general. Nevertheless, Xu Huang admitted Yan Liang was formidable, both as a leader and a fighter. Which was why Lord Cao had called for Guan Yu.

Lord Guan was fresh as a plum the next morning when we stormed out of the packed city and spread our six thousand men in front of a baffled enemy. Their panic was a sight for sore eyes.

"Do one of you see him?" Guan Yu asked, hand over the eyes to help him scan the battlefield.

"No," Guan Yu's second, Mi Fang, the younger brother of Mi Zhu, replied almost immediately.

I didn't, either. The ground was unusually dry for this time of the year, and the milling of Yan Liang's regiments raised vast dust clouds. Even from our vantage point, we could barely distinguish the officers among the enemy ranks. The Yellow River was rather low, which made the dike nothing more than an obstacle for Yan Liang's men. Most were on our side of the structure, and it would serve as an anvil to our hammer. But first, we had to take their leader out, not only to assure our victory but to send a message to every fighting man within Yuan Shao's army. If Yan Liang fell in the chaos of the battle, they would fight to avenge him, but if a champion defeated him, they would lose heart.

Guan Yu's victory had to happen before our men charged into the enemy lines.

"There," One-eye, riding a little on the side, said, his finger pointing somewhere close to the path of rock connecting the dyke to the lower ground. "Just follow the flow of messengers, and you'll see him."

The archer was right; he was easy to spot this way. In the middle of a thick corps of shield-bearing soldiers, themselves standing behind a six-men-deep company of crossbows, Yan Liang struggled to get a semblance of order, shouting orders left and right atop a stocky white horse.

"I see him," Guan Yu said. Something in his voice made me shiver; a will of fire I would witness a few times in my life.

Guan Yu never wore helmets, but he readjusted the green turban keeping his hair away from his face. I, however, adorned my winged helmet, as much for protection as for my lord's benefit, a reminder of the pride I took in wearing his gift.

"Ready?" Guan Yu asked me.

"No," I replied, working the thong under my chin. The next few minutes would probably be the most dangerous of my life, and I could not believe how quietly Guan Yu behaved. My men, the few I had chosen for this suicide mission, looked no better. I had picked the best cavalrymen among them, except for Guli, who remained in Xuchang. Du Yuan tilted his head meaningfully when I exchanged a glance with him, and One-eye clearly wished to be anywhere but here.

"Would you feel better if I asked you to serve me some hot wine first?" Lord Guan asked, a smile he only wore before battle, reshaping his regal beard.

"Damn waste of wine," I replied, which made him chuckle.

"Lord Cao," he then called, twisting on his saddle to check my lord, who rode a few steps behind us. "When Yan Liang loses his head, please call for the charge."

"Are you speaking metaphorically?" my lord asked, his signature smirk in place.

"No such thing in the army," Lord Guan replied a second before kicking his monstrous stallion down the light slope.

"Scorpions! With me!" I shouted, taking Yingzhao from its scabbard and ordering Qilin after Red Hare.

My mare was faster than Guan Yu's from a dead start, but some of my men would struggle to keep up. I wished he would slow down a little, but we needed to throw caution to the wind and use all the speed given to us by the inclination of the slope, and the effect of surprise, if we were to accomplish our mission.

I closed my eyes to fight the wind but lost Guan Yu when he penetrated the cloud of dust. I whooshed in right behind and forced Qilin ahead, though she would not like running blind. Soon, I heard men screaming ahead and felt the familiar sensation of bolts buzzing past me like angry bees. None came close, and they just as soon stopped.

Qilin emerged from the cloud to the sight of archers scrambling about confusedly, a clear path of dead at the center of their unit. Guan Yu was already on the other side. I engulfed myself in his path of death, slashing my sword a couple of times to widen the way for my men.

This was utter madness.

By the time I had pushed through the crossbowmen, Guan Yu was already folding the guards from his reach, bringing his massive halberd in wide arcs that sliced through the solid straight-edged shields as if they were made of paper, and still managed to cut their bearers down. I forced Qilin into their ranks to give Lord Guan the support he barely needed and plunged my sword into the neck of a bewildered soldier. The poor man had probably woken up that day with different ideas on how he would spend it.

The Scorpions followed through, and the guards all but disbanded when the last of my horse riders joined the chaos, leaving a livid Yan Liang to meet us, spear in hand.

We had to act fast, kill the bastard, and retreat before the rest of the army realized what had happened to their leader, so I kicked Qilin forward, but Guan Yu would not let me. He blocked my path with his blood-dripping weapon, and one look at him sufficed for me to understand where my place was.

"This one's mine," he said before tugging the reins to force Red Hare to a walk. It was astonishing how well the beast behaved once in its element. Maybe it could feel the aura of strength evaporating from Guan Yu's sweating skin.

"Fight me, Yan Liang," he told the enemy leader, who remained ten *bu* further, mouth agape and eyes wide with fear. I'm certain in usual circumstances he was as fearsome as they come, but the image I got from Yan Liang that morning was less than flattering.

Yan Liang did not reply. Instead, he made a fatal mistake; he checked around for support, then over his shoulder.

Guan Yu was on him before his attention came back to us, and Yan Liang's head kissed the ground a few seconds before his body toppled like a bag of grain. Once it stopped rolling in the dirt, this head looked in my direction, an air of painful confusion forever painted on his face, even as Guan Yu trotted back to his victim and planted the tip of his blade in the stump of the neck. He lifted his trophy until he could grab it and slowly tied the head to the mane of Red Hare, using his victim's hair to do so.

"You should close your mouth," Guan Yu said as he trotted back to us, "you might swallow some dust otherwise."

As I watched the back of Guan Yu riding peacefully back toward Lord Cao while our army slammed into the panicking enemy trapped against the dyke, I was left to wonder how in the world I had once managed to defeat such a monster.

"What do you think would happen if Liu Bei were to die?"

This is how my lord started our face-to-face.

Boma had been buzzing like a beehive after our successful battle, the name of Guan Yu on everyone's lips. No one seemed to remember he had been our adversary not long ago, and they hailed him as the greatest champion of the realm for his audacious killing of Yan Liang. The Scorpions also received their fair share of accolades, and for the first time in months, we felt appropriately used.

Then, as anticipated, Lord Cao sent Guan Yu back to Xuchang with the order to present Yan Liang's head to the Son of Heaven. This was obviously an excuse to get our new hero back to the rear, where he would not reduce his debt any further, but, to my surprise, Cao Cao asked me to remain in Boma with my men. Less than a *shi* after Guan Yu's departure, I was invited to the house my lord occupied. There was no such thing as a palace in Boma, nor even what would be considered a mansion, so he had to make do with the city's chief house, a building half the size of our compound in Xuchang.

Cao Cao was deep into observing a map of the region when I entered. I took a knee, announced my presence, saluted my leader, kept my head down, and waited in complete silence. My lord made me wait for a couple of minutes, the motion from the lamp's flame in his hand the sole indication the man himself moved. The friction of his robes marked the moment he turned around.

"You may rise," he said in an imperial fashion.

Then he peered through my mind with those clever eyes that missed nothing, as he had so often in the past. I buried my rancor deep inside my chest and tried to remember the dashing young colonel of cavalry who had saved me from the pits. Digging for it, I unearthed some of my respect for the man and filled my mind with the admiration he used to inspire me.

"What do you think would happen if Liu Bei were to die?" he asked.

"My lord?" I asked, confused.

"To Guan Yu? What do you think would happen if his brother died?" he repeated. "I presume you do not believe he would really die as well, bound by the sacredness of their oath?"

I scoffed a little.

"No, I do not think so," I answered. "That *they* do is embarrassing enough."

"What then?" he asked before plugging the tip of the lamp. The light from outside was still strong enough to notice how his features remained unperturbed by my friendliness.

"Are you asking me if I think Guan Yu will then serve you or if he will join his brother?" I asked.

"Well?"

I thought about it briefly, wondering if Cao Cao had

received news of Liu Bei's death. This would be terrible for my plan, and I felt my bowels twist at the idea that I might be stuck again.

"I believe he would remain on our side," I said honestly. "Though not for you. No matter how well you treat him, you must have realized Guan Yu is not a man to be bought." My lord nodded in agreement.

"Go on," he said.

"He will serve you for as long as you serve the emperor," I went on. "And as long as you treat Liu Bei's women with respect. You will also need to give him chances to shine, as you did with Yan Liang. But, yes, I believe he would remain on our side."

"Good," Cao Cao replied, "because you are going to kill Liu Bei."

And just like that, my great plan backfired. I had, it seemed, regained Lord Cao's trust, and my prize was the murder of the one man I needed the most after Guan Yu. I knew there would come a time when I'd have to decide between following my lord or betraying him; I just hadn't expected Cao Cao to force the decision.

"When?" I asked before my hesitation showed.

"Tomorrow," Cao Cao replied.

I had one day. One day to decide if I was to save Liu Bei and use him as my way out or kill him and bind myself to Lord Cao for the remainder of my life.

CAO CAO DESIGNED ONCE AGAIN a simple yet cunning plan that I believe will make his fame last for centuries. He had long realized the weakness of Boma, which stood too far from our base for long-term defense. Sure enough, the enemy realized it as well, which is why, right after we dealt with Yan Liang, the enemy general Wen Chou, his men, and Liu Bei crossed the Mother River a few *li* south and west from us at Yan ford. A few *li* might not sound like much, but it put them right between us and Xuchang, and as such, they would cut our supply route.

We left Boma in a hurry, taking everything of value with us and marching so close to the enemy still crossing the river that they had to see us. They first saw six hundred cavalrymen, then a few thousand foot soldiers, and a baggage of a hundred carts filled with bags of grains, trunks of gear, and whatever their imagination let them picture. Then they saw how our men panicked upon sighting them and how they fled, leaving those carts and their horses on the plain without a single soldier to protect them. For a few *shi*, none of them acted on the unattended hoard, but they gathered at the edge of their yet unfortified area, peeling slowly away from the dyke serving as a protection for their division. A few of them, fearing their commander's bastinado less than the others, crawled to the carts, peered through their contents, and returned to their camp arms full of well-crafted materials, from armor to knives. The rumor spread, more left the cover of their units, and soon the plain was swarming with Yuan Shao's soldiers searching through our baggage.

I knew this for two reasons. First, it was my lord's plan. Second, scouts were reporting the enemy's movements as it happened.

While our officers in charge of the rear organized this feigned rout, we, the cavalry, kept going, then veered once away from the enemy's eyes and found cover behind a curve in the dyke, putting us three *li* from Wen Chou's men. Knowing that our time to act drew near, a wave of anticipation passed through the riders and their horses. I gripped Qilin's reins tighter, the thought of what I was about to do turning my bowels to a mess of tangled ropes.

Liu Bei's presence had first baffled me. I had thought him in hiding after his defeat in Xu, but he had apparently found refuge at the court of Yuan Shao. I don't know what the lord of the north planned for the imperial uncle, but when he heard of Guan Yu's actions against Yan Liang, Yuan Shao decided to put Liu Bei on the front line. I can only assume the man thought to lure Guan Yu with his brother's presence or have Liu Bei killed in the action if he turned out to be a spy. Whatever the case, my lord heard about it and meant to seize this chance to get rid of a cumbersome foe. Liu Bei was still secondary on his list of priorities for the coming battle of Yan ford. Killing Wen Chou took precedence. This is why he tasked me and my men to make sure Liu Bei died while he would focus his effort on Wen Chou. That I knew Liu Bei and would recognize him easily had pushed him to trust me with this mission.

There was still a big chance my sword would not be needed on that day. If my lord's plan came to fruition, the enemy's commanding circle would be the only ones not taking the bait of the abandoned baggage. They would be easy to spot at the back of their mass of soldiers and few in number. Six hundred cavalrymen would be enough to take Wen Chou and his guards down, and Liu Bei, who we assumed had a limited retinue, would fare no better. Chances were high that he would die during our charge. If he didn't, I was to end him.

Except that I still had no clue if I would accept my lord's order or follow my own path. I prayed for the gods in heaven to show me the way, then my lord's sword left its scabbard, the scrap of the metal on the lacquered wood calling me to the now before he lowered it toward our target. I nodded at my closest comrades, wondering for the first time what would happen to them if I truly betrayed Cao Cao. Then we left.

We abandoned any idea of discretion, moving from a stop to a gallop in a matter of heartbeats, staying as close as possible to the dyke to gain a few precious seconds of coverage before we came in view of Wen Chou's army spread like a swarm of locusts on a field of wheat. The whole plain came to life at once. Wen Chou's soldiers abandoned their looting, rushed to whatever weapon they had carried, and ran away from us for the most part. The bravest, or most obedient, came in our direction, but they would never reach us in time to protect their leaders.

Wen Chou and his guards were mounted as well, and as I rode close to my lord, at the tip of our cavalry, I saw them kicking their mounts the other way, thirty seconds or so before we could get to them. Not all fled on time, and my lord, jubilant from his victorious strategy, chopped the head of a panicking horse rider as we slammed the few of them who had remained on their spot. Cao Cao, despite all his faults and being well in his forties, was still a decent warrior and a great horseman, as he reminded us on that day. I managed to slip through the few stragglers without killing any of them but knew they were all dead anyway.

Then started one of the craziest chases I ever took part in. Wen Chou's riders numbered in the hundred. Not nearly enough to face us. They rode well, and the distance hardly shrunk for a long minute at full speed. But soon, we knew, they would meet a wall of spears and shields, for they were unknowingly riding inside my lord's palm. The last part of the trap was about to spring up.

Zhang Liao's men stood from the cover of the wild grass,

and the whole cavalry of Wen Chou reared, the neighs of their mounts announcing their fright. Zhang Liao's men charged and, being so close, would take a good number of foes before we punched from the back. The distance now vanished with each step of our horses. In ten seconds, I would have to do my part and kill whoever stood in front of me, even if it was the one man who could change my future.

However, just as I adjusted the grip of my blade, a big chunk of our target managed to slip away southward. Our cavalry was too big to react at once. That was it, I thought; if Liu Bei was within those dozens of riders, he could make it to safety.

My lord crushed my feeble hope, though.

"Chun!" he called, pointing his blade toward the escapees.

I nodded and regrettably tugged Qilin's reins, taking us away from the massacre about to take place in pursuit of whoever thought to get away from my lord's grasp. Those riders pushed their mounts to their limits, especially when they climbed the closest hill. A rather large wood stood on the other side of it, and if they managed to reach it, they would be lost to us. Not knowing of the small forest's presence, some split in other directions, but I remained on the tail of the group of seven men rushing toward it. I risked a look over my shoulders and saw that only five of my comrades had followed me.

"Is that him?" Du Yuan called, his voice barely reaching me, even if he rode so close I could see his gelding's muzzle breathing warm clouds of air.

I nodded in reply, for I was now certain Liu Bei stood among those seven riders. Fate had pushed me in his wake, though for what purpose, I still did not know.

The woods came closer. In a minute, Liu Bei would lose

himself there, and we would be lucky to see him again. Nature was still young this early in the year, but the trees had leafed enough to hide the inside of the forest. Without my men nearby, I would have given up the chase, but they were witnesses, and while I trusted them with my life, I did not want to involve them in my potential betrayal. If I had to choose between my plan and their lives, I would choose them. So I kicked my mare for more speed, knowing she had some more to give.

Liu Bei's six men suddenly came to a halt and reversed their course. They came at us to gain their leader some time. They were brave men, some of them I probably even knew. This was my chance. Using one of the few cavalry tactics my men and I had worked on, I gestured for them to split on both sides, hoping to divide those riders as well.

From the corner of my eye, I saw Du Yuan and Pei Yuanshao ride away on my left while One-eye and the Meng brothers went to the right. It did the trick, and five out of those six riders went to intercept my comrades. It only left Liu Bei and the one who had chosen to come at me.

"Move out!" I yelled at him as the young man locked his spear under his armpit to skewer me. I didn't know him but had no wish to kill him. I reversed my grip on Yingzhao to strike with the back of the sword. In one swift movement, I dodged his thrust and slammed my blade on his forehead, hoping that the shock wouldn't be enough to kill him. I heard his body drop to the ground but paid the young man no more attention, for Liu Bei was penetrating the woods, and I was right behind. Maybe, I thought, I could do better than just let him go.

"Liu Bei!" I shouted as Qilin passed between two saplings. "Stop!"

I doubt he heard me, and if he did, he ignored my calls.

The forest quickly grew thicker, the trees wider, and what had been a furious chase turned into a careful trot. Liu Bei rode well, and it took all my skills to catch up with him, but slowly I did. Qilin was shorter than Liu Bei's mare, an advantage in this environment.

"Liu *huangshu*!" I then called, hoping that using his imperial nickname would help him realize I came in peace. It didn't, though he noticed me this time.

Liu Bei pushed his mount a little harder. A few seconds later, as the imperial uncle checked for my progress, his mare caught herself in the root of a venerable tree and fell. Her neighing lasted for a long time before she stood up again, riderless. Liu Bei rolled on his shoulder and faced me in one agile movement, unsheathing his second *jian* sword before I could tell him it was useless.

"If you come for my life," Liu Bei snarled as I stopped my mare five steps from him, "you should know it will come at a price, young Liao Chun."

Liu Bei wore a face I did not think existed in his repertoire, a mix of anger and hatred. The last months had been hard on him, and sleep must have become a rarity, judging by the hollowness of his cheeks. To be honest, he scared me a little. Liu Bei could fight and now stood on the *sidi*. A corner of my mind wanted me to fight him and let our duel decide my path.

"Lord Liu Bei," I said in a soothing tone.

"Save it!" he barked. "If this is to be my end, so be it. I've lost everything! Zhang Fei is gone, and Guan Yu has betrayed me. The Han dynasty is as good as dead with your lord in charge, and your men are fighting with the last of my comrades. So, do it, Liao Chun, take my head and earn your—"

"Will you shut up!" I said. "We don't have time for this."

I dismounted before Liu Bei could resume his speech full of self-pity and removed the sheath from my belt, into which I slid my sword before tugging the lot in a loop of my saddle. Liu Bei's confusion was evident on his face as I took a series of quiet steps in his direction, hands held high in a show of peace.

"Guan Yu didn't betray you," I said, stopping at an arm's length from the man. "He joined Cao Cao to protect your family. They are safe in Xuchang, and he doesn't know you are with Yuan Shao; otherwise, he would never have fought Yan Liang, believe me."

"Why should I believe you?" he asked, refusing to release the tension. "You wanted us dead, your lord wants my head, and I know you think I'm just a naive dreamer."

I couldn't argue any of those points, so I didn't.

"Listen, I don't have time to explain everything, but you have to trust me. My men are coming here anytime soon, so just listen, all right? Guan Yu made a pact with Cao Cao that whenever he hears of your location, he would be free to join you. Cao Cao agreed, but if you are with Yuan Shao, he will never accept to let Guan Yu go, as you can imagine."

Liu Bei slowly loosened the grip on his swords and let his arms dangle.

"You need to distance yourself from Yuan Shao. Find another place to go."

"My brother really still follows me?" he asked, eyes tearing up.

"Yes," I answered, slightly annoyed because I thought I heard someone calling my name. "Listen to me!" I snapped again because I could see Liu Bei was losing himself in the thought of his brotherly bonds. "Go away, don't send us any message; it would be intercepted. Instead, make as much noise as you can, and wait. We'll come for you."

"Why do you do this?" Liu Bei asked, his frown from before back between his eyes.

"Chun!" someone called from my back. He was still far, but I recognized Du Yuan's voice.

"I'm doing this for the emperor," I said. It wasn't the truth or not all of it, at least, but I didn't want to waste any more time, so I used the one argument I knew Liu Bei would not discuss. "Now go, toss your cloak and your helmet first."

While he did, my name resonated in the forest, closer and closer. Sadly, as Liu Bei meant to climb on his mare, I noticed she was keeping a hoof from the ground. The root from earlier had made her limp. I sighed, knowing what I had to do.

"Take her," I said, offering the reins of my loyal mare to the imperial uncle. Liu Bei took them but could see how much it hurt me. "She was chosen by someone precious to me, so you take care of her, all right?"

He promised he would, but parting with Qilin wasn't the only thing that had made me sigh. If I came back to my men without my horse but otherwise looking as fresh as the winter snow, they would know something odd had happened. So I told Liu Bei to hit me.

"Make it believable," I said as I closed my eyes.

"The emperor is right to think of you as a friend," he replied.

Then came pain.

Oh, he made it believable. Liu Bei broke my nose in one straight punch that sent me on my ass and made me see blimps of lights long after he rode off on my mare's back.

"Chun!" Du Yuan called.

"Here!" I answered, my voice distorted by my hands keeping my nose shut.

"*Tian-na*," my comrade said as he jumped from his gelding. "What happened?"

So I told him the story I would later tell my lord. Liu Bei's horse had tripped, her rider tumbled, I thought he had died of the fall, but when I approached him, he hammered me with a stone, then took my horse and left.

I could see Du Yuan didn't like my explanation, and neither did Lord Cao, but since he had just earned himself another victory and killed Wen Chou, Yuan Shao's second most famous general, he quickly let it go. He even went as far as offering me a new horse because Liu Bei's would never recover. His gift made me feel ashamed of my actions against him. Somewhere, deep within, the Lord Cao of my childhood still existed. Then I thought of the emperor's favorite he had strangled and shut my heart again.

I owed everything to that man, but fate had let me save Liu Bei's life, and when the time came, I would join him.

16

Xuchang, capital of the Great Han
8th month, 5th year of Jian'an era (200), Han Dynasty

THAT SUMMER, the heat rose to amazing heights in our part of the empire. The night offered no respite to the scorch, and no cold air seemed to find my bedroom windows. As I struggled to please my lover, our sweat mixing at the base of our bellies, I told myself this was why she did not match my efforts. Then again, I was tired of finding excuses and being the only one trying.

It had been a year since she came back to Xuchang after I sent her to save Ma Dai, one year that I failed to arouse her in any way. I knew women could be mysterious creatures but never thought the northern ones to be so impossibly difficult. I had given her everything. Time to heal from whatever ailed her, then comfort during her recovery. I had kept her from the Scorpions' missions, though those were not many anyway. And, following some advice from my men, I bought her jewelry of jade or gold. I knew she wouldn't care much about any of it, but I was desperate.

Her embrace had no strength, not even when we made love. Her eyes were fleeting from mine. Even our breathing no longer matched. This had been the case with each attempt from me to rekindle our lust, but this time was worse; I could feel it like a bucket of cold water over my head.

Yet I could not see what could have soured her mood even more.

Nothing had happened. Nothing since my return from Boma. The Scorpions had resumed their boring task of surveilling Guan Yu's mansion. Cao Cao and Yuan Shao had reached a stalemate near Guandu, the great fortress protecting the capital in the northwest. I had yet to go there, but I heard the whole area was now covered with trenches, pits, and the carcass of innumerable siege engines. So far, we had gained one victory during those long months, when Xu Huang and the Brothers managed to burn one of Yuan Shao's supply depots near a town named Gushi. But the enemy leader snapped his fingers, and more supplies came from the north, which he crammed into a stronger fort at Wuchao. This war was going nowhere.

As far as I was concerned, the greatest news came from Runan, which Man Chong administered, and where Liu Bei had been spotted a few days ago.

According to the reports I heard, Yuan Shao had given Liu Bei a small troop with direct orders to destabilize Cao Cao's rear. He took his new soldiers to Runan, one of the closest cities to Xuchang, and allied himself with local bandits calling themselves Yellow Turbans. Whether they truly belonged to my former creed, they, and Liu Bei, were mounting a form of resistance against my lord. I guessed the imperial uncle did so to follow up my plan rather than actually trying to battle Cao Cao. I would have preferred him to cut ties with Yuan Shao completely, but Liu Bei had done what he could with what he had. Whatever his reasons, Liu Bei and the Turbans disturbed my lord enough that he sent Cao Ren and the Third to deal with them.

I had to act fast if I wanted Guan Yu and me to join Liu Bei before Cao Ren annihilated him. Yet I could not just tell Guan Yu about his brother's whereabouts, or he would simply force his way out of Xuchang. Too many details had yet to be arranged for my plan to have a chance. I wasn't ready. I had yet to find how to broach the topic with Guan Yu or trick Cao Cao. I needed time, and I needed hope. Thus I had kept my plan from my men, only confiding in Guli simply because the silence between us had become too heavy.

I was actually close to giving up on my attempts for that morning, Guli's blank, fleeting stare taking my pleasure away, when Pox barged into my room.

"Sorry, Chun," he said, red and breathless. "You got to come. It's Guan Yu."

That he did not even linger on Guli's naked chest told me something serious had happened.

I never ran so fast in the streets of Xuchang before. In usual times, this could be considered a minor criminal offense to disturb the capital's peace the way we did. But, with Cao Cao and most of his staff being near Guandu, the law had slightly relaxed in Xuchang. No one stopped us anyway, and I arrived at Guan Yu's mansion panting and sweating in equal measures.

The shouts guided me from the entrance, still guarded by two of my men, to the western side of the courtyard, near the stable, where Du Yuan stood his ground in front of a menacing Red Hare, its master dressed up for war. I have to give it to my second-in-command; he was brave beyond words, standing so close to the monstrous steed and refusing passage to Lord Guan.

"And *I'm* telling you, you are going nowhere until Lord Cao agrees to it," Du Yuan shouted back at Guan Yu, whose face squinched.

Behind the Lord of the Magnificent Beard, a wagon pulled by two more horses waited. I saw Mi Zhu climbing down from it and guessed his sister would be inside.

"What is happening?" I asked.

"Thank you for showing up," Du Yuan said with a tone of reproach. More than any other member of the Scorpions, he hated this assignment. Du Yuan would have preferred to be near the frontline, reaping the rewards from dead bodies and possibly sampling their camp followers.

"Your man refuses to let us go," Guan Yu answered from the bottom of his cavernous voice.

"Where are you going, Lord Guan?" I asked, fearing his answer.

"To my brother, of course," he boomed. "As Cao Cao promised I could."

"You know of your brother's whereabouts?" I asked.

"And so do you," Guan Yu replied, a tone of murder in his voice.

"Chun?" Du Yuan asked. "What is he talking about?"

"Can we speak in private?" I asked Guan Yu, hoping that *my* tone would be enough for him to understand the difficult position he was putting me in.

"Why?" Du Yuan asked as he grabbed my arm by the biceps. "Chun, what's going on here?"

"Captain," I replied, using the rank I had recently been allowed to bestow upon him, "you'd better let go of me now." Du Yuan was my friend, but I made my stare cold and hard for him to understand he was overstepping. He challenged it for a few seconds before finally releasing his grasp. I knew a conversation with my second would soon happen, though whether he or I would start it remained undetermined.

"We still need some time to get the wagon ready," Mi Zhu commented, cutting through the tension like a knife through a piece of tofu.

"Very well," Guan Yu said, nodding. "Let's talk while the servants ready the vehicle."

Du Yuan hissed like a snake in my back as I followed Guan Yu to the garden. As if guessing our purpose, a servant carried a platter with some cups and a fuming pitcher of hot water toward the small gazebo lost at the center of a small pond. It was too early for wine, but it was way too hot for boiled water, so I left mine on the side while explaining the situation to Lord Guan, telling him of my encounter with Liu Bei and keeping only my purpose from the conversation.

"You not only knew where my brother was but also met him and told me nothing of it?" Guan Yu asked, barely containing his ire.

"If I had told you, what would you have done?" I asked.

"I would have ridden to Liu Bei through wind and rain," he answered, fist hammering the table between us.

"And you think my lord would have let you?"

"He promised," Guan Yu said.

"Guan Yu," Mi Zhu, the only other person inside the gazebo, said, his soft voice once again doing wonders to the rising tension. "Surely you understand why Cao Cao cannot simply let you go to Liu Bei as long as he remains with Yuan Shao?"

The bearded warrior grunted, as close to an admission as we would get.

"Lord Guan," I went on, "I have a plan. And your brother

is following it as we speak. You need to trust me and give Liu Bei and me some time."

"What is your plan?" Guan Yu asked.

I would have preferred to keep it to myself for a little longer, but I also needed to make Guan Yu trust me. So I told him.

I told him I would use Liu Bei being a thorn in Cao Cao's side to our advantage. When the moment was right, I would let my lord know of Guan Yu's intention to rejoin Liu Bei and offer to accompany him to get Liu Bei to stop fighting and leave Yu province. I would then remain with the imperial uncle and Guan Yu. Cao Cao would be tempted to refuse, but I would push him to accept.

"How?" Guan Yu asked.

"Because I will go with you," I answered. "Because my lord still believes I hold a grudge against you and will truly believe that I remain by your side as his spy."

"Why are you telling me this?" Guan Yu asked, his frown suggesting how little he liked my idea.

Guan Yu could be really thick. Contrary to Cao Cao or Liu Bei, he was simply incapable of judging people's motivations and inner thoughts. It was oddly refreshing but could be plain annoying as well.

"Because he will not be his spy," Mi Zhu said.

"I will not be his anything," I went on. "I am leaving his service." That was it. I had finally told someone of my intentions. The weight of it floated out of my chest.

"You would betray Cao Cao?" Guan Yu asked. He still wore his dark frown.

"May we ask why?" Mi Zhu asked as well.

Why? Such a simple question with no easy answer. Some issues cannot be expressed in words, especially those that torment the heart. I could not stay with Cao Cao because that would make me an associate to many people's suffering. I always knew my lord followed his ambition first, but for a long time believed this ambition matched a greater purpose. Serving him, I thought, would help end the chaos disrupting the empire. There was a time I also thought of myself first, and Cao Cao was a sure way to fame and glory. I could no longer do that. Once you look into the eyes of an innocent in pain, there is no coming back to holding the knife hurting them. I didn't expect them to understand the exact nature of my anguish, so I summed it up in as few words as possible.

"Because it's the right thing to do," I said. "I cannot serve a monster anymore."

It was a weak argument, but I hoped my honesty would convince Guan Yu. They looked at each other; Mi Zhu, I knew, would want to believe me. Lord Guan, on the other hand, needed some seconds of pondering, which he spent slowly drinking his cup of fuming water. Nothing mattered more to him than loyalty, and even for good reasons, he would think lower of me for betraying Cao Cao. I hoped he would still find it in him to understand me or at least realize I was his best chance.

"Very well," Guan Yu said after a smack of his lips, his cup now empty. "We will give you some time. But if I hear nothing from you in one week, I will take my leave with or without the approval of you—of Cao Cao."

I thanked him and assured both men one month would be enough. As I left the mansion, though, I wondered if I had gained enough trust back from Lord Cao to move on with my plan. The failure in capturing Liu Bei would weigh against me, but Cao Cao had little more to complain about in my case. However, as I returned to the compound, I pushed this issue from my mind. I had other things to think about.

Guan Yu knowing of his brother's location was one thing I could understand. The reports mentioning it might have been confidential, but I was hardly the only one to know about it. However, Guan Yu knew that I knew, and there was only one person in Xuchang at the moment with this particular knowledge.

It was time for me to have a serious conversation with Guli.

I DIDN'T EVEN NEED to put Du Yuan back in his place as I stormed out of the mansion, and simply informed my men everything would return to normal. Alone, I retraced my steps to the compound, stomping more than walking as I entered the building. The staircase cracked under the weight of my burning anger. How dare she go over my head and tell Guan Yu of information I had trusted her with? Guo Wen observed me from the first floor. He meant to say something, but I opened my hand to order his silence. My heart was beating like a war drum as I slammed the door of my bedroom open.

And there she was, her back to me, looking out the window, just as the first time I entered that room. She was dressed now and even wore a cloak. She was as beautiful as ever, or as she used to be at least, and my ire just vanished. In its stead was a thirst for comprehension. I needed to know why she had told Guan Yu. Why she had been so gloomy and cold to me over the past year.

"Why—" I asked.

"I did it for you," she said, looking over her shoulder.

"You've been suffering for too long. I just wanted to make things move on for you."

"I needed more time," I said. "You knew I needed more time. Why did you have to tell him so soon?"

"Because—" she said, interrupting herself with a tremor announcing her internal struggles. "Because I needed to do something nice for you. Before I go." She sobbed upon her last words and brought her hand to her mouth. I then noticed the bundle in the corner of the room. Her possessions. Clearly not all of them.

"Go?" I asked as I crossed the room. "Why would you go?" I found that my voice was shaking as well. A sharp pain made itself known at the center of my chest. A cold, stabbing pain right under the sternum.

"Because I did something bad," she said. Her whole body shook. I put my hands on her shoulder to reduce the tremor. I could not see what she could have done that deserved her departure and said so after dropping a kiss on top of her head.

"Chun, I lost a child," she said as I slid my hands to her hips. It froze me to the spot.

How could I have been so stupid? It must have happened while she accompanied Ma Dai back to Liang and I went to end Yuan Shu's life; either on her way back to Xuchang or soon after. No wonder she could not get any better. Guli had never wanted a baby, but it was her baby nonetheless. She had no one here to grieve with, especially with me away or so absorbed with my own issues. Even worse, it probably happened because I asked her to ride so far with Ma Dai. Riding a horse is one of the worse things a pregnant woman can do. I had not known she was expecting our child, or I would never have sent her. This was my fault more than it was hers.

"No, Chun," she replied when I said as much. "I lost *a* child."

Guli spoke our language as well as anyone born in the empire by then, but I didn't understand her meaning and made her look at me so that she could explain better. The guilt in her eyes, the way she looked away, told me what she had meant.

"Who?" I asked, every ounce of compassion vanishing from my chest as the fire coursed through my veins.

"Chun," she feebly said, looking away from me again.

"Who?" I shouted, shaking her so that she would look me in the eyes. "Tell me, who did you sleep with?"

"Chun. It's not his fault," she said. The worst thing that could have come from her mouth. She defended the bastard who had taken my woman instead of defending herself. I was enraged at the thought of my sweet Guli having sex with another man and made myself menacing.

"Guli, by the Sky, tell me or ... or I will hurt you."

"Ma Dai," she said, stopping me with my hand in the air, ready to strike.

I did not hit her but found myself being the one shaking.

"Ma Dai?" I asked, a piece of my mind refusing to believe what I had just heard.

Shy, discreet little Ma Dai? That Qiang bastard, whom I had welcomed with open arms, whom I had treated better than anyone had ever done in his life, repaid my kindness by sleeping with my woman? How could he? How could she?

Suddenly, Guli's beauty vanished. She was a mess of tears and snot, falling on her knees and begging my forgiveness. There would be none. How many times had she told me I would never marry another woman because they didn't act like this in her culture?

I remained stone to her pleas, focusing all my strength on keeping my rage inside rather than taking it out on her. She had meant the world to me. I used to think we would eventually have a family together. If she hadn't lost her baby, I would have raised him as my son or daughter unknowingly. This was no way to treat one's lover, not after everything we had gone through together.

Guli let go of my robes and slumped even deeper on her knees, hiding her shame inside her palms. I moved to the corner of the room, grabbed the bundle, returned to her, and dropped the bag in front of her.

"Get out."

"Chun, please—"

"Get out! Get out before I kill you!" My voice no longer belonged to a human being but to a wounded beast.

She crawled to her bundle, then stood with pain, her sniffling interrupting her sobs. Head down, she passed by me, the smell of her skin filling my senses for the last time as she walked toward the door.

"Chun, I really wish it went differently," she said.

"And I wish I hadn't stopped Du Yuan when I first met you," I said.

Never in my life had I voiced such awful words, and for many years I regretted them being the last I spoke to the first love of my life.

Guli left.

I did not throw a tantrum this time. I didn't have the energy for it. Instead, I remained by the window, my nails digging into the wooden frame while the day drank my pain minute after minute.

When someone entered the room, I did not need to turn to guess who it was.

"How come you are always here when I am at my lowest?" I asked.

"That's what friends do," Guo Wen answered, a forced yet warm smile on his lips.

He stood next to me, silent, for a while. We watched the sun bathing the city in gold. The shadow of the palace extended over the capital, almost to the point of touching the eastern wall.

"Is it going to hurt for a long time?" I asked.

"I don't know," he replied. "I guess it will fade away like every pain," Guo Wen said, massaging the stump of his arm as he spoke. "She loved you, you know." I did not reply. "He loved you too. Like a brother. They just loved each other more."

"You knew," I said.

"Not about the baby. I swear."

I believed him.

"And she tried. For a long time, even when her feelings were clear to her, she tried to stay true to you. When you came back from Xu, she tried her best to love you again, like before, and Ma Dai tried to stay away."

"Why wasn't I enough for her?" I asked, not wanting my friend to bring the image of the young traitor into my brain.

"Chun, we are talking of love. There is no such thing as enough or not enough. In love we just are, that's it, and sometimes we are no more. You and Guli have grown together, but it was time for it to end. Everything ends, even if we don't want it to."

Despite his lack of education, Guo Wen was the wisest of my friends. Yet a part of me wished he would just curse her with me. I so needed to make it her fault, even though I knew it was as much mine, or no one's really.

"I miss her," I said, as finally I could take it no longer and dropped my head on his shoulder to cry in peace.

"I know," he replied, patting the back of my head with his one hand and hugging me closer with his amputated arm.

"I said horrible things to her," I went on through my tears.

"And she did horrible things to you. Now, you're even, and you can move on to the next step of your life."

Guo Wen was right; more than he knew. This was the last straw. Guli's departure was the sign that my old life had reached its end. It would take me three days before my mind stopped asking the same question over and over again. Now what?

Now was the time to do something dramatic.

Now was the time to move on.

17

Ningqiang county, Yi province
12th month, 4th year of the Jingyuan era of the Cao Wei empire (263)

"My apologies," I tell the scribe as I fold the cloth into which I had to blow my nose.

"None needed," he replies, using this break to clean his brush inside a square of silk. "The sadness of a heartbreak never really goes away."

"Don't get coy on me," I go on, snorting a fake laugh. "I'm not tearing up; I'm still sick, that's all."

Chen Shou makes a face suggesting how little he believes me. He is right to doubt my coldness toward my own story. It took me many years to stop thinking about Guli and even more to forgive myself for my last words to her. I may not hold the same grudge against her or Ma Dai, but the pain never truly left, and thinking about our separation has this magical way of making me twenty-three years old again. I can still remember the scent of my room as she left me to my own self, or the sensation of Guo Wen's arm on my back. Though he died a long, long time ago, I miss my old friend dearly.

"I wasn't apologizing for that, but because I spent too much time recounting a story that has little to do with your task. An old fool's love story, nothing more."

"I doubt it will make it into the official history," Chen Shou agrees, "but I am glad you confided in me."

"Me too, my young friend, me too."

Now that I think about it, I don't think I have told this story to anyone for more than three decades. It gives me a warm feeling of relief to speak of Guli after so long.

"Did you ever see her again? Or maybe hear from her?" Chen Shou asks, his indiscretion accompanied by a light blush.

"If I did, would you really want me to tell you all about it now?" I ask, taking solace in my audience's interest.

"Now, who is coy?" he says.

"Guilty," I reply after a short giggle. "But I think it's time we go back to the story you are supposed to write about instead of losing time on such a trifle. As far as you are concerned, Guli left me for good, which is good because I might very well have stayed with her and thus would have never married my wife."

"I heard she was an amazing woman."

"She was the best," I reply right away, the prickle of tears threatening to shame me again. "Strong but sweet. Clever but silly. And beautiful beyond words. No such woman ever walked the earth before her, and none will ever after, of that I'm certain."

"Do you want to talk about her now?" Chen Shou asks, a smirk drawing itself at the corner of his lips.

"In due time," I answer. "All in due time."

He sighs, and I laugh, but the truth is I don't think I

could speak of my Ladybug so soon after ending my story with Guli. It would be disrespecting her memory.

"So," the scribe goes on, blowing on the tip of his clean brush, which can be used again. "How did you approach Cao Cao with your plan?"

"You're going to like this story," I tell him, even daring a friendly wink.

To this day, I still believe the events about to be retold are some of my greatest battles. I was young, strong, and determined. Cao Cao was desperate. And together, we would shift the balance of the war.

Guandu, frontline of the war between Cao Cao and Yuan Shao
9th month, 5th year of Jian'an era (200), Han Dynasty

Guli had taken a piece of me with her; the piece that worried about the future. So when I approached my lord as he stood motionless on the ramparts of Guandu, I wasn't nervous. I knew what needed to be done, what I had to say. The night air was refreshing and the sky clear besides a few clouds lazily treading between us and the realm of the gods. Cao Cao was by himself, which suited me fine. I had come with half of my men but came to him alone.

"Liao Chun?" he asked, surprised to see me here since he had not requested my presence in Guandu. "Everything all right in Xuchang?"

"Yes, my lord," I replied, giving him my most reassuring smile. "I just needed to speak with you."

"And decided to take a few days' journey to the front?" he asked.

"Well, people say the view from Guandu is breathtaking," I answered, which made him laugh a little. It was good to approach Cao Cao in a friendly manner. Since his son's death, I had never spoken with the man without a ball in my belly. And the view was truly breathtaking, though not because of its beauty.

The night sky was clear enough to get a good sight of battlefield. It was indeed marked with dozens of trenches cutting the land at regular intervals and hundreds of small fires lightening the places where soldiers waited for the next assault in a mixture of mud and blood. Between those rows, innumerable carcasses of siege engines and fallen mounds for archers gave the land a bit of relief, while the river Bian naturally separated us from Yuan Shao's main camp, twenty *li* to the north.

"And now that you have taken the sight in," Cao Cao said, "why did you really come here?"

I breathed in, knowing the following conversation might be the most difficult of my life.

"Guan Yu asked to leave Xuchang," I said. Cao Cao sighed and slumped a little forward, using the wall for support.

"He has heard about his brother then?" he asked.

"He did."

"Do you know how?"

"Does it matter?" I asked, using my lord's favorite form of communication, a question to answer a question.

"It does not," he said.

"What should I tell him?" I asked.

"What do you suggest?"

"Is Liu Bei a threat?" I asked. I knew the answer to that question, but I needed Lord Cao to answer it first.

"Not really, but he could prove troublesome," he replied, shaking his head slightly.

"Then let Guan Yu go," I said. "Surely you've understood he will never abandon his brother, no matter the gifts you bestow upon him or the potential rewards."

"Chun, you have seen what he did to Yan Liang. Imagine he stands on the other side next time."

"He promised never to harm you," I reminded my lord. "Guan Yu is a man of honor; he won't go back on his oath."

"Men of honor also lie," Cao Cao said.

"No, they don't," I replied.

He did not like that. I had basically just called him an honorless man, but he knew I was right about Guan Yu.

"Tell him as soon as his brother surrenders, or retreats at

least, then he will be free to go," Cao Cao said. "Just say this is to guarantee his sisters-in-law's safety or something. That should keep him quiet for a while."

"My lord, may I suggest something else?" I asked.

Nervousness came back at this point. I suddenly found my throat dry, and the words came with difficulty when he told me to go on. I still managed to explain my idea.

I would volunteer to accompany Guan Yu to his brother, who would persuade Liu Bei to stop fighting, then I would remain with them under the pretense of betraying my lord. I said my frequent outbursts with Cao Cao were no great secret, and it would be easy to fool Guan Yu and his naive brother. From there, I could spy on the brothers and their next lord, and work however my lord saw fit.

Cao Cao remained quiet for a while, but his intense gaze never left me. I could not read him, but I thought he could hear the ruckus my heart made in my chest.

"You would be gone for a long time," he said. "How about your responsibilities in Xuchang? Do you really believe you would serve me best under Liu Bei rather than at the head of my Scorpions?"

"Lord Cao," I said, "I can no longer lead the Scorpions."

"How so?" he asked.

"I've lost their respect."

I told him how the last couple of years had robbed me of my position within the Scorpions. It was all my fault, I said. I even mentioned how my lover had betrayed me for nearly a year, which they all knew but never informed me of.

"I can give you new men," Cao Cao simply replied.

"Thank you, my lord, but they are the best. They will serve you well under someone else's command. If you allow me, I still wish to ask some of them to accompany me on my new assignment, but I doubt many will follow."

"Is it really what this is about?" he asked. I had guessed Cao Cao would sniff something of my motives and had decided to give him a bit of honesty if it came to that.

"My lord," I said, "while I want to help your cause, I cannot do so from Xuchang anymore."

"Is this about Lady Dong?" he asked, his unwavering gaze making me feel small. Even more so because I was about to lie through my teeth.

"I understand why you had her and her clan killed," I said, "but I still cannot stomach it. I don't blame you for anything, Lord Cao. It is just that I helped you bring the emperor to Xuchang and feel responsible for his pain. Do you understand me?"

I wondered how many people had ever asked this question to Cao Cao. Probably not many. And he was a little baffled.

"I do," he replied. "But you just admitted your feelings of guilt and your displeasure of my actions against the concubine of Liu Xie. How could I send you away for possibly several years to work with a member of the imperial family?"

Good, I thought, now I could really explain the reason for my presence. I went on one knee and held my fist inside my hand in salute.

"You know me, my lord, I might be blunt, but I am your man. I have bled and fought for you since my childhood. We may often disagree, but I have never betrayed your trust. I only ask that you remember my successes and judge me fairly, despite our recent arguments."

I was afraid it all sounded rehearsed, which it was, but Cao Cao's pause led me to believe I had scored a point.

"You have served me well," Cao Cao acknowledged, "but that was before. How can I be sure where your heart lies?"

"How can I prove myself to you, my lord?" I asked.

He scoffed and laughed as he said, "How about you win me this war?"

"Consider it done," I said, which cut right through his laughter.

"Are you joking?" he asked.

"No such thing in the army," I replied.

Cao Cao's face, a mixture of confusion and doubt, will remain with me until the day I die. I don't believe many men managed to make him look as such, and in itself, it was a victory. The best part was that I hadn't spoken through my ass. I actually had a plan to tip the scale of the war a little, one only the Scorpions could manage.

So, for the last time, I led my brave comrades between the jaws of war and would make the name of Cao Cao resound like a terrifying howl through the Empire.

We were going to storm Wuchao. We were going to kill Yuan Shao's hopes of victory.

"Tight as a walnut," is how Pei Yuanshao described Wuchao. I knew to trust our certified burglar when it came to assessing the penetrability of a fortified camp. "The kid hasn't lied."

The said kid, who was actually a couple of years younger than us at most, slumped in relief. We had tied his hands behind his back, so he used his shoulder to wipe some sweat from his face. This had been a long morning for him.

"So, no entry points, back door, or even a slightly floating plank to slip through?" I asked.

"None," Pei replied. "As far as I could see, they don't let their soldiers out, even to visit the camp followers."

"Poor bastards," Meng Bobo commented.

"How about the password?" Du Yuan asked.

"Couldn't get close enough to hear it. But the kid said they change it every watch. There's no way I could learn it and then get us back in time to use it."

"I swear, they change it every two *shi*," the kid said, a face imploring us to believe him. I did. We had caught him as he took an impromptu break from his sentry mission, five *li* from the supply depot of Wuchao, where the result of the war would be decided, if I could get us inside. We had prevented him from raising his flag to alert his comrades, dragged him down from the flimsy tower where he held his post, and replaced him with Meng Shudu, just for the look of it.

"When I left, it was *mogu*," the kid went on.

"Mushroom? That's your password?" Du Yuan asked, thinking very little of this choice.

"You stay on watch for a whole day," One-eye said. "How do you do if passwords last only one watch?"

This was a good point, and as we all switched our attention back to the kid, he melted a little inside.

"We give our name and that of our direct officer. He is then called to the gate to make sure of our identity. Please, I'm telling the truth." The kid folded in half until his forehead touched the ground, his sobbing barely under his control.

"Should we ask Stinger to make sure?" Pox asked, leaning on the pole of his dagger-ax. On cue, Stinger took a step forward, his hands already working the case of instruments strapped from his shoulder.

"No need," I replied. "Even if he lies, we can't do much about it." I doubted we could get all in pretending to be scouts or sentries anyway. Even then, it was doubtful we could fulfill our mission in time while sneaking into the supply depot. We had until midnight to act, or my lord's troops would head back to Guandu. He had taken a huge risk in removing a whole division from our main base and advancing them through the trenches until they reached the limits of our digging. Upon seeing the flames devouring Wuchao, they would get in position to intercept Yuan Shao's reinforcements, for surely the general of the north would attempt to rescue his supplies, or so I believed. In one strike, we would burn all his food and crush a large portion of his army. The latter part of the plan was offered by Guo Jia, while burning Wuchao was my idea. Xun Yu, the second of my lord's tacticians at Guandu, believed Yuan Shao would rather use our attack on the depot to send men to Guandu, which would be less defended, so Cao Cao left Zhang Liao in charge of it. Cao Cao himself would be present with the interceptions forces, along with Xu Huang's Brothers and Yue Jin's independent regiment. If they saw no fire in the night sky, though, they would head back. We had to act fast, and we were nowhere closer to infiltrating Wuchao.

"Tell me again of the inside," I asked the kid.

"It's, uh, it's a large camp. Bigger than the others on the march."

"Thank you, mister obvious," Du Yuan said.

"It used to be a village," the poor sentry went on. "So there are some houses of earth used by the officers. The rest is like usual, just rows and rows of tents."

"How about the silos?" One-eye asked.

"Oh, right, the silos. Well, there are a good dozen of them. Huge things, those. Almost as tall as the watchtowers. By the way, there are ..." Here his eyes went up as he remembered the layout of his camp. "Twelve of them. There are twelve watchtowers with big crossbows."

"The silos," I repeated.

"Right. There is a dozen of them. Each has a large trap door on the top, with a ladder to access them. But the ladders are always guarded by a tent section of men."

Du Yuan's tongue clicked in his mouth. I shared the feeling. It would be a tough nut to crack, indeed.

"How about the man in charge?" I asked.

"General Chunyu Qiong? What about him?" the kid asked, eyes round with renewed fear.

"How is he? Cruel? Lax?" Du Yuan asked for me.

"No, he is ... well, to be honest, he is drunk more often than not." The kid thought we would appreciate his humor, which we did, but not for the reason he thought. They had a weakness, after all.

I was surprised to learn that Chunyu Qiong had been put in charge of a supply depot. Now that we had dealt with Yan Liang and Wen Chou, he was Yuan Shao's most experienced officer. That he had been given this post was either proof of the depot's importance or a punishment to the man. This general being a drunkard led me to believe it was the latter. From what we had gathered, Wuchao was guarded by a little under two thousand men. Not much for a vital spot, too much for my half platoon.

"Chun?" Pox asked, probably worried by the vicious grin Du Yuan and I shared at the moment. We hardly agreed on anything recently. That we now did could not be a good sign for the others.

"Are you thinking what I'm thinking?" Du Yuan asked.

"If you're thinking we'll get in from the front door, then yes," I answered.

"Gods in heaven," Pei Yuanshao said, which summed it up perfectly. We would need their help, for my plan was very likely to get us all killed.

"What do you need?" One-eye asked.
"Some ink," I replied.

The unlucky captain went over the document for the third time as if the answer to his current problem hid somewhere along the lines I had written earlier. He wiped the sweat pearling on his bald head with the back of his sleeve, the constant tapping of my foot doing nothing for his nervousness.

"Well?" I asked, obtuse to the extreme.

"My apologies, sir. If you would just let me get one of the senior officers, I'm sure they—"

"And what would be the point of sending the army controller if I let you inform your superior of my visit, uh?" I asked, a voice so petulant you would think it was born between the dowager's legs. "This is worse than expected," I went on, closing my eyes and bringing the tips of my fingers to my forehead. "Write it down," I then told Pei Yuanshao standing next to me, a brush at the ready and bamboo slips stretched over his left forearm. "Complete lack of cooperation from the captain of the guards. What is your name?"

"My, uh, my name?" the poor captain asked.

"Yes, your name!" Du Yuan barked, the perfect hound to my petulant officer act. "Are you deaf on top of being stupid?"

"Li Miao, sir, captain of the—"

"It's *Army Controller Liao* for you," Du Yuan replied, taking a bold step toward the hapless captain, who took one back.

"Enough, Major Du," I said in a tone that could not be

bothered. "I am certain Captain Li will remember how to address his superiors. Won't you, Captain?"

"Yes, Controller Liao," the man replied in a clear, obedient voice.

I made a small gesture toward Pei Yuanshao as if to ask him to cross out the name he had just written and heard a snicker from the Meng brothers, who enjoyed the show very much.

"So," I went on, clapping my hands palm to palm, "are you finally going to open the door, or should I ask the general-in-chief himself to come here? Surely you would believe him, then? Not sure you would have much future in the army afterward, of course."

The captain hesitated but must have understood he had little choice in the matter. And the idea to let a dozen people in might not have looked like much of a threat anyway.

"Let me take you to the colonel in charge then," he said, nodding to his soldiers for them to open the camp's door.

"We did not travel all the way here for a colonel," I snapped. "Take us to General Chunyu."

"But, uh, Controller Liao. General Chunyu is ... on his watch of rest."

"You mean he is drunk, isn't he?" I asked, pursing my lips with contempt. "Just as the general-in-chief feared." I invited Pei Yuanshao to take more notes. "Even better. I insist, take us to Chunyu Qiong right away."

Captain Li found nothing to reply to and turned on his heel before stepping inside Wuchao camp, the supply depot he was just letting his enemy infiltrate. *So far*, I thought, *so good*.

I lifted my chin as I followed the good captain, putting my hand in front of my nose in an exaggerated attempt to fight the dust of the place. My act, if I do say so myself, was quite brilliant. I wondered if most pettish officers or ministers I had ever met started off joking about it and found themselves enjoying the role so much it became part of them.

When the idea came to my mind, I wondered for a few seconds if some of my men would be more convincing in the role of the army controller. I was still young for such a rank, especially in Yuan Shao's more traditional army, but my companions could hardly pass for one either. Plus, I told myself, the helmet marking me as a man of high standing was mine, and I would be damned if anyone else wore it. I borrowed Pox's blanket, the cloak of a now long-dead target from the Scorpions, and used it as it was supposed to be once more. It had seen better days, but after six months of war, no one wore clean clothes anymore, so it had found my back and now dusted the floor of Wuchao with each of my peevish steps. My left hand rested lazily on the ring of Yingzhao's pommel, and I avoided as many gazes as I could to complete my act. No one interrupted us until we reached General Chunyu's house, into which went the captain after telling us to wait outside. I told him to be quick about it.

There was a shout, then something crashed, a jug probably, followed by a series of curses. One minute later, the captain came out, then stood straight as a spear pole. His general followed a few seconds later, struggling with a difficult belt and eyes half-closed against the sudden light, even though we were close to dusk.

"Who're you?" the general asked as he stepped out of the farmer's house.

"Who am I?" I asked, dropping my hand on my chest. "Didn't your captain just tell you? Captain, the document?" I snapped my fingers toward Captain Li, who then rushed to hand his superior the small roll of bamboo.

General Chunyu blinked hard several times as he attempted to decipher my perfect imitation of Yuan Shao's calligraphy. While I would never write naturally as Yuan Shao or Cao Cao did, I could still more or less copy their style if I applied myself to the task. The tone might have been slightly off, as was the choice of words, but for a half-drunk, half-awake officer, it would suffice. Cao Cao would be proud of me, I thought, before catching the idea by its tail and remembering my lord's acknowledgment was no longer my concern.

Chunyu Qiong had a paunch to make the late Gongsun Zan jealous, small veins that popped all over a tired face, and eyes standing apart that showed neither intelligence nor cunning. His camp, which we had crossed from south to the center, was well-maintained, and the men boasted an air of professionalism. The defenses were solid, the archers alert, and the silos well-protected. Whoever had prepared Wuchao was a good officer and was clearly not the general.

"Where's the seal?" Chunyu Qiong asked. "There's no seal."

"The seal?" I asked, stupefied. "Are you seriously asking me about the seal? Where were you at the last war councils? Were you even there? Or were you drunk on that day too? We don't use seals since they have been counterfeited on several letters. *I am* your seal as far as you are concerned."

"And you are?" the general asked, as he took a couple of steps to hand me the scroll back. I nodded for Du Yuan to take it for me.

"The document just informed you who I was, General. I am Liao Dun, controller of our great army, as you should know."

"Last time I heard, that wasn't you," he replied as he finally managed to buckle his belt.

"My promotion followed the sad passing of my predecessor, Controller Gao," I said.

"Old Gao died?" Chunyu Qiong asked, not looking cross about it. "What was it? Arrow? Bolt?"

"Dysentery," Du Yuan replied.

"Poor bastard," the general went on, shaking his head. "That's no way to go."

"While I agree with you on that point," I said, "I don't have time to lose in sorrow. Shall we?"

"The missive says you're here to check the camp's security?" said Chunyu Qiong, who had already forgotten about the lack of seal. *Confuse the leader, confuse the army*, Master Chen Gong had taught us.

"Yes, among other things," I replied, looking down at him so he would feel the implied threat of my presence. "General Yuan Shao and other staff members fear a repeat of Gushi's failure would prove too much for our soldiers to bear."

"Not my fault *that* depot was taken by the enemy," the general said.

"Nevertheless," I went on, "*I* have work to do and wish to report to our illustrious leader before sunrise. Shall we?" I asked again, and this time, grumbling through his teeth, the general led us away from his command center, which reeked of cheap wine by then.

Chunyu Qiong did not let his scowl rest for as long as we moved from one silo to the next, then along the wall. Every stop was the occasion for me to dictate some notes to Pei Yuansho, who I could see barely wrote a decent character of the inspection. My men climbed the ladders, now accessible thanks to the kind orders of the general. One-eye and Guo Huai, in turn, inspected the trap doors, then the grain, before ultimately coming back down and informing me of the perfect condition of the structures. They were smooth, and no one noticed the little *gifts* they dropped inside the silos.

It went as hoped until the last of them, where an officer with a mean-looking scowl expected us.

"My apologies," he said, sounding as sorry as I was glad for the interruption. "May I see your orders?"

"Colonel!" the general barked. I believe he was more hungover than drunk at that point. It didn't make him nicer. "How dare you interrupt Controller Liao?"

"I am just following the protocol," the officer replied, not even flinching at his superior's outburst. No love lost between those two.

"It is fine," I said as Du Yuan handed the man the roll. "And you are?"

"Colonel Lü Weihuang," the man replied with a perfect salute, which I returned. I knew then he was the man really in charge of Wuchao.

"Colonel Lü," I replied, smirking. "Finally, a name to report positively to the general-in-chief."

Lü Weihuang kept his face of stone, unmoved by the flattery. *Whatever,* I thought, this wasn't for his benefit. *"Whenever two men lead, divide them,"* Cao Cao used to say.

"The controller is very busy; step aside," General Chunyu told his subordinate, who agreed after a couple of tense seconds. I gestured for One-eye to climb up the ladder, knowing he possessed our last *hot box*, as Stinger called them. This competent colonel did not let my archer from his sight as One-eye examined the trap door, then the quality of the grain. I needed to get his attention. Fortunately, Lü Weihuang was the one who got the conversation going.

"Apologies," he said again, "I do not recall you from the staff of our general-in-chief. Did we meet before?"

"Unlikely," I replied. "I recently came back from convalescence after the battle of Boma."

"You were at Boma?" Lü Weihuang asked, finally a hint of respect in his voice. I had chosen to name this battle because few people from their side survived after Guan Yu slew Yan Liang. The panic had been total, and my lord's men eager to score this war's first victory.

"I was. And if poor General Yan had listened to my words of caution, he would still walk among us. Truly, Cao Cao is a scoundrel, but his men are vicious in their fighting." I thought he would comment that he didn't think anyone had actually survived the battle, but he let it go as One-eye came back down. I needed to prevent him from asking too many questions.

"Colonel," I said, "could you please call for the men to gather by the forum? Those not on watch, of course. I have new directives to share with them."

"Surely an announcement to the officers would be enough," the man replied.

"While I do not doubt the quality of some officers," I went on, almost whispering, "others give me little confidence if you know what I mean. I would rather speak to the men."

"Of course," he said, bowing before leaving to fulfill his order. Lü Weihuang might have been an efficient leader, but he bore the same ambition as any other. Getting on the good side of the army controller was a fairly safe path to promotion.

"Before I address the men," I told the general, who had started sweating heavily despite the cooling of the evening air, the lack of alcohol getting on his nerves, "let us review the instruments."

"The instruments?" the general asked, mouth agape.

"Yes, the instruments. The drums, the gongs, the bells, I assume you have heard of them? Well, some soldiers who made it out of Gushi claimed they couldn't hear the alarms. A bunch of nonsense from cowards if you ask me—"

"Rankers ..." the general commented before spitting a rich gob of saliva.

"Yes, well, even if the general-in-chief insists we check the instruments."

So, as Lü Weihuang crossed the camp and sent men to gather the soldiers in front of the forum, we methodically played with drums and gongs. At first, it caused a ruckus, and soldiers ran to their weapons in droves until the word spread that this was just an inspection. By the time we banged the last gong, they did not even react anymore.

The night was nearly full when I stepped on the stage of the forum, where the general and his four colonels in their best attires expected me, along with half of the soldiers crammed into the supply depot. I hoped the hot boxes would soon fulfill their role, for I did not believe my improvisation skills would keep the crowd for long. Stinger's absence, I told myself, had been a mistake. I had left him in charge of our prisoner and manning the watchtower in our absence. Stinger had offered to make the young man silent, which was his way of suggesting to kill him quietly, but I refused. He had done nothing to offend us, and I wished him no harm. Since we needed to leave one man behind, it might as well be the scariest-looking member of the Scorpions. He had taught us how to use his precious boxes, but since we had no experience with their timing, I could only rely on his guess.

The boxes were rather simple devices; fairly thin logs of damp wood into which we dug holes, with special care in carving a plug from the waste. At the bottom of the hole, we dropped glowing pieces of ember. They would keep burning for a long time, and when the humidity of the wood dried out, the log would quickly heat up. The thickest boxes were dropped into the first silos, and Stinger calculated they all should start the fires pretty much at the same time. This was a wild guess, but I had learned to trust that man's peculiar skills. When Pox asked him where he had learned to make those items, Stinger answered that we didn't want to know, and there too, I trusted him.

I nodded to Lü Weihuang when General Chunyu introduced me to the three other commanding officers, but the colonel did not react. Something was off, and I prayed once more for those damn boxes to fulfill their role as soon as possible. My hope was feeble, but our only chance to make it out alive from Wuchao was for chaos to spread before the enemy realized who had started the fires. Lü Weihuang, I thought, was the greatest threat to this plan. So far, though, I did not think he had spotted the disappearance of two of my men.

For once, luck was on my side as far as the weather was concerned. The night was shrouded in thick darkness born of low-hanging clouds. Not the kind that would smash my plan to pieces with a sudden rain, just those which shielded us from the moonlight. Darkness would prevent the most alert soldiers from seeing the smoke rising from the silos, and by the time the flames burst bright, it would be too late. At least for the supplies. What happened to us Scorpions remained in the hands of fate.

"Controller Liao," General Chunyu called after clearing his throat. "Would you like to speak?"

"Yes, yes," I replied, brushing the bottom of my armor as if about to address the ministers at court.

"After your address," Lü Weihuang said, "we would very

much like to hear your account of Boma's battle." *We,* I understood, were the four colonels, who presently looked at me with something like hunger in their eyes. Hunger for the truth. I felt the trap ensnaring me as I replied that I would be much obliged to do so but would have to make it short on account of my return to headquarters. *When deceiving the enemy, get your plan down to the smallest details, but keep your words vague,* Cheng Yu had taught us. Boma, I now realized, had been the wrong choice. Few of them had survived, meaning they knew each other to some extent. Worse still, I had been there, on the other side, wearing the same helmet as I did in Wuchao. I rarely wore a helmet when riding and had only done so that day to impress Cao Cao and regain some of his trust. This detail might come biting me on the ass as I deceived Wuchao's soldiers. Now I truly hoped the boxes would prove their usefulness quickly.

One thousand pairs of eyes dropped on me as I took a step toward the front of the stage, my mind struggling between the content of my address, which I still ignored, and the possibility of having to explain my presence at a battle the team of colonels knew I had not attended. I still thought the destruction of Wuchao would take place, but my faith in us surviving the night dwindled dangerously low.

I was about to open my mouth when an alarm rang. A bell from the eastern side of the camp, where we had dropped the last of the boxes. The soldiers looked at each other with questioning gazes, but since they had heard similar sounds for the past thirty minutes or so, none reacted. The colonels also shared a confused look with their leader.

"Two of my men are still inspecting the bells," I said, jumping on the absence of the Meng brothers to explain those sounds. Chunyu Qiong accepted the excuse and gestured for his soldiers to remain quiet.

When he did so, I heard the scrape of Du Yuan's sword regaining the bottom of its sheath. My friend was on edge, knowing as well as I did that one step in the wrong direction meant our imminent death. The bells kept going, so I took the center of attention.

"Soldiers!" I called, using all the strength of my commanding voice. "Defenders of Wuchao! I am Liao Dun, controller of the army under direct order from our grand leader Yuan Shao."

From the corner of my eyes, down the stage, at the back of my few men, I noticed the return of Meng Bobo, whose nod indicated he had successfully accomplished his task.

"I am pleased to tell you I approve of Wuchao's defenses!" I said, which was met with a wave of relief, both on and down the stage. "But let's not forget the importance of this place. The enemy will try anything to take us down here, as they did in Gushi. Will we let them?"

"No!" the soldiers shouted back in unison, covering the sounds of a second alarm from the west this time as they raised their fists in the air.

Du Yuan was right by my side, but all the others stood in front of the stage. My second and I were dangerously outnumbered. I also had no clue how we would get out of the camp, especially before Yuan Shao's reinforcements came to try to salvage their supplies.

"Soldiers of Justice!" I called, but another voice interrupted me just before I could tell them of some spurious reward in case Wuchao held for the length of the war.

"Fire!" a breathless soldier shouted. "The silo is on fire!"

We all looked toward his outstretched arm and noticed the first flames appearing on top of the furthest silo, neither the first nor the last one we had "inspected." If I remember correctly, it was filled with the horses' fodder.

The rumble from the soldiers' panic spread fast, and soon reached the stage.

"Colonel Lü," I called, "send a company to extinguish that fire."

"A company?" the colonel asked, confused beyond words. "We should send every soldier not on duty!"

"Controller Liao, I concur," the general said, for the first time agreeing with his subaltern.

"One company is enough to take care of one silo," I replied. "Or do you mean to say your men are not trained for the occurrence of an accidental fire?"

"No, but—"

"Then one company. What are you waiting for?"

"Second regiment, first company! To the fire!" Lü Weihuang shouted, his eyes never leaving mine, even as his men obeyed with alacrity. I had hoped he would go with them, but Lü Weihuang thought otherwise.

Even if he had sent the whole regiment, it wouldn't have mattered. Their tanks of water, the ones needed to take the fire down, would be nearly empty, courtesy of Meng Bobo's adept hand with a chisel.

"My friends!" I went on, stepping out of character in an attempt to regain some of the soldiers' attention. The ruckus remained as strong. Strong enough to cover the appearance of more bells.

"Soldiers!" I then snapped, to no avail. The chaos of men searching for a semblance of direction engulfed the forum. Because I knew where to look, I spotted the lines of smoke floating above a couple more silos.

"Sir," Lü Weihuang said in a tone that could have earned

him the bastinado. "I insist. We need to send more men; this could be an attack."

"Nonsense," I replied, returning my attention to the slowly panicking crowd. His sword came out of his scabbard before he spoke again.

"Guards!" he called, and I didn't need to look at the colonel to know his blade was pointed at me. "The enemy is here!"

More blades came to life, those of the three colonels, Du Yuan's, my men down the stage, and the guards who stepped from the front of the crowd to surround them. I kept mine where it rested because I still hoped to gain some time. One fire would not destroy the camp.

"How dare you point that blade at me?" I asked, turning around to face my foe. In the process, I saw the light from another fire erupting from another silo.

"Colonel?" Chunyu Qiong asked, taking a step closer to us.

"General, step away from that man!" Lü Weihuang barked.

The whole camp came to life as three more *whooshes* birthed almost at once. The closest was so near that I felt the heat licking the side of my face and saw its burning light giving depth to the lines of Lü Weihuang's face. His three comrades stepped up, Du Yuan came next to me, and the half-circle of guards tightened around my men, backing themselves against the stage. And in all of this, Chunyu Qiong remained helpless.

I knew then that I could keep the masquerade going no longer.

I nodded with respect toward Lü Weihuang, then let my crude smile creep onto my lips. Time to be the leader of the Scorpions for the last time.

Spinning on my heels, I put myself behind General Chunyu Qiong, drew my sword out in a smooth gesture, then drove its tip under the fat general's chin.

"One more step, and he dies!" I shouted.

They froze, even Lü Weihuang. The sudden stillness allowed the chaos of Wuchao to make itself known to us. Suddenly it was as if dozens and dozens of bells were ringing. Gongs too. The fires multiplied and spread to other structures. The soldiers had naturally dropped their standing position and rushed to their comrades' help. The forum was near empty, with only the guards' corps in our presence. The heat grew so fast I had to half-close my eyes against the pain. It was all too late for them. Wuchao was condemned. But unless a miracle took place, so were we.

"What's the plan now?" Du Yuan asked.

"Get on the stage!" I told the others while the guards remained in their spot under threat of their general's life.

"You bastard!" Chunyu Qiong barked.

"General," Lü Weihuang said, his face turning uglier from the maelstrom of hatred he shouted at me. "My apologies, but the law is clear. Military officers are never considered hostages."

"No," Chunyu said, his body slumping with the realization that he was about to die, betrayed by his subaltern. Sadly, it also meant the older man protected me from nothing.

"Kill them!" Lü Weihuang shouted, but his bellow was interrupted by the sounds of neighing horses. And just as the panicking beasts came into my visual periphery, crossing the empty forum without anyone to control their stampede, their liberator charged from the other side of the stage, roaring with delight as he slammed into Colonel Lü, shoulder first. Lü Weihuang had not seen Meng Shudu rushing his way and found himself ejected from the stage, then kissing the dust of the forum under the uncomprehending stares of his guards.

"Sorry," Shudu said as he unsheathed his blade and took a spot next to me. "The stables were well-guarded." Nothing spreads hysteria in a camp faster than frightened horses, and nothing frightens those animals more than roaring fires.

"You!" I called, ignoring my comrade's excuses. "You're done already! Wuchao is lost. Get out now, and you still have a chance to make it out alive."

The three colonels looked at each other, the sense of what I had just said obvious to their defeated minds.

"Please don't kill me," the general said, a few drops of blood dripping along the length of my blade.

"Kill them!" Lü Weihuang shouted as he stood back up, his left cheek caked in dirt. "Their heads will be our redemption!"

The three colonels' eyes turned to steel. Words would take us no further; it was time to let the blades speak.

"Scorpions," I called after I slammed the pommel of Yingzhao against the back of Chunyu Qiong's neck to quiet him. "On me!"

Du Yuan moved first, Guo Huai by his side. I moved next, and between the three of us, those colonels stood no chance. I killed my target with an upward slash that cut right through his face. I never learned his name, and he died in the blink of an eye. Then I moved my attention to the borders of the stage, from where the unit of guards attempted to swarm us.

I took one with a thrust through the shoulder, then kicked him back from where he came. From the gap of his presence came a spear, which I parried away with a bout of luck. Pox slammed the perpendicular blade of his dagger-ax into the spearman's skull and twisted it out in time to strike another soldier with his foot already on the stage.

A scream behind me stole my attention for a second, fearing it had come from Guo Huai. Instead, I saw our youngest member singing a song of death with a succession of reels from his *dao*. He repainted the stage red, claiming lives faster than any other platoon member. Though I could not linger on his exploit, I was proud of him. Not so long ago, he had been a child pleading with me to train him in using the *dao*. Now he showed the world he had mastered the damn thing. One-eye took a step aside to avoid the young man's savage attack, himself holding his ground well despite not using his loyal bow.

"Always stay focused!" Cao Ren had drilled into us, using any chance we had given him to teach us this lesson with a well-placed whip of his bamboo cane.

His lesson saved my life. I felt the tip of a spear jutting toward my abdomen and caught its pole a finger length from my armor. I yanked on it, forcing the spearman to let go as he hit the stage, then reversed the grip and returned the weapon to him through his open mouth.

"Shit," I heard Pei Yuanshao bark, but I had learned my lesson and kept my eyes locked in front.

We kept the stage for ourselves, slowly stepping back to avoid the many blades stabbing the air for our death. Had they been smart, they might just have thrown them or simply used some bows. But they were not smart; they were enraged. Wuchao was crumbling around us, the silos, the stumps of what they had been at least, vomiting flames without control. Horses were slamming into powerless soldiers. The cacophony of bells, drums, and gongs would not stop, though at this point their purpose was dubious.

Our blades met theirs, adding to the sounds of metal on metal.

I was at the center of the turmoil, right where I was meant to be. I was born to fight on that stage. Each man by my side was born for the same purpose. We were killers, we were proud warriors, and we had bent Wuchao to our will. We were invincible.

One guard managed to climb between me and Pox, who was too busy keeping the volley of spears and swords from his legs to bother with one man. That man chose me and quickly got within my reach.

"When the enemy gets too close, don't use a blade, you'll be too late. Use his momentum," Xiahou Yuan had taught us. On that day, he had used a naive Xu Chu to demonstrate. At Wuchao, I crouched as my foe meant to skewer me with his *jian* sword, then let his momentum carry him one step before I kicked his ankle.

"Bobo!" I shouted as the guard fell face-first. The younger Meng brother twisted on his heels and kicked the head of the fallen guard like a ball of *cuju* with so much strength that the neck bent at an odd angle. Bobo returned to his killing as if nothing had happened. He was in a warrior trance, his canine teeth flashing through a vicious snarl.

The bells and gongs from the southern wall seemed to pick up in strength, but I gave them no more thought. Instead, I focused on the rhythm of the cries and shouts, the metal on wood, the screams and curses. I stood on the *sidi*, the death ground, home.

"And if any of you ugly inbred bastards break the line, we're all dead," Yu Jin shouted as we sweat under the midday sun of our first summer in the ranks, pummeling our comrades facing us during a mock battle. *"So, never, I repeat, never*

break the line. Protect it as if the courtesans of your favorite brothel stand behind you, and by the gods, they will be very grateful for your protection."

"Come on! Keep the line!" I shouted after slicing through the wrist of an eager soldier.

Du Yuan's laughed on my back, and soon Pei Yuanshao joined in. We were going to die eventually, but none of us thought about it.

"That's for Liang-the-broken," Shudu yelled. "And that's for Two-Knives!" A scream welcomed his second gift. None of those men had anything to do with our two fallen comrades, but they would pay nonetheless.

The image of those we had lost within the Scorpions flooded my mind. I struck for them. It was their rage I let speak on that night. This was my last chance to fight in their memory. The last time I would lead those hard bastards to the chaos of war, no matter the end of this battle.

Guo Huai's voice came in short yelps as he reeled, struck, and killed. Pox spat in the face of his direct opponent. The Meng brothers pushed a man who had also managed to make it on top back into his ranks. At this instant, I missed all of them already.

A structure fell on the forum, making the ground shake with the shock. It got the attention of those men, and soon the first of them, knowing they would never get on that stage, took a step back. His closest comrades followed suit. Then those around them. In front of our very eyes, the guards, the few dozen who had survived our fury, peeled away from us.

The Meng brothers cursed them and called them cowards in many variations of the noun as the others whooped and laughed. Not one part of Wuchao remained untouched by fire, except the stage, where a dozen men hugged and embraced each other for having survived the craziest battle of their existence.

"Pei, you're all right?" Pox asked.

"It's nothing," my comrade answered, though the nasty cut on his cheek let too much blood run to be considered *nothing*.

One-eye took Guo Huai by the shoulders as the young man dropped his sword and started shaking from the sheer stress of what he had just done.

"Chun," Du Yuan said. "Maybe it's time we go."

"Couldn't agree more," I replied.

"Oh, shit," another of my men said, pointing his gore-covered blade toward the south, from where a whole regiment of soldiers came running. At their head, I saw a furious Lü Weihuang call for our death, blade held high. I had forgotten about him and guessed he had gone to gather his men while the guards died.

"Well, it's been a pleasure," Meng Bobo said as he peeled away from his brother's arms.

"It's been an honor," I replied, whipping the sweat from my forehead and shoving the helmet back in place.

We formed a line on the stage as three or four hundred men rushed through the main path of the camp, keeping to the center to avoid the inferno. I felt no regret, not even for bringing my friends to their doom. I don't think any of them regretted being here, either.

Lü Weihuang reminded me of those fierce-looking guardian gods with his flame-shaped helmet and muscular arm brandishing a straight blade reflecting the golden blaze of his defeat. His fish-scale armor was glistening like hundreds of tiny mirrors, and his shout could be heard above any other.

"You want to say it?" Du Yuan asked me. An honor, considering how much he hated me for abusing my call.

"Scorpions!" I shouted, a wide grin splitting my face. "On me!"

My men, my friends, took over my shout and welcomed the approaching enemy snarling.

A loud *boom* interrupted us, then a wave of screams, not of pain, but of panic. Lü Weihuang heard it. All his men did as well, and they stopped. They turned around, but how many saw the archers of the wall running from their posts, or the southern gate opening out of nowhere, I wonder. They, however, understood faster than I did who was rushing through the opening, and scrambled as one while my lord and his mounted soldiers broke through Wuchao.

"It's Cao Cao!" Guo Huai shouted with delight.

"I can't believe it," I said, my blade dangling without strength at my side. And yet it was truly him. The man himself slashed his marvelous blade through Lü Weihuang's chest a few seconds before reaching our location, his smirk the most pleasant surprise of the night for me. For a few seconds, everything was forgiven.

"My lord?" I asked.

"Had to make sure not one husk of grain remained," he joked as he turned his mare sideways. Behind and around him, our comrades were spreading throughout Wuchao under the command of Xu Huang and Yue Jin, the latter, as was his habit, running in front of his comrades.

"I think it's mostly unhusked grain, sir," Pox commented.

"All the more reason then," my lord replied. Cao Cao was a god, sitting straight on his horse, flames making his every move more pronounced, and not one scratch on his armor or his person even though he had fought at the gate and surely before.

"What about Yuan Shao's reinforcements?" I asked as he checked left and right to assess the situation.

"*I* am betting they will not come here," he replied.

Cao Cao was partially right. Yuan Shao made his worst decision of the war that night. Instead of committing his men to save his supply depot or attack Guandu while we fought at Wuchao, he split them into two groups, one for each. The one supposed to rescue Wuchao turned back when they understood the depot was gone for good; as for the second, they would never be enough to storm Guandu. At least, not before we came back to our base.

My lord and his men took less than twenty minutes to clear Wuchao. By then, every soldier of Yuan Shao was either dead, gone, or on their knees. Chunyu Qiong came back to his senses as the last of his silos toppled pitifully, and he probably regretted his consciousness dearly, for my lord had his nose chopped off before letting him go. I felt a little sorry for him, but his pain did not last long. Yuan Shao had him executed the next day.

The Scorpions took no part in cleansing Wuchao, choosing instead to enjoy the view from outside the burning camp. And what a view it was. Not only the depot going up in flames, but the whole region covered in fleeing soldiers was a sight for sore eyes. They climbed out of the trenches in the thousands and spread toward their main base, suddenly aware of the dramatic shift in the war. The only soldiers of Yuan Shao who did not flee were those unlucky men who had been sent against Guandu. Their leader, the young officer Zhang He, had not even called the assault, knowing better than his general-in-chief how doomed such a tactic was from the start.

When we reached our base, he came to Cao Cao and knelt in submission, calling Yuan Shao a fool for thinking this strategy had any chance of success and for so easily dispatching *him* to this foreseeable failure.

Zhang He was the last of Yuan Shao's four great generals, and now he offered his blade to the service of Cao Cao, who welcomed him and his men with open arms. Thus my lord gained the service of the last of his future *five elite generals*.

I barely saw the man that night, too eager for some deserved rest, but one day he would become one of my most eager enemies. They all would.

Cao Cao pushed all his divisions after the fleeing mass of Yuan Shao's soldiers, and my comrades achieved such an efficient pursuit that the governor from the north crossed the Yellow River in the morning with less than one thousand soldiers.

I had thought to tip the scale of the war with the loss of a supply depot, but Yuan Shao so badly handled this debacle that he lost any advantage he used to have over Cao Cao.

My lord was now the most powerful man in the empire, and I was about to betray him.

18

Xuchang, capital of the Great Han
10th month, 5th year of Jian'an era (200), Han Dynasty

It is a strange experience to leave a place we inhabited, knowing we will never see it again. My room filled with the ghosts of Guli and me sharing some intimate moments, both pleasant and heartbreaking. I took the view of the palace from my window one last time, breathed the morning air of the capital as the sun reached the side of the great hall, and remembered how I had pulled my former lover into my arms in this very place.

"Will you miss it?" Guo Wen asked as he came to pick up the second of my trunks. Clothes mostly in this one. The first, already waiting for me inside a cart parked in front of the compound, welcomed my armor, blades, helmet, and all my cash. Where I was born, it would be considered a hoard.

"I will," I replied as I stepped to my servant and stood on the other side of the trunk, ready to grab one of the handles. He didn't need my help, but I wanted to offer it anyway. "Not as much as the bath, though."

"They don't have baths where you go?" Guo Wen asked.

"I still have no idea where we are going," I told him. We were leaving for Runan, where Liu Bei was mounting a form of rebellion against Cao Cao. But Runan wasn't our final destination. Knowing Liu Bei only acted to get our attention, Guan Yu promised Cao Cao he would persuade his brother to give up the fight and go somewhere else.

"But wherever we end up going, it won't be Xuchang," I went on. There would be no baths in compounds, wherever we ended up. No court of blood, nor emperor either.

"Should I get some things transported to you when you arrive?" he asked.

"Nah, it can all stay," I answered, thinking that besides my furniture, there wasn't much to send anyway. "Besides, I thought you would not remain here either?"

"Just a few days to help the boy," Guo Wen said.

When Cao Cao asked who I would consider as my replacement, I told him to name Du Yuan as the new leader of the Scorpions. He was the natural choice for this role and had acted as such more often than me over the last couple of years. However, to my great surprise, Du Yuan asked to remain with me when I gave my men the choice. I told him Liu Bei would never ask us to do any of the things he favored, but Du Yuan claimed it was of little importance; staying with his old companions mattered more. I never pictured Du Yuan as the sentimental kind but was glad for his presence. Pei Yuanshao would also accompany me to my new life. I knew I would have to tell them the truth at some point, but for now, I was just glad to have my oldest friends by my side for a little longer. As far as they were concerned, we were on a spying mission for Cao Cao that could last several years. Besides the honesty of my defection, I had been frank about what awaited us.

I then offered the role to Guo Huai, and judging by the grins from my companions, they had guessed I would do so. Not the boy, though, who blushed and spluttered his thanks as I officially handed him his staff of command. Guo Huai had fought like a demon at Wuchao and had grown with us. He could now read, showed discipline, and knew loyalty. In time, I believed, he would become a great leader. I pointed out to Cao Cao that the young man was slightly older than Cao Pi, his eldest living son, and would thus serve him well for many years.

"Then I will finally head back home," Guo Wen went on. "I haven't seen my wife in so long I worry she might try to find a husband with two hands."

"That would be her loss," I joked.

"You will miss me too, won't you?" Guo Wen asked half-seriously.

"By my ancestors, I will," I replied with a burst of exaggerated laughter. "Not sure I can still tie my boots by myself."

"You will learn," he said.

A relaxing silence sat between us. Guo Wen had grown old, and I was relieved he was returning to his wife and two other children in good shape. I had given a fat purse to his son to be given to the father as a well-deserved bonus. If I gave it to him directly, he would refuse, but with the contents of the purse, Guo Wen would live well for a couple of years at least.

"You've been a good friend, Soldier Guo," I told him as I held my left arm for him to take.

"And watching you grow has been my pleasure, kid," the man replied as he took my offering.

Guo Wen owed me his life and his family's good fortune, but in my mind, I owed him at least as much. We carried the trunk to the cart together, and I used the next few minutes to salute those good brothers of mine that would stay behind. Most of those present in the courtyard as we shared a last joke were remaining within the Scorpions. One-eye had decided to leave the army but agreed to stay a few more weeks until Guo Huai, our grown Sparrow, managed to fill the gaps of our departure with fresh blood. Then, the archer would be off to whatever the next step of his life happened to be. He had often mentioned his will to start a family, and I hoped he fulfilled this particular ambition. He would make a great father and had often acted as such to us younger men of the unit.

They all offered to accompany me to Guan Yu's mansion, where the others waited, but I refused. The place would be cluttered enough, and saying goodbye once was already too much. The compound would not even be half-full after our departure, but I still sighed with nostalgia as I walked out. My new horse, a rather beautiful gelding with a chestnut coat and blond mane, pawed impatiently before I climbed on it. The Meng brothers, who had unanimously decided to come with me, drove the cart where all our belongings had been dropped. As usual, I could hardly guess their motivation in choosing to follow me, but Meng Bobo simply claimed that I was the only officer crazy enough to put up with them and ask for more of their service. They would make the journey more lively, and to be fair, they were right; few commanders could handle them.

They cracked the reins of their two horses and called for the cart to move. My gelding followed gently, and I waved one last time at my brothers.

I never saw Guo Wen again, but still think about him as my greatest friend from that time under Cao Cao.

As I took in the sight of Xuchang in for the last time, I let my mind wander in the meander of a city I had called home for a few years. The last days had been less moving than I would have thought, but it was mostly due to the absence of so many friends. Most of my comrades in the army were gone after the remnants of Yuan Shao's army, clearing Yan province of their presence while Lord Cao prepared his journey across the Yellow River to push his momentum.

Xiahou Yuan was leading his cavalry all the way to Boma, so I could only say goodbye to his son, Xiahou Ba, who remained in Xuchang because of a light injury. The young man had respectfully promised to give my farewell to his father, then told me he was sad about my departure. I warned him to choose his opponents more wisely and wished him a glorious future.

I managed to share a few cups with Xu Chu, who was never far from Lord Cao, and asked him to raise a toast in my name when he and Yue Jin next met. Man Chong and Cao Ren were presently stationed in Runan, our destination, and I hoped fate would allow us some time together, though how it would happen, I could not imagine.

However, I did not speak with two people dear to me. Lady Bian was the first. She had meant the world to my young, foolish heart, but I was now a grown man; it was time I let her go. The Son of Heaven was the second. If he still cared about me, he must have felt betrayed by my departure, but I could not risk meeting him. Instead, as I trotted to Guan Yu's mansion, I told him in my heart that one day I would return for him and truly help him as a friend.

A big wagon waited outside the walls of Guan Yu's

temporary lodgings, two gentle horses pulling it. Lady Mi and Lady Gan, two plain women with good hearts, would occupy it. The cart with our things was already being loaded with some more trunks, bags, and baskets filled with Mi Zhu's and Guan Yu's belongings, though the latter traveled lightly on account of him giving back anything Cao Cao had ever offered, down to the seal of marquisate marking him as a nobleman. He only kept two things, Red Hare, and a warm cloak of dark blue silk Lord Cao was just handing him as I reached them. Guan Yu thanked Cao Cao and promised to use it well on this journey back to his brother, a comment that did not please Cao Cao, though he hid it well.

My men, those who would remain with me, were also present by the convoy, all accounted for, even Pox who seldom arrived anywhere on time. Since Guan Yu had sent Mi Fang and his few soldiers toward our destination to inform Liu Bei of our coming, the nine former Scorpions that we were made the greater part of our forces. We were so few that Mi Zhu had to drive the wagon harboring his sister, and I must say I was impressed such an educated man could actually manage this task. As I stopped my gelding by Guan Yu's side and dismounted, this advisor stood there as well.

"Master Mi," Cao Cao was saying, "my offer still stands. You would be a marvelous administrator for Taishan."

"I am grateful for your kind words," Mi Zhu replied as he bowed deeply, "but my place is by my brother-in-law."

"Liu Bei is a lucky man," Lord Cao said, "to be surrounded by loyal and talented men. Even those who I thought loyal to me end up following him." The last he said with a sneer aimed at me. We had agreed he would behave as if my departure displeased him, to sell the "lie" of my defection better. Of course, Cao Cao was the one being lied to, and Guan Yu knew this was all an act. The bearded warrior had told me he fared badly in deception and would remain as quiet as possible rather than betray our plan.

It was a dangerous game, and I can't say I particularly enjoyed it. Cao Cao could not have trusted me entirely, and Guan Yu might assume I was still working for Cao Cao; this would not have been the hero of chaos's strangest scheme after all. Even my men must have had doubts about our departure's real motive. However, more than any other, Lord Cao's son, who stood right behind him, made me feel like the most despicable being in the empire.

Cao Pi must have been about thirteen years old and looked so much like his dead brother that it pinched my heart to look at him. He wasn't as warm or friendly-looking, but he was his father's blood just as well. He also had his mother's more angular chin, and the gods knew where he got those cold, stabbing eyes that reminded me more of his half-brother, Man Chong.

"I thank you for letting me go so gently, my lord," I said, staring away from Cao Pi.

"You have earned the right to choose your master," Cao Cao replied without enthusiasm. "Guan Yu," he then went on, "could anything make you change your mind? I will respect my promise, but I would much rather have you stay with me. With a man of your caliber by my side, the empire would be as good as united again."

"I am flattered," Guan Yu replied, "but if I accepted your offer, I wouldn't be, as you said, a man of my caliber."

"Well said, Yunchang," Cao Cao said, using the bearded warrior's *zi* name with respect. "Well said. In that case, I only ask that you take good care of my student here." My heart skipped a bit when Cao Cao mentioned me with such gentle words. They were, I understood, for me. "He is foolish, stubborn, hot-headed, and all too inclined to insubordination, but few are more worthy. If it weren't for his complete lack of poetical senses and his fondness for my wife, I would have fought harder to keep him."

I felt the threat of tears as we all chuckled. I had hardly seen his friendly grin over the past few years, but it sent me back to the best days of my childhood. Guan Yu did not share our laughter, but I often noticed how rarely he did so. The bearded warrior had his issues when it came to humor.

"Talking of her," Cao Pi said as he dropped his right hand inside his luxurious golden *hanfu*, "my mother sends you her farewell and wanted me to give you this for the journey."

Even though Cao Pi clearly wanted to have nothing to do with me, he retrieved his mother's gift and slapped it inside my hand. A green apple, my favorite kind since a beautiful concubine had peeled such fruit for a ten-year-old boy struggling with poetry and turned him into a love-struck teenager.

"Give her my thanks and tell her I will enjoy it before Xuchang vanishes from my sight."

"If you'll excuse us," Guan Yu then went on, saluting my lord and his son. I was about to follow his example when a loud voice interrupted us.

"Liao Chun!" Xiahou Ba called from further down the street, right after the boy appeared at the corner of the mansion. "Wait a minute."

"What is it, nephew?" Cao Cao asked as the boy searched for his breath, his face glistening from the effort of running here. In his hands, he held a basket deliciously smelling of freshly made *shaobing*.

"My sister made these for your journey and hoped you would give her regards to Zhang Fei," Xiahou Ba explained as Mi Zhu took the basket from his hands. The young man sounded as sorry as I was, for few people had suffered more than Lady Xiahou Yu from the rift between Cao Cao and Liu Bei. She should have been married to Zhang Fei by now, and their strange love would have flourished. Instead, she remained hidden in her father's house, and neither I nor anyone I knew had seen her outside of her compound since Liu Bei had betrayed my lord. In giving us those flatbread buns, Zhang Fei's favorite, I believe, she sent her regards to her lover. It was an awkward situation, so I thanked Xiahou Ba and told him to give my regards to his sister.

Mi Zhu left to drop the basket inside the cart, and Guan Yu used this chance to remount Red Hare.

"Chun," Cao Cao called as I was about to do the same.

Lord Cao waited for Guan Yu to ride to the head of the small convoy, then dropped his hand on my shoulder. We were of the same height, but I felt shorter, as I always did by his side. I thought he would give me some instructions or share a story of our common past. However, Cao Cao had other plans.

"Remember what happens to those who betray me," he said.

The temperature dropped suddenly. A cold grip tightened around my heart as my former lord directly threatened me. It was the first time I felt this eerie sensation of quiet menace every man who once crossed Cao Cao suffered. Not the last, though.

"I will remember everything you taught me," I replied.

He nodded; I bowed, then put my fist inside my hand as I extended my arms in front of me. Saluting as we do is a way to make ourselves vulnerable. We drop our sight from our superiors and offer our scalps without any means of defending ourselves should they decide to get rid of us. I was giving Cao Cao a last chance to do so. When I raised my head again, he was my enemy.

Cao Cao, his guards, his son, and his nephew walked with us until the city gates, though no other word was shared between us.

A weight vanished from my chest as the shadow of the walls was replaced by the mid-morning sun. I was done with cruelty and would now fight for a man who believed in respect over fear. Liu Bei was naive, but maybe some of it had infected me. Besides, Liu Bei might be my new lord, but Guan Yu was the man I followed.

"So," he said just as I took the first bite of the apple. "Now that your new life has begun, what do you want to do first?"

"Last time my life changed," I said after a long *hum* of pondering, "I changed my name. Maybe it's time for another one?"

"Any idea?" my new lord asked.

"I'll think of something," I replied. "By the time we reach Lord Liu Bei, I will have a new name."

"You'd better think fast then. It will be a short trip."

How wrong he was. How very wrong he was.

EPILOGUE

Yingchuan commandery
10th month, 5th year of Jian'an era (200), Han Dynasty

THE SUN HAD JUST SET on our first day on the road. We had moved as expected and should have reached Runan three days later. If they had found him, Mi Fang or some of his men would ride back to us to lead us straight to Liu Bei. The atmosphere was light around the evening fire, the smell of the boiling soup making us impatient and prompting my men to behave as they always did, like children. Once the meal finished, I knew Hu Zi and Duck would sneak somewhere private and share the night together. I don't think Guan Yu had understood the nature of their relationship and wondered if it would be an issue. The way their elbows always met when they sat next to each other made me smile, and I wasn't the only one finding them amusing despite having witnessed this scene hundreds of times.

"No wonder they wanted to stay with you," Stinger said, sitting next to me on our saddles dropped on the ground. "Cao Cao's army is no place for this kind of partnering."

"And why by the sky did *you* decide to come along?" I asked, for I truly could not understand what Stinger of all people could hope from his decision. In fact, I assumed if there was a spy in our odd unit, it was him.

"Because you told me to spare the boy," he replied frankly.

The light of the fire danced quietly inside his placid, dark eyes. Whenever Stinger looked at nothing in particular, you could see all the pain he had inflicted on others make waves of guilt across them.

"The boy?" I asked.

"At Wuchao," he went on. "You didn't want me to kill him, even when I offered. And you took care of Yuan Shu, even though I offered then as well."

"So you think you can get lazy on me?" I asked, chuckling.

"You never ask me to hurt anyone if it's not necessary," he said, which cut right through my laughter. He threw the twig he had been triturating into the fire, where it fizzed because of the humidity. From the corner of my eye, I saw Mi Zhu leaving the cooking pot with two bowls for the ladies. "I'm done with torture," Stinger said.

That got me quiet. I had always thought Stinger took, if not pleasure, at least pride in his talents and had never even asked if it bothered him. I felt a little ashamed but thought that maybe he and I were not so different after all. Maybe I was his way out.

"We'll find something else for you," I said, lifting my calabash of yellow wine to fill his empty cup.

"Thank you, I—"

"*Tian-na!*" a voice shouted near the closest wagon.

The whole circle of warriors interrupted their conversation, taken by the panic in Mi Zhu's voice and the ruckus of movements by the wagon.

I rushed to his help, thinking we were being attacked, but only found the advisor fighting with the wagon doors, which the ladies struggled to keep closed against his will. Pox, who got there before me, helped the thin man and nearly flung one side of the small doors from its hinges.

"Heaven," Meng Shudu, who rarely called for that place, said.

Inside the wagon sat a third woman. A young, pretty, tired woman with pale skin, disheveled hair, and silk robes of good quality, though one pang of it hung under her left breast from where a baby was quietly feeding. She looked through the open door, panic making her chest rise and fall in rushing breaths, her eyes scanning through the small crowd gathering speechless by the wagon. When she found mine, she looked like a desert dweller would when stumbling upon a water well.

"Liao Chun!" she called.

"Shit," I said.

Xiahou Yu brought her robes over the babe before shuffling toward the door. All the while, the ladies whooshed us away and called us thugs for staring at the girl.

"What are you doing here?" I asked the young lady when she stood out of the wagon. She was a far cry from the dazzling girl I had last seen. The past few months must have been terrible for her, and seeing the baby in her arms, an event I had not been made aware of, I realized something awful must have happened.

"I'm coming with you," she said, biting her lips to keep the tears at bay.

"No, you're not," I replied in a high-pitched voice.

"I'm coming with you," she said again, stronger this time.

"Anyone know you're here?" Du Yuan asked.

"No," she lied. "My brother," she then said.

"Shit," I said again. "That's why he made this fuss with the basket of bread. No wonder I thought that was odd." Xiahou Ba had helped his sister sneak into the wagon, and she had been lucky the ladies were good women who kept her hidden for the rest of the day.

"Chun, if they ask him where his sister is—" Du Yuan said.

"I know," I interrupted him. "Lord Guan, we need to get back. They'll come after us if they find out where she is. I'll take two men and catch up with you as fast as possible."

"Agreed," Guan Yu said. "I'll send riders to tell you where we are."

"I'm not going back!" Xiahou Yu said.

"Xiahou Yu, don't be stupid!" I barked back. "I'll tie you to my horse if I have to."

"I'll bite my tongue off then," she said, her stare challenging me.

The young lady breathed hard, and the baby started fussing inside her robes. She patted his back a few times to keep him quiet, to no avail. I had only seen him for a few seconds but guessed he was a little under a year old.

"Lady Xiahou, whose baby is this?" Mi Zhu, who thought he was doing the right thing, asked. I wish he hadn't. While I understood his will to defuse the situation, the less we knew, the better.

"It's Zhang Fei's, of course," she replied, looking cross. The baby answered her temper with a bout of gut-wrenching crying.

"My lady," Guan Yu said, taking a step toward Xiahou Yu and making her look very small in comparison. "You haven't seen my brother in almost two years. This could not be his."

"And what do you know of women?" she asked, looking right back at him with more verve than most warriors would be capable of. "Tell me if this isn't your brother's?" she asked as she took the baby out and shoved his crying face close to Lord Guan's. Even with the growing darkness, the resemblance between the squirming infant and the mighty warrior of Liu Bei could not have been more obvious. Down to the volume of his voice, the baby was a worthy heir to his father. Guan Yu found nothing to say, and I could see he got lost in his thoughts.

"Chun," Du Yuan said, standing sideways next to me, "it doesn't matter who the kid is. They'll come for us and arrest us for kidnapping. Let's take her back."

"Can't we say we didn't know?" Pox asked.

"They'll find out the truth," Stinger answered, and of course, he would know.

"Are you sure it's Zhang Fei's?" Meng Bobo asked the girl, who replied with a murderous stare. I knew she was speaking the truth. Just as I knew her father probably knew nothing of the baby's existence.

"Please, Chun, they'll kill him," the girl said, echoing my thoughts.

"Or turn him into a eunuch," Pei Yuanshao unhelpfully went on. Her eyes turned wide with despair at the idea, and she nearly threw herself at my feet. I did not let her, and while I helped her back on her feet, she dropped the kid in my arms. It was a low blow, and I angrily shook my head as she stepped back, leaving the boy against my chest.

"Chun," Du Yuan went on, grabbing me by the elbow. "I know you don't like kids being hurt, but this is not our problem. *She* isn't our problem." His hand looked dirty next to the baby, who was anything but clean himself.

"Lord Guan?" I asked, happy to have someone to defer to for once.

Guan Yu snapped back to the now as if I had interrupted him during a dream. He checked the baby in my arms, frowned, and said nothing for a while.

"She isn't married," Mi Zhu said. "She still belongs to her father." He did not look happy to remind us of the law; this was simply the way of things.

"How can you be so daft?" his sister's voice shouted from within the wagon.

"I don't make the law!" he barked back at her.

This was getting out of hand. My men started arguing with each other, the baby was threatening to throw a tantrum again, and in all of this, the only three people who remained silent were me, Lady Xiahou, and Guan Yu.

"Enough!" he finally roared. It got very quiet, very fast. Even the babe sucked his breath in and stopped fussing. His big, bright eyes turned to his uncle with a mixture of fear and awe.

"The law is clear," Guan Yu went on. "The girl belongs to her father, but the kid belongs to his. It's father against father. Xiahou Yuan or Zhang Fei. They should decide the fate of those two."

"Lord Guan," I said, "neither of them is here. This is not helpful. Do I bring her back to her father? You take the kid to Zhang Fei?"

"Chun!" the lady screamed. "Don't take my baby from me."

"We don't even know where Zhang Fei is," Mi Zhu reminded us.

The baby grabbed my beard and pulled on it with strength. I didn't find it funny, but he did.

"Liao Chun," Guan Yu called.

"My lord?"

"You know her well?" he asked.

"Since she was a child herself," I answered, thinking it had not been so long ago.

"And her father?"

"Since I was a child myself."

"Then, I will ask you something I hope never to ask you again," Guan Yu went on gravely. "You decide what to do with them."

This was unfair. I had saved the girl's life once and now had the responsibility of her baby's as well. I was also the one who had introduced Zhang Fei to her, so it was, in fact, a little my fault too. None of this, of course, was the baby's fault. He was born into a world cruel to bastard boys. But my men, who would be pursued if we kept going, were for once innocent of any crime. I thought to transfer the responsibility back to Guan Yu, but the intense stares of everyone around the wagon told me they agreed I should decide on our next course of action.

"So?" Guan Yu asked.

"Chun?" Du Yuan said, shaking his head in a warning.

"Liao Chun," the girl pleaded, eyes filling with tears.

"Shit," I said for the third time, thinking that I really had to change my name.

My next words, as it turned out, would draw a lot of blood.

To be continued in

FOREST OF SWORDS

BOOK FOUR
of
THE THREE KINGDOMS
CHONICLES

A Three Kingdoms Chronicles' Novella

AUTHOR NOTES

Still with me? You, dear reader, are amazing. Thank you so much for being part of this adventure and following the life's tale of Liao Hua. In the blink of the eye, three novels were published and we are nearly done with the first cycle of the series. Liao Hua is fully grown by now, and this has been a fairly painful experience for him, especially in *Dynasty Killers*. Our main character discovered a lot about himself through some pretty daunting moments and through the demise of people around him. I often consider that a person only truly becomes an adult when they awaken to the suffering of others. Empathy is an astonishing sign of maturity, one that many never truly develop. Liao Hua did, and with it came the realization that his path had to change.

The reason for Liao Hua's betrayal escaped me until I started this book three. I knew it wasn't going to go down to one single moment, but rather a series of events, or rather a natural evolution that made him take another road than Cao Cao's, and even now it is not easy to define what exactly made him say "enough." In *Dynasty Killers*, Liao Hua's pain

Author Notes

is mostly psychological, and while he suffered, maybe unknowingly to himself, the benevolent attitude of Liu Bei and the righteousness of Guan Yu offered him another way. Will it be enough? We will see. But for now, Liao Hua has veered from the cold and calculating manners of Cao Cao and is moving on to his historical self.

I'm excited to dive into the part of the legend that actually mentions Liao Hua, and while it means dealing with some constraints, it will also give me some clear directions to follow.

Talking of historical accuracy, I want once again to apologize for any mistake that I committed in this novel. As usual, I try to remain as true to the history as possible while keeping in mind the entertainment part of your reading experience, and its ease. Here are some points I can mention. When the Scorpions meet with Sun Ce, the Little Conqueror is surrounding the city which Taishi Ci is defending. In my novel, this city is Xuancheng, while in reality, it was a place called Jing. Because I didn't want any confusion between Jing the province and Jing the city, I moved the location of Taishi Ci to Xuancheng, which stood fairly close to Jing (the city).

A lot has been left out from the war between Cao Cao and Yuan Shao, and I'm sad not to develop the conquest of the north by the Hero of Chaos. Maybe a bonus chapter or two from characters such as Guo Jia and Yue Jin will do the trick?

On the characters' side, I was pleasantly surprised by the space taken by Ma Dai, whom I did not intend to be so important to begin with. Xiahou Ba was also a great addition, and I look forward to bringing those two back. We also got to say goodbye to some big names in this third novel. Lü Bu, Chen Gong, Yuan Shu, and, even more important to our

Author Notes

main character perhaps, Dian Wei, Cao Anmin, and Cao Ang. The latter one's demise was a painful moment. This being said, I never enjoyed writing a battle scene as much as Wan's. I wrote the whole of it in one session that left me thirsty, shaky, and exhausted, but damn, it was worth it! I hope you enjoyed reading it as much as I enjoyed writing it.

We had some heavy battles in *Dynasty Killers*, Wan being one, but Xiapi and Wuchao had a very significant impact at the time. It could even be argued that those two had a more pivotal role for the future of the empire. Wuchao happened quite differently in reality, but it was first and foremost an occasion for me to give a last hurrah to the Scorpions, a last chance for them to shine before saying goodbye, or even farewell, to some of them.

Nine of them remain as they leave Xuchang to wherever they will find Liu Bei, and what should have been an easy journey will, of course, offer its set of challenges. Who knows how many of them will remain by Liao Hua's side by the time this journey ends?

The next volume, entitled *Forest of Swords*, is the first novella of this series and will thus close this first cycle of the *Three Kingdoms Chronicles*. Some big names of the legend/history will pop up in that one, while others will leave the stage. So be ready, it's gonna get bloody, it's gonna get brutal, and it's gonna get real!

ACKNOWLEDGMENTS

I wrote *Dynasty Killers* while *Yellow Sky Revolt* was released, and as such it is the first novel I wrote while my work was already out there. It took a conscious effort to avoid taking reviews and criticism (both positive and negative) into account while writing it, or at least not too much.

This being said, I want to thank all the gentle souls who took the time to leave a review and drop some stars for my previous books (and hopefully will too for this one). Some amazing reviewers shared the word about my series and helped me remain confident in my art. Thank you, dear friends. Thank you, Tori, Kyle, Allen, Rachel, Kate, William, and many more.

A couple of months after the release of *Yellow Sky Revolt*, I sent a copy to a man I deeply respect and whose life work had made this series possible, Dr. Rafe de Crespigny, probably the greatest authority on the late Han dynasty and Three Kingdoms in the world. Rafe was not only kind enough to accept my small gift but even shared with me his positive impression of the novel. I cannot tell you how happy I was to know the master approved of my work. His support means the world to me and I thank him from the bottom of my heart, not only for his kindness but for all his passionate work. If you, dear reader, want to know more about the Three Kingdoms, check his books, *Fire Over Luoyang*, *Generals of the South*, and *Imperial Warlord*, among others.

I received the support of too many people to name all of them here, even in the superbly generous writing community. Walking among peers is a fabulous experience. Thank you, guys. Angus Donald, *the* Angus Donald, has been a great source of inspiration and positivity over the last few months. Thank you, Angus.

The poem in the foreword was written by Wang Can, one of the Seven Scholars of Jian'an. Among them I have briefly mentioned two; Kong Rong (in Yellow Sky Revolt), and Chen Lin (in Dynasty Killers). I found this particular poem extremely poignant and conveying the exact tone I was looking for for this novel. For copyrights reasons, I decided to translate it myself, but I wish to thank Professor Paul F. Rouzer, whose very own translation served as a base for mine, and who so kindly helped me in this linguistic endeavour.

And, as usual, I need to thank my beautiful, patient, brilliant wife for being my everything and the pillar of my world. She still hasn't read any of the books in the series, by the way... But, since I'm working on a historical romance spinoff set during this book three, there's hope. Oops! Spoiler alert. *wink, wink*

ABOUT THE AUTHOR

I always feel a little silly talking about myself in the third person, so I'll keep it in the first here. I am a French author, publishing stories set in ancient China, written in English, from the comfort of my apartment in Tokyo. Ancient cultures have always fascinated me, and studying East Asian ones has been a pleasure of mine since early childhood.

As you may have seen in my previous dedication, I have two sons and a wife who I love more than life itself. So, nearly as much as Kung Pao Chicken.

I write for them, you, my characters, and myself, not necessarily in that order, but the point is I love writing and you're not done with me by a long shot.

If those previous three books are not enough for you, please visit my website, subscribe to the newsletter, and receive the bonus chapters I share every two months.

Never hesitate to reach out on Facebook and Twitter either.

Amicalement,

Baptiste Pinson Wu

THANK YOU

If you have enjoyed Dynasty Killers, Heroes of Chaos, and/or Yellow Sky Revolt please give them a review on Amazon and/or Goodreads. Not only it would mean the world to this hopeful writer, it would be *your* stone on the Three Kingdoms Chronicles' edifice.

In any case, know that I am extremely grateful you gave these books a chance.

See you very soon!